No Law Against Angels

Doll for the Big House

Chorine Makes a Killing

Three Novels by
Carter Brown

INTRODUCTION BY JEREMY YATES

Stark House Press • Eureka California

NO LAW AGAINST ANGELS / DOLL FOR THE BIG HOUSE /
CHORINE MAKES A KILLING

Published by Stark House Press
1315 H Street
Eureka, CA 95501, USA
griffinskye3@sbcglobal.net
www.starkhousepress.com

ISBN-13: 978-1-944520-70-0

Book design by Mark Shepard, SHEPGRAPHICS.COM
Cover art taken from the Ullstein Bücher edition
of *Leiche—Oben Ohne* by Carter Brown

First Stark House Press Edition: March 2019

NO LAW AGAINST ANGELS

In which Lt. Al Wheeler investigates the murder of two young ladies—

+ both of whom worked at the Haven of Rest mortuary
+ both of whom had a tattoo on their upper shoulder in the shape of a dollar sign which turns into a snake
+ and both of whom worked as part-time call-girls for the mysterious fellow known as Snake Lannigan, a man no one has ever seen.

DOLL FOR THE BIG HOUSE

In which Lt. Al Wheeler is reassigned to the Eight Precinct under Captain Bligh in order to—

+ find Lili Hertz, whose sister has reported her missing
+ track her to the Big House of Absolem Kirch, despotic owner of a newspaper empire and the man behind a lot of dirty politics
+ and crack the kidnapping ring that provides Kirch with the young girls he keeps in his mansion against their will.

CHORINE MAKES A KILLING

In which Lt. Al Wheeler turns in his badge to become a private investigator for a lawyer's firm in order to—

+ investigate an open-and-shut murder case involving Walter Byrne, friend of the lawyer and now married to the lawyer's ex-wife
+ determine just who really did kill the chorus girl, who was also Byrne's mistress
+ figure out who is trying to kill Byrne's wife, Myra, while fending off the advances of the man's sexy daughter.

Contents

Carter Brown
An Introduction

by Jeremy Yates

Carter Brown (previously known as Peter Carter Brown) (aka Alan Geoffrey Yates) was my father.

He abounded in a love of life, of searching and finding, of extreme generosity and had a brilliant mind and sense of humour.

May I take you on a tour of my experiences?

I was born on the 25th of September, 1951.

The first Peter Carter Brown book – *The Lady is Murder* was published in September, 1951. I obviously had an early impact on my father's success!

Dad had been an Able Seaman in tactical Landing Craft from 1942 in the British (Royal) Navy in the 2nd World War. Later he was sent for officer training becoming a sub-lieutenant on a light cruiser the HMS Euryalus. His role was cipher officer. To fulfil this role he was taught and needed to be proficient in touch typing.

Thus it was that he touch typed all novels gravitating from manual typewriters to the IBM electric golf ball typewriter in later times.

Having met and married my mother – Denise in Australia, they returned to England where my older sister – Priscilla was born.

Then they 'boomeranged' back to Australia.

Shortly after the commencement of the Korean War in 1950 Dad joined the Royal Australian Naval Reserve undertaking several intelligence courses. A good friend of his in the RANR was Paul Trimble who had two sons – Christopher and Michael. Michael was my age and we were often allowed to come to the Navy training area (outside secure areas) where we (at the age of about 6 years) were given money to keep ourselves busy downing a can of coke ("Champagne American") and a meat pie with tomato sauce (staple Australian diet)!

The locations for the Carter Brown books was the U.S. Dad had not been there before and so in 1958 both my parents took a trip there with Dad's Australian publishers.

They had a great time there and brought back a range of advanced U.S. products including striped tooth paste which looked like candy cane. So much so that I even started brushing my teeth!

My younger brother – Christopher was born on the 27th of December that year.

We moved to another (larger) house with a half size Olympic swimming pool (as the previous owner had a daughter who had an eye on competing in swimming in the Olympic Games).

Given the size of the pool and Dad's nautical history, he thought I would appreciate a wooden canoe for my Birthday. Mum and Dad had an appointment with the publishers on the morning I received the gift. Dad was dressed in a suit for the meeting but was insistent that he show me how to get in and out of the canoe before leaving. Dad lined up the canoe along the side of the pool, grasped the paddle, put his right foot into the canoe and.................fell out the other side!

One more try with the same result before changing for the meeting!

An attraction 'Down Under' is the Sydney Royal Easter Show. This originated as an agricultural show but developed to include side shows, amusement rides and sample bags. It is heavily attended and despite my sister and my supplications to Dad, he was not keen to go. So we struck a deal – we would go and buy a lot of sample bags for the two of us and come home. Dad found a gourmet food sample bag which he bought and, I think, may have been the beginning of his gourmet cooking sub-career (details coming!).

In 1960 it was decided to gain more understanding of the U.S. We flew initially to Honolulu and had a magic 4 days there. Then on to Los Angeles.

Dad bought a 7-seater Buick and we then proceeded to drive from California to New York staying overnight at a number of cities (including Cheyenne, Salt Lake City and Ogallala). The number of stops was attributable to my brother being 2 years old.

We arrived in New York initially living on West 86th Street and later East 72nd Street. Priscilla and I went to the United Nations School where I met (at the age of 9 years) my first heart throb. Dad said that from my description, he was expecting "a cross between Marilyn Monroe and Jane Russell".

I invited my girlfriend and her friend to dinner. We had steak. Dad asked me if my girlfriend's friend had enjoyed it given the cost. Apparently, I said – 'yes – it was the first time she had tasted it. Her mother and father are vegetarians'.

While we were living in New York, the family was requested to be interviewed by a television show called PM East/PM West. It was a very interesting show. On that night there was also an interview with the Von Trapp family, famous in relation to the Sound of Music.

After a year in the U.S. we returned to Sydney.

In 1963, we headed to Europe on board the P&O ship "Oriana".

We arrived in the U.K. and spent some time with my father's parents – Tom and Linda. Tom was the cook and ensuring that we were ok on a day that they needed to go out, prepared a 'Shepherd's Pie' (lamb mince and mashed potato) for us. Unfortunately, Dad's gourmet tastes led us to a country pub with Italian cuisine. The Shepherd's Pie was planted in a hedgerow for posterity.

After our European trip, Mum and Dad wished to adopt a fourth child. This led them to Hong Kong where they were to live for one year due to government regulations regarding the adoption process. Priscilla was at University and I was at school so we lived with our maternal grandmother Grace in Sydney and went to Hong Kong on our holidays.

My (Chinese) brother Andrew was adopted and became part of our family.

He could not originally speak any English so Mum and Dad started learning Cantonese. Unfortunately, when they were telling Andrew about coming to Sydney, the method of transport was described as via 'a flying chicken'.

In terms of transport, Dad had a passion for British quality cars, originally enjoying driving a range of MGs – models such as TD, TF, MGB and MGA Twin Cam. On one occasion when I was quite young, a truck driver pulled into our lane in front of Dad's car causing him to take very quick evasive action. When we got home Mum asked if I was alright. I told her the story and then stated that Dad had said 'that bloody barse nearly got us'! I think I learned the meaning of 'barse' later on.

He was also fond of Jaguar motor vehicles. One day he said he would take us on a picnic so we drove to a leafy spot, put down the tray tables and drink holders in the current Jaguar and had sandwiches and soft drinks in the car!

During the 1960s and early 70s we lived in a very nice house in St. Ives in Sydney. It was here that Dad developed his culinary skills.

He decided one night to cook a chicken and to enhance it with white wine. The chicken had been frozen but was now thawed. Unfortunately, Dad did not realise that the neck and giblets were inside the chicken in plastic bags. He also poured a whole bottle of white wine over the chicken and placed it in the oven to cook. About 2 hours later he took it out of the oven and 'voila' we had a meal resembling (and feeling) like a football with a melted plastic centre! Take-away time!!

On a later occasion he found a recipe for Cheese Fondue. Not exactly knowing much about garlic, he put the whole bunch into the Fondue (about 15 cloves). The Fondue was marginally edible but we had to keep all the doors of the house open during the day for a week.

One New Year's Eve Dad decided to invite guests to a party. He had read in his *Playboy Cookbook* about 'Hero' sandwiches. He made these with great flourish but again not knowing a lot about chilies he decided to be generous with their application. I seem to remember there was a lot drunk on that night!

Dad was very keen on good wines and cocktails also.

I was allowed to try wine in my early teens.

Dad's rules were – dry red, dry white, champagne but he also didn't mind 'black velvet' = champagne and stout + cocktails = bloody Marys, martinis, stingers (cognac and white crème de menthe) margueritas and more. I had to obey these rules! Someone had to do it!

Talking about *Playboy*, Dad used to buy a copy quite often – obviously for the articles, recipes and gaining more insights into the American culture!

Old copies were stored in bookshelves along with copies of Carter Brown novels. In my early to mid-teens I would charge my friends a small fee to review some of the *Playboy* magazines and the CB book covers.

Dad's writing of CB books had the main hero as Lieutenant Al Wheeler but he also had some other heroes and one heroine – Mavis Seidlitz. He wrote in the first person for all of these hence having to write for Mavis as a woman. Mavis was Blonde, Buxom, (inclined to be a Blonde of the types often mentioned in jokes) and the Personal Assistant to a Private Detective. In the opening paragraph of one of the books with her as the heroine, she says 'I knew it was going to be a bad day when my left bra-strap broke'.

I completed secondary school in 1969 and applied to the Sydney Metropolitan Universities Admission Centre to attend university in Sydney. I gave 8 possible choices at one of (then) 3 Sydney-based Universities largely based on Arts, Law or Economics.

It was therefore a total surprise when I was awarded a place to attend a Sydney University to attempt a Science Degree with a focus on 'Wool Classing'. As usual, Dad was pragmatic and helped me to get into a country New South Wales university (University of New England) to do Arts and then combine it with Law at Sydney University.

I attended the course for 18 months but Dad's father (Tom) had become ill in the U.K. With the exception of my sister Priscilla we all flew to Hong Kong, joined a very small (5000 ton) Russian vessel (the 'Baikal') and sailed to Yokohama and then to Vladivostok to catch the Trans-Siberian train to Moscow.

On the ship we hit two typhoons (one on each leg). Mum had always espoused brandy and dry ginger ale as a stomach settler. The bar on the Baikal only had Russian brandy and no dry ginger ale but they did have ginger beer so we invented a new drink (not too bad either!).

The Trans-Siberian rail trip took 8 days with 84 stops. There were 5 classes of carriages. There was an 8 hour time difference between Vladivostok and Moscow but the dining car worked on Moscow time. The stewards and stewardesses in the dining car did not speak English so we would wait until food was delivered to another table, point at it and then point at ourselves to get the message across. An interesting but somewhat confusing trip!!

We arrived in London and found a very nice maisonette to live in in South Kensington. I re-started my Arts degree at London University but at a college in North London and at night.

After a while, I thought I really need to get a job so I started searching 'wanted' advertisements. I applied to be a clerk at a Burglar Alarm manufacturing company amongst others but with no success.

Dad said I should try for a job in Banking and Finance. I said –'why?' and he said 'why not?'

I found an advertised position as a Trainee Representative for Citibank Trust which had recently purchased an existing finance company to commence operations in the U.K.

Dad helped me write a resume and I sent this off to Citibank. About 2 days later he said 'why don't you call them?' I said 'what do I say?' He said 'tell them that they might not understand your Australian academic history and you can explain it to them'. Eventually I called Citibank and spoke to a very nice Canadian gentleman who turned out to be both the hiring manager and the boss. I gave him my pitch and he responded 'so you want an interview?' I was astounded but quickly said 'yes please'.

So a time was agreed. Dad then said you now need to go to Companies House and find out as much as you can about the company. I went and reviewed a number of microfiches taking notes as I went through them.

At the interview the big question came –'what do you know about us?' I was ready! I think my interviewer's jaw was dropping until I told him that he was Canadian born, married, had two children and had been instrumental in setting up operations in the U.K

I got the job on the spot and have been involved in corporate and institutional banking and finance ever since. Thanks – Dad!

On the 5th of October, 1973 I met my wife to be – Margaret who was born in Cardiff, Wales.

We were married on the 15th of June, 1974 at a church in Kensington with the reception being held at my parents' place in South Kensington.

On the 6th of December 1975 Margaret and I returned to Australia (Margaret for the first time). The temperature on Christmas Day was 100 degrees Fahrenheit. We were invited to the Pittwater side of Palm Beach (one of Sydney's Northern beaches with wonderful scenery and water views and no clouds on that day). We had a cold meal mainly consisting of fresh seafood. Unfortunately, not what Margaret was used to!

We returned to London for a trip in December 1979 and had several wine tasting dinners with Mum and Dad.

Mum and Dad returned to Australia in 1982 and stayed with us for a little while. They then found a townhouse at Cremorne (an upmarket Sydney suburb near to Sydney Harbour). This was very convenient as we could park there on New Year's Eve, walk down to the harbour, watch the fireworks and stay over.

Mum and Dad always thought the world of Margaret with Dad signing a copy of his autobiography to us saying "For Maggie and Jeremy – I made a deal for Jeremy but Maggie was a kind of bonus! – Alan Yates alias Carter Brown".

Dad died in May, 1985. He taught me a whole lot!

He was a prolific and successful author but more so – a kind and generous person with an abounding love of life.

—December 2018,
Pymble, Australia

No Law Against Angels

Carter Brown

CHAPTER 1

"Hey!" the blonde said sharply.

"What's the matter?" I asked her.

"It's just that you're so—well, unorthodox!"

"Ain't it the truth!" I agreed.

She pushed me away. "I should be going home," she said.

"Give me one good reason!"

"My husband," she said nervously. "He's an all-in wrestler and…"

I handed her her hat and coat: "That's two good reasons—I only asked you for one."

"It's so late," she said. "I never even noticed the time."

"I would have been insulted if you had," I told her. "Let me know when your husband takes a trip to Europe—I'll call you again."

I rang an all-night cab service and ten minutes later she rode out of my life—I would have been sorry about that if it hadn't been for her husband. Why didn't she tell me before? I shivered as I poured myself a drink. It's dames like that blonde who can make mangled corpses out of guys like me. An all-in wrestler yet! I would have had no faith in the police preventing any mayhem, even if I am a cop.

I settled down in a chair, nursing my drink for a change, and the last disc on the turntable was piped through the walls. Peggy Lee and *Black Coffee*. I thought maybe it was an idea.

The 'phone rang. I looked at it suspiciously. It might be a husband wanting the best of three falls. I picked up the receiver gingerly, cleared my throat and said in a sing-song voice: "Li Still's Chinese Laundry."

"I had hoped," a weary voice said, "that for once I might find you sober."

"Why, Commissioner," I said, "I'm glad to hear your voice!"

"Now I know you're drunk!"

"It's a lie!" I said. "Well—an untruth, anyway. I haven't had more than four drinks all night."

"That means you've got company then?"

"Just left," I said. "Do you know a wrestler by the name of Kychinsky?"

"No," he said. "Do you?"

"I do not. Furthermore, it is my burning ambition not to know him—ever!"

He made a growling noise into the 'phone: "I didn't ring you to talk about female wrestlers! Get into your car and get down to the morgue. I'll meet you there."

"What are you going to do?" I asked him. "Put me on ice?"

He hung up, of course.

I backed the Healey down the driveway, straightened it out in the street and headed towards the morgue. One of the bigger disadvantages of being the Commissioner's personal assistant is that he doesn't realise a working day ends—like now.

He was waiting for me when I got there. With two other guys with him. One was a guy with a chalk-white face, an overall coat to match, and eyes that permanently started out of his head. Charlie Katz, the head mortician.

"Hi, Charlie," I said. "How's business?"

"I keep a drawer empty all the time," he told me. "Anything happens to you, Al, I always got a place for you here."

"Well, thanks," I said. "My haunting rates are cheap, too, if you want to rent me out."

Commissioner Lavers glared at me: "Wheeler!"

"Good morning, sir," I said. I looked pointedly at my watch, which said it was one forty-five—a.m. "Off to an early start this morning, aren't we, sir?"

"This is Lieutenant Hammond," he said, "from Homicide."

Hammond was a thin guy, with a beak of a nose and the trusting look of a second-hand car salesman. He nodded curtly.

"I've heard of you, Wheeler," he said. "The unorthodox cop, they call you? What do you do—eat your meals standing upside down?"

"Only when I'm in Australia," I said. "I haven't heard of you, Hammond—that's understandable, of course."

"Let's go inside," Lavers said. "There's something I want you to look at."

"A cadaver?" I asked. "Isn't it a little early in the morning to look at a stiff? Before breakfast even!"

I followed him and Hammond into the storage-room. Charlie pulled one of the drawers out of the wall and switched on an extra light. It was a girl. A girl who had been young and pretty with long dark hair framing the waxen oval of her face.

Lavers pulled back the sheet gently, exposing her right arm. There was a tattoo mark on it—high, just below the shoulder. Something like a dollar sign, only the bar through the S weaved and had the head of a snake.

"That's the second one this week," Lavers said. He pulled the sheet back into place, then motioned to Charlie to close the drawer.

We walked back into the outer office and I lit a cigarette, feeling the chill of the storage-room still in my blood.

"How did she die?" I asked.

"Knifed," Lavers said laconically. "And so was the first one. Hammond has been working on the first case, without getting anywhere. Not his fault—there's no lead, nothing."

I didn't have to be psychic to know what was coming.

"I'd like you to take a look at it," the Commissioner went on. "Hammond can give you the details. He'll still work on both cases, of course. You just might in your crazy, illogical Marx Brothers way, come up with a new angle."

"Yes, sir," I said dutifully.

"The only connecting link between the two is the tattoo mark of course. We don't know much about the first one—and this body was only discovered three hours ago. Tell him about the first one, Hammond."

The Lieutenant shrugged his shoulders. "Her name was Angela Markon. She got into town three weeks back—had a room in a boarding-house. The old dame who runs it said the girl never talked about herself at all. She went out three or four nights in the week—nobody ever called for her or brought her home. She told the old dame she was looking for a job, but, she didn't seem to look very hard—she deposited two hundred dollars in a bank close by the day she arrived in town, and another two hundred a couple of days before she was murdered."

"The deposits were cash, I take it?" I asked him.

Hammond nodded: "That's right. We can't find out where she came from or anybody who knew her. We've circulated a description and her prints, of course—but we haven't heard anything."

"How about the girl in there?" I asked.

He shrugged his shoulders. "So far we've got her name—Leila Cross. Her purse was on the sidewalk where she must have dropped it. There was twenty bucks inside, a pack of cigarettes and matches, lipstick, handkerchief—a social security card and another card."

"What was on the other card?"

"The name and address of a mortician," he grinned. "Maybe she had a premonition!"

"What have you checked so far?"

"The address—another boarding-house. She had been there a month. She worked for the mortician, they told me."

"And the mortician?"

"A guy by the name of Alexi Romonoff. I talked to him. The girl worked for him—a cosmetician."

"A what!"

Hammond grinned sourly: "That's right—pretties up the faces of the departed so they look nice. She was good at it, he told me. She'd only been working for him the last three weeks. He didn't know much about her, except that she was obviously experienced in the job and she was a good worker. That's about all I got from him. The dame who ran the boarding-house didn't know anything about her, either."

"Where were they both killed?" I asked.

Lavers cleared his throat: "Both in an alleyway—not the same one, but there isn't much basic difference. They're within half a mile of each other in the Rockton district. Both of them stabbed through the back by someone who knew what they were doing. Death would have been practically instantaneous in both cases."

"I never knew two dames that people could know so little about!" Hammond said disgustedly.

Lavers grunted: "It's the connecting link between them—that and the tattoo mark. Does it mean anything to you, Wheeler?"

"No," I said. "Maybe they both had a low opinion of money, hence the snake?"

"Maybe it's some cult they both belonged to?" Hammond suggested. "How about that?"

"Maybe," Lavers grunted. "You've got to find out between you, and quickly. I don't like two unexplained murders hanging over the department."

I lit myself another cigarette: "Just how do Hammond and I handle this thing between us—exactly?"

"Hammond continues his routine investigation," Lavers said. "I'm giving you a free hand to follow any line of investigation that occurs to you. I expect you both to exchange any information you have, of course."

"You don't object to me back-tracking over ground that Hammond's already covered?"

"No. If you think you've anything to gain by it."

"I'll be grateful for any points the Lieutenant thinks I've missed!" Hammond said coldly.

"And I'll put them in words of one syllable for you, too," I said cheerfully.

And that broke up the party. Lavers and Hammond went back to town in a prowl-car and I drove the Healey back to my own house. I had a couple of drinks to keep out the morgue-cold and went to bed.

I spent the night in nightmare where I was stuck in one of those refrigerated drawers and every time I tried to get out, a pretty girl with Charlie Katz's face tattooed on her arm would come along and close the drawer again.

For once in my life, I was glad to wake up.

CHAPTER 2

Haven of Rest, it said in neat letters across the front of the establishment. I opened one of the glass doors and stepped inside. The silence was broken only by my footsteps as I crossed the parquet floor to the reception desk.

The receptionist was a pallid blonde wearing a black frock. She gave me a pallid smile: "Can I help you?"

"I'd like to see Mr. Romonoff," I said.

She looked doubtful: "He's very busy."

"Business is good?"

"I said he's very busy!"

"I'm a police officer," I said. "I am also busy. I would like to see him now!" I showed her my shield as a clincher.

She picked up, the ivory 'phone and dialled a number, then whispered into it. She listened while somebody presumably whispered back, then she hung up.

"Mr. Romonoff will be down in a moment," she said.

"Thanks," I told her. "This is quite a place you have here."

"We do our best for the Departed," she said. "One cannot say more than that, can one?"

"If one is one of the Departed," I said brightly, "one cannot say even that much, can one?"

That finished our conversation.

A couple of minutes later Romonoff appeared. He was short and fat, with thick, curly black hair and a luxuriant curling moustache to match. He looked aggressively alive and therefore out of place.

"Cops!" he said. "The whole place is getting loused up with cops—soon I got no room for stiffs!"

"I'm Lieutenant Wheeler," I said. "I wanted to talk to you about Leila Cross."

"Sure," he said. "What else? No cop could afford one of my funerals! Okay, Lieutenant—I'll give you ten minutes. Let's get out of here and have a drink—there's a bar across the street. This place always gives me the creeps!"

"I'm with you there," I agreed.

He looked at the pallid blonde. "I'm out for ten minutes," he said. "And, honey—while I'm gone, why don't you get yourself a pint of blood?"

The blonde closed her eyes, dropped a mental nickel in a slot and a pained expression appeared on her face.

Romonoff shrugged his broad shoulders. "One of these days," he confided to me as we walked towards the door, "I'm going to shoot her with a silver bullet and if she crumples right away to dust, I'll know my first guess was right!"

We settled down in the more cheerful atmosphere of the bar.

"Scotch?" Romonoff asked me.

"On the rocks," I agreed.

He ordered, then turned back to me: "Like I told the other Lieutenant when he dragged me out of bed last night—I don't know nothing about the kid. She was a good cosmetician—she knew her job all right."

"I find it hard to get used to the idea of a cosmetician," I said. "In your line of business."

He drank some of his Scotch appreciatively. "You need 'em in my line of business," he said. "And the dough they cost me! Leila came to me about three weeks back and asked me for a job. Said she had done the work before—didn't have any references. I had her give me a practical demonstration and she convinced me. So she started right in that day—good cosmeticians in this business are hard to find. I don't know why, it's the only business where the customer never talks back!"

"Did you talk to her while she was working for you?"

"I'd say good morning a couple of times," Romonoff said. "I'm a busy man, Lieutenant ... people keep on dying all the time. I didn't have the time to do anything else. I didn't know a thing about her except she was a good worker."

"That's bad luck," I said. "What about the people she worked with? Anybody she was friendly with at all?"

He thought about that for a moment: "She worked alongside Drusilla Peace."

"That," I stared at him, "is her real name?"

"Why shouldn't it be?" he demanded.

"No reason, I suppose," I said. "It's just a little sudden first time up, I guess."

"I don't think Leila talked much to anybody," he said. "But you could talk to Drusilla if you want."

"I'd like to do that," I told him.

He finished his drink. "We'll have another one and then go back," he said. "The weather's been good lately."

"It's been raining and cold," I said. "East winds howling from all points of the compass. People have been dying like flies!"

"Yeah," Romonoff nodded complacently. "Like I said—good weather!"

I ordered the drinks, the cold damp air seemed to be creeping into my bones all of a sudden.

"Maybe she had a past?" Romonoff said suddenly. "You ought to check on that, Lieutenant?"

"I'm trying to," I said. "Maybe if the weather had been sunny the last three weeks, somebody like you might have had time to talk to her and find out about her past!"

"Can I help it if business is good?" he asked plaintively.

Ten minutes later we were back inside the *Haven of Rest*. The blonde still looked pallid, so maybe she hadn't taken Romonoff's advice after all.

He took me past her desk to an elevator and we rode up to the second floor. We walked down a corridor and then stopped outside a closed door.

"Excuse me a moment," Romonoff said, and opened the door and peered into the room. "It's all right," he said. "It's vacant."

He walked into the room and I followed him. It was a small room, nicely furnished in the modern manner. The only things that seemed out of place were the numerous urns and bowls of flowers, and the oversized sofa.

"I call this the *Tranquil Room*," Romonoff said. "Good name, huh?"

"Wonderful," I said. "What do you use it for?"

"Private viewings," he said, waving an arm towards the sofa.

"We put 'em there before they go into the casket so if anybody wants to make sure we've done a good job, they can take a look."

He walked over to the sofa and sat down, picking up a 'phone from the small table beside it. "Why don't you sit down?" he asked. "Make yourself comfortable?"

"No, thanks," I took another look at the sofa. "I think I'll stand if it's all the same to you."

"Suit yourself," he shrugged. "Ask Drusilla to come up to the *Tranquil Room* right away," he said into the 'phone. He put the receiver back on the cradle and looked at me. "She'll be here in a minute, Lieutenant. You mind if I leave you to it? You want me afterwards, the receptionist will find me."

"Okay," I said. "Thanks, Mr. Romonoff."

"No trouble," he said.

He got as far as the door, then seemed to hesitate a moment.

He looked back at me. "When your department's finished with Leila," he said, "I'd like to have her—I'd sort of like to do things right for her—you know, the works! On the house, of course!"

"That's very generous of you, Mr. Romonoff," I said gravely.

"It's nothing," he said modestly. "I just don't like the thought of her—being a professional—being fixed up by amateurs!"

He went out, closing the door behind him. I put a hand to my forehead and it came away slightly damp. I lit a cigarette and felt slightly better as the nicotine soothed my nerves.

They needed soothing—or bracing. I imagined what Drusilla would be like—a bat masquerading as a female. Something that makes a swishing noise in the dead of night and talks in scream overtones!

There was a slight tap on the door, then it opened and the female bat walked in. She looked at me and smiled: "Lieutenant Wheeler? I met Mr. Romonoff in the corridor and he told me what it was about."

If she was a female bat, I was going to swing by my toes off the nearest tree from here on. She was a redhead with a mane of hair that she let fall to her shoulders. Her lips were full and red and spoke a different language to the words they framed. Her eyes had a greenish tinge and promised more than a thousand words from a second-hand car salesman.

She wore a white uniform which made no attempt to hide the full, generous curves of her figure. In fact, it seemed to be in full sympathy with it, clinging where it could cling to the most advantage, and moulding where it thought a point could be accentuated to advantage. The word *Haven* made a left-hand curve around the front of the uniform.

She stood there, waiting patiently for me to recover from the shock. I guessed it happened every time she met a guy she hadn't met before. She had to wait for him to recover from the stunned shock, then probably hit him over the head with a baseball-bat once the recovery was complete.

I felt the adrenalin pounding through my veins like crazy and wondered how any corpse could keep still for her. If you kept still while she was around, you'd know you were dead for sure!

"You wanted to talk to me about poor Leila?" she prompted.

I recovered my voice: "That's right. I understand from Mr. Romonoff that you worked with her?"

"That is correct," she said. Her voice was the warm sigh of the Trade Wind fluttering the palms ... the overtones identical with the voice of Eve saying, "Have a bite?"

I was finding it hard to concentrate. I stubbed out my first cigarette in a vase of white lilies and lit another one.

"You know about Leila Cross?" I mumbled.

She nodded: "Mr. Romonoff told me ... I didn't really know her very well, but it's shocking when it happens to someone you know even slightly, isn't it?"

"Yes," I said, and puffed hard on the second cigarette. The pattern of her uniform changed considerably every time she breathed in and every time she breathed out. It was unsettling.

"Did she talk to you at all?" I asked her.

She shook her head gently: "Hardly ever. She was pleasant enough, but she kept herself to herself."

"Did she talk about where she had lived before she came here to Pine

City? Where she had worked—anything like that?"

"I'm afraid not."

"Did she mention any relatives—parents, husband, brothers or sisters?"

"No, I'm afraid not."

"Did she mention any of her friends—their names—maybe a boy-friend?"

"I'm afraid not."

I took another drag on the cigarette: "In three weeks she must have said something!"

"The work we do requires a lot of concentration," Drusilla smiled sympathetically. "We don't normally talk very much to one another. I'm sorry, Lieutenant."

"Did she talk about anything—anything at all! The sort of food she liked—books she'd read—movies she'd seen—anything at all. Don't worry about how unimportant it sounds ... just anything at all!"

She thought hard for a few moments: "She did say once, I remember, something about how she hated the cold weather and how nice the Californian climate was."

"That's something," I said. "Anything else you can think of?"

She concentrated some more while I concentrated on watching her concentrate.

"There was something else," she said finally. "It was about three or four days ago. She said she had a date and she'd just as soon not keep it, but the fellow was meeting her outside after we finished for the day and she wouldn't be able to dodge him, so she supposed she'd have to keep the date."

"Did she mention his name?"

"Douglas," Drusilla said. "She said his name was Douglas and if ever a name didn't suit a man, it was with him. We left together that night and I saw her meet him." She smiled faintly. "I must confess, Lieutenant, that I was a little curious."

"What did he look like?"

"About medium height—somewhere about forty, I'd say. He was thin with fair hair and big glasses with horn rims, thin ones."

"How was he dressed?"

She shrugged her shoulders which set up a new pattern in the uniform: "I didn't really notice, so I guess it was just average—he looked like a clerk or something. Nothing very exciting."

"Did she talk about him next morning?"

"Nothing. She didn't speak at all the next day—only to say hello first thing in the morning."

"Nothing else?"

"I can't think of anything else."

"Thanks, anyway," I said. "If you do think of anything, let me know, will you?"

"Of course, Lieutenant."

"And I'd better have your address in case I should want to get in touch with you in a hurry."

"You can always reach me here."

"You don't live here, do you?"

"Oh," she smiled. "I see—I have a small apartment on Summer Boulevard—apartment nine and the house number is 824."

"Thanks," I said, and wrote it down carefully.

"I hope you catch whoever did it, Lieutenant," she said, then walked out of the room, the uniform a poem of flowing motion.

I thought I needed a change of scenery. I went down the corridor to the elevator. I rode the elevator down, then walked past the reception desk where the pallid blonde smiled in her own pallid way, and then I was in the street again amongst the living.

I went back to City Hall, back to my desk in Commissioner Lavers' office, which had never been the same since a certain stenographer by the name of Annabelle Starr had left three weeks back.

She'd told the Commissioner she had been offered a good job in New York and was taking it. She'd told me that although she loved me, loved me, loved me, I obviously wasn't the marrying type ... And she wasn't a career-girl. So she was taking her broken heart to New York, where she hoped that soon a nice young man with a name like Rockefeller would sew her heart together again with gold thread by proposing marriage.

But the office wasn't the same somehow without Annabelle around. In her place was a female tartar—age vague, but acid approach unmistakable. She didn't approve of me. I don't think she approved of anything, but I was a priority rating on her list of disapprovals. Her name was Fern Gulley and she looked like one around the head. I gave her a couple of hints about how romantic Yul Brynner looked, didn't she think, but so far she hadn't done anything about it. I lived in hope.

She looked at me disapprovingly as I came into the office.

"You're late today, Lieutenant," she said flatly.

"But that's only for today," I said. "For tomorrow and all of next week, I'm early."

I left her there trying to figure some sense into it and knocked on the Commissioner's door. He told me to come in, so I went in. He looked up at me with that remarkable lack of enthusiasm he has whenever he sees me.

"Are you just starting work?" he asked.

"I have been working, Commissioner," I told him with quiet dignity. "All morning. I've been visiting the *Haven of Rest*. If you haven't made provision for your ultimate future, I would be happy to book you a casket any time and ..."

"What did you find out?"

"Not much," I admitted. I told him what little there was.

Lavers sucked his teeth: "It's something—she had a date four nights back. The guy's name was Douglas ..."

"Medium height and medium dressed and wearing medium rimmed glasses," I said. "There wouldn't be more than half a million guys who'd answer that description, would there?"

He grunted: "It's a start, anyway."

"Has Hammond found out anything?"

"Why don't you ask him?"

"I don't think he likes me, Commissioner."

"Which is understandable," he said. "The routine's gone ahead—morgue photographs are being circulated of both of them. We don't have their prints on file and neither does L.A. The prints have gone with the photos. He checked on the bank where the first girl, Angela Markon had her money ... the two deposits, remember?"

"Two hundred and then another two," I nodded.

"One of the tellers remembered her quite well. But she didn't tell him anything of any interest."

"That's great!"

"You can't blame Hammond for that!"

"No," I agreed. "How long had they been dead before they were found in these alleyways?"

"The Markon girl had been dead about four hours—the Cross girl a little longer, around five. Why?"

"Curious," I said. "The marks on their arms—a definite tattoo job?"

"Yes, according to the surgeon. A skin-graft would have been necessary to erase them—that would be the only way, he said."

"We don't seem to get very far, do we, sir?"

"You don't!" he said brusquely.

And on that tender note I left his office.

I went over to the Homicide Bureau and found Hammond at home in his office. He didn't seem to be particularly excited to see me.

"The Commissioner's boy!" he said as I walked into his office: "Case all wrapped up and ready to make an arrest, eh?"

I hooked a chair with one foot, then sat down and lit myself a cigarette. I thought I'd try and play fair with him anyway, so I told him the story of my morning's activities.

"I've been trying to get a lead on the first one," he said. "I'm not making much progress!"

"You and me both, pal," I said. I got onto my feet. "Let me know if somebody comes in and confesses!"

His 'phone rang and he answered it. "For you," he said, then handed me the receiver.

"Lieutenant?" It was Fern's sexless voice. "A Miss Peace rang you five minutes ago, said it was very urgent and wants you to ring her back. It occurred to me you might be in Homicide."

"Thanks, Fern," I said. "I'll buy you some fertiliser!" The 'phone slammed down in my ear a moment later.

"Anything interesting?" Hammond asked.

"Some guy I owe ten bucks," I said.

"Life's tough!"

I picked up my hat from his desk. "See you around, Hammond."

"Sure," he grunted. His eyes were still narrowed suspiciously. "Sure—why not?"

I went out of the Bureau fast and picked up the Healey, then drove back to the *Haven of Rest*. The pallid blonde gave me a look of hopeless resignation.

"What now, Lieutenant?"

"Tell Drusilla Peace I'm here, please."

"She's in the embalming room, Lieutenant."

"Just tell her I'm here—I'll wait if I have to."

She rang through, then told me Miss Peace would be down to see me in a couple of minutes. I put a cigarette into my mouth and was going to light it, when I caught the look on the pallid blonde's face and put the cigarette hastily back in my pocket.

Drusilla appeared a little while later. She smiled when she saw me: "It was nice of you to come in person, Lieutenant."

"A picture is worth a thousand words," I said. "Who wants to listen on a 'phone when he can see you?"

"I rang because Douglas rang," she said, slightly breathlessly. "About half an hour ago."

"Douglas—the guy who had a date with Leila Cross?"

"The same! He just asked for the cosmeticians' room and the call was put through. I answered it and it gave me goose pimples when somebody asked to speak to Leila. Then I realised it isn't in the papers yet, is it? And I thought you'd want to know who it was, so I said she was out for a little while and could I get her to call him back when she came in. So he said to tell her it was Douglas Bond calling and he'd meet her after work—outside."

I shook my head admiringly: "Drusilla, you're a genius!"

"Did I do the right thing?"

"One hundred and ten per cent!"

"I'm glad."

"What time do you finish work?"

"Five o'clock."

"I'll be here at a quarter to five. I want you to meet me here so that we can both watch the street. I'd like to see if you can identify him as the guy she met before."

"All right, Lieutenant," she said. "Do you think he's the one who ..."

"I have no idea," I said. "But maybe we'll find out at five tonight."

CHAPTER 3

Drusilla was dressed ready for the street when she came down to the reception desk to meet me at a quarter to five. She was wearing a light grey suit with a white silk blouse underneath. My adrenalin supply got out of hand again.

She stood beside me and looked through the plate-glass doors onto the street. "I can't see him yet," she said.

"There's plenty of time," I said. "If he turns up. I found out the story was released for the afternoon papers on the murder. It was too late to even try and stop it. If he's read his paper yet, I don't imagine he'll be here."

She gripped my arm suddenly: "There he is!"

I looked up and saw him, standing there directly outside the doors. A guy of medium height, thin with the blonde hair and horn-rimmed glasses—like she'd said. A character you wouldn't look at twice—like she'd said.

"The same one?" I asked her.

"It's the same man, all right," she said eagerly. "The one she met the time before."

"Thanks, Drusilla," I said. "Thanks a lot."

"You don't want me anymore?" She sounded disappointed.

"I'll take it from here," I told her. "And thanks again."

I walked out of the *Haven of Rest*, onto the sidewalk, up to the character who stood waiting patiently, with his paper rolled under his arm—waiting for a girl who'd been dead for the last thirty hours.

"Mr. Bond?" I asked him. "Mr. Douglas Bond?"

"Yes," he blinked at me. "Who are you?"

"I'm a police officer, Mr. Bond," I said. "Lieutenant Wheeler."

"A police officer?" He blinked more rapidly. "What do you want with me?"

"I wanted to have a talk to you, about Leila Cross."

"Leila! She's not in any trouble, is she? I mean nothing has happened to her? I ..."

I took his arm and pushed him gently towards the parked car. "Get in, Mr. Bond," I told him. He got into the car obediently and I got in beside him and drove out into the peak-hour traffic.

"I was supposed to meet her," he said plaintively. "She will wonder what's happened to me! I ..."

"She won't be there, Mr. Bond," I said. "I'll tell you what it's all about as soon as we arrive."

"Arrive?" There was a squeak in his voice. "Arrive where? Are you arresting me for something?"

"No," I said. "We're going out to my house where we can be comfortable, Mr. Bond. I'd like to ask you some questions, that's all. It won't take long—another ten minutes."

"But Leila! What's happened? I demand ..."

"I'll tell you all about it as soon as we get there," I repeated. "It won't be long."

He slumped back in the seat and stared unseeingly through the windscreen. I concentrated on driving. It took us fifteen minutes to get to my place and I took him straight inside, sat him in an armchair, then went on into the kitchen and poured two hefty measures of Scotch. I took them back with me into the living room and gave him one.

He looked up at me: "I don't understand, Lieutenant. I don't understand this at all!"

"Drink that," I said. He raised the glass to his lips obediently and drank. "Have you read your paper?" I asked him.

"Paper?" He looked down automatically at the newspaper still rolled and tucked underneath his arm. "No—why?"

"I think you better had," I told him.

He looked at me again for a moment, then put down his glass on the table beside him and slowly unrolled the paper. It was front-page stuff, with the morgue photograph reproduced and a request that anybody knowing anything of the deceased should contact Lieutenant Hammond of the Homicide Bureau.

Bond's face went a chalk colour as he read through the story. His hands started to tremble violently and he put the newspaper down on his knees.

"Finish your drink, Mr. Bond," I said. "I'm sorry—there isn't an easy way to tell a person about a murder. You were close to her?"

"We were going to be married," Bond said tonelessly. "Or I hoped we were, at least."

He finished his drink and I took the glass out into the kitchen and poured him another. When I got back, he took the glass and drank some more.

"I still can't believe it really happened," he muttered. "I knew something was wrong—dreadfully wrong. I pleaded with her, but she wouldn't listen to me."

"Why don't you tell me about it, Mr. Bond?" I suggested.

He looked at me dully: "She lived in Vale Heights ... that's where I come from."

"That's about forty miles out of Pine City, isn't it?" I asked. "On the coast?"

"That's right, Lieutenant. Leila worked in the local beauty parlour—she was a cosmetician. I guess you know that?"

"Yes."

"Everything was all right until about three months ago, then she got in with a new girl at the shop. I never did like her—she was a bad influence on Leila. They started going out together at night. Leila would put off a date with me and I'd ask her why, and she'd say it was none of my business. It worried me. I felt there was something wrong about it. If there was nothing to it, why wouldn't Leila tell me what she was doing? And she had money. The clothes she started wearing cost more than she could afford out of what she made at the beauty parlour."

I offered him a cigarette and lit it for him and one for myself.

"Then what?" I asked.

"She disappeared suddenly, without a trace. A little over three weeks ago. Her parents had died about four years ago and she had a small apartment of her own in Vale Heights. The woman who owned the place didn't know where she'd gone. Leila left her a note saying she'd had to leave suddenly, and left the rent up to the end of the week. I nearly went crazy for a while— the other girl didn't know where Leila had gone. I had a feeling she might be lying, but I couldn't do anything about it.

"I thought wherever she'd gone, she would have to find work and she'd find work as a cosmetician. She could have gone anywhere—the two nearest and biggest cities were here and L.A. I spent a week-end in L.A. checking all the beauty parlours, and drew a blank. I spent the next week-end here and drew a blank. When I got back to Vale Heights, I suddenly remembered that she'd sort of fixed up a couple of people who had died."

He finished his second drink: "You know it happens in that business. A woman dies who's been going to the beauty parlour for years and the mortician asks the girl who used to attend her, would she mind fixing her up for the funeral. I remembered there had been a few times Leila had done that. And I thought she just might have taken a job with a mortician instead of a beauty parlour, to make it harder for me to find her—if it was me she'd run away from. I couldn't really believe that."

I nodded: "That was smart thinking, Mr. Bond. Your hunch paid off, of course."

"I finally located her. I came down here and booked into a hotel. I rang her and she agreed to meet me after work one night. She wasn't pleased to see me. She told me she'd finished with her life in Vale Heights and that included me. I told her I didn't believe it, there was something more to it than that. Something she was hiding from me. Then she got mad and walked out on me. I rang again today, hoping she might have changed her mind even a little ... and she was dead before I even lifted the 'phone!"

I waited for a moment. "She had a tattoo high up on her right arm," I said. "Do you have any idea what it meant?"

"Tattoo?" He stared at me. "Leila never had any tattoo on her arm!"

"She did when she was found—like a dollar sign, but the bar was wavy and had the head of a snake. Does it have any meaning for you at all?"

He shook his head vigorously: "She must have had it done very recently. I can't think why she would. A tattoo mark!"

"This girl," I said. "The one Leila became friendly with and went out with. Her name would have been Angela Markon?"

"Why, no," he said firmly. "That was Olga Kellner."

"Have you ever heard of a girl named Angela Markon?"

"No," he shook his head.

You can't have everything.

"What's the name of the beauty parlour where this Olga Kellner works?"

"Vale Heights Beauty Parlour."

"That's original, anyway," I said. "Would you know Olga's home address?"

"No," he shook his head again. "I'm sorry, Lieutenant."

"Your impression was that Leila ran away from Vale Heights, because something was worrying her?"

"I think so," he said. "Yes, I'm quite sure of it! I don't think it had anything to do with me, Lieutenant. I'm not exactly the dominant male type," he smiled ruefully. "I didn't scare Leila out of Vale Heights!"

"But you think something or somebody else did?"

"Why else would she suddenly vanish like that?"

"You have no idea what it might have been?"

"None," he said limply. "Over the last few months I haven't known much about her private life, Lieutenant. I wish now that I had—that I'd made it my business to find out! I might have saved her this...." He shook his head wearily. "There's not much point in developing hind-sight, is there? She's dead now, and nothing will change that!"

"I'm afraid not, Mr. Bond," I said. "There's nothing else you can think of at the moment that might be a lead? However slight, it might help."

He thought for a few moments: "I'm sorry, Lieutenant ... I can't."

"Would you give me your address here?"

"Of course. I'm staying at the *Wagner Hotel*—you know it?"

"I know it."

"Not a very good hotel, I'm afraid," he smiled ruefully again. "But the best I can afford."

He took out his billfold and handed it to me: "I guess you'll want to check on that. There's a receipt there and identification and so on."

"Thanks," I told him.

I checked through the contents of his billfold. There was a driver's licence, letters, the receipt he mentioned, about thirty dollars in bills. I gave him back the billfold.

"I realise this must have been quite a shock to you," I said. "I'll drive you back to your hotel in a minute, Mr. Bond. I'd like you to go down to the Homicide Bureau in the morning and make a formal statement of everything you've told me, to Lieutenant Hammond. He'll have a stenographer record it and you can sign the statement afterwards."

"Of course," he said.

I gave him one more drink and then drove him back to the *Wagner Hotel*. I asked him what were the bright spots in Vale Heights on the way.

"There's a new hotel on the waterfront," he said. "It's called the *Beachcomber*—it's very bright and very expensive, I believe. There are half a dozen bars, too, which are quite good—and a couple of nightclubs. The town's expanding fast the whole time—all on the tourist trade, of course."

"That's interesting," I said,

"I'm not quite sure it's a good thing," he said carefully. "The town is losing its identity and there are a lot of unsavoury characters coming in. The tourist money attracts them, I guess. And there's talk of building a casino on the waterfront as well."

"It always happens," I said.

I pulled in out front of the *Wagner Hotel*.

"Thank you, Lieutenant," he said earnestly. "It was good of you to drive me."

"Think nothing of it," I told him. "And don't forget to go in and see Lieutenant Hammond in the morning .... I wonder if you'd do something for me?"

"Of course," he said. "What is it?"

"Well," I told him carefully. "Officially, this is Lieutenant Hammond's case ... I'm attached to the Police Commissioner's office and the Commissioner has me looking into the case ... unofficially. I wouldn't want to hurt Lieutenant Hammond's feelings."

"I understand, I think," he said.

"If you wouldn't mention our conversation tonight. The story will be in the morning papers. You could tell him you read it and went straight down to the Bureau to see him. He won't question it and it will save his feelings being hurt."

"Certainly, Lieutenant, I'll do that," Bond said warmly. "No trouble at all."

"Thanks very much," I told him.

I drove home again, put a call through to the *Beachcomber Hotel* in Vale Heights and booked a room for the night, packed a few things in a suit-case and went back to the car.

It was seven-thirty when I left for Vale Heights. And that gave me a good fifteen hours start over Hammond, I thought. I had a strong desire to show him that even on my hands, walking upside down, I could still travel one hell of a lot faster than he could!

CHAPTER 4

I made the forty miles to Vale Heights in about three-quarters of an hour, with the Healey's rev-counter not extended much beyond three and a half thousand.

I drove past the front of the *Beachcomber*, and it looked everything that Bond had said it was. Three blocks further down I found the Vale Heights Beauty Parlour. I parked at the kerb and got out of the car.

The beauty parlour was closed, of course—but there was an apartment above it and a stairway which led to the front door. I pressed the buzzer and the door was opened quite quickly by a woman in her fifties, with impossible pink hair. She wore a satin robe which bulged almost everywhere—she looked like the booby-prize in a sweepstake.

"Yes?" she said coldly.

"I wanted to contact Olga Kellner," I said. "It's urgent, and I wondered if you could help me. Could you give me her address, please?"

"No!" she snapped. "And nobody in Vale Heights could, either!"

"I don't understand," I said. "She works in the beauty parlour, doesn't she?"

"She did, you mean!" the woman said triumphantly. "Until a week ago, then she just vanished. Without collecting the money owing to her, either. If you ask me, she was in trouble!"

"You have no idea where she went?"

"None at all! So I can't help you—sorry!"

I tried an encouraging smile that stretched my facial muscles, but that was about all. "Could you describe her to me, please?"

"If you're looking for her, you know what she looks like!" Her beady eyes glistened. "Or don't you?"

"I'll come clean," I managed a leer. "She skipped owing some back payments, and I'm trying to locate her for the finance company."

"Oh!" She seemed pleased. "And I'm not surprised, neither. Always giving herself airs, she was! She's a blonde—you know, ash-blonde. Nearly white, I'd call it. Well-built sort of girl. Pretty, I suppose," she sniffed loudly. "If you go for that type! Too brassy for my liking!"

"You wouldn't have a photograph of her?"

"Of course not! What would I want with something like that?"

"It was just a thought. Could you give me anything else to go on—tall or short?"

"About medium, I'd guess," she sniffed again. "Sexy to look at—if you know what I mean! Something about the way she walked and the clothes she wore. Nothing you could put your mind to definitely, but some girls have just got it."

"Some sure have," I agreed. "I know what you mean."

"That's all I can tell you," she said. "And she skipped owing money, did she? I'm not surprised! She was just the type. She might owe money here for all I know. I wouldn't be surprised if she did!"

"Neither would I," I said. "Thank you for your help."

"That's all right," she said. "I hope you find her. She left me in a nasty spot, she did. Walking out like that. It was the second girl I've lost inside a month! I don't know what gets into their heads—no sense of responsibility to their employers, that's their trouble! No thought for me, with bookings a couple of weeks ahead and clients expecting to get their treatment as soon as they walk into the shop! That's the trouble with the girls of today—they just haven't got any ..."

"Yes, indeed," I murmured, and beat a swift retreat down the stairs again.

I got back into the car and lit a cigarette. Maybe that fifteen hours start didn't mean very much, after all. Olga Kellner had skipped, the way Leila Cross had skipped. Only not so fast—she had stayed on a couple of weeks. Then why had she suddenly decided to run? If the danger—if there was danger to her—had suddenly grown greater? Or maybe, I thought, it might have caught up with her the same way it had caught up with Leila. Maybe Olga Kellner hadn't skipped very far. Maybe she was a corpse in a Vale Heights alleyway waiting to be found.

It wasn't a cheering thought. I made a U-turn in the Healey and drove back to the *Beachcomber*. An attendant parked the car for me. A bellhop grabbed my case and escorted me into the hotel. I signed the register, picked up the key of the room, and the bellhop took me up to it.

I gave him a dollar which didn't make him a friend, and then decided I needed a drink. I rode the elevator back down to the ground floor and found I had quite a choice ... There was a Continental diningroom, a grill service, a clubroom which stayed open to four a.m. and had three floor-shows, and two bars. I took the smaller bar which was nearly empty.

I sat on a chromed stool and ordered a Scotch on the rocks. The barman was young with eyes that were twenty years older than the rest of him. If Satan ever needed a barker, this character had just the face for it.

He served the drink and asked if I was a house guest. When I told him I was, he pushed a pencil and a chit across for me to sign. A nice gesture that made me feel I really belonged.

"I haven't been here in a while," I said. "Vale Heights has changed quite a lot."

"Yes, sir," he grinned. "The place is getting some life in it!"

"You live here?"

"All my life," he said. "It was like a morgue when I was a kid—now it's getting some pace!"

"They tell me they're thinking of building a casino on the Waterfront?"

He nodded eagerly: "That's right, sir. There's a vacant lot just a couple of blocks down from the hotel. I figure it's pretty right too, because Eli Kaufman moved down here three months back and he wouldn't come just to get the sea breeze!"

"Kaufman?"

The look on his face told me I was a square for sure.

"Kaufman's one of the biggest operators out of L.A.," he said in a slightly condescending voice. "He's bought a house up on the hill and he's living there right now. He's got three cars up there! Man! You should see 'em standing there on the driveway. A white Caddy, a new Thunderbird and one of those Bentley Continentals!"

"Sounds like he isn't pushing for a buck?"

"Kaufman?" He laughed. "He wouldn't be pushing it for a million, the way I hear it!"

"Nice, if you can get it."

"Yes, sir!"

He moved down the bar to serve a newcomer, and I sipped my drink. I thought I could have drunk a lot cheaper at home and played some hi-fi at the same time. But there it was—Vale Heights—so I might as well enjoy it.

I had four more drinks and the bar had filled up quite a bit in the hour I'd been there. I finished the last drink and reached for a new chit and the pencil. The barman was down at the other end of the bar, serving half a dozen people who'd just come in, so it looked like I would be kept waiting for quite a while.

I made out the chit and sat looking at it. The barman was still busy. I started doodling unconsciously while I waited. Maybe five minutes later the barman was back.

"Sorry, sir," he apologised. "Same again?"

"Thanks," I said.

He refilled the glass with Scotch and crushed ice and placed it on the bar in front of me. His hand came down onto the bar to pick up the chit and stopped suddenly.

I looked at him. His face was completely blank as he looked at the chit. "Don't worry about my doodling," I said. "I do it all the time."

"Yes, sir," he said.

I looked at the chit. I'd drawn a car the way a child of five would. I'd ringed around my room number and I'd drawn the face of a bearded man with a look of pop-eyed surprise—and I'd drawn a dollar sign, with the bar a wavy line with the head of a snake.

That was the doodle the barman was staring at.

His fingers picked up the chit and placed it under the counter.

"Room two-o-five, sir," he said respectfully. "At what time, sir?"

"Time?" I said blankly.

"Whenever is convenient to you, sir, of course," he said in a low voice.

We were playing a game and nobody had told me the rules. I glanced automatically at my watch. It was a quarter after ten. "Eleven o'clock," I said hopefully.

"Eleven, sir," he nodded. "Thank you."

He moved away to serve somebody else and left me staring blankly at my reflection in the mirror on the wall opposite me. The sign had meant something to him. He had mentioned my room number and asked at what time.

I wondered if Hammond's vague theory of the tattoo mark representing a cult membership was right. Maybe at eleven, the barman would appear in my room wearing a voodoo mask and we'd have a jolly time sticking pins into little wax figures.

Maybe ... There was one sure way to find out.

I finished the drink without hurrying it, then left the bar and went up to my room. I rang room service and asked them to send up a bottle of Scotch and some ice. It arrived five minutes later. Then I unpacked the suitcase and stowed it away in the wardrobe. I'd packed my gun in the case and I un-buttoned my jacket, put on the shoulder-holster and slid the thirty-two into it, then put on my jacket again.

It seemed a sensible precaution.

Then I poured myself a Scotch on the rocks and sat down to wait. I didn't have to wait very long. At eleven precisely there was a knock on the door. I walked across and opened the door, and a cool-looking blonde stepped past me into the room.

I closed the door, then turned around to have another look at her. She was tall and nicely built, wearing a sharkskin dress with a low neckline. The dress fitted her closely all the way down to her knees and then spread out just enough to allow her to walk. She was carrying a big black purse in one hand and a couple of slave bangles dangled on her right wrist.

"Hi," she said brightly.

"Hi," I said cautiously.

She looked at the Scotch and nodded approval. "You can pour me one of those, Mr. Wheeler!" she said.

"I can?" I walked over to the table and poured her the drink.

"I'm Frankie," she said. "And don't pull that gag about you being Johnnie—if you don't mind!"

I handed her the drink: "I won't. The name is Al."

"Here's luck, Al!" She raised her glass and eyed me appraisingly. "You look a nice sort of guy."

"Thanks," I said.

She looked around the room with what seemed to be an expert eye. "This your first time in the *Beachcomber?*"

"Check."

"Next time get a room on the floor above this—they're much better and only two dollars difference," she said. "And talking of money, we might get that settled first, huh? Then we don't have to worry about it anymore."

"Money?"

"Fifty bucks," she said.

"What for?"

"Mister!" She raised her eyebrows. "Are you kidding?"

I didn't need a comptometer to figure that one out.

"Are you sure you got the right room?" I asked her.

Her foot tapped the floor impatiently. "Now don't give me that!" she said sharply. "This is two-o-five, isn't it? And your name is Wheeler, isn't it?"

"I guess so."

"Then that settles it! Just give me the fifty, honey, and we can forget all about money!"

She dropped her purse onto the dressing-table and started to casually unbutton the top of her dress.

"Hold it!" I said.

"What now?"

"I'm Wheeler," I said, "and this is two-o-five. But that's as far as it goes. The only thing I asked room service for was the bottle of Scotch—and that's delivered."

"Look!" she said tightly. "Did you or did you not draw the snake sign on a chit in the bar about half an hour ago? And did you or did you not tell the barman eleven when he asked you what time?"

"I guess I did," I said. "We must have been at cross-purposes."

She put her hands on her hips: "You mean you changed your mind now? That's fine! Where does that leave me?"

"Take off that dress," I told her.

Her face cleared: "Well—now you're talking sense, honey!" Her fingers made short work of the remaining buttons and a moment later, she stepped out of the dress carefully and put in on a hanger in the wardrobe.

She wore a nylon slip, lace-trimmed around the neckline, and the whiteness of her bra and pants showed through it. But it was her arm that interested me—her right arm. High up, close to the shoulder was the tattoo mark.

She bent down and took hold of the hem of the slip, then started to pull it over her head.

"You can leave it on," I told her.

"What?" She let the slip drop again. "I never knew a man change his mind so fast as you do!" she said bitterly.

"And you can put your dress back on," I added.

"Now, look!" she said in a hard voice. "You ought to know enough about Snake Lannigan's girls to know you can't get away with this, mister!"

"I don't," I said. "But you can tell me. I'm a good listener."

"You give me fifty bucks!" she said. "Or I walk out of here and inside half an hour you'll have some other visitors! Big guys! Guys who work for Snake and don't like seeing a girl pushed around. You don't want a beating, mister, do you? For the sake of fifty lousy bucks!"

I dug my hand into my hip pocket and found my shield, and held it out so she could see it.

Her face lost its colour suddenly. "A cop!" she said faintly. "A lousy cop! I knew it wasn't my lucky night tonight!"

"Put that dress on again," I said. "Then we'll talk!"

She walked listlessly over to the wardrobe and got the dress out, then stepped into it. She started doing up the buttons again.

"Sergeant," she said, "I ..."

"Lieutenant."

"Lieutenant!" she moaned. "That's worse! Look, Lieutenant, it was just a gag—honest! Supposing you let it go at that, huh? I guess I've wasted your time. How would a hundred bucks go, huh? A hundred for pulling a silly gag like this ..." Her face brightened hopefully. "If you don't know the town, I could show you the sights—for free!"

"No dice," I said.

Her face dropped again. "Okay," her voice was resigned. "I guess it's a pinch! What are you—vice detail? Ain't you got enough vice in Pine City, you got to come all the way up here looking for it?"

"Sit down," I said, "and I'll pour you another drink."

"Huh?" Her mouth made an O of surprise.

"Sit down," I repeated. "We'll talk."

I took the two glasses across to the table and refilled them. I carried them over to where she still stood, not believing it. I gave her the drink and told her to sit down again. She sank into a chair, the glass in her hand and looked at me blankly.

"Cigarette?" I held the pack out to her.

"Thanks," she took one hesitantly. I lit it for her and one for myself.

"What is this?" she asked. "Is it a pinch or isn't it?"

"That depends on you, Frankie-girl," I told her.

"How do you mean that?" A gleam of understanding came into her eyes. "You mean if I up the ante? I can go to a hundred and fifty, but I don't have any more dough than that. That's honest, Lieutenant!"

I was starting to feel sour inside. A lieutenant was worth one hundred and fifty bucks! If I'd been a sergeant as she thought at first, she would have probably offered fifty. Because she was for sale, she figured everyone else was, too—including any cop she bumped into along the way.

"Just listen, Frankie," I said. "I'm not going to repeat this. I don't want your money. I don't want you to show me the town for free. I don't even want you! All I want is information. That's simple, isn't it? Information! You give me the story I want and I'll do a deal with you."

I walked across to the dressing-table and picked up her purse.

"Hey!" she said anxiously. "That's my purse!"

"I didn't think it was mine," I said. I opened it, up-ended it, and shook the contents onto the table-top.

There was the usual junk every woman carries. Handkerchief, powder, lipstick, comb, cigarettes, matches, a roll of notes that looked better than a hundred and fifty—and a pocket diary. I picked up the diary and opened it.

There were names and addresses under different dates. There were never less than three in one week; and sometimes six. A regular entry was *Check Beachcomber*, with a man's name beside it. Tonight's entry was *Check Beachcomber, Joe.* Joe would be the barman, of course. There was an entry for tomorrow's date. *Party at Kaufman's. Wear formal.*

I put the notebook in my pocket and tossed the other things back into her purse. She watched me with a sullen look on her face.

"What was this deal you were talking about?" she asked.

"That's right," I picked up my drink from the dressing-table. "Information! You answer me some questions—and there's no pinch. You can walk out of here as free as when you came in."

"What sort of questions?"

"The snake sign ... the tattoo on your arm. What does that mean?"

"You know that," she said. "You know the sign. It means I'm one of Snake Lannigan's girls."

"Who is Snake Lannigan?"

"I don't know."

I shrugged my shoulders: "The deal depends on me getting answers, Frankie. That isn't any sort of answer."

"Honest, Lieutenant! I don't know!"

"You're one of Snake Lannigan's girls, but you've never met Snake Lannigan—is that it?"

"That's it," she said. "I ain't even sure there is such a guy as Snake!"

"Try and make sense out of that one, Frankie," I said. "Tell me something I could just try and believe!"

She gulped down the remainder of her drink. "I've only been working for him the last three months," she said in a worried voice. "Before, I was working as an usherette at the drive-in just out of town. Not much of a life—selling hot-dogs and ice-cream and running around with a tray all the time—in a blouse and a pair of tights. And every guy who buys a hot-dog seems to think you're included in the price!"

"I'll cry tomorrow," I said. "What about Snake Lannigan?"

She looked indignant: "I was telling you! One day I'm in the beauty parlour having a facial and a set, and—like it is in a parlour, you get talking to the girl who's doing the facial for you—I got to telling her how tough it was at the drive-in."

"This girl," I said. "That would be Leila Cross?"

"No."

"Olga Kellner, then?"

"If you know that much, I don't know why you're bothering to ask me about it."

"I like to hear you talk, Frankie. Go on."

She shrugged her shoulders: "Well, anyway, I told her how tough it was and how I wished I could find a guy with some money ... and I wouldn't care whether he married me or not! And she said it could be done if a girl knew her way around. I thought she was joking at first, then I looked at her face and I saw she wasn't. So I met her that night—it was my free night and we had a couple of drinks at her apartment and she tells me."

She crossed her legs, not bothering to hitch down her skirt which rode up. They were nice legs. Sometimes being a cop has its disadvantages.

"She tells me she works for this Snake Lannigan and how he's got the biggest call-girl organisation on the West Coast. She says it's easy. The organisation makes the contacts and gives the girls the names and addresses of clients. They charge fifty dollars a night, and twenty goes to Snake and the rest the girl has for herself. Two nights a week and I'm making a lot more than I make six nights a week at the drive-in, and I got the days free.

"So I tell her it sounds good to me. She says there's just one thing more. This Lannigan, she says, is a tough guy. You treat him right and he treats you right. You don't treat him right and he's a bad enemy. And then she tells me about the tattoo. All Snake's girls have to have it, she says.

"Because Snake reckons that nobody will try and take his girls away because they'd be too frightened of him. So the tattoo tells anybody that a girl belongs to Snake. And the same sign is used by clients who are travelling around and don't know where to contact the local girls—if they show that sign around, somebody will cotton on. Like the way you did tonight. Most of the bar tenders in town are in it—and a lot of the bellhops and hack drivers. It's the same all over the West Coast, she told me."

I nodded: "Olga Kellner left town a few days back. Who gives you your contacts now?"'

"I got a 'phone number," she said. "I ring it at eleven every morning, unless he gives me jobs a few days ahead."

"Who is he?"

"I don't know, Lieutenant—and that's the truth! It's just a man's voice on the other end of the line. When he answers I tell him my name and then he tells me what jobs he's got. If there's nothing definite, then I get a job like tonight. Check with the barman here or at one of the other hotels. If I don't get anything at the hotel, I'm supposed to go home and ring the number again. Then I'm on call ... they might get a late call from some guys having a party or something like that."

I finished my own drink: "Did you know Leila Cross?"

"She worked in the parlour too, didn't she?"

"That's right."

"She fixed my hair a couple of times, but I didn't know her."

"Did you know she was one of Snake's girls, too?"

"No," she shook her head. "I didn't."

"Ever know a girl called Angela Markon?"

"No. The only one I ever met is Olga Kellner, Lieutenant. And she rang me one night and told me she had to go to another town for Snake and wouldn't be back for a while, and she gave me this 'phone number to ring and told me I'd be okay."

"What about the twenty dollars from each fifty you get? How is that collected?"

"Each week I put it into the mail. Send it to a box number at the mail office in Pine City."

"What's the box number?"

"LJ-1126," she said reluctantly.

I made a note of it: "And the 'phone number you ring?"

"You won't ever let them know I told you these numbers, Lieutenant? They'd kill me if you did!"

"I won't," I said. "So long as you level with me. The 'phone number?"

She gave me it and I wrote it down.

"What's this Kaufman—formal thing, tomorrow night?"

"That's Eli Kaufman," she said. "I guess you've heard of him?"

"Yeah," I said.

"He's got a big house up on the hill. He has parties up there pretty regularly. I have to wear a formal up there."

"Been there before?"

Frankie shook her head: "This is the first time."

"Anything else you can tell me?"

"That's all of it, Lieutenant. Honest!"

"Okay," I said. "You've got yourself a deal, Frankie. You can walk out of here. Keep quiet about this—for your own sake!"

"I will!" she said.

There was a knock on the door and a moment later, before I had a chance to answer, the door flew open and Hammond strode into the room, followed by a couple of other guys.

"What the ..." I started to say.

"Wise guy!" Hammond said. "Thought you'd play it smart, huh? Do the boy-scout act on your own, huh?" He looked at Frankie. "Who's the dame?"

She looked at me venomously. "You dirty double-crosser!" she said. "I hope Snake Lannigan kills you for this!"

CHAPTER 5

Commissioner Lavers' voice sounded irritable over the 'phone.

"I told you in the beginning, Wheeler," he said. "Officially, it's Hammond's case. You were to see what you could hunt up on your own. But you were both to co-operate with each other. As I understand it, you didn't. You got some information and went tearing off to Vale Heights alone, without telling him anything about it. Then he got the information and followed you."

"Sure," I said. "But the point is, Commissioner, that ..."

"As far as the girl is concerned," he said sharply. "Your duty was to arrest her, not make any sort of a deal with her. The information she gave you could have been got from her by routine questioning after arrest. Hammond has made a formal arrest and I understand is now questioning her. His actions have my full approval!"

"You don't understand!" I almost yelped into the 'phone. "He will queer the whole deal if he's not very careful! The girl isn't important—it's this Lannigan character who is!"

"I've had quite enough from you, Wheeler, for one night!" he roared. "This call has already cost the department far too much! Just understand this. Hammond's actions have my full approval. He is officially in charge of the case. You didn't co-operate with him, you can't expect him to co-operate with you. You'd better be in the office at nine in the morning—I'm taking you off the case!"

"But ..."

"That's final, Wheeler!" He hung up in my ear.

I put the 'phone down and lit a cigarette. The desk sergeant looked at me sympathetically.

"Having a rough time, Lieutenant?"

"You can say that again," I agreed.

"That's what comes of being unorthodox!" he grinned. "Look at me—I'm orthodox! Thirty years on the force and I finally get to be a sergeant, putting my flat feet up on a desk! How long you been on the force, Lieutenant?"

"Eight years," I said.

"And you're only a Lieutenant!"

I sucked smoke into my lungs: "Hammond still questioning that girl?"

"Yeah—him and those two sergeants he brought up with him. Ain't had so many cops from Pine City in town in a long time!"

"I hope you're enjoying it," I said. "Is there a mail box near here?"

"There's one just outside."

"Got an envelope?"

"Sure, Lieutenant." He opened his desk and found one, then handed it to me.

"Stamp?"

"Anything you want, Lieutenant."

"Thanks," I took the stamp and stuck it onto the envelope.

I walked outside the main precinct of Vale Heights, took the notebook out of my pocket and sealed it inside the envelope. Then I addressed the envelope to myself at home and mailed it.

I walked back inside the precinct again.

"Find it okay?" the sergeant asked.

"Thanks," I said. I looked at my watch. It was twelve-thirty a.m. "How long has Hammond had that girl in there now?"

"Around forty minutes, Lieutenant." The sergeant winked at me. "Always takes longer questioning a nice-looking dame like that!"

"Sure," I grunted.

Somewhere, around the bend in the corridor, I heard a door open and close and then the sound of feet walking down the corridor towards us.

Frankie came into view, escorted by a police matron. She glared at me savagely. "Do a deal!" She called me a name my mother would have resented.

"That will be enough of that!" the matron said firmly, then took Frankie's arm and hurried her off.

Heavy feet tramped down the corridor this time, and then Hammond came into view, followed by the two sergeants he'd brought with him from Homicide.

"Still around, Lieutenant?" He sounded pleased with himself. "I thought you'd be on your way to Pine City before now!"

"You booked the girl?"

"Of course!"

"I'd just made a deal with her before you busted into my hotel room," I said. "No pinch for the information she gave me."

"That was your deal, Wheeler," he said. "Not mine!"

"I hope I can do you a favour sometime!" I told him.

"The Commissioner supports me," he said smugly. "In fact, I understood from him that he's taken you off the case, Wheeler?"

"Yeah," I grunted. "It's all yours!"

"It shouldn't be very hard," he said. "We're going to follow up that 'phone number here—and then the box number in Pine City. I figure we should have this Snake Lannigan by this time tomorrow night and the case will be finished!"

"You think he killed the two girls?"

"Who else?"

"I wouldn't know who else," I said. "But what evidence have you got that this Lannigan killed them?"

"They worked for him," Hammond said contemptuously. "He is running a call-girl racket. Like the little guy Bond says—his girl got frightened and ran. I guess she wanted out of the racket. The same with the Markon girl. So Lannigan knocks them off, as a warning to the others. They can't get out of the racket unless he tells them they can. And I guess he don't tell 'em that till they're old and grey!"

I let it ride: "How did you find Bond?"

He laughed: "He found me! After you left him, he suddenly got suspicious. He thought it was a funny kind of story for a cop to tell him and maybe you weren't a cop, after all. So he hotfoots it around to the Bureau and tells me all!"

He laughed again: "I had to admit to him that you were a cop, but that you got some funny ideas at times. I said to him, maybe it comes of sitting around the Commissioner's office all day with nothing to do!"

Both the sergeants had broad grins on their faces. Or, counting the Vale Heights sergeant on, the desk, all three of them had.

"What are you going to do now?" I asked him.

"It's not really any of your business—is it, Lieutenant?" He studied his fingernails for a moment. "But I'm not the sort of guy to hold a grudge. We already checked that 'phone number here and got the address. We're going along there right now, to arrest whoever's sitting at the other end of that 'phone. Like to come along, Lieutenant? See how an orthodox cop works?"

The sergeants chuckled appreciatively. The Commissioner's boy was being put in his place and they were loving it.

"No, thanks," I told him. "I wouldn't want to waste my time."

"What do you mean?" he asked suspiciously.

"You don't expect to find anybody at that 'phone now, do you?"

"Why not?" he barked.

"This call-girl racket," I explained in the sort of voice you explain things to a backward child, "needs more than call-girls. It needs clients. It needs even more than that—it needs people to bring the clients and the girls together. People like barmen, hack drivers, bellhops ..."

"So what?" he said loudly.

I smiled at him: "So when you made your big play of being an orthodox cop and thumped all over the *Beachcomber Hotel* with two sergeants trailing you like hound-dogs, you let everybody know you were a cop! In capitals! And when you took the girl away with you, you let everybody know she was under arrest. For sure, somebody who works for Snake Lannigan's organisation saw you! What do you think would be the first thing they'd do, Lieutenant? Buy themselves a drink, or pick up the nearest 'phone and ring that number to tip off the guy at the other end that one of his girls has been pinched?"

Hammond glowered at me for a moment, then turned and looked at his sergeants. "C'mon!" he said savagely. "What the hell are you standing around here for? Let's get going!"

They stomped out of the precinct and I lit another cigarette as I watched them go.

I walked out of the precinct onto the street, then down half a block to the nearest bar which was still open. I ordered a drink and thought about things, and didn't like any of it very much.

Hammond would have killed the leads we had. The 'phone would be deserted—nobody would collect any mail from the box number in Pine City from tomorrow on. And all that would happen to the organisation is that the girls would be given a new 'phone number, and a new box number to send the money to. Because a copper like Hammond had to play being a copper, with bells on!

I finished my drink and went out onto the street again, then walked back to the *Beachcomber*. I went into the same bar I'd been drinking in before. There was a different barman on duty.

"Yes, sir?" he asked politely as I came up to the bar.

"Scotch on the rocks," I said. "What happened to Joe?"

"He was taken sick, sir—had to go home."

"You know where he lives?"

"No, sir. Sorry, sir. Joe's a friend of yours?"

"He might not think so," I said.

"Sir?"

"Skip it," I said. "Let's have the drink."

Joe would be lamming it out of town by now, thinking of himself as public enemy number one or something. He probably couldn't have told me as much as Frankie had, anyway. The hell with Joe! The hell with Hammond and his sergeants! The hell with Lavers, too!

The barman put the drink in front of me: "Are you a house guest, sir?"

"Sure," I said.

He gave me the chit and pencil. I signed it, wrote my room number, drew the snake sign on it, then handed it back to him. His lips tightened slightly as he looked at it.

"That sign mean anything to you?" I asked him.

"Why—no, sir. Should it?"

"Why don't you just call me Lieutenant?" I suggested.

I drank the Scotch and went up to my room. I got into a pair of pyjamas and then got into bed. Contrary to my expectations, I went straight to sleep and woke up at nine the next morning.

It was ten-thirty when I left the hotel, eleven-thirty when I walked up the steps of City Hall.

Fern looked at me with an air of triumph as I walked into the office. "Commissioner Lavers wants to see you, Lieutenant," she said. "Right away, he said. The minute you came in!"

"Thanks," I said. "I see you haven't shaved your head yet?"

Her lips tightened until they disappeared. "I wouldn't keep the Commissioner waiting if I were you, Lieutenant," she said. "I don't think he's in a good mood!"

I knocked on Lavers' door and walked in. He looked up from his desk and put down his pen carefully onto the holder.

"Well, well!" he said. "Lieutenant Wheeler, as I remember! Didn't I give you implicit instructions to be in this office by nine this morning?"

"You did," I agreed.

"And what is the time now, Lieutenant?"

I glanced at my watch: "Eleven forty-three and a half."

"You're just two hours, forty-three and a half minutes late!"

"You're on the ball, Commissioner," I said. "You must have been up bright and early this morning!"

His head jerked upwards another couple of inches as he stared at me. "Wheeler," he said softly. "You know what I can do to you, don't you? What I will do if this sort of thing goes ..."

"Look!" I said. "Why don't you make up your mind? Do you want an unorthodox cop around this office, or don't you? Once upon a time about eighteen months ago, I was very happy in the Twelfth Precinct working under Captain Parker. It was you who yanked me out of there and put me into Homicide. It was you who made me Lieutenant-in-charge of Homicide, and then changed your mind because I let the paperwork pile up. It was you who brought me into your office, because you said I was unorthodox—when something unorthodox came along it might be useful to have me around to handle it.

"But on this case, you tell me first to be unorthodox and see what I can find. When an orthodox cop comes barging in on me, gumming up the work I've done, you tell me he's a great cop and he's dead right all the way down the line—so much so, that you're taking me off the case right away! Then you tell me at twelve-thirty a.m., when I'm forty miles out of town, to be here by nine o'clock!"

His jaw was sagging slightly as he looked at me.

"All I ask," I said with great restraint, "is for you to make up your mind. If you give me a traffic detail, I shall be on time when I start work. I shall also finish work on time. I shall have things like nights and week-ends all to myself. I was working on that case from nine yesterday morning to a little after midnight. If I'm going to do that, I am not going to leap out of bed at six-thirty in the morning in Vale Heights so I can be here at nine, simply because you tell me to do so when you're in a mood to play Police Commissioners! Do I make myself clear?"

A faint gurgling noise came from somewhere inside his throat and his Adam's apple moved spasmodically a couple of times.

"Just one more thing," I said in a pleasant voice. I was told in Vale Heights that the majority of the force considered you were out of your mind when you attached me to your office. I am rapidly coming to the conclusion that you are out of your mind—period!"

I sat down in one of the visitors' chairs and lit a cigarette. I was wondering how I'd look in a blue uniform again and trying to remember the correct signal to tell a line of traffic to move around a left-hand turn of an intersection.

The silence seemed to go on for a long time. Finally I looked up and saw Lavers was still there behind his desk. His face was a complete blank. Then his lips moved.

"You've been taking lessons from my wife," he said in a mild voice.

"Your wife is a woman I would gladly take lessons from," I said. "I have the greatest respect for your wife. She made only one mistake in her life!"

"You've been taking lessons from her," he repeated. "Nobody else could talk to me like that and get away with it!"

He cleared his throat with a rasping noise: "Sergeant Moore was one of the sergeants Hammond took with him last night. The sergeant and I have known each other for a long time. He repeated a certain conversation to me, which I believe took place between you and Hammond in the Vale Heights Precinct."

I smoked my cigarette and didn't say anything.

"You were right, of course," he went on. "The 'phone was in an apartment. And the occupant had obviously left hurriedly. Hammond has men staked out all over the General Mail Office. One of the countermen told us the box is always cleared by ten each morning. It hasn't been cleared this morning—and it won't be."

He grinned again, almost sheepishly. "You put it on the line, Wheeler. I apologise. I should have remembered some of the other things you've handled in your own crackpot way and come up with results. I was wrong to back Hammond last night. I was wrong to order both of you to work on the same case, without giving you clear authority over him. I made a botch of it—and Hammond made an even worse botch of it last night. What do you want me to do—give you the case now? Or would you rather just forget it?"

I sat there, not believing my ears. "Well, sir," I stuttered. "I, I ..."

"Whatever you want, Wheeler?"

I made up my mind he was really saying these things.

"What I'd really like," I said, "is for you to leave things as they are, or appear to leave things as they are. You've suspended me before enough times for it not to come as a surprise to anyone if it happens again. What I'd like, sir, is for you to suspend me right now—officially. And unofficially, I'll dig around some more and see if I can pick up any other leads."

"All right," he nodded, "I'll do that. Do you have any ideas?"

"I'm going to a party tonight," I said. "Maybe I'll get some ideas there."

"Now we're back to your favourite subject," Lavers growled disgustedly. "Women!"

CHAPTER 6

I got back to Vale Heights around five that evening. I found a smaller hotel six blocks away and booked a room. I went out again, had a meal and then a couple of drinks in a bar. The time got around to eight o'clock.

I had debated the issue quite a lot—got into a huddle with myself—the two most important guys in the universe—Wheeler and Wheeler, and made a decision. No gun, no shield, nothing. They stayed behind at the hotel, along with Frankie's notebook which had arrived in the early afternoon mail before I left Pine City.

After I left the bar, I picked up the Healey and followed the coastal road through Vale Heights. It started to climb once it left the town and climbed for maybe eight hundred feet, and there was quite a view if you were in the mood for a view.

The road wound around and around the cliffs, doubling back on itself at times and I could have had some fun with the Healey if I'd been in the mood for it, but I wasn't. And I was looking for Eli Kaufman's place.

I found it fifteen minutes later and like Frankie had said, you couldn't miss it. It stood perched on the edge of a cliff, with the Pacific rollers breaking on the rocks way down beneath it. It was a two-storey house of about fifty squares—it would have held a Marine division.

There were two imposing wrought-iron gates that stood wide open, on either side of a wide gravel driveway. I drove down the drive slowly for about half a mile, until I rounded a bend and saw half a dozen cars parked just ahead of me. I parked the Healey in line and got out.

I made my way to the front porch up eight marble steps, and heard the music blaring inside. The front door stood wide open, the whole house was ablaze with light. Kaufman liked to live it up a little, apparently.

I stepped inside the mansion and stood there for a moment, looking around. There was nobody else in the hall. I dropped my hat onto a bronze lion who was crouched at one side of the door, and walked down the hall.

Double-doors stood wide open leading into a ballroom, where maybe a dozen people were standing and talking and drinking. That last activity convinced me this was the room I was looking for. I walked in and up to the huge cocktail bar that flanked one wall. There was no one serving, but the bottles were lined up. I poured a generous measure of Haig and Haig over some ice in a glass and got a firm grip around the glass.

Then I turned around and looked at the people. Or I was going to, but

I was distracted.

"It's like a zoo, isn't it?" a voice said beside me.

I turned around and looked at the speaker. She was blonde, tall and willowy. She wore what I guessed Frankie would call a formal. But it didn't look formal. There was a large scoop of no-gown, all-blonde in the front, and the rest of it was black something or other which looked rich and strokable. It hugged her with the enthusiasm of a coal-black mammy, and in its place, I had to concede, I would have done exactly the same.

The blonde's hair was swept around her head, tight against her head on one side, leaving a shell-pink ear all exposed, and on the other side it cascaded down to her shoulder. Her eyes were a vivid blue and her lips full and delicately-shaped. You only had to look at her once to see she was a woman.

"I said," she repeated, "it's like a zoo, isn't it?"

"I'm sorry," I apologised. "I was too busy looking at you."

"Are you satisfied now?"

"I've gone as far as an eye can go," I said. "I wouldn't say was satisfied—impressed might be the word."

"You can't be a friend of Eli's," she said. "They don't use words of more than one syllable."

"I'm an acquaintance," I said cautiously. "In a vague sort of way."

She looked me up and down carefully. "I was going to leave early," she said. "I may change my mind."

"Are you a friend of Kaufman's?" I asked her.

She shook her head vigorously: "I'm a friend of Marlene—his wife. If I'd known she wasn't here, I wouldn't have bothered coming."

"Oh," I said.

"I'm Jo Dexter," she said.

"Al Wheeler," I said.

"We must see more of each other," she said.

"I've been trying to see more of you ever since we met," I said courteously. "Only that gown gets in the way."

"I see you believe in the bludgeon rather than the rapier as a technique?"

"Girls as outspoken as you," I explained, "are either kidding or they aren't. The quickest way to find out is with a bludgeon."

"You seem to have made a study of these things," she said.

Someone stopped in front of us. A big character—heavy, but light on his feet. Black hair with a widow's peak and a craggy jaw. And eyes that looked all ways at once.

"Hello, Eli," Jo Dexter said. "I didn't know Marlene was away?"

"Been gone the last few days," he said indifferently. "Went down to L.A. to do some shopping or something." He looked at me curiously.

"You know Al Wheeler?" Jo Dexter said.

"Oh—sure," he said, and held out his hand. "How are things in your business, Al?"

"Fine," I said. "How's the casino coming along?"

"A little trouble with the City Fathers at the moment," he said. "I expect to get over it." He backed off a pace. "Have fun, folks."

Jo Dexter wrinkled her nose critically as she watched him walk away. "Why Marlene married that man, I'll never know!"

"Could money be a reason?" I suggested.

"She had plenty of her own."

"Maybe the zoological appeal?"

"It must have been," she said. "Would you pour me another drink, please?"

"Sure! What is it?"

"Whisky."

"And?"

"Just whisky."

I poured the drink and handed it to her. "Do you live around here?" I asked her.

"I've got a place down the road a couple of miles," she said. "Only for a month. I just shed a husband in Reno and I thought a month of sea-air might clean up my system."

"A husband?"

"My third," she said easily. "I like men—but as husbands, they tend to become monotonous."

"I must remember that."

"For when you marry?"

I shook my head: "For when some dame wants me to marry her."

"Dame? Really, Mr. Wheeler! What a vulgar word!"

"If I applied it to you," I said, "I should put the word dizzy in front of it."

She smiled complacently: "You'd probably be right. Do you know any of the other people here, Mr. Wheeler?"

"No," I said.

"I thought not," she said. "And you didn't know Eli, did you? You weren't even an acquaintance of his?"

"What makes you say that?"

"Neither of you recognised the other. And Eli thought you were with me and he must have met you before somewhere. I think you're a man of mystery, Mr. Wheeler!"

I took time out to refill my glass. She had been very useful in getting me accepted by Kaufman without question, but she seemed to be getting a little too curious.

I picked up my refilled glass and turned back to her.

"Why don't you believe in husbands?" I asked her.

"Don't change the subject," she said. "I want to know why you're here!"

"There's a party," I said. "I never can resist food and drink, and beautiful dames." I looked at her closely. "Even beautiful, dizzy dames!"

"I think you're one of the newer products," she said thoughtfully. "The semi-literate racketeer who doesn't look like something that should never have been allowed to stray from the garbage-can in the first place! And Eli is a racketeer, of course. I wonder if you're a rival of his? No!" She shook her head. "He would've recognised you if you were. I've got it!" She snapped her fingers. "You've been specially imported by his rival—from New York or Chicago or some place East. You're a triggerman, a torpedo! And you've come to bump off Eli!"

I felt the pained look on my face. "That sort of jargon went out with Capone!" I said. "A hood covers the ground adequately for the sort of character you're trying to describe ... and they don't bump off people anymore. They've gone polite like the dictators did—they liquidate or remove!"

"You see!" she said triumphantly. "You do know all about it!"

"Hobby of mine," I said. "But second to women, of course!"

"I think you're a most intriguing man," she said. "This is going to be a lousy party—Eli's parties always are. Why don't we go back to my house and have a party?"

"I'd love to," I said. "But I can't go right away."

"Oh?" she said a trifle coldly.

"I have to talk to Kaufman first."

"Are you really going to ... liquidate him?"

"I just want to talk," I said. "I'll do that first and then I'll be free to go whenever you feel like it."

"Don't take too long," she said. "I might change my mind!"

"You can probably change that even quicker than husbands," I said. "I'll hurry!"

Kaufman was talking to a small, podgy man in one corner of the room. I took my glass with me and walked across to them slowly. Kaufman frowned as he saw me coming and the podgy man gave me a dirty look. I didn't let it worry me.

"I'd like a word with you," I said to Kaufman.

"Yes?" he answered impatiently.

"Alone," I looked at the podgy man.

"This is Porky Smith," he said. "He's my right hand. There's nothing you'd want to talk about that he couldn't hear."

"Okay," I shrugged. "I have a message for you—from Snake Lannigan!"

"Snake Lan ..." Kaufman grabbed my elbow and hustled me towards the door. "Save it till we get somewhere private!"

The three of us finished up in his library. Kaufman closed the door carefully, then came back towards me. "All right," he said, "What is it?"

"You're a girl short tonight," I said.

"Yes?" He shrugged his shoulders. "I hadn't counted. I wanted four. If we only got three, then one of the boys is going to be unlucky, that's all."

"Aren't you worried your wife might walk in on you?"

He looked at me curiously for a moment. "She won't," he said shortly. "She'll stay down in L.A. a while yet. When she goes shopping, she spends money like it grew on trees!"

"This girl who's missing," I said. "The cops picked her up yesterday—last night, in fact."

"Yes?"

"Snake's a little worried about it. There were two lieutenants and two sergeants up from Pine City in Vale Heights last night."

"Nothing you can't cover, is it?" he asked shortly.

"No," I said slowly. "Only Snake is wondering if the girl told them she was due here tonight—maybe she's got it written down in her diary and maybe the cops found it."

Kaufman and Smith looked at each other for a moment.

"He's got a point there," Porky grunted. "We don't want 'em picked up here. Better get 'em out of the place right away!"

"Seems hard," Kaufman said. "But I guess you're right. How do we get rid of 'em?"

"Easy!" Porky said. "Our friend here can gather 'em up and take 'em away right now." He looked at me. "Can't you?"

"Oh—sure," I said wanly.

"I'll go with him," Porky added. "When he's got 'em rounded up, I'll make sure they're well clear of the house before I come back."

"Sure," Kaufman said. "Thanks—er, Al. And tell Snake not to worry!"

"Okay," I said.

"Let's go," Smith said.

We made our way back to the ballroom. There were maybe twenty people there by then—ten or eleven women ... and the only one I knew was Jo Dexter. I stood there looking around, wondering desperately if I could persuade them all to show me the tops of their arms.

"Let's hurry it, Wheeler," Porky growled.

"Sure," I said. "Just sorting them out."

"Where are they?"

I looked around desperately. "There's one!" I said quickly and made a dive in Jo Dexter's direction.

"Well!" she said. "Back so soon?"

"I just realised what a wonderful idea you had!" I grabbed her elbow and propelled her towards the door. "And I couldn't pass it up!"

"Hey!" She was almost running. "Slow down, will you?"

"I can't," I said. "It's the wild blood of the gypsies coursing through my veins!"

We came level with Smith, who was staring blankly at me.

"Wait a minute!" he said, and put a hand on my arm.

"Can't!" I said, shaking off his hand. "Be back in a minute, Porky. Explain everything then!"

I got Jo into the hallway and raced down to the front door. Another twenty seconds and she was beside me in the Healey and I was reversing down the drive.

I spun out into the roadway with a shower of gravel spraying out from the rear wheels. I accelerated forward and by the time the Healey was in third gear, Jo had managed to push herself off the windscreen back into her seat.

"You must be crazy!" she said. "I left a drink back there! My car's back there! Will you slow down?"

"When we reach your house," I said. "How far is it?"

"About two seconds at this speed!"

I slowed down a little and took a quick look in the rear-vision mirror. There was nothing in sight behind us.

"Around the next bend," Jo said. "There's a dirt road off to the right and for Pete's sake take it slowly! It goes down to the beach with a gradient of about one in five!"

"Okay," I said.

I made the turn-off and the nose of the Healey dropped away so fast I thought it was going to disappear altogether. I dropped into second and we whined our way down the dirt road to the beach.

"That's it," she said, pointing. "That house over there."

I drove the Healey in under the carport and switched off the engine.

"You're crazy!" she said. "And I need a drink!"

"Me, too," I said. "I didn't think I was going to get out of there in one piece!"

"You mean they were going to kill you?" She clutched my arm tight. "How wonderful!"

"Thanks!"

"I mean how exciting! Why?"

"It's a long story and I'm not sure I know the details even," I said. "How about that drink?"

We got into the house, which was small only by comparison to Kaufman's house. She switched on the lights and we went into the living-room, then she led the way to the bar in the corner.

"You pour us a drink and have yours, while I put on a new face and get my breath back," she said. "I need to get my breath after that hair-raising ride!"

"Okay," I said.

She went out of the room and I poured myself a drink—a long one. I lit a cigarette to go with it and thought that Wheeler was certainly a smart character. I had hoped to bluff Kaufman into disclosing something about Snake Lannigan and all I'd done was to warn him that something was wrong. Once I couldn't pick out the girls from the crowd, Porky would have known I was a fake. I began to wonder what they were doing about it.

I finished the drink and renewed it. And then Jo Dexter came back into the room. She was wearing a powder-blue negligee—a fragile thing that looked as if it would fall to pieces at the touch of your hand. Fortunately, Jo herself didn't give me that impression.

I stared at her admiringly: "I always wondered what they meant in the women's magazines when the heroine says she's going to slip into something cool. Now I know!"

"I always thought they meant a swimming pool," she said. "Is that my drink?"

"That is your drink," I agreed. "The one with the undiluted Scotch in the glass."

She sat down on a wide, comfortable-looking divan: "Bring the drinks over here, Mr. Wheeler."

"Call me Al," I said. "After all, we've known each other for the last hour."

I took the drinks with me and sat down beside her on the divan and gave her the one with the undiluted Scotch. She took a long pull on it and shuddered slightly.

"That's better," she said. "Much better!"

"Which do you get through more of during a year?" I asked interestedly. "Scotch or husbands?"

"It depends on the mood I'm in that year," she said. "Would you like to be my next husband?"

"You mean—any time I'm not doing anything special one week-end?"

"It could last a whole week with you," she told me. "You're dynamic!"

"Is that catching?"

She leaned back and looked at me through half-closed eyes. "You're a man of mystery, Al—like I said before. Tell me about it."

"Would you excuse me a moment?" I said carefully.

I pushed the sleeve of the negligee back to her shoulder and looked carefully at her right arm. There was no tattoo mark.

"What are you looking for?" she asked coldly.

"It's nothing important," I said and picked up my drink again. "I just had a momentary thought that your name might be Olga Kellner, but it isn't."

"If you don't stop talking in riddles, Mr. Al Wheeler," she said menacingly, "I shall hit you with something hard!"

I finished my drink and put the glass down on the floor.

"How long have you known Kaufman?" I asked her.

"Only since Marlene married him, which is about two years ago. We—Marlene and I, that is—have been friends for years."

"I see," I said.

"Why?"

"Kaufman had three call-girls at his party tonight ... there should have been four, but one couldn't make it."

"I'm not surprised," she said. "He's a first-grade louse!"

"Would that worry Marlene if she knew?"

"I don't know," she said slowly. "I think it would. I don't think she knows he's going in for that sort of thing."

"I thought he was taking a chance," I said. "She could come back any time."

"I can't understand why she went down to L.A. again," she said musingly. "We both went on a shopping spree there when I got back from Vegas, and that was only a few weeks ago."

"It's all very confusing," I said.

I noticed her glass was empty. "Can I get you another drink?"

"No, thank you," she said firmly. "I didn't slip into something cool because I expected to stay that way. If you don't make a pass at me fairly soon, Al Wheeler, I shall send this negligee back to where I bought it and demand my money back!"

"Yes, ma'am," I said humbly.

We met in the centre of the divan and Jo melted into my arms. Her lips were warm and demanding and they fused with mine and I began to feel that a cop's life had its compensations, after all. She moved her lips two inches away from mine to tell me some vital information.

"The light-switch," she murmured, "is beside the door."

"Yes, ma'am!" I got up from the divan and started across the room towards the door.

I was halfway across the room when the visitor arrived. Porky Smith, with a gun in his hand pointing straight at my ribs. I did the heroic thing you'd expect a cop to do ... I lifted my hands high in the air and kept them there.

CHAPTER 7

Jo Dexter sat up, her eyes shining. "Well!" she gasped. "This is really something!" She looked at Porky expectantly. "Are you going to shoot him down?"

"Shut up!" he said coldly.

He came closer to me and frisked me expertly. "All right," he said. "You can drop your hands."

"Thanks," I said. "What's this all about?"

"That phony line you pulled about being from Snake Lannigan," he said. "What was the idea?"

"I was just interested to know how well Eli Kaufman knew Lannigan," I said.

"He don't know him," Porky replied. "He knows about him. That's different."

"If you can believe it," I said.

Jo straightened out her negligee. "Why don't you jump him, Al?" she asked wistfully.

"Didn't you notice?" I asked her. "He's holding a gun!"

"Take him by surprise," she said.

"It'll be the last surprise he ever gets if he tries it!" Porky said.

"That I'll believe," I said quickly. "I'm happy right where I am!"

"You won't be for long," he said. "We're going back up to the house. Kaufman wants to talk to you."

I'd felt pretty silly when I'd run out of the house in the first place. Going back into the house with a gun in my back would make me feel sillier still. I put a hand into my pocket and got out the key of my hotel room and tossed it over to Smith.

He caught it with an automatic reflex: "What's this?"

"The key to my hotel room," I said. "In the *Starlight*. Drive down there and take a look."

"What for?"

"In a drawer you'll find a cop's shield with Lieutenant on it," I said. "And right alongside it is a Smith and Wesson thirty-two police special and holster. And alongside that is an identity card which says that Lieutenant A. Wheeler belongs to the Pine City Police Department."

He stared at me for a moment. "It's just a gag!" he said. "I go out of here and you'll take it on the lam!"

I pulled the keys of the Healey out of my pocket and tossed them across to him. "Now I got to walk," I said. "Believe me, Porky, I want to talk to

Kaufman!"

The hand holding the gun sagged. "I never hit something like this before!" he muttered. "A guy gives me the key to his room so I can go check on whether he's a cop or not!"

"Why don't you try it?" I suggested.

"Okay," he said slowly. "But you stay right here!"

"You think I want to go any place?" I asked him, looking at Jo.

Porky's eyes followed my gaze and there was a concentrated silence for maybe ten seconds. "I see what you mean," he said finally. He put the gun in his pocket and walked towards the door. "I'll pick you up on the way back," he said.

"I'll be here," I told him.

The door closed behind him and a few seconds later there was the sound of a car engine turning over. I walked back to the divan and sat down beside Jo.

"Now," I said, making a lunge. "Where were we?"

"You were terrific!" she said. "He fell for that story all the way down the line. You really convinced him, Al!"

"Story?" I looked at her. "What story?"

"It was a riot!" she said. "I nearly died laughing inside. Just imagine you being a cop!"

"What's so funny about that?" I asked stiffly.

"A Lieutenant yet!" She rocked with laughter. "I never heard anything like it in my life!"

"I am a cop!" I grated.

She was still laughing: "You don't have to keep it up with me, honey. I'm on your side!"

"Why shouldn't I be a cop?" I demanded.

"Al! I've met real live lieutenants of police! You have no idea how different they are from you!"

"This gets funnier all the time!" I said sourly.

"What are you really?" she asked in a confidential voice. "A pickpocket?"

I suddenly felt the pressing need for a drink. I got up from the divan and walked over to the bar.

"What are you wasting time walking away from me for?" she asked in a surprised voice.

"It's that negligee," I told her. "There isn't one pocket in the whole damned thing!"

I poured myself a drink and one for her and took them back with me. Jo took the drink and looked at me with soulful eyes.

"I'm sorry if I offended you, Al," she said. "I was just kidding about you being a pickpocket. I think you're a hoodlum at the very least!"

"Thanks a lot," I said. "It feels great to be put back into the social register!"

"The thing is," she said. "You aren't going to wait here till he comes back, are you?"

"What do you suggest I do?"

"You'd better take it on the lam!" she said. "Scram out of here while the going's good!"

I winced: "Haven't you been to the movies at all lately?"

"Not in ten years," she said. "Did a good film come along?"

"The dialogue," I said. "It's outdated!"

"Never mind the dialogue, honey," she replied. "Let's think about you. Don't you have a gat?"

"Gun!"

"Same thing! Don't you have one?"

"Not with me."

"He's got a gun!" She thought hard for a moment. "There's a carving-knife in the kitchen, if that's any use to you?"

"Don't tempt me!" I said. "Aren't you nervous, being here all alone with a hoodlum—or a pickpocket at the very least!"

"I think it's thrilling!" she told me. "My last husband was a company accountant. His idea of excitement was long division!"

I took a gulp of my drink. "Just ease down," I said. "I'm going to wait here till Porky gets back."

"I think you're being very foolish," she said. "Supposing he brings a real lieutenant of detectives back with him and has you arrested for impersonating a police officer?"

"Jo," I said. "Why kid around beating up a cyclone in that vacuum inside your head? Just relax, huh?"

"You think I'm dumb?" she said coldly. "Didn't I pick you as a phony right from the moment you walked into Eli Kaufman's house tonight?"

"I guess so," I said. "But that wasn't brains—it was intuition!"

She started and finished her drink in one neat swallow, then handed me the glass. "I wish that man hadn't come in," she said. "He's spoiled my mood. I don't feel romantic anymore!"

"Too bad!"

"What can we do, Al?"

"If you've got a few spare pockets around the place," I said, "I could practice for a while."

"What started you on your life a crime?" she asked. "Tell me about yourself, Al. When did you stop being honest?"

"The first time a blonde slapped my face," I admitted. "After that I decided the truth was for the birds!"

"Seriously! Tell me about yourself. What made you become a criminal?"

I leaned back against the divan and lit a cigarette. "It's hard to say what makes a criminal," I admitted. "Maybe the question of environment comes into it—I was born in a railroad tunnel and never saw the light of day till I was four years old."

"Why not?"

"The railroad sent another train through the tunnel—the folks had to pack up and move."

"I wish you'd be serious!"

I frowned at her: "I am! Then there's the hereditary angle. I could have been influenced by the fact that my mother was a poisoner and my father a strangler. When I was only six, they murdered my uncle between them. My uncle had one of the most original deaths you ever saw. And there was my elder brother, of course."

"What about him?"

"He was the most stable of the lot of us. Never stole a dime till he was nine years old. Then he sort of broke out—knocked over the National Bank in Chicago and got away with five million."

"Dollars?"

"Years. The judge said he was being lenient. He's a foundation member at Alcatraz. There was my sister, of course. My sister Lizzie—they called her Lizzie after my mother's family—the Borden side. Lizzie specialised in getting married, insuring her husband, and then having an accident when she was chopping wood. She was doing all right too, until she had a real accident one day the axe slipped and that was the end of her. She got through three husbands...." I looked at Jo carefully. "You wouldn't be my sister Lizzie, by any chance?"

The sound of an approaching car grew louder and louder.

"That's him!" Jo clutched my arm. "He's back!"

"I heard."

"Well!" She shook my arm agitatedly. "Aren't you going to do something? You aren't going to just sit there, are you?"

"I was thinking about standing up," I admitted.

The door swung open and Porky Smith came into the room. He came towards us and dumped the things he was carrying on the coffee table in front of us. Then he handed me back my car keys and the key to my hotel room.

Jo sat bolt upright and looked wonderingly at the thirty-two in the shoulder-holster. She picked up my shield and studied that for ten seconds. Finally she picked up my identity card and read it through carefully—twice. Then she just sat there looking at me.

"My mistake, Lieutenant," Porky Smith said uneasily. "I sure am sorry about the whole thing."

"Forget it," I said. "My fault in a way." I got onto my feet and took off my jacket. When the shoulder-holster was in place, I put the jacket back on again.

"I'll come back with you," I said to Smith.

"Sure," he nodded. "Anything you say, Lieutenant."

"Lieutenant!" Jo breathed. "This is the most wonderful thing that ever happened to me in my whole life!"

"It didn't happen!" I said hastily. "We were just sitting there on the divan and ..."

"A real live lieutenant of police!" Jo interrupted. "Whatever it is you're investigating, it must be pretty important to have a lieutenant on the case!" She got to her feet. "I'm coming with you!"

I looked through her negligee pointedly: "In that?"

"Oh!" She looked down at herself. "I see what you mean—it could be cold out there, huh? I'll change. I won't be a moment."

"You're staying right here," I said. "And what's more ..."

"I'm coming with you!" she said firmly. "Don't try and argue with me— you're just wasting your time!"

She walked towards one of the doors leading off the living room into the other wing of the house. I waited until the door had closed, then said to Smith: "Let's get going before that dizzy dame comes back. I'll follow you in my own car."

"Anything you say, Lieutenant."

Ten to fifteen minutes later I parked the Healey behind the Cadillac in the driveway of Kaufman's property. The cars that had been parked there earlier on in the night had vanished. I imagined the party had ended abruptly.

We walked into the house and down to the library, where Eli Kaufman was waiting for us.

"I owe you an apology, Lieutenant," he said uneasily. "If I'd had any idea ..."

"Skip it," I said. "I'm just glad Porky had the forethought to ring you from the hotel and let you know I was a cop."

They looked at each other for a moment, then looked at me with an intimation of a smile on their faces.

"I'm looking for Snake Lannigan," I said. "I want to find him. I knew you were having some of his girls up here tonight and I wanted to find out how much you knew about Snake. Hence the act earlier on that misfired. That was my mistake. We can forget what's happened to date, so far as I'm concerned. I won't even ask Porky if he's got a licence for that gun he waved at me half an hour ago!"

"Well!" Kaufman said heartily. "We appreciate your attitude, Lieutenant! Don't we, Porky?"

"Sure do!" Smith agreed.

"And if there's something we can do in return?" Eli asked.

"There certainly is," I said. "You can tell me all about Snake Lannigan. Who he is and where I can find him."

There was a short silence after that.

"I'm sorry, Lieutenant," Kaufman said finally. "I wish I could help you, but it's impossible!"

"Don't let's spoil this friendly atmosphere we just got," I said. "I don't want to have to start remembering things again. Things like you hiring call-girls for your party tonight. Or things like Porky waving a gun at me—that's worth five to seven years in Alcatraz on its own!"

Kaufman lit himself a cigarette. "You misunderstand me," he said quickly. "It's not that I don't want to help you—I can't. I don't know who Snake Lannigan is, or where you could find him. I've never met him in my life!"

"When I said to you I had a message from Snake, you didn't act as if you'd never met him in your life before," I said. "You brought me in here right away—remember?"

Kaufman winced: "I remember. I wish I could forget. I know the name Snake Lannigan all right, Lieutenant—but I never met the guy! I don't think anybody ever met him. I'm not sure if he even exists—it's a cover for the call-girl organisation and means of identifying people connected with it at the same time."

I stubbed my cigarette out in his beaten silver ashtray.

"Supposing you keep on talking?" I said. "Tell me everything you know about the call-girl organisation? And maybe Porky could pour us a drink while you're talking?"

"Sure thing!" Porky said quickly and moved over to the drink cabinet in the corner.

Kaufman lit another cigarette from the butt of his first. "You know who I am, Lieutenant," he said. "What I do. I'm probably the biggest gambling operator on the West Coast. I'll be honest with you, but I'll deny it of course, if you quote me in court!"

"Go on," I told him.

"My operations are legitimate," he said. "My places are run squarely. When you're taking out ten per cent of the turnover in a casino, you'd be a fool to try and chisel your customers at the same time. But I'm the fall-guy for every clean-up campaign that comes along. I'm a safe target for politicians who want to beat a big drum about cleaning up a city.

"No clean-up campaign lasts very long, but it can be expensive for me if they raid my places even once. They probably break up the tables, do a lot of damage to the place—frighten off a lot of my clients ... I prefer it not to happen. That means I have to sweeten some of the politicians—the ones that can be sweetened. I have to be nice to them, entertain them—and all their hangers-on."

Porky put the drinks in front of us on the small table.

"I'm of age," I said to Kaufman. "So this is what the big wide world is like—when do we start talking about Snake Lannigan?"

"I was coming to that," he said, "You give a big party for some of these people and they want girls there. I had to have a reliable source to supply the girls when I wanted them. And a discreet source, too.

"It was about eighteen months ago I got a telephone call. A woman's voice. She told me that Snake Lannigan was operating the biggest call-girl racket on the West Coast that there ever had been. She quoted me the rates, the sign of the snake which would identify his girls ... she talked to me for about fifteen minutes straight. When she'd finished I said it sounded fine, but why tell me. She said because I could mean big business to them and they'd look after me. I wasn't sure whether it was a gag or something. She said what could I lose—next time I was throwing a party, why not contact them. She had given me four 'phone numbers—call any one of them, she told me. Day or night. A twenty-four hour service."

I picked up the drink and tasted it. It was a nice brand of Scotch. "Then?" I asked him.

"I'm sorry, Lieutenant," he shrugged his shoulders. "But up to now it's been as simple as that. The service always worked fine. All you had to do was ring one of the numbers. When I took this place, I had a call three days after we moved in. A voice told me the service was now operating in Vale Heights and gave me a local number to call."

"What number was that?"

He told me and it checked with the number Frankie had given me. "That's all there is to it, Lieutenant," he said.

I drank some more Scotch: "Does Snake Lannigan operate in Pine City?"

Kaufman shook his head: "Not to my knowledge, Lieutenant. I don't get into Pine City very often," he grinned faintly. "Your city ordinances make it tough for a guy like me to make a visit worthwhile."

"And that's all you know about Snake Lannigan?"

"That's all of it, Lieutenant. I swear it! Whoever runs the organisation knows what they're doing. Up to now, we've never had any trouble with the police. This must have been the first slip-up Snake Lannigan ever made."

"That could be," I said, with more conviction in my voice than I felt.

Feet pattered down the hallway and the door was suddenly flung open. Jo Dexter stood there, panting, her eyes dancing with excitement. She looked around the room and then looked disappointed.

"Haven't you arrested them yet?" she asked me.

"Not yet," I said.

"Aren't you going to?"

"I don't think so," I said. "I thought you'd stay home."

"A fine thing!" she said. "Walking out on me like that!"

I looked at Kaufman again. "You could be telling me the truth," I said. "I don't know. For the time being, I'm going to think you are. If you aren't you'll be in trouble. I'll see to that."

"Believe me, Lieutenant," he said. "That was the truth."

"If anyone from Snake Lannigan's organisation contacts you, 'phone me right away."

"I'll do that," he said.

"Okay," I said. "I'll take myself out of here. Thanks for the drink."

I walked into the hallway and headed for the front door.

Jo caught up with me on the front steps. "Don't walk so fast," she said breathlessly. "I have to run to keep up!"

"It was a lousy evening, one way and the other," I said. "So no thanks for it."

"You don't think I'm letting you get away with that!"

"What are you talking about?"

"Where do you think you're going now?"

"I'm going back to Pine City," I said. "Why?"

"I'm coming with you!"

"Are you crazy?"

"This is the first real excitement I've had in years!" she said. "And if you think I'm going to miss out on it now, it's you who are crazy! I'm staying right alongside you until this investigation is finished, Lieutenant Al Wheeler! And if you try and stop me, I shall report you to your Commissioner!"

"Report me! For what?"

"Abduction, that's what!" she said fiercely. "Have you forgotten how you forced me out of this house earlier on tonight? You grabbed me and ran me out of the house and threw me into your car. Me, a defenceless woman with no man to protect me! I'll tell your Commissioner, all right! How you drove like a maniac back to my house, took me inside, threw me onto the divan and then ..."

"Wait a minute!" I yelped. "That's a pack of lies—and you know it!"

"I know it," she said sweetly. "But your Commissioner won't! And think of the witnesses I'll be able to produce who saw you rush me out of the house away from the party tonight!"

I knew when I was licked. "Okay," I said. "This has been my lucky night, all right. I could have just fallen down and broken a leg—but no! I had to meet you, instead!"

"You drive down to the house," she said, "and I'll follow in my car. I'll pack some things and then we'll drive back to Pine City."

"Yes, ma'am!"

"And let's get one thing right from the start," she said firmly. "I guess we'll see a lot of one another during the next few days or so, until your investigation is finished. I just don't want you to misunderstand, Lieutenant Al Wheeler! This isn't going to be..."

"That's okay," I said. "There's plenty of room in my house and you don't need to worry, I'll ..."

"This is not going to be," she ignored my interruption, "one of those stupid platonic arrangements! So far as I'm concerned, half the fun of this investigation is going to be the investigator!"

CHAPTER 8

There's nothing like a blonde to decorate a kitchen. Jo stood at the stove, poaching eggs while the percolator burbled. She was wearing an ivory-coloured sweater and a pair of black television slacks ... They call them television slacks because when a girl like Jo wears them, you watch the slacks and not the TV.

Bright sunlight streamed through the windows and my watch said it was ten-thirty in the morning.

Jo flipped the eggs out of the pan onto the waiting toast and brought two plates across to the table. She went back for the percolator and I started in on the eggs. She could cook, too.

When we had finished eating and were on our second cup of coffee and first cigarette, she looked at me. "You look sort of worried," she said. "What were you thinking about?"

"I was wondering," I said. "Where would you hide a corpse?"

Her face, paled: "Do you have to think about things like that? So close to breakfast, too!"

"This is what you wanted," I reminded her. "To be close to an investigation."

"That's what I said," she nodded. "I like being close to the investigator ... so why shouldn't I like being close to the investigation?"

"The only reason I can think of is this corpse," I said. "If I ever find it."

"If you're going to keep dragging it into the conversation, I suppose we'll have to talk about it," she said. "What corpse?"

"A girl," I said. "An ash-blonde by the name of Olga Kellner. She left Vale Heights suddenly a few days back. I'm almost sure she's been murdered—but where's the corpse?"

"There must be a million places you can put a corpse and it will never be found," she said.

"Name one," I said.

"The sea."

"No dice. They float—they get washed back in with the tide."

She thought again: "You could bury it."

"Then the ground's disturbed," I said. "Somebody walks past and sees there's a six-foot plot of ground with freshly-turned earth on top. It looks too much like what it is for them to forget it. Nobody tries to get rid of a corpse by burying it—you might as well carry it around with you for the attention it attracts!"

"Somebody could hide it in their cellar … or a cupboard or something!"

I shook my head: "I don't want to dwell on the point so close to breakfast, but the older a corpse gets—well! It's not a thing to live with!"

Jo's face changed colour to a watery-green. "Give me another cigarette!" she said.

"Sure," I gave her another cigarette and lit it for her. "This character, Snake Lannigan, is the key to the whole problem," I said. "The guy nobody has ever seen. We don't even know if he exists!"

"It sounds very complicated to me," she said.

The 'phone jangled in the living-room and I went to answer it. It was the Commissioner.

"Hammond picked up a line on Angela Markon," he told me. "She came from Palmerstown … you know it? About twenty miles south?"

"I know it," I said.

"She worked there for a couple of years—waitress in a diner. Suddenly quit her job about three months back, but kept on her apartment. Never talked much to anybody, but seemed to have plenty of money although she wasn't working. Last seen there nearly a month ago."

"Familiar story, Commissioner," I said. "Anything else?"

"Nothing else," he said. "Hammond's still in Palmerstown at the moment, but I don't see him learning any more there. The stake-out is still in the General Mail Office, but I'm sure no one's going to try and collect the mail from that box. Incidentally, the mail today that was delivered was only about a quarter of what it normally has been."

"Lannigan's passing the word around fast," I said. "That was to be expected."

"I think so," he agreed. "How about you, Wheeler? Got any leads?"

"None I'd stake a dime on at the moment," I said. "I'm going out to look for a corpse in a little while."

There was a short silence, then he asked cautiously: "Why? Did you lose one?"

"The Kellner girl," I said. "I'm sure she was knocked off. She disappeared out of Vale Heights about a week ago the same way Leila Cross disappeared. Nobody has seen or heard of her since."

"That sounds interesting," he said. "Where were you thinking of looking?"

"I'm not sure, sir," I said. "I have a hunch she won't be too far from Vale Heights. She stayed there a fortnight after Leila Cross had run. So the Kellner girl must have thought she was safe from whatever the menace was. And if the menace left her alone for a fortnight, he must have thought so as well. Then something happened to change the menace's mind suddenly. So he probably acted in a hurry. If he hurried, he maybe killed her while he was in Vale Heights or close by."

Lavers' grunt didn't sound impressed. "You said it was only a hunch," he said. "There's an awful lot of guesswork in that and no facts whatsoever. But you might as well try it—we're up a blind alley with this case and unless we get a break, we'll stay that way."

"Yes, sir," I said.

"Incidentally, everyone knows you're suspended," he told me. "The word's gone around fast. I told Miss Gulley in the strictest confidence that I had suspended you, and now every precinct in the city knows about it!"

"Has she shaved her head yet?"

"Not that I noticed!" Lavers sounded startled. "Why—is she thinking of it?"

"I wouldn't want to undermine your confidence in your secretary, Commissioner," I said earnestly. "But she has an obsession. Just casually mention the name Yul Brynner to her—say how much you admire him, and see what reaction you get."

"You think she's a little—er, unstable?" he asked anxiously.

"I wouldn't like to say, sir," I said. "But if you just try that little experiment, I think you'll see for yourself. I also understand that the Mayor is in need of a secretary at the moment, should you consider ..."

"Thank you, Wheeler," he said. "I'll bear that in mind."

I went back into the kitchen.

"Anything exciting?" Jo asked.

"Routine," I said. I slumped into a chair and wondered if it was long enough after breakfast to have a drink. I thought I could give it another ten minutes.

"You're thinking again!" she said accusingly.

"Tell me something," I said. "You've known Kaufman for a couple of years—what sort of man do you think he is?"

"I think he's a louse!" she said. "A heel!"

I nodded: "What about Porky Smith? Do you know anything about him?"

"Only that he's Kaufman's right-hand man," she said. "And what Marlene has told me about him. Marlene's just a little frightened of him, I think. She said once that Eli was only a child compared to Porky Smith ... an amateur compared to a professional. Whenever Eli has to get tough with somebody, it's Smith who does it. She told me that."

"Makes sense," I said.

She looked at me enquiringly: "Why are you asking me all these questions?"

"I was thinking about last night," I said. "I bust into their party ... I give them a phony story about being from Snake Lannigan and when they call my bluff, I run out on them. Smith follows me and finally catches up with me in your house. He has a gun in his hand—he looks as if he can use it. He frisks me like an expert.

"He's the tough, competent professional—right up to the time I tell him I'm a cop. Then he goes to water. He says sure he'll run the errand down to the hotel and bring back my things that prove I'm a cop. When he gets back he's only anxious to oblige, nothing is too much trouble."

"What are you driving at?" she asked curiously.

I leaned back in my chair: "When I got back to the house, I questioned Kaufman—I was rude to him, I threatened him. He takes it all lying down. Yes-sir, no-sir, Lieutenant-sir! Anything you say, Lieutenant! That's the truth, so help me, Lieutenant! And Smith just stands around pouring the drinks, with a polite smile on his face like the hired help."

"I still don't see ..."

I lit myself a cigarette and thought it definitely was time for a drink. "'Let's remember a couple of things," I said. "First up, Kaufman is a big boy in L.A. He'd have a finger in all the graft around the coast—he's got connections, plenty of connections. I busted into his house, gave a false name and pretended I had a message for him. When they found out I wasn't what I pretended to be, I ran out of the house taking you with me. Smith had every right to follow us—and to pull a gun on me. He could say in a court—and nobody would doubt him—that he was worried about your safety. If it was proved in a court that I acted as I did, the least that would happen to me would be me getting kicked off the force.

"But does Kaufman threaten me with that? Does he thunder and shout and talk about getting his tame lawyers—and he'd have a dozen of those—onto it, right away? Does he tell me to get the hell out of house and he'll fix me but good? No! From the time I tell Porky that I'm a cop, both of them are so busy cringing they don't have time for a drink, even!"

Jo nodded: "I see your point—it was out of character?"

"Exactly!" I said. "And why? Because maybe they had something to hide. Something they didn't want a cop nosing around, because it was too big. Once I said I was a cop, they thought I was after the big thing and it scared them to death! And when they found I wasn't, they were so relieved, they could've kissed me, maybe!"

"Gosh!" Jo told me enthusiastically. "You sound just like a detective!"

"I am a detective!" I snarled.

"I keep forgetting," she admitted. "Although I must say you can certainly find your way around in the dark!"

"Let's go have a drink," I suggested.

We went into the living room. I put some Peggy Lee onto the turntable and let her voicepipe gently through the walls. I poured the drinks and gave one to Jo, then sat down in an armchair. She sat on my knee and curled herself up like a ball of wool.

"Where does all this deduction get us?" she asked.

"They were scared stiff," I said. "Of a cop. Of a cop doing what? The only thing I can think of was they were scared of a cop being in that house. It wasn't expected."

"You mean you think they're hiding something in the house?"

"Sure," I said.

"This gets more exciting every minute!" she said. "It leaves long division for dead! What do you think they're hiding?"

"The body of a girl named Olga Kellner," I said soberly.

Good Scotch spilled out of her glass onto my knee.

"Don't say things like that," she said faintly, "even as a joke."

"I wasn't joking."

More Scotch got wasted. She closed her eyes. "What are you going to do about it?"

"I'm going back to Vale Heights," I said. "Tonight. I'm going to try and get into that house and take a look around."

"Isn't that dangerous?"

"Depends," I said. "After their scare last night, if it was there they might shift it. That's why I've got to get inside the house tonight. If they have moved it, there should be signs of where it was."

"I won't ask you any details," she shuddered.

"So you go to a movie tonight, honey," I said. "Or sit home and play the hi-fi."

"I'd like to do that," she said. "I really would—but I can't."

"Why not?"

"Because I'm going with you!"

I pushed her off my lap and got onto my feet, holding her shoulders. "Now, look!" I said. "This is one thing ..."

She put a finger on my lips. "You listen," she said. "I know that house— I've been there many times. I know it well, and you don't know it at all. And another thing ... Marlene is my best friend and if the man she's married to is a murderer, I've got to do my best to help prove it before she comes back from L.A.!"

I thought about it and it made sense. With Jo along with me to guide me through the house, it would halve the time, and the risk.

"Okay," I said. "You made yourself a deal."

"That's fine," she said. "When do we start?"

"Not till tonight. Latish, I guess. If there was some way we could get them out of the house ..."

Jo snapped her fingers: "I've got it! I'll call him!"

"Now you're going crazy again!"

"I could call to see if Marlene is back yet," she said. "That's a natural thing for me to do. Eli wouldn't think about that. I could maybe find out what he's doing today."

"Maybe," I said. "You could tell him I've gone to Palmerstown because I found out a girl who was murdered a few days back came from there, and I won't be back for a couple of days. You could imply I had brushed you off and you were on your way back to your house. That would take care of me."

"I could tell him I was lonely," she said. "He's never actually made a pass at me, but I've seen that look in his eye a few times. I think he didn't make a pass because he knew I was Marlene's best friend and it would go straight back to his wife."

"It would be better if we could get Porky out of the house as well," I said. "Supposing you ring him. Ask about Marlene first, then tell him about me. Sound annoyed—as if your pride's been hurt. Then tell him you're in the mood for a party. Say why doesn't he bring Porky down to your house tonight and you'll bring a girl-friend back from Pine City with you—for Porky! That should be bait!

"If he agrees, tell him you expect to arrive at the house at eight-thirty and for them to come at that time. When they get there and find the house empty, they'll think you've been delayed on the way and they'll wait—for a while, anyway. Long enough for us to take a look at their house."

"Okay!" she said.

I poured us another drink and gestured towards the 'phone.

"It's all yours, ma'am!" I told her.

She got the call through about five minutes later.

"Eli?" Her voice was warm. "It's Jo Dexter here. Is Marlene back yet? Not yet? Oh, I just thought I'd give her a ring—I'm in Pine City on my own-some with nothing to do ... Him! He's had to rush off to Palmerstown—something about a girl who was murdered a few days ago—they discovered she came from Palmerstown and he's gone there to make enquiries. Take him a couple of days he said, and he quite obviously didn't want little me along with him ... so another of my budding romances has ended tragically!

"Eli ..." her voice dropped an octave and became warm and promising. "Eli—I'm bored! Why don't we have a party tonight at my place? You're a grass widower, and I'm just out of Reno without a husband—and I don't even have that cop I thought I was going to have. I'm in the mood to whoop it up a little, Eli!"

She gurgled with laughter: "And if we have a gay time, Eli, there's one thing for sure—you won't tell your wife about it and I won't, either! You will? That's great! Bring Porky with you and I'll have a girl for him—no, I don't particularly want Porky along, but if he doesn't come it'll make things sort of awkward. I ran into a girl-friend of mine this morning and asked her back with me. I don't want to put her off suddenly now—she's very bright. She's a brunette with a figure like Jayne Mansfield's—I know Porky will like her. And, Eli darling, that's quite a big house I've got—we won't need to see anything of them after a couple of drinks ... You're nice to me! We'll be there around eight-thirty. You arrive then and we get the party started right away! That's fine, Eli. See you tonight ... 'Bye!"

She hung up and looked at me with a smug smile on her face.

"Okay?" I asked her.

"Of course!" she said. "What man could resist me?"

"You mean what man could you resist!" I told her.

CHAPTER 9

We had an early dinner in Pine City before we left and we reached Vale Heights around a quarter to eight. I took the road through the town and the Healey took the climb over the other side without any effort at all.

I went past Kaufman's house at a steady thirty miles an hour so that the engine noise was small and kept on going up the hill. Half a mile further on I got the Healey around on full lock on the narrow road and switched off the engine, then let the car coast back downhill.

I stopped the car a hundred yards from the gates of Kaufman's drive, running off the road until the nearside brushed against the trees. We got out and I left the car without any lights. It was off the road and wasn't any danger to other cars coming down the hill, and Kaufman wouldn't spot it unless he drove right past it—and if he did that he'd be heading in the opposite direction to where Jo's house was situated.

We walked down the road fifty yards and then stood in the shelter of a tree and waited. I checked my wristwatch—it was eight-fifteen.

"Who else is likely to be in the house when they've left?" I asked Jo.

"I'm not sure," she said. "I don't think he's got any servants there. When he holds a party, he hires the help. But always he seems to have a couple of men hanging around. They were at the party last night, and they're always around in L.A. They must be bodyguards, I think."

"He won't be taking them down to your place tonight," I said. "Not unless he's crazy, and he's not crazy except like a fox. So they're still in the house probably."

"In the kitchen drinking—for sure!" Jo said confidently. "Or maybe upstairs somewhere. We can get into the house without bothering them or having them bother us."

Another ten minutes went by and then headlights lit up the driveway and gates. A few seconds later a magnificent Bentley Continental swung out into the road and headed in the direction of Jo's house.

"Let's go!" I said. I grabbed her hand and started off at a fast trot towards the gates.

By the time we reached them, I was out of breath. About the only physical exercise I get normally is changing the discs on the turntable of my hi-fi set-up.

"Let's just walk from here?" I suggested.

"You aren't out of breath?"

"I've got plenty of breath," I said hoarsely. "It's just that my lungs aren't big enough to keep up with the intake!"

We walked down the drive until the house loomed in front of us. There were no lights showing in the front.

"What did I tell you?" Jo asked triumphantly. "They'll be in the kitchen drinking—for sure!"

"Okay," I said. "Show me some more genius—how do we get in?"

"There must be a window open some place?" she suggested doubtfully.

I closed my eyes and counted up to ten. It didn't make any difference. "There must be a window open—for sure! Let's start with the one to the left of the front door, shall we? Shouldn't take us more than half an hour to work around the house to the front door again!"

"I thought you'd know how to break into a house," she said defensively. "Don't policemen know those sort of things?"

"You're confusing cops with burglars," I told her. "But I have a better idea—we'll knock!"

"Huh?"

I took her arm and hustled her onto the front porch. "Would those two characters inside recognise you?" I asked.

"Not right away, I don't think," she said. "But why?"

"When someone answers the door you give 'em the big smile," I said. "You say you're one of Snake's girls, and Kaufman rang and said he wanted two girls to come up tonight to entertain his friends while he was out. They'll think their boss is a pal!"

"What then?" she asked nervously.

"You say the car stalled at the gates and the other girl is still with it. One of them will go to assist—I shall wait for him!"

"What about me with the other one?"

"You play catch-as-catch-can with him until I get back—it won't be long."

"How will you get in?"

"I shall ring the bell, stupid!"

"Al," her voice quavered. "Isn't there an easier way?"

"I am not going to walk around the house trying windows!" I said firmly. I jabbed my finger onto the bell-push and left it there.

When I heard someone coming down the hall, I backed off the porch fast and hid behind a convenient rose-bush at the start of the drive.

The character who opened the door was short and broad-shouldered, wearing an aloha shirt and tan slacks. He looked Jo up and down in one comprehensive sweep: "Yeah?"

"I'm one of Snake's girls!" Jo said. She put her hands on her hips and took a deep breath. That convinced him.

"You must have the wrong night, sister!" he said. "The boss is out!"

"Ain't that the truth!" Jo said. "He rings Snake and says to send a couple of nice girls up here for company for two of his buddies in the house."

"He did?" The character's face brightened. "Say! That's nice of him!"

"My girl-friend's got trouble with the car down at the gates," Jo went on, chewing a wad of imaginary gum. "Be a gentleman, huh? Go and help her fix it!"

"Sure!" He turned his head and yelled: "Hey, Mack! Look what Santa Claus Kaufman just had delivered!"

Feet thudded down the hall and then Mack appeared—he was tall and broad-shouldered. That was the only significant difference between the two of them, I noted. The first guy explained the situation.

"I get it!" Mack said. "I'll go help the dame bring the heap up the drive. You go organise us some drinks, huh? Man! This is what I call living! Getting paid for looking after a call-girl!"

The first character put his arm around Jo's waist and escorted her inside the house. Mack started off at a loping run and when he was just past the rose-bush, I caught him on the back of the head with a loping gun-butt.

There was the minor problem of what to do with him. For the time being I let it ride and went back to the porch. The front door was open, so I walked in and down the hall. I heard a quick scampering of feet from the living-room and I took a look.

Jo was backing off around the table, a faintly desperate look on her face, while the short character was edging around trying to get closer to her. His back was to me, and Jo hadn't seen me either … she was concentrating too hard on staying out of the clinches.

"Whatsamatter, baby?" the short character asked plaintively. "You're the screwiest call-girl I ever did meet! One call and you start running!"

"It's just that I'm new to the business," Jo said jerkily, then made another three yards around the table. "You'll have to give me time!"

I came up behind the short character and used that loping gun-butt again. It made the customary crunching noise and the short character stopped taking an interest in anything.

"Well!" Jo said coldly. "It's about time! Another five minutes and …"

"You'd be starting to earn your fifty dollars?"

"I suppose you think that's very funny, Al Wheeler!" she said bitterly. "I've a good mind …"

"That is the remark of the week," I told her. "I shall treasure it!"

I picked up the short character's feet and dragged him out of the room and along the hall to the porch. Jo followed, a look of mild expectancy on her face,

"What are you going to do?" she asked. "Cut their throats?"

"Please remember I am dedicated to the task of upholding law and order," I said. "I think!"

The Cadillac was under the carport, alongside the Thunderbird. The keys were in both cars. One thing about a Caddy—nothing is stinted—and that does include the luggage-space. It took both the short character and the tall character without any trouble at all.

I slammed the lid shut and locked it, then put the keys in pocket.

"Won't they run out of air?" Jo asked anxiously.

"Not for a while, anyway," I said. "I'll open it up when we leave."

We went back into the house.

"Has this place got a cellar?" I asked her.

"I think so. There's a flight of steps goes down to some place, just before you get to the kitchen." Her voice quavered slightly. "That was a gag, wasn't it, Al? You know—what you said about looking for a body?"

"As the vampire said to his victim," I widened my eyes so that the whites showed. "It was a joke in a different vein!"

"Al!" Jo closed her eyes. "Don't!"

We found the steps that led down to some place, just before you reached the kitchen. I walked down the stairs with Jo close behind me. There was a door at the bottom with a heavy chain and padlock locking it.

I mentally recounted the things I could be charged with ... Breaking and entering, armed assault ... an added charge of damaging property didn't seem to matter very much. I took the thirty-two out of its holster and blew the padlock apart. In the confined space, it sounded like the end of the world had just happened.

"Do you have any earplugs?" Jo asked in a muffled voice, when the last reverberations had died away. "I need them to fill two holes in my head where my eardrums used to be!"

"Aren't you forgetting about that great big hole right in the top of your head?" I asked her.

"Why didn't I stick to a quiet life just working my way through husbands!" she muttered.

The door sagged open a little. I gave it a heave with my foot and it swung open wide. I felt around till I found a light switch and flicked it on. Bright neon light flooded the cellar. I walked a little further inside. Jo clutched my arm and went with me.

It was a wine cellar. A prosaic place with bins stacked along the walls and standing in rows, evenly-spaced across the whole width of the cellar.

Jo gave a shuddering sigh of relief: "At least there isn't a corpse here!"

"We haven't looked properly yet," I said. "If you'd rather wait upstairs ..."

"No!" she said definitely. "My imagination would be worse than any reality you could find down here. I'll look with you, but I'm not going to like it!"

I walked up and down the cellar. Kaufman must have spent a small fortune on the liquor he had stored down there. With a couple of bodyguards loose in the house, it would be logical to padlock the door. A couple of guys could have had a three-year drunk down there and still have some bottles left over.

In the far corner we came upon a long metal chest, painted black. It was also locked. I told Jo to stuff her fingers in her ears and blew the lock open. This was getting to be kid's stuff. I just hoped Commissioner Lavers never got to hear of it.

I put the gun back into its holster and looked down at the chest, feeling a curious reluctance to lift the lid.

"Do you think," Jo asked in a small voice, "that it ... might be in there?"

"There is," I said with my years of police training coming to the fore, "one way to find out!" I got hold of the lid with both hands and threw it back.

There was a girl inside the chest. She lay there quite peacefully with her hands crossed on her bosom. She wore a lamé gown, the colour of gunmetal, which must have cost an awful lot of money.

She had a milky-white skin which looked even whiter by comparison with her black hair that curled softly about her face. She was really very beautiful—and she was dead. I touched her cheek with my fingers and it was cold and unyielding.

"I found my corpse all right," I said. "But I was looking for an ash-blonde!"

Jo didn't answer. I turned around to find out why and saw she had passed out neatly without any fuss and lay in a heap on the floor.

I had another look at the girl in the chest. I pushed back the sleeve of the gown and looked at the top of her arm. There was no tattoo mark.

I heard a hollow groan from beside me and Jo tottered back onto her feet. She looked down at the chest and closed her eyes tight.

"She looks so beautiful," she said faintly. "Just like an angel!"

"There's no law against angels!" I grunted. "But there's a law against people keeping a corpse in their cellar!"

"The poor darling!" Jo said. "And all the time I thought she was in Los Angeles!"

"You mean you know her?"

"Of course I know her," she said. "That's Marlene!"

"Kaufman's wife?"

"My best friend!"

I took another look. I uncrossed the hands gently and found no sign of a bullet hole or wound underneath. The doctor could find out how she died, anyway. I recrossed the hands and then shut the lid.

I lit two cigarettes and put one into Jo's mouth.

"Thanks," she mumbled. "I—the shock, it's—Marlene! He's a fiend! A fiend!"

"Could be you're right, honey," I agreed. "This is one hell of a complication for a poor hard-working cop to find of his own account!"

"Don't you have any heart?" she asked fiercely. "You stand there moaning about your petty troubles when ..."

"I'm sorry," I said. "But it still is one hell of a complication. It just doesn't fit! I ..."

"Stop drivelling!" she said. "What are you going to do about Kaufman?"

"That's easy," I said. "Wait here till he comes back and then arrest him. I ..."

There was a faint sound from behind us.

"I hope we haven't kept you waiting long, Lieutenant?" Eli Kaufman's voice said. "I was stood up by a blonde tonight, so I came home again. For once my timing looks right."

I turned around and saw the two of them standing there ... Porky with a gun in his hand, Kaufman with an expressionless face.

"Why did you kill her, Kaufman?" I asked.

He smiled: "She came home at the wrong time. There was a party going on. She made quite a scene. I suppose I'd had a little too much to drink. I hit her. I only meant to shut her up, but I hit her a little too hard and she fell. She struck her head against the edge of the table as she fell ... I didn't realise until about five minutes afterwards that she was dead."

"Murderer!" Jo said.

Kaufman shrugged his shoulders: "Technically, I suppose you are right."

"If you have any witnesses, you can plead manslaughter," I told him. "But I'm booking you on a homicide rap, Kaufman, and ..."

"You aren't booking anybody, copper!" Porky interrupted. "You stuck your nose in too deep and now we got to cut it off for you—at the back of the skull!"

CHAPTER 10

Kaufman handed me a drink.

"What happened to my two men, Lieutenant?" he asked casually. "I don't see them around."

"The local boys took them down to Vale Heights Precinct," I said just as casually—I hoped. "I imagine they've talked their heads off by now."

"You're lying, of course," he said easily.

He reached out suddenly and grabbed himself a handful of the front of Jo's blouse and pulled her towards him. He slapped her face hard with the palm and then the back of his hand.

"I can keep this up for a long time, Lieutenant," he told me. "Right up to the time you tell me the truth!"

"Okay," I shrugged my shoulders. "They're locked in the boot of the Cadillac."

He let go of Jo, pushing her suddenly so that she stumbled backwards and nearly fell.

"I'm glad you see reason, Lieutenant," he said. "The keys?"

"In my pocket," I said.

I pulled them out and tossed them over to him. Porky had relieved me of my gun before we left the cellar, so I had nothing in my pockets more lethal than a box of matches.

"Thanks," he said. "I think I'd better let them out, they might be running short of air. Porky you keep an eye on these two until I get back."

"Sure," Smith nodded. "A pleasure!"

Kaufman looked at me with a sort of puzzled look, then went out of the room. I saw two angry blotches were staining Jo's cheeks.

"You all right?" I asked her.

"I'm fine," she said. "Just contaminated, that's all!"

"She always makes with the witty dialogue," Porky said. "I love a dame that makes with the witty dialogue!"

"What's her name?" I asked him.

I offered Jo a cigarette and lit it for her and one for myself.

She glared at me. "Can't you do something?" she demanded.

"I forgot to bring my records along," I admitted. "But if you like, I'll sing."

Kaufman came back into the room, followed closely by two dishevelled characters in Hawaiian shirts.

"Just let me at him!" the short one said murderously. "Just let me beat his head into the ground for a little while!"

"And after you finished," the tall one pleaded, "I'll jump on his face— just for kicks!"

"Calm down!" Kaufman said coldly. "A couple of bright bodyguards you are! You let a cop and a dame jump you!"

"They tricked us!" the short one said passionately. "The dame makes out she's one of Snake's girls, and that you sent her and another dame up here just to keep us company!"

"You think I'm another Dale Carnegie?" Kaufman asked him. "Endowing the hired help with call-girls!"

"Hell!" the taller one said apologetically: "We didn't know, boss. We thought maybe you'd gone crazy and ..."

"Just keep your big mouth shut, Mack!" the short one said wearily. "We got enough trouble, already!"

Kaufman looked at me: "Where's your car?"

"Along the road a little," I said. If I hadn't told him he would have started in with the slapping routine again, and I thought I had a certain responsibility to get Jo out of this in one piece.

"You want the keys?" I dragged the keys out of my pocket and threw them to him.

He passed them to Mack. "Go and bring his car in," he said. "You'd better take him with you," he pointed at the short guy. "So you don't get lost!"

"What are you going to do with them?" Porky grunted.

Kaufman lit himself a cigarette carefully. "They present quite a problem," he said. "The cost of disposing of a body is going up all the time!"

"You listened to me before, we wouldn't have that problem," Porky grunted again. "What's the matter with the sea?"

"We've been through that," Kaufman said. "The Lieutenant will tell you. Corpses float—get washed in with the tide—fishermen fish them up instead of fish!"

He looked at me: "How would you dispose of a corpse, Lieutenant?"

"I'd send it to the morgue," I said.

He grinned. "That's a very good answer," he said. "You see, Porky? The Lieutenant knows what he's talking about!"

He was talking skid-talk so far as I was concerned. It didn't mean a damned thing!

"The last person you ever murder is a cop," I told him. "You must know that, Kaufman. The reason's simple. All the cops get together when one of 'em is knocked off, and they find the guy who did it. They don't want anybody setting a precedent. You aren't seriously thinking of killing me?"

"I'm afraid I shall have to," he said. "Nothing personal in this, Lieutenant, you understand?"

"You'll never get away with it!"

"You might be right," he said. "I can only try. If I let you go now, you take me in a straight line towards the gas-chamber. By disposing of you, I at least have a chance, even if it isn't a very, good one."

"Why don't we stop horsing around?" Porky asked. "What are we going to do with them?"

I heard the Healey come up the drive and stop somewhere close to the house. I started to calculate the odds—they weren't very bright. Four to one, and they had all the guns. Maybe I should have been an orthodox cop, after all.

The two bodyguards came back into the room, looking quite pleased with themselves—at last they'd done a job right.

"Anything else, boss?" Mack asked eagerly. "Maybe we can jump on the cop a little, huh?"

"You can take the girl out into his car," Kaufman said, "and drive her down to her house. And you can wait there with her, until we arrive. And don't let her out of your sight!"

"Sure thing, boss!" Mack said confidently. "Leave it to us!"

"You slip up on this job," Kaufman said softly, "and it will be the last mistake that either of you make!"

They grabbed Jo and hustled her out of the room. A minute later the sound of the Healey's motor died away in the distance.

"Pour us another drink, Porky," Kaufman said. "We all need one—particularly the Lieutenant!"

"Okay," Porky said sourly. "You thought of something yet?"

"Sure," Kaufman nodded. "I think it's good, too. Just get that drink!"

Smith poured the three drinks and handed me mine. I took a grateful sip and concentrated on Kaufman. I didn't think I was going to like his good idea, but I was anxious to hear it.

"Porky," he started. "This guy may be a cop, but he's really nothing but a woman-chaser!"

"So what?"

"You remember the first time he was here?" Kaufman went on. "How he just grabbed Jo and hustled her out of the house?"

"Yeah?"

"We had a party going, remember?" Kaufman asked him. "A lot of witnesses to that. Then he took her down to Pine City with him. And then he came back up here with her—to her house."

"This I know!" Porky grunted.

"So tonight she gets tired of him and gives him the air," Eli went on. "And he can't take it. Not a woman-chaser like him. And he goes berserk. Maybe he didn't mean to kill her but in a blind fury, he does!"

"And then what does he do?" Porky didn't sound impressed.

Kaufman finished his drink and put the empty glass, back on the table, carefully. "Figure it out for yourself, Porky," he said gently. "He's a cop. And he's just murdered a woman in a blind fury. He can see the headlines describing him as a sex-maniac—him a cop! What would you do if you were him?"

"I guess I'd blow my brains out!" Porky guffawed.

"Sometimes you're almost smart," Kaufman told him. "That's exactly what he is going to do!"

Porky stopped guffawing: "You just might have something there!"

"I think it's good enough," Kaufman said. "They must have been seen together in Pine City. We can produce witnesses who saw him yank her out of the party the other night. We can build a story that will stand up. The cops won't want it played up in the newspapers, they'll want to hush it up as much as they can." He looked across at me and grinned: "How does it sound to you, Lieutenant? If you see any holes in it, I'll listen!"

"I've been thinking about you," I said slowly. "Maybe you didn't mean to kill your wife. But when you found out you had, you realised there were witnesses you couldn't trust. Witnesses who might talk. The call-girls at the party. And they'd thought of that one, too. So they disappeared, or tried to. But you caught up with them—you or Porky. You knocked off Angela Markon and Leila Cross to make sure they never would give evidence against you. What about Olga Kellner? Have you got her corpse tucked away some place as well?"

The grin broadened on his face. "You know," he said, "for a copper, you aren't bad!"

"There is more to the theory," I said. "I also think that Eli Kaufman isn't the only name you have."

"I have an alias?" He raised his eyebrows. "This is getting to be really interesting, Lieutenant. What is the other name I have, the one I don't know about?"

"Snake Lannigan!" I said.

The grin disappeared from his face. "Not bad," he admitted. "Not bad at all. How did you work that one out, Lieutenant?"

"When I arrived at the party," I said, "I told you that Snake Lannigan had sent me. You picked me as a phony right away. Why? Because you knew that Lannigan couldn't have sent me, for the simple reason you were Lannigan!"

His face was a careful blank: "Let us stay with the current problem, Lieutenant. Do you see any holes in this theory of mine on how to get rid of you and the girl permanently?"

"It's shot right through with holes!" I said. "You'll never get away with it!"

"Why?"

"You just won't, that's all. You're crazy to even think of it!"

The grin came back on his face as he looked at Porky: "You hear that? The Lieutenant can't pin it down. Not one thing that is wrong. The only thing he can do is sound off like a cop and fan the breeze!"

"Okay," Porky nodded. "So you're a master-mind! If we're going to do it, let's do it and get it over with!"

"That's what I intend," Kaufman said. "Take him out to the Cadillac. You can sit in the back seat with him and I'll drive."

"Okay," Porky nodded again. Then he looked at me. "Just try anything, copper, and you'll only try it once!"

We went out to the Cadillac. Me first, then Porky's gun, then Porky. We sat in the back seat and waited. A couple of minutes later, Kaufman came out and sat behind the wheel. It wasn't a very exciting trip down to Jo's house; nobody said anything. I tried to think of some bright conversation and found I was all out of bright conversation.

What I really needed was a little help ... something like the Marine Corps.

Out of the car and into Jo's house in the same order—me first, Porky's gun and then Porky, with Kaufman behind Porky.

Jo sat on the sofa in the living-room with the two bodyguards watching her. They looked pleased with themselves when they saw Kaufman.

"Okay, huh, boss?" Mack said. "We got here with no trouble and we ain't taken our eyes off the dame once!"

"You can say that again!" Jo said bitterly: "I don't know why I bother to wear clothes!"

I lit myself a cigarette: "Kaufman!"

"What?"

"You wanted me to shoot holes in your theory. The biggest hole is the simplest fact. I'm a cop. I'm working on a case. The Police Department knows that. They just won't believe that I'd commit a murder and then kill myself."

"I think they might," he said easily. "But we'll find out soon enough."

He looked around him slowly: "Lucky we were here before, Porky. Maybe we weren't wasting our time, after all."

"I don't get it!" Smith grunted.

"We know the layout. The bedroom would be better. And it wants to be mussed up quite a lot."

"How about the dame?" Porky asked.

"In the bedroom," Kaufman said.

"Hey!" Jo sat bolt upright. "What's going on?"

"They're going to kill you, honey," I said. "And then kill me. Only they think it will look like I killed you, then shot myself. So Kaufman thinks."

"He's crazy!" she said.

"I know," I agreed. "I told him."

Kaufman shrugged his shoulders impatiently: "Well, let's get it over with!"

"Boss?" Mack looked at him, frowning. "You serious? We going to croak the dame, then the cop?"

"You don't have to worry," Kaufman said crisply. "Porky and I are quite capable of handling it!"

"It doesn't make any difference of course, Mack," I said. "You and your pal have got equal responsibility with Kaufman and Smith. Four guys can go to the gas-chamber for a double murder just as well as one."

The two bodyguards looked at one another uncertainly. I had a sudden hunch. "You guys been down the cellar lately?"

"Huh?" the short guy said.

"The cellar in Kaufman's house?"

"You think the boss is crazy?" He laughed. "He don't let us loose with all that liquor down there!"

"That's not the only thing there," I said.

"Shut up!" Kaufman said coldly.

The two bodyguards looked at each other, then back at me.

"All right," Mack said. "What's down in the cellar?"'

"You two boys don't need to stay here," Kaufman said. "You can walk back to the house."

The short guy wasn't paying him any attention he was still looking at me. "Just what is down in the cellar?" he said slowly.

"His wife's body," I said. "I thought you knew."

"I told you two to get the hell out of here!" Kaufman said in a thin voice.

"So you did," the short one agreed. "But I ain't going yet!" He took a deep breath. "Me and Mack, we like to get our facts right. Don't we, Mack?"

The tall one nodded solemnly: "We sure do!"

"So we got to think about this deal," the short one went on.

"We sure have!" his partner agreed.

Porky moved his shoulders impatiently. "Okay!" he said. "So if you're through with the vaudeville routine, do what the boss says—get the hell out of here!"

The short one still stared at me: "You really are a cop? A Lieutenant from Homicide?"

"I really am," I agreed. "Right now, I've got nothing against either of you boys. But you walk out of here and leave the girl and me to be murdered by Kaufman and Smith ... then you're candidates for the gas-chamber, like I said."

"I figure this cop could know what he was talking about," Mack said slowly. "What do you figure, Jackson?"

"I figure the same way, Mack," the short one agreed.

Porky swivelled the gun in his hand a little so that he covered the two bodyguards. "You guys turning chicken on us," he said softly. "Won't do you no good! Could do you a lot of harm. Be sensible—get out of here, like the boss said. Wait in the car for us—we won't be long."

"You guys will have a bonus coming," Kaufman said. "I'll see to that!"

I looked at the short one, "Ever see inside the gas-chamber, Jackson?" I asked conversationally. "They strap you in a chair, then they drop the pellets into the acid and the gas starts to rise. Funny, but every guy who gets that seat holds his breath when he sees those pellets drop! They should know it won't do 'em any good, but they can't help it! You can imagine how it would feel—holding your breath till your lungs start screaming at you, knowing the next breath you take will be your last!"

His face was completely devoid of expression. After about five seconds, he shifted his gaze to the tall one. "Let's do what the boss says, Mack," he said. "We'll go wait in the car."

The tall one looked uncomfortable. "Well, I ain't sure. I don't like the way that cop talks ..."

"Did I ever give you a bum steer in my life?" Jackson asked impatiently. "C'mon!" He started towards the door and after a moment's hesitation, Mack went with him.

And with them went my chances of living to a ripe old age—and Jo's chances, too.

The expression on Porky Smith's face relaxed a little. "Now you guys are being sensible!" he said. "Just sit in the car—five minutes and we'll be with you!"

"Sure!" Jackson said easily. "I'm remembering what the boss said about a bonus ..." He came up level with Porky and then suddenly moved sideways, driving his elbow hard into Porky's kidneys.

Porky grunted painfully as he was knocked off-balance. His gun wavered as he tottered, trying to regain his balance. Then Jackson's hand dived into his hip pocket and came out holding a gun.

"Kaufman, Mack!" Jackson called out crisply, and the tall one dived a hand into his pocket.

I made a dive towards Porky, which was a mistake. I realised it was a mistake when I was still only halfway across the intervening space and I found myself looking down the barrel of his gun.

A shot sounded loud, and Porky suddenly lost interest in me and dropped his gun. I altered the direction of my dive and grabbed the gun off the floor.

I heard another shot and, straightened up to see Mack folding up slowly like an ironing-board ... and the smoking gun in Kaufman's hand. Mack's reaction hadn't been fast enough, when Jackson had shouted at him to take Kaufman. It looked as if it was his last mistake.

In the split-second before I had Kaufman in line with the gun in my hand, I got a picture of everybody. Porky was stretched out on the floor, Mack was toppling towards it. Jackson had had his back turned to Kaufman and was swinging round desperately to face him, but he was never going to make it in time. Kaufman was moving his gun through a short arc to shoot the second of his former bodyguards.

I steadied the gun in my hand and pressed the trigger twice. I felt I owed it to Jackson to make sure. And then the whole million bucks that Kaufman was worth weren't worth a dime to him anymore. Both bullets hit him in the chest, knocking him back against the wall so that he seemed to stay upright too long, his eyes fixed on me, staring.

I was all set to let him have another one when I realised it was only the wall keeping him up. And just to prove it, his legs gave way suddenly and he slid sideways down the wall onto the floor and rolled over onto his back.

"Lieutenant!" Jackson's voice was hoarse. "How does it feel to kill a millionaire?"

CHAPTER 11

"Three of them!" Jo's voice rose an octave. "And all dead!"

"All dead, lady," Jackson said. He got up onto his feet and looked down at Mack's body. "He was a dumb slob, but he trusted me. He always did what I told him to do."

"You told him right," I said. "Better this way than winding up in that gas-chamber!"

"I guess so," he said. He didn't sound as if he was sure he believed it.

Jo put a shaking hand to her forehead. "If I really believed this," she said, "I'd pass out!"

"What're you waiting for?" Jackson growled. "Rigor mortis to set in?"

There was a soft moan as Jo kept her word and crumpled onto the sofa. I headed towards the liquor cabinet and poured two healthy-sized drinks and gave one to Jackson.

"Thanks," he said.

"No," I shook my head. "Thank you!"

"You weren't kidding me?" he asked. "About that body in the cellar? Really his wife?"

"Really and truly," I assured him. "Have you got a record in this state?"

"Two convictions," he said. "Why?"

"Are you hot at the moment?"

"Not exactly," he glared at me. "What's the pitch?"

"What do you mean by not exactly?"

"Well," he shrugged his shoulders. "I do believe the 'Frisco cops want to talk to me about a heist-job. It's strictly a case of mistaken identity, of course!"

"Of course!" I agreed.

He finished his drink and helped himself to another. I held out my empty glass silently and he splashed whisky into it.

"What's the pitch?" he asked again.

"I was just thinking," I said. "If you have no objections, Mack and I had better be the heroes in this set-up."

"How's that again?"

"I'm suggesting that you gather up your tents and fade into the night," I said. "Three corpses aren't going to argue and I can guarantee the dame won't. So far as this business is concerned, you never were. There was only one bodyguard ... Mack. He decided to join the angels' team and gave me a break. He got Porky and Porky got him, and I got Kaufman. Nobody ever heard of a guy called Jackson."

He nodded: "That sounds like a break."

"You earned it, friend," I told him. "Why don't you take that Cadillac back to Kaufman's place, get your stuff together, then head for a different climate?"

"Sounds like good advice," he said. He put his empty glass on the bar. "Maybe Florida could use a guy like me?"

"Just so long as it's a long way from either Vale Heights or Pine City," I said. "Good luck, Jackson—and goodbye!"

"I'll tell my grandchildren," he said. "Supposing my wife ever catches up with me ... I'll tell 'em that once I met a cop who was a right guy!"

"Thanks, Jackson," I said. "Now get out of here before we start to slobber over one another!"

He went out of the room and a few seconds later I heard the Cadillac move away from out front of the house. I found my gun in Porky's pocket and put it back into the shoulder-holster.

"I heard nearly every word you said!" an accusing voice told me.

I turned around and saw Jo had left the sofa and was busy pouring herself a drink.

"And I don't know that I will go along with your story," she went on. "Unless you're very nice to me!"

"You're the other half of the story," I said, "You were never here, either."

"Huh?"

"Don't argue!" I said. "Grab a suitcase, then take the Healey and drive back to Pine City."

"At this time of the night!"

"You want to spend the, rest of the night with three corpses and a couple of carloads of cops?"

"No!" she said quickly. "I don't!"

"Then do as I say, honey. You were never here, either. The reason Kaufman brought me here was because you're a friend of his wife's, and he knew you weren't here—okay? It will save an awful lot of complications!"

"All right, Al," she said. "I won't argue. Give me five minutes and I'll be on my way."

She went into the bedroom to get her things. I poured myself another drink, then took it across to the 'phone. I dialled Lavers' private number and waited. After a couple of minutes, his wife answered.

"Sorry to disturb you, Mrs. Lavers," I said. "But would you mind telling that worthless husband of yours that while he's been sleeping, I have solved the mystery of Snake Lannigan and the tattoo marks on the girls' arms, and I'm sitting in Vale Heights surrounded by corpses, waiting for him to come along!"

"This would be Lieutenant Wheeler," she said. "I'll tell him. You don't mind if I add a few adjectives of my own to that 'worthless' of yours?"

"It would be a pleasure, ma'am," I said. "You might find it helpful to kick him in the ribs to waken him. Just so that he's awake before you start on the adjectives."

"I always use a broom-handle," she told me. "Have no fear, Lieutenant. He shall hear every word!"

I waited.

Jo came out of the bedroom with a suitcase in her hand. "When do I see you?" she asked.

"Tomorrow morning probably—or later this morning," I said. "You just relax when you get there." I dug into my pocket and found the key and tossed it to her. "Bye, honey!"

"Bye," she said and went out of the room, walking carefully and being even more careful not to look at the floor as she went.

A noise that sounded as if it could only have come from a sex-starved hippopotamus sounded in my ear. The Commissioner had awakened.

I waited until he ran out of breath, then got in my piece.

"The case is all washed up, Commissioner," I told him. "I'm corpse-sitting with three stiffs and I'd like company. Someone to hold my hand."

I gave him instructions on how to find the house and hung up quickly while he was still in mid-sentence.

I looked at my watch and was surprised to find it was only midnight. I poured myself another drink and then turned on the radio. Someone was playing an oldie—*I'll Be Glad When You're Dead, You Rascal You!*

I looked at Kaufman and said: "Hi, rascal!" But he didn't say anything back. Which was probably just as well. Even a cop's nervous system can only stand so much.

It was five to one when they arrived. Lavers came in first, closely followed by Hammond. A lot of other guys came in behind them. Lavers stopped and everyone else stopped and waited while he looked around the room.

After what was quite a long pause, he looked up at me and swallowed twice. "What are you starting here?" he growled. "A branch of Murder Incorporated!"

"Satisfaction guaranteed," I assured him. "If the wound isn't fatal, we return your money!"

"All right, Wheeler," he said. "Start explaining!"

"With the Commissioner's permission," I said politely, "I'd like to show you something else before I explain."

"Where is it?"

"About ten minutes away," I said. "Shall we go?"

"What about these?" He made an all-embracing gesture with his hand. "What about this litter you've left here?"

"The boys can take care of them," I said. "There are no clues or anything they can trample on, so it's safe to let them loose!"

"All right," he growled. "I'll give you that extra inch of rope! Ten minutes from here?"

We went back up the hill to Kaufman's place in one of the prowl-cars. Lavers and Hammond came into the house with me, leaving a sergeant and a couple of officers outside. I took them down to the cellar.

"Trust you to find a liquor cache like this!" Lavers said. "This where you've been the last couple of days?"

"I almost wish I had," I said. "But the liquor isn't really what I wanted to show you."

I took them over to the chest and threw back the lid. They stared down at the body of Marlene Kaufman in silence, then Lavers lifted his head slowly.

"All right," he said. "Do you want to start at the beginning?"

"You remember the girl with me in the hotel?" I asked. "The one Hammond so brilliantly booked?"

"Now wait a minute!" Hammond said throatily. "You don't need to go throwing mud at me just because I did my job! Just don't forget you got suspended over that deal and ..."

"There is a vast amount of liquor here," Lavers said heavily. "Why don't you try some of it, Hammond? Get drunk ... or something! Anything to keep you quiet!"

He looked back at me: "Yes, I remember."

I told him a story that skittered close to the truth. I left Jo out of it. I told him I had a hunch about Kaufman. He was the big wheel in the district— the millionaire from L.A. I told him about the party and how I'd pretended to be a messenger from Snake Lannigan and how they'd picked me right off.

I told him how they acted when they discovered I was a cop, and the way they acted wasn't right. I said I'd felt they must be hiding something in the house so I'd sneaked back to take a look and they had jumped me after I found the corpse of Kaufman's wife.

I said Kaufman had mentioned a house belonging to a friend of his wife, who was away, and that would be an ideal spot to get rid of me. I said I had worked on the bodyguard by telling him he would get the gas-chamber for being associated with my murder, and how he had seen the light and pulled a gun on the other two.

I said that he and Porky had shot each other simultaneously and Kaufman had been momentarily dazed, giving me a chance to grab Porky's gun, and I had just beaten Kaufman by a split second in pulling the trigger. I said I was very sorry I'd killed Kaufman, but I guessed the Commissioner knew how it was.

Lavers didn't say anything for a while. I could see Hammond trying to work out the holes in it. I lit a cigarette and gave my impersonation of a character being nonchalant.

"Why did he kill his wife?" Lavers asked.

"She came back from L.A. unexpectedly," I said. "She found he was having a party—with call-girls. They had a fight and he hit her, knocked her down and she hit her head against the table as she fell—and that killed her."

"He could have pleaded manslaughter," Lavers grunted. "Why hide the corpse away down here?"

"I agree it would have been a stupid thing to do for anybody else," I said. "But he wasn't only Eli Kaufman, the millionaire; he was Snake Lannigan, the biggest call-girl operator in the state as well. He couldn't take the chance.

"And when he cooled down a little, he realised he couldn't take the chance on the three girls who had seen it happen—he couldn't rely on them keeping their mouths shut, so he decided to make sure of it. That's why he killed them. They must have realised he might get around to thinking that way ... so they skipped. But he caught up with them—Leila Cross and Angela Markon."

"You said something about three girls?"

I cleared my throat: "That's right—there was a third. A girl named Olga Kellner. She was an active member of the racket—used to recruit the girls for him. She must have figured she was safe because she stayed in Vale Heights afterwards up until a week ago. Then she must've decided that caution was the better part of staying alive and she skipped."

"Where is she now?"

"Your guess is as good as mine, Commissioner," I said. "I'd say Canada probably by now. She's had a week!"

He rubbed his chin thoughtfully: "It makes sense."

"If I might say so, sir," Hammond said, looking righteous, "I don't consider Wheeler had any right to work on his own the way he has. If he'd called in assistance from the Bureau before he entered the house, none of this would have happened."

"And if I hadn't told him to follow his own nose on this case, we'd still be no closer to a solution!" Lavers snarled. "The story of Wheeler being unofficially suspended was a fabrication—and I fabricated the story, Lieutenant! There are times when orthodox police methods are not good enough. And this was one of those times! I don't waste the taxpayers' money in paying Wheeler's salary, to have him sit around my office doing nothing all the time! But perhaps you hadn't thought of that?"

Hammond smiled wanly. "I hadn't seen it that way, sir," he admitted hastily. "But now you've explained the whole thing, of course I can appreciate that ..."

"Go and find the telephone," Lavers said wearily. "Better still, take the prowl-car down to the other house and tell the meat-wagon when it arrives that there's another customer to pick up here. And then come back here and pick us up."

"Yes, sir," Hammond said unhappily, then left the cellar. Lavers glared at me. "I ought to ..." Then he shrugged his shoulders helplessly. "What would be the use?"

"I did think of asking for a search warrant," I said. "But you know how long it takes to get one, sir ... and I thought with Kaufman's connections it would be possible somebody could tip him off. A clerk in the judge's office—anybody."

"Yes," Lavers grunted. "I have to admit that there's always an advantage in a murderer being D.O.A. into the Bureau. It saves us wondering whether some smart lawyer might get a verdict from a dumb jury. It means the whole case is sewn up."

"Yes, sir."

He looked down into the chest. "She was almost beautiful!"

"Yes, sir."

"A great pity!"

"Yes, sir."

I looked down at Marlene Kaufman's tranquil face and felt an uncertain feeling in my stomach. Kaufman and the other two hadn't worried me—but with her, it was different.

"If you'll excuse me a moment, Commissioner," I said. "I need a drink! And it fortunately so happens this cellar ..."

"Is loaded with it!" he interrupted. "All right, Wheeler!"

I grabbed the nearest bottle I could see. It was three-quarters full and the label said a good brand of Scotch. Someone else had needed a swig before me. Kaufman, I wondered? Porky Smith, maybe? It didn't make much difference. I pulled the cork out and tipped the bottle to my lips. I took a good swig while the Commissioner watched me with idle interest.

The liquid hit the back of my throat as I tossed it down. For a split-second nothing happened, then my throat closed convulsively. I spat the mouthful out on the floor and felt my stomach churn. My throat with a sense of outraged indignation, refused to believe what it had just tasted.

Lavers guffawed: "Having trouble, Wheeler? What is it—a bathtub brand of whisky?"

"Whisky, nothing!" I shuddered. "That was embalming fluid!"

CHAPTER 12

It was four-thirty in the morning when I got back to my own house in Pine City. I let myself in and walked into the living-room. The Healey had been under the carport, I noticed.

Jo was on the divan.

She was sleeping peacefully and it seemed a pity to disturb her. I went through to the kitchen and got the coffee percolator going—I still had a faint taste of embalming fluid in my mouth. When I got back into the living-room, Jo was sitting up, wide awake. Well—awake, anyway.

She yawned and changed the yawn into a smile: "How are things, master-mind?"

"Fine," I said. "Everything is just fine. Everything is neat and nicely tidied up, filed away in triplicate."

"Then, we should celebrate!"

I shook my head: "I don't feel like celebrating, somehow. I'm making some coffee—want some?"

She pouted: "You're the most unenthusiastic man I ever met!"

"Depends what you want me to enthuse about, honey," I said. "Right now, I can enthuse about coffee and then the thought of getting some sleep."

"Coffee and sleep are things I can get at home!"

"With three corpses for company?"

She shuddered: "They aren't still there, are they?"

"No," I admitted. "They've been taken down to the morgue."

"What about Marlene?"

"Her, too," I said. I lit myself a cigarette.

"Tell me something, Al," she said after a while. "Remember when you started talking about the gas-chamber and frightened those two bodyguards into helping you?"

"I remember every long second of that time!"

"What would you have done if they hadn't decided to help you?"

"Died," I said. "Next question?"

"What about me?"

"You would have died, also," I said. "Death and murderers, honey—they both don't play favours. Go and pour us a cup of coffee and we'll celebrate our return to the land of the living!"

She got up and stretched. "This is exciting," she said. "The way cold spinach is exciting!"

"You can't have everything ... as the principal of the girls' college said to the music master when he wanted a piano!"

"And here in glorious Pine City," she said, walking towards the kitchen, "I get gags for free as well!"

I realised she was wearing something I had only seen before in advertisements. The sort of advertisements they publish in virile magazines for men. You know the sort of thing:

> *Tiny-tiny fabulous nightie in sheer, sheer nylon.*
> *Choice of three colours, black, flame and Grrrr!*

Jo was wearing one. Hers came in two colours ... flame and Grrrr! She disappeared into the kitchen. I found myself staring at the door hopefully, waiting for her to return. She came back in a couple of minutes, carrying a couple of cups of coffee.

"Where did you pack that thing you're wearing?" I asked her. "In a cigarette-case?"

"Well, I'm glad you noticed it," she said. "That's something, anyway."

"Noticed it! I looked at you for a couple of minutes before I realised you were wearing it!"

"Maybe you'd better drink your coffee," Jo said thoughtfully.

So I drank the coffee. I drank two cups and it didn't seem to make any difference. It's wonderful what a rejuvenating effect nylon can have. I finished my second cup in three scalding gulps and put it down on the table.

I walked towards Jo with a purposeful look in my eyes.

"Lover," she said firmly. "You have a five a.m. shadow, and your suit is all crumpled, and you look tired." Then she sniffed gently. "What on earth have you been drinking?"

I knew when I was beaten. I made a detour around the divan and headed for the bedroom.

"It smells awful!" she said after me. "What was it you were drinking?"

"Embalming fluid," I told her, then closed the bedroom door behind me.

It was eleven in the morning when Jo woke me.

"There's somebody on the 'phone," she said. "Says he must talk to you."

"Probably the Commissioner," I growled. "Tell him—no," I dragged myself out of bed. "I'll tell him myself!"

I picked up the 'phone. "Now, listen!" I said coldly. "I have worked a hundred and twenty hours this week, already! If you expect me to get into the office at nine, after ..."

"Lieutenant Wheeler?" a polite voice asked. I could tell by its politeness it wasn't the Commissioner.

"Yes," I said. "Who's this?"

"Douglas Bond," the voice said nervously. "Do you remember me, Lieutenant?"

"Sure, I remember you all right," I said. "You were the guy who thought I should be locked away in a padded cell!"

"I'm terribly sorry about that, Lieutenant," he said. "It was an unfortunate mistake! I hope you'll accept my apologies?"

"Sure," I said. "Anything else?"

"I read about it in the papers, Lieutenant. I wanted to thank you for finding the murderer of Leila. I guess it's hard to put it into words, Lieutenant, but ..."

"Sure," I said hastily. "Well, thanks." And I hung up.

Jo looked at me with one eyebrow lifted: "Are you going to eat breakfast now or go back to bed?"

"I'll drink breakfast," I said. "You know—coffee?"

"I'll make you a deal," she said. "I'll drink coffee with you if you shave first. That beard of yours is starting to cast a shadow across the room!"

So I showered, shaved and dressed, and around mid-day I was drinking coffee with Jo. She made good coffee—she looked good to go with the good coffee. She wore a white silk shirt and a tight-fitting black skirt. The sort of outfit for a dream secretary to wear.

"I suppose all this has just been routine for you?" she asked.

"Yes, ma'am just routine. Taken from the files of the Los Angeles ..."

"You're not very funny late at night," she said. "But in the morning!" She shuddered.

I got the drift.

"A man called Lavers rang earlier on," she said. "He seemed to think you ought to be up, so I told him that was ridiculous. Then he asked me if my name was Annabelle, by any chance. What do you think made him ask that?"

"He has a fixation about Annabelles," I said hastily. "In the dim distant past when he was young man, a girl called Annabelle frightened the life out of him."

Jo looked interested: "What did she do to him?"

"I think she suggested marriage," I said. "What else did he have to say?"

"He said to tell you to come into the office this afternoon and that the District Attorney was very pleased with the results."

"He would be," I said.

"What will I do while you're gone?"

"You could play some records."

"In Vale Heights, I was a grass widow," she said. "More or less. Now, in Pine City, I'm a hi-fi widow. I don't call that improving my situation."

"Honey," I said, "I shan't be long inside the office—I promise. I'll be back early and then we'll do the town!"

"Can you afford to do that?"

"No," I admitted. "But I thought you could."

"That's the punch-line written for a trio of husbands!" she said. "They all had the same theme-song ... you can afford it, can't you?"

"Can't you?"

"Of course I can!"

"Then what are you worrying about?"

"You say the most romantic things!" she said bitterly. "Have you got time for lunch before you go to that office?"

"I have time," I said. "But not for lunch!"

"Why, Al!" She brightened a little. "You do have a romantic streak, after all!"

It was three in the afternoon when I got into the office. I noticed that Miss Gulley's desk was vacant. I knocked on the Commissioner's door and walked in.

"What happened to Fern?" I asked interestedly.

"She now works for the Mayor," he said. "I mentioned that name to her—Yul Brynner, wasn't it?"

"That's right. What happened?"

"She had hysterics all over my office," he said, shaking his head slowly. "I must have been overworking the poor woman!"

I sat down in the visitor's chair and made like a visitor.

"Anything new, Commissioner?"

"No. Except the girl's voice that answered your 'phone this morning. You must have untold reserves of energy, Wheeler!"

"Yes, sir."

"The D.A. is quite pleased—he gave a big spiel to the papers. Did you read it?"

"No, sir."

"I think he's going soft in the head—he actually mentioned your name!"

I lit myself a cigarette: "Anything else, sir?"

"Nothing at the moment," he said. "If you want a couple of days free of the office, you're welcome."

"Thank you, sir."

"That's about all," he said.

I went out of his office and sat behind my desk for half an hour and thought. It was something I don't do very often and I need to sit down while I'm doing it.

When I'd finished thinking, I went down to Homicide. The boys I saw when I got there were all nice and friendly, proving that they'd read the newspapers. I found the guy I was looking for—Johnny Cuttle. Doctor J. Cuttle, the police medico and a nice guy in spite of all the corpses he sees.

I went into his office and closed the door carefully behind me.

"Well, well!" he grinned. "The unorthodox cop triumphant again, huh? You should hear a certain Lieutenant by the name of Hammond on the subject!"

"I imagine," I said.

"Have you come to recount your exploits?" he asked.

"I've come for some advice," I said.

"That won't cost me anything," he said. "You've come to the right place!"

"Advice on being unorthodox," I said.

"Sounds interesting!" He lit his pipe and puffed ferociously. "Though I'm not sure I know anything that Kinsey didn't put in his book ..."

"Not that sort of unorthodox!" I interrupted hastily. "This is different."

"How different?"

I lit a cigarette in self-defence against that pipe.

"Supposing you wanted to put somebody to sleep and make it look as if they were dead," I said. "For a period of say, five or six hours. Can do?"

"I know you don't like the D.A.," he said. "But why not put some castor oil in his coffee?"

"This is serious, Johnny," I said. "Cross my heart!"

He puffed his pipe for a few seconds: "I don't have anything that will stop somebody breathing for six hours, then let them start up again. I could give you something that would knock somebody out and leave them so relaxed that their breathing would be very slight. You could think they weren't breathing at a casual glance."

"That sounds good enough," I said. "How about it?"

"Well, okay," he said. "Only I shall deny it if anybody asks!"

Five minutes later he gave me a small phial with a colourless liquid inside. "Give it in a drink," he told me. "It'll take about twenty minutes to work."

"Thanks," I said. "Thanks very much, Johnny."

"I don't want to hear what you're going to do with it," he said. "In fact, I'm beginning to regret I didn't say no in the first place."

"It's directly in the interests of justice," I told him. "And Al Wheeler, of course."

"Of course!"

"Now all I need is to call into a drugstore on the way home and I'm organised!" I told him. From the blank look on his face it didn't make sense to him, but what the hell? It made sense to me.

I stopped off at the drugstore around the corner from the Bureau and bought what I wanted. I used their pay-booth to make a 'phone call, then I climbed back into the Healey and drove home.

Jo had changed her clothes. She was wearing what you could call a formal. In some ways it was informal. It was backless so far down her back that I didn't know a gown could go that far and still be a gown. It was cut low enough in front to emphasise that Jo owed nothing to artificial aids of any kind.

She gave me a big smile as I came in. "Hurry up, lover-boy!" she said. "Get changed. Tonight we do the town—remember?"

"Were you pouring me a drink?"

"Well, just one before you change!" She made action with the bottle and glasses and handed me a drink.

"Thanks," I said. "Here's to crime!"

"Here's to our night on the town!" she said.

"Yeah," I said thoughtfully. "I have to tell you something about that."

She lowered her glass and looked at me suspiciously: "If that Commissioner ..."

"It's my own idea, really," I said. "I'm sorry, Jo, but things have altered since lunch-time."

"In what way?"

"Well, I've got another date for tonight."

She didn't have any violent reaction. Well ... apart from the contents of her glass hitting my face, and the ribbons of skin her high heels tore off my shins. And there was an odd scream or two ...

Ten minutes later Jo had departed on her way back to Vale Heights, complete with suitcase. I was sorry it had to be that way, but there it is. A man can't date two dames at the same time—not in the one house, anyway.

CHAPTER 13

Came a quarter to eight and I was prepared. The drinks were organised, the bottles and ice waiting. There was a stack of discs on the turntable and the first one had just dropped. The Kenton theme was oozing out from the walls as I poured myself a drink, lit myself a cigarette and waited for the buzzer.

The buzzer went at five after eight. My date wasn't late—unless it was a process-server. I went to the front door, opened it, and there she was. If you closed your eyes and dreamed of the most gorgeous redhead you could dream of—that was the redhead who stood on the doorstep, smiling at me.

"Come on in," I breathed, "before I wake up and you vanish!"

"I take that as a compliment, Lieutenant!" she smiled.

We went into the living-room and she slipped off her wrap. She was wearing a black evening gown. I wondered how the maker had made such a basically small piece of material stretch so far. It looked as if one deep breath would disintegrate the whole thing ... It was a nice, sort of hopeful thought to carry around with me.

"What will you drink?" I asked her.

She had her head cocked slightly to one side: "Kenton?"

"But you can't drink him," I said.

"I'll have something on the rocks please, Lieutenant," she said. "Something like whisky, I think."

"Fine," I said. "And the name is Al—remember?"

"Of course," she smiled. "I'm sorry."

I poured her a drink and refilled my own, then took them to where she'd thoughtfully sat on the sofa.

"Thanks," she said. "I'm flattered by this date, Al."

"You are?"

"Being dated by a hero, no less!" she said. "That funny, little man—Douglas Bond, rang me and told me all about it."

"I wouldn't pay too much attention to what he said about me, Drusilla," I said. "Even if it was all strictly true!"

She smiled: "I'm glad you cleaned everything up, Al. I didn't have time to get to know Leila very well, but I liked her. It gives you a sort of satisfied feeling to know that her murderer was caught, and that he's dead."

"It gives me a satisfied feeling that the case is wound up," I said. "And now I can relax. You, I might add, are my idea of what relaxation should be!"

"Thank you!"

She sipped her drink: "I like your hi-fi set-up, Al. It's really something!"

"It keeps me poor," I told her, "but honest."

"I like your house, too."

"Why don't you spend a week here? Really get to know the place!"

Her smile broadened. "That sounds like a leading question! I'll take a raincheck on the answer!"

"We have plenty of time," I told her. "Would you like some food?"

"No, thanks," she shook her head. "I had dinner around seven. But if you haven't eaten ..."

"I'm not hungry," I said.

We sat looking at each other. Her smile was still warm, and maybe getting a little warmer.

"How's business?" I asked her.

She pulled a face: "Let's not talk shop!"

"It fascinates me in a macabre sort of way," I said. "I never realised how expensive and complicated a process getting buried was, until I saw the *Haven of Rest!*"

"It's a business," she shrugged her shoulders—I thought maybe the material would split, but it didn't. "Like any other business."

"You've been in it a while?"

"A few years," she said. "It pays very well."

"I can imagine," I said. "How did you start?"

"I was a cosmetician in a beauty parlour," she said. "Then I heard I could make another twenty dollars a week working for a funeral parlour, so I switched. I needed the money."

I glanced across to where her wrap was draped carelessly over the back of a chair. "It certainly looks as if it does pay more," I said. "That's mink, isn't it?"

"Come now!" she said huskily. "You aren't going to ask for all a girl's secrets, are you?"

"Only a couple, honey," I said. "And if the mink is a secret you prefer to keep, I won't pry!"

I took her empty glass over to the table with me. I glanced at my watch and saw that it was eight-thirty. I had a long night's programme ahead of me, and I thought I'd better get started. I didn't really feel enthusiastic about it ... it was going to be an awful waste of a gorgeous redhead.

I refilled her glass and took it back with me to the sofa and handed it to her. "Aren't you drinking?" she asked.

"I'm a couple of drinks ahead of you, already," I explained. "So I'm giving you the chance to catch up. Don't thank me, it's part of the Wheeler service!"

She took a sip of the drink and her eyes were thoughtful as she looked at me over the rim of the glass. "You're a peculiar character, Al!"

"I know it," I admitted. "But usually my friends don't mention it while I'm around."

"You aren't a very good actor," she went on slowly. "Your heart isn't in it. You're pretending hard that you've nothing on your mind except me and a nice cosy evening ahead of us, but you aren't pretending very well. What's the punch-line, Al?"

I grinned at her feebly: "Well, I have to admit you're right, Drusilla. So you picked me in one! You were so helpful to me over fingering Douglas Bond and you seemed so interested in police work, I thought you might like to help me with a little experiment, maybe?"

"What sort of experiment?" she asked cautiously.

"It's quite painless, believe me," I said. "But there's no hurry for that." I picked up my glass and drained it, then held out a hand towards her. "Hurry up and drink that—remember I'm still one ahead."

"All right," she finished the drink and handed me the glass. "Are you trying to get me high—is that the experiment?"

"Perish the thought!" I said.

I took the two glasses back to the table and refilled them. I had my back to her while I did it. It wasn't hard to slip the Mickey Finn into her glass.

I got back beside her on the sofa and gave her the drink, then lifted my own glass. "Bottoms up!" I said. "Last drink before the experiment commences!"

"Al!" She shook her head. "You really are a character!"

"I'm going on television," I said, "just as soon as they make me an offer!"

Drusilla poured the drink down her throat with a practised movement and gave me the empty glass. "Bottoms up! Now tell me about this experiment. I'm fascinated!"

I drained my own glass: "It's quite simple. Only we can't hold it in here. We have to move a little—not very far—just to the bathroom."

"The bathroom!"

"Shall we go?"

"Well, I suppose I can always scream for help if I have to!" She got onto her feet and smoothed down the skirt of her gown with the palms of her hands. "Lead on, MacDuff!"

We got into the bathroom and she looked around, then looked at me. "I may be dumb, Al," she said. "But it looks just like a bathroom to me."

"Have you observed, Watson," I said in a dramatic voice, "the hand-basin?"

She walked over to the hand-basin and looked at it. "It has water in it?" she said.

"Correct! And not only water. Another substance has been added to the water."

"Something gruesome like cyanide, I suppose?"

"The substance is definitely not lethal," I said. "It guarantees it on the packet."

I walked over to the cabinet and opened it, pulling out the empty packet.

"It says here—and I quote," I said, reading from the label, "Guaranteed to remove all traces of any hair dye and restore the hair to its natural colour. Contains no injurious substances … etcetera, etcetera!"

The smile had gone from her face: "Are you crazy?"

"It's possible," I admitted. "But this is a serious experiment, Drusilla honey. I want you to dip your beautiful hair into the basin for me. It's quite a simple experiment, really."

"What for?"

I lit a cigarette carefully: "Well, I have a theory that the full properties of a hair-dye remover have never been investigated thoroughly before. According to my theory, that stuff will not only remove hair dye, but it will make a complete personality change as well!"

She took a couple of quick steps towards the door and then stopped. Maybe because I had shut the door and was leaning against it.

"My theory is revolutionary," I continued. "I'm just crazy to see how it works out!"

"And how do you think it will work out, Lieutenant?" Her voice was suddenly harsh.

"Well, I think that a beautiful red-headed doll by the name of Drusilla Peace will stand in front of the hand-basin and start to rinse out her hair," I said slowly. "And when she's finished!" I snapped my fingers. "Drusilla Peace will have vanished—and in her place will stand a beautiful ash-blonde doll by the name of Olga Kellner!"

The only sound was her breathing, and if she didn't control it, that gown was just going to have to give up and fall down.

"I think you are crazy!" she said harshly. "I'm getting out of here! And if you try and stop me, I'll scream!"

"Who for?" I asked interestedly. "A cop?"

She made an effort and smiled at me. "I know you're just clowning, Al," she said. "But enough is enough! Why don't you stop kidding and we'll go back to Kenton and that sofa?" Her smile deepened. "You know, a sofa always does something to me—takes away my resistance. I never could say no on a sofa!"

She came really close to me then and leaned against my chest, her red lips pouting up at me. "Kiss me first, Al," she murmured breathlessly. "Then carry me back to the sofa!"

"Honey," I said gently, "if you haven't got your head down in that hand-basin within one minute from now, I'll ring and get a police matron to come and hold it for you!"

For a long moment she stared up into my eyes. "All right," she said slowly, then turned away towards the hand-basin. "This gown was expensive, Al—I wouldn't want to ruin it!"

I watched as she undid the zipper at the side and wiggled her way out of the gown. She had a figure to make a banker forget all about his balance once he came to grips with it.

She looked at me appraisingly: "The hand-basin, Al? Or the sofa?"

"The hand-basin," I told her. "Within twenty seconds or the police matron to assist. Take your choice, honey!"

"I thought you were a sucker for a dame," she said. "I must have been mistaken!"

"Mistimed, maybe," I said. "Make with that hair-dye remover, honey—

we're running out of time!"

She walked over to the hand-basin and bent down, starting to rinse her hair. I checked with my watch—seven minutes since she'd had that drink.

Ten minutes later she was towelling her head dry. There were still a couple of faint red streaks left, but the rest of her hair was a beautiful ash-blonde colour.

"Well now, Olga," I said. "Would you like to unburden your soul and talk a little?"

"About what?"

"About you—and the other girls and Snake Lannigan."

"He's dead! I don't know anything about any girls—and why call me Olga? Since when has it been a crime to dye your hair?"

"Okay," I said. "If you've finished towelling your hair, how about getting back inside that gown?"

"I worry you like this?"

"I never was any good with a zipper," I said.

She shrugged her shoulders and wiggled her way back into the gown. "Now what?" she asked.

"Let's go back to the living-room—to that sofa," I said, "and sit down. If we hurry, we might just make it."

"You're talking double-talk, Al. I don't understand a word of it!"

"You will!" I assured her.

I took her arm and propelled her back into the living-room, then gave her a push so that she sat down suddenly on the sofa.

"This was my idea in the first place," she said, with a baffled expression on her face. "What made you change your mind?"

"I want you to be sitting down when you feel tired, honey!"

"Tired?" She looked even more baffled. "Why should I ..." A huge yawn cut off the rest of her words. When she had finished yawning, she looked at me again. "I do feel tired—quite suddenly. I ... You! You doped that drink! Why, you ..."

Then her head dropped forward onto very adequate support and thirty seconds later she started to snore gently.

The doctor had been quite accurate in his timing. I poured myself another drink because it was going to be a long night. When I'd finished it, I put on my shoulder-holster and checked the Smith and Wesson before I put it into the holster.

I came back into the living-room where the ash-blonde still snored peacefully and went through her purse. I found two sets of keys and put them in my pocket. I picked up the ash-blonde and carried her out to the carport and put her into the Healey. I put the hood up so she wouldn't catch cold, then got in beside her and started the motor.

"Honey," I said, "I'm going to do right by you. The *Haven of Rest* is going to surpass itself tonight! You're going to have the de-luxe treatment. I'm going to see you have the best casket I can find!"

It took me twenty minutes at a legal thirty miles per hour to get there.

Moving around in a funeral parlour at night on your own, wasn't my idea of fun. I wondered how the ash-blonde could sleep so peacefully through it all.

One set of keys did belong to the *Haven of Rest*, and one key opened the front door without any trouble at all. I carried the ash-blonde inside, closed and locked the door again, then carried her upstairs.

I found the room where I had first interviewed her and felt relieved; after I'd switched on the light, to see there wasn't any other occupant. If there had been, I would have gone screaming home for mother.

I stretched her out neatly on the sofa, her hands crossed over her bosom, her feet together. She had stopped snoring and as the doc had prophesied, her breathing was very slow and shallow. Unless you looked very closely, you would have thought she was dead—and that was the idea.

There was a bunch of flowers in a vase. I took them out and put them in her hands. It was the final touch needed to complete the picture. If I'd been an insurance man, one look at her and I would have paid the claim without question.

I lit myself a cigarette and went over to the 'phone on the small table and lifted the receiver. As I'd hoped, it had a direct line through the switchboard. I used the old gag and placed my handkerchief over the mouthpiece to distort my voice, and then dialled a number.

I heard the 'phone ring the other end for a while and then the click as someone lifted the receiver, and a moment later, a voice saying; "Yes?"

"Snake?" I asked.

"What?"

"Snake?" I repeated. "Snake Lannigan, isn't it?"

There was a silence for a few seconds, then his voice said: "I think you must have the wrong number!"

"I got it right," I told him. "Listen, Snake—this is a tip-off. Somebody got Olga Kellner tonight ... and they got a sense of humour, maybe—because they dumped her body in the funeral parlour, in one of them waiting-rooms!"

"Who is this?"

"Santa Claus," I told him. "I'll bring you a new baby doll for Christmas—in place of Olga!"

I put the 'phone down and the handkerchief back into my pocket. I lit myself another cigarette from the stub of the first and wished I'd been smart enough to think of bringing a bottle along with me for company. The ash-blonde was no company at all.

The room was quiet, the whole building was quiet—quiet as the grave. That was a logical thought—the *Haven* was only one step removed from the grave, anyway.

I took a last look at Olga who was still sleeping soundly; then switched off the light. I stepped out of the room and into the corridor, then walked down to the next room and tried the door. It opened easily and I stepped inside, and at the same moment I heard the faint sound of the front door closing downstairs.

I shut the door of the room and put my ear to it, not daring to switch on the light, and waited. After a short while, I heard the even footsteps coming down the corridor. They went past my door to the door of the rest-room and then stopped for a moment. I held my breath, straining my ear against the door to catch the slightest sound.

I heard the door open suddenly, then another silence, followed by the click of the light switch. Then the measured footsteps walking across the floor of the next room. I eased the thirty-two out of its holster and held it firmly in my right hand. With my left hand clutching the door handle, I waited for the next sound.

There was nothing to herald its approach ... It came with a staccato hammering sound that seemed to beat into my temples. The same hammering sound twice ... two shots from a heavy calibre pistol.

I swore wildly to myself as I wrenched open the door and dived into the corridor. I should have thought of that! I should never have taken the risk. I ...

I kicked the door of the rest-room open and took two quick steps that brought me inside the room. .

Olga Kellner still lay peacefully on the sofa, her hands still holding the bunch of flowers and crossed over her bosom. There was only one material difference between now and when had left her. Now she wasn't breathing. There were two neat holes in the side of her forehead, discoloured by powder burns. Two shots at point-blank range.

I realised something else. Other than the body of Olga, the room was empty. And that was impossible. He had to be inside the room. I refused to believe that Snake Lannigan could make himself invisible, even if I hadn't found anybody in the whole course of the investigation that had actually seen him.

It took me two seconds to discard the theory of the invisible Snake Lannigan, and that was one second too long. One second I tossed away while logic told me there was only one place he could be.

And in that one second, the barrel of a gun jabbed into my back and his voice said harshly: "Drop your gun, Lieutenant!"

I knew he meant it. I had Olga Kellner's body right in front of my eyes to prove it. I dropped the gun onto the floor.

"Now kick it away from you, Lieutenant!"

I kicked and the gun skidded across the floor and disappeared underneath the sofa.

"It was the elementary psychology of the situation, Lieutenant Wheeler," he said. "I knew you would be hiding somewhere. I thought that you wouldn't have killed Olga ... even a career lieutenant doesn't murder people to further his career. So I made up for your omission, knowing that the sound of the shots would bring you racing in here, forgetting all your elementary training in handling situations like this!"

"And you stood behind the door," I added. "So that when I flung the door open, you were hidden from my view. And I came charging in like a wounded buffalo!"

"You're so right," he agreed.

There was a hiatus. A hiatus is a period of nothing in between two periods of action. The first period of action had resulted in Olga Kellner alias Drusilla Peace being murdered. I had a nasty feeling about the way the second period of action might pan out.

"It was so thoughtful of you to bring Olga here for me," he said: "It could hardly have been more fitting, could it?"

"I guess not, Snake," I said.

"You were really quite clever to work it out," he went on in a conversational voice. "I imagine that it would have given your career quite a flip with the Homicide Bureau. Fortunate for me, you being a career cop, Lieutenant. Otherwise, you would have arrived here with a posse of prowl-cars instead of by yourself. And you keeping the whole thing to yourself makes things much simpler for me, doesn't it?"

I shrugged my shoulders. I tried to anyway, but with that cold gun-barrel boring into the small of my back, the shrug became a spasmodic jerk—like me. From here out I was going to be known as Twitch Wheeler.

"You know, Lieutenant," he went on, "I can dispose of both you and Olga and no one will ever know. You'll just disappear, completely!"

"There's no way of getting completely rid of a corpse, Snake. Too many guys have ended up in the gas-chamber, who thought that!"

"Lieutenant!" he said reproachfully. "There are dozens of corpses disposed of every day completely disposed of, except sometimes for a few ashes that the more sentimental relatives like to place on top of a bureau—in an urn."

He'd made his point—and how!

The gun-barrel jabbed against a couple of my vertebrae painfully. "I'd like to get this finished with, Lieutenant," he told me. "You could do me a favour and lie down on the sofa alongside Olga—it's quite big enough for the two of you."

"It appeals to the sense of the dramatic in you, Snake?"

"Just being practical, Lieutenant. That way there won't be much blood and less cleaning up afterwards. You can please yourself, of course. Only a bullet through the head is a painless way of dying, whereas a bullet through the spine is not ... and takes much longer, of course."

"You've got a strong selling-point there!" I said. "I guess it comes easy after selling caskets."

"You prefer the sofa then, Lieutenant?"

"Like I said—you just sold me!"

I walked over to the sofa and stood there looking down at Olga for a moment. She looked just as peaceful as she had when she'd been breathing.

"I'm sorry I can't run to flowers for you," he said. "Like the ones you so thoughtfully provided for Olga. A nice touch that, Lieutenant. I appreciated it."

"No flowers by request," I said. "Tell Ma I died with a smile on my lips."

"I suggest you save the corn, Lieutenant," he said. "You might need a harvest of something to take with you wherever you're going!"

"You could be right at that," I said. "Only I've got a nasty feeling that wherever I'm going, I won't need to take a harvest with me—I'll reap it when I get there!"

"The sofa, Lieutenant!"

"Yeah," I said. "I knew there was something I'd forgotten."

It was one hell of a way to die. To lie down meekly beside a corpse and have a gun pressed into the side of your head and wait while someone pulled the trigger. It wasn't in the tradition of the Marines—it wasn't in any tradition that I knew of. And unorthodox I might be, but I had no ambition to start a new tradition.

"Maybe I'm squeamish, Snake," I said. "You mind if I move Olga over a little before I lie down? There isn't much room for me right now."

"Okay," he said impatiently. "But hurry it!"

I bent forward and slid one arm around her shoulders and the other under her knees and lifted her. One arm fell and dangled uselessly, the bunch of flowers dropping onto the sofa.

I straightened up and swung around quickly in one motion. I knew I wouldn't have a chance of getting around to face him before he pulled the trigger, but I banked on something else.

The something else was Olga.

As I swung, her head and shoulders hit his arm, jolting him off-balance. The gun exploded and I felt a searing hot pain down my side. I kept on turning and he was forced further off-balance and then I was around far enough to see what was happening. He was staggering sideways, fighting to retain his balance long enough to swing the gun-barrel-back in my direction.

I heaved Olga bodily at him and as her dead weight hit him, it knocked him right off-balance so that he went down onto the floor, the gun dropping from his hand, and finished up with her on top of him.

Grotesquely, both her arms encircled his neck as he lay there, and her face was inches away from his. He screamed thinly and pushed her away from him, so that she rolled onto the floor and lay there on her back, not looking peaceful any more but somehow triumphant.

I could have bent down and picked up his gun. But I didn't. There's a limit as to what can pass as a human being and Snake Lannigan had passed that limit.

I hated him right then as I've never hated any man. I hated him because he had murdered Olga Kellner in cold blood and it was partly my fault for making him the opportunity ... And I hated him for having been going to murder me the same way a few moments before.

I stamped down hard with the heel of my right foot into his solar plexus and he jack-knifed convulsively. I did it twice more and the last time he didn't jack-knife. He just lay there making bubbling sounds somewhere in the back of his throat.

I picked up the gun then and put it into my pocket. I picked up Olga gently and put her back onto the sofa and arranged her arms the way they had been before. And then I picked up Snake Lannigan and lay him on the sofa beside her.

I took the gun out of my pocket and he looked up into my eyes and then he knew. Somehow he found his voice—a hoarse, tortured whisper: "No! You can't! You wouldn't!"

"Why not, Snake?" I asked. "You've murdered lots of people. Angela Markon, Leila Cross ... Olga Kellner. You were going to murder me a couple of minutes ago and it didn't worry you one little bit!"

"You wouldn't!" His eyes were frantic, dilated with fear.

"Judge, jury and executioner, Snake!" I said. "I'm giving you the same break you gave Olga! So long, Romonoff!"

I put the barrel of the gun against the side of his head and squeezed the trigger.

I took the white handkerchief from my top pocket and wiped the gun clean, then held it by the handkerchief. I bent his arm upwards, closed his fingers around the butt of the gun, then let go. The arm dropped to dangle listlessly over the side of the sofa and the gun dropped to the floor.

I retrieved my own gun from underneath the sofa and put it back into its holster.

Then I became aware of two things. The burning pain in my side was really burning—and I needed a drink.

CHAPTER 14

The door opened and Mrs. Lavers stood there, with her hair in pins and a woollen robe wrapped around her.

"I thought so," she said placidly. "It would only be Lieutenant Wheeler that comes calling at three in the morning."

"And a bright good morning to you, Mrs. Wheeler!" I said. "Would you like to wake the Commissioner and tell him I want to talk to him?"

"I'll try," she said doubtfully. "I doubt if even Gabriel lent me his trumpet, it would make it any easier!"

"Alternatively," I said. "You could take your hair out of pins and we could elope!"

She patted her grey hair complacently. "I couldn't do that, Lieutenant," she said. "It would break the iceman's heart!"

"How can I love you so much and hate your husband so much at the same time?" I asked wonderingly.

"That's easy," she said. "I'm a woman—he's just your boss!"

She turned around: "You'd better go into the living-room and I'll awaken His Majesty and then make you some coffee. I seem to spend a lot of my life lately making you coffee in the early hours of the morning, Lieutenant!"

"It's just because you love me," I said. "Admit it!"

Lavers came into the living-room ten minutes later.

"You look like you've seen a ghost!" he growled.

"Commissioner Lavers at three-fifteen a.m. in a purple robe is the next best thing!" I shuddered.

"What's it about, Wheeler?"

"Snake Lannigan."

"You mean Eli Kaufman?"

"I mean the founder and owner of the *Haven of Rest*," I said slowly. "One, Alexi Romonoff. Who now rests in peace in his own *Haven!*"

"Make sense, Wheeler," he growled. "And make it fast!"

I told him the story—of the date I'd made with Olga Kellner alias Drusilla Peace. Of the Mickey Finn I had gotten from the doctor. How Alexi Romonoff had done the one thing I'd never expected him to do—murder her in cold blood. I prevaricated with the truth a little towards the end of the story.

I told him that I'd had the drop on Romonoff and he'd begged me to allow him to shoot himself, and I had. From the way the Commissioner's mouth tightened when he heard it, I had the feeling he didn't believe it. Right then, I didn't care very much.

He stared at me, then said: "Why the hell go into a crazy routine like that in the first place?"

"I had some hunches and they all added up to Romonoff," I said. "But no proof. I didn't really have any proof about Olga Kellner—she'd dyed her hair, sure—but that's no crime in itself as she reminded me. Playing it the way I did, brought Alexi out into the open. By coming to the *Haven* after I'd phoned him, he admitted he was Snake Lannigan."

The Commissioner grunted: "Hunches, you said. What sort of hunches?"

"The way he told me in the first place he hired Leila Cross. She had no references so he let her give him a practical demonstration of her competence—he said. Can you imagine any guy running a funeral parlour doing that? Then Olga Kellner—she hadn't run when the other two girls had run. She stayed right on where she was in Vale Heights for a fortnight after they'd disappeared. Only then did she follow them.

"That started a train of thought. I found out in Vale Heights that Olga had been a recruiting officer for Snake's organisation. So maybe she hadn't run for the same reason the other two girls had. Maybe she'd gone back to Snake to do a job. Which was, of course, to help take care of the other two girls.

"Then the way she set up Douglas Bond for me. She did it too efficiently. It was too easy, too neat. She wanted to set up Bond for me because he couldn't harm them and he could be a red herring to take my mind off that funeral parlour."

Lavers grunted: "Thin! Very thin!"

"And there was the body of Marlene Kaufman in the cellar," I continued. "According to our evidence, she would have been dead then for nearly three weeks—but the body was in perfect condition. And I found out why when I drank some embalming fluid in mistake for whisky. Her body had been embalmed, of course. And that's an expert's job. A job for a guy who runs a funeral parlour, maybe?"

"Maybe," he said. He wasn't sounding quite so disbelieving. "But why?"

I lit a cigarette and hoped Mrs. Lavers was going to be quick with the coffee. "Alexi Romonoff was Snake Lannigan" I said. "Running his high-class call-girl service throughout the state. Eli Kaufman was backing him, being the sort of guy who could never resist making an easy, dishonest dollar. And Olga travels the countryside working in a cosmetician's shop here and there, recruiting girls for the service.

"They supply three girls for one of Kaufman's parties while his wife is away. His wife comes back unexpectedly and there's an argument—a scene.

Kaufman loses his temper and hits her—maybe he kills her when he hits her or maybe he told the truth about her striking her head as she fell. Either way, the result is the same—he's left with a corpse on his hands and witnesses that he killed her. If that leaks out, he's a broken man, facing at least a manslaughter rap.

"So while he's panicking, Olga Kellner takes charge. She takes the girls back to Vale Heights and then points out the obvious moral to them. When Kaufman sobers down a little, he won't want any living witnesses to what's happened, hanging around, ready to talk to the police any time.

"So Olga organises them out of Vale Heights in a hurry. She organises them down here to Romonoff. She tells Alexi what has happened and he starts organising. And the first thing he sees, is that if he handles this thing right, he can bleed Eli Kaufman of every cent the man has. Alexi, being a smart character, doesn't rush this.

"He makes a deal with Kaufman. He'll get rid of the three witnesses at a price. And Kaufman agrees. Then Alexi probably tells him it would be too risky to get rid of his wife's body until they're sure the police don't suspect anything has happened to her. So he goes up to the Kaufman house and embalms the body and leaves it there. It makes his bargaining position very strong!

"Then he takes care of the two girls. And then he takes care of the third, so he tells Kaufman. Actually, he brings Olga down from Vale Heights to work in his funeral parlour. She dyes her hair, adopts a new name and she's disappeared completely. That's what Kaufman thinks. But Olga is Romonoff's ace in the hole. If Kaufman proves difficult about parting with all his money in large lumps, Alexi has a witness he can still produce to testify against Kaufman, if necessary."

Mrs. Lavers came in with a tray, poured out the coffee and passed it around.

"There still isn't one word of evidence that would stand up in a court!" Lavers snorted.

"I said I had hunches," I told him. "That's why this crazy scheme of mine tonight was the only way I could think of to find out if my hunches were right."

He snorted violently, "Why do you always have to be a lone genius!" he thundered: "Why don't you confide in somebody once in a while! I wrapped up the Kaufman case smartly for two reasons—one because the D.A. wanted it done that way, and secondly because it would lull the real Snake Lannigan into a false sense of security."

It was my turn to look surprised: "Then you thought ..."

"I know you have a poor opinion of scientific work done in a lab!" he snarled. "But we were well aware the body of Marlene Kaufman had been embalmed—by an expert. I've had Romonoff tailed twenty-four hours a day since the night Kaufman died. He slipped the tail tonight for the first time.

"And Olga Kellner," he went on. "You force her to rinse the dye out of her hair and she turns from redhead to ash-blonde. But that isn't evidence, you say no law against dyeing your hair. It never occurred to you that if you'd formally booked her for the first thing that came into your head, we could have held her long enough to take her back to Vale Heights. And we must have found a dozen or more people there who'd identify her as Olga Kellner!"

I was feeling very tired and the pain in my side seemed to be getting worse. "Okay," I said wearily. "So I boobed."

"Are you going to shout at him all night?" Mrs. Lavers turned on her husband suddenly. "Just stand there and shout at him—while he's bleeding to death!"

He gaped at her: "While he's what?"

"What's that, then?" She stabbed out a finger in my direction. "Tomato sauce!"

I looked down and saw the trickle of blood that stood out against the whiteness of my shirt, and the wet patch that was staining my jacket.

Lavers moved across the room quickly and undid the jacket, then unbuttoned my shirt and pulled it back.

"You've been shot!" he said.

"I don't think it's anything much," I said.

"You were lucky," he said. "It burned your side, tearing up some skin on its way. Another three inches and it would have been in your heart. Ma! Get some hot water, and bandages!"

"Of course!" she said breathlessly, hurrying towards the door. "What else would I be doing?"

The door slammed shut behind her and Lavers straightened up onto his feet again: "So you had the drop on Romonoff all the time? He begged you to let him blow his brains out, and you did? Then who fired that bullet at you—Davey Crockett!"

I gulped down the rest of the coffee. I was too tired to argue.

"Okay," I said. "I killed him. I murdered him, if you like. He murdered Olga Kellner in cold blood and it was my fault—I put her there for him. I put her on that sofa in a drugged condition, all set for him like a sacrificial lamb! Then he told me to lie down on the sofa beside her, while he put a gun against my head and pulled the trigger. For sure he murdered one, if not both of those girls. And he murdered Olga. So I murdered him!"

He paced up and down the room once, then stood in front of me. "I think you'd better take a holiday, Al," he said quietly. "Rest up for a while."

"And then?"

"Come back to work when you feel up to it. Just remember, the odds are that the Kellner woman probably killed one of the other two girls. Even if she didn't actually strike them down, she knew it was going to happen and helped bring it about. In the eyes of the law, she was just as guilty as Romonoff!"

"I guess so," I said. "It'll just take me a while to get used to the idea, that's all."

"You will," he said.

I lit a cigarette: "What about Romonoff?"

"What about him?"

"You booking me for murder?"

"Sometimes I think I should retire," he said heavily. "Take up chicken farming, maybe. I left Hammond to clear things up at the Kaufman house that night. He reported the body had been embalmed. I knew it. I remembered you drinking that fluid. The bottle of embalming fluid had been down in the cellar. I told Hammond that, and I said that obviously Kaufman had done the job himself, to give himself time to get rid of the corpse safely."

It was my turn to stare at him: "Then what made you suspect Romonoff?"

"I didn't suspect Romonoff!" he said coldly.

"Then why put a twenty-four hours a day tail on him?"

"Damn it!" he roared. "I didn't! That was fiction—I couldn't stand listening to you anymore. I have my pride—what use it is to me, I'm not sure. You think I liked standing here, hearing an impudent youngster like you telling me how I'd fallen down on my job? I had to say something!"

He grinned at me suddenly: "I should resign and give you my job, Wheeler. But I won't, of course," he added hastily. "You had every moral right to kill Romonoff, even if you had no legal rights. The story of the suicide will stick. The story Homicide will hear is that you and I were suspicious and closing in on Romonoff and he panicked—murdered the Kellner woman just before we arrived on the scene and when he heard us coming, he shot himself!"

"Thanks, Mr. Commissioner," I said slowly.

"Don't thank me," he grinned. "I'm taking the biggest part of your glory and you won't be able to do a thing about it!"

The door opened and Mrs. Lavers bustled in, carrying a basin of hot-water, bandages and a sponge.

"What about this holiday?" Lavers asked me. "Anywhere in particular you want to go?"

I thought about it while Mrs. Lavers cut a great chunk out of a hundred and fifty dollar suit: "There's a certain blonde who lives in Vale Heights," I said slowly. "If you were to ring her and tell her the date I had tonight was strictly in the line of duty, she might consider sharing her house with me for a while."

Lavers sniffed: "A strictly immoral arrangement, I presume?"

"Why, Mr. Lavers!" his wife said fondly, looking up at him. "To hear you talk! Don't you remember that summer in Maine? The year before we were married, when you told me we ought to try a new design for living and the next thing I knew ..."

"All right!" Lavers said hastily. "All right! I'm sorry I said a word!"

"The blonde's name is Jo Dexter," I told him, "and the 'phone number ..."

THE END

Doll for the Big House

- - - -

Carter Brown

CHAPTER 1

It was a nice bright morning with the sun shining outside and it didn't help my hangover one little bit. The phone rang and that helped my hangover even less. I pressed one hand down on top of my head so that my scalp wouldn't lift off and float away. Then I picked up the receiver with my other hand and croaked hoarsely into it.

"Wheeler," Commissioner Lavers' voice barked into my ear. "I have come to a decision."

"If you drive carefully," I told him, "you shouldn't have any trouble getting around it."

"You have lived too long in the rarefied atmosphere of my office."

"Huh?"

"I don't think it's good for you. I think you have forgotten what it's like to be a cop."

"I'm only following your example, sir," I said politely. "If you didn't want me to be a slob, you should have said something about it before now."

The silence was only punctuated by the sound of his heavy breathing for a while.

"That," he said finally, "illustrates exactly what I mean. Your familiarity has reached the nauseating stage. So we are going to have a change."

"A change?" I asked cautiously.

"You are going to do some work," he told me. "Nice, solid, routine, orthodox work. From this morning on, you are going out to the Eighth Precinct to work there."

"That's Captain Bligh, isn't it?"

"That's right."

"Any difference between him and Bligh of the *Bounty* is hardly noticeable?"

"Captain Bligh is a strict disciplinarian, yes."

I closed my eyes. "You aren't serious about this, sir?"

"I was never more serious in my whole life," he said. "Being an orthodox cop for a while is going to do you a world of good, Wheeler. I shall be most interested to read Captain Bligh's report on your progress at the end of the month. Good morning. I won't keep you—you wouldn't want to be late for your first day out at the Precinct, would you?"

Then he hung up before I could even scream.

I had a shower and a shave for breakfast, got dressed and then drove the Healey out from under the carport and pointed its bonnet in the direction of the Precinct.

One thing I had learned the hard way was that when Lavers made up his mind, you couldn't change it with a charge of dynamite. I had to face it—if I wanted to keep on eating steady, I was working out at the Eighth Precinct from here on.

The Eighth Precinct covered mainly the Cone Hill district, I remembered. That's an area so plush that it costs you money to breathe the air. Every house has its own minimum of two acres of land, a butler and four Cadillacs. I wondered if I'd have to wear a tuxedo to work.

I got there at ten after nine and went into the Precinct house.

The desk sergeant stood up and bowed as I came in.

"This is an honor, Lieutenant," he said.

"Don't let it throw you," I said. "I go slumming all the time."

"The Captain is desirous of your presence in his office," the character went on. "If you would be so good as to grace his presence, I guess he'll take up the little matter of his lieutenants getting here on time if not before. His office is the second door to the right, Lieutenant—and you knock."

I thought he'd keep till I'd got rid of this hangover and hadn't collected another—in between hangovers was the time to take care of the desk sergeant.

I knocked on the second door to the right and what sounded like a trained seal barked inside. I debated whether I should go out and buy some raw fish first and then thought the hell with it, so I opened the door and stepped inside the office.

Captain Bligh looked up from his desk as I came into the office. He was a big, fat guy, completely bald and with the coldest blue eyes I ever saw outside an aquarium.

"So glad you could get along this morning, Lieutenant," he said in a bleak voice. "Just remember in future that when you work a day shift out of this Precinct, you start at nine o'clock, and that doesn't mean five past or even one minute past. It means nine o'clock at the latest."

I thought about it and decided he must be for real. "Yes, Captain," I said. "Sir."

"You don't have to call me 'Sir'—I'm only a lieutenant."

He pursed his lips. "Let me tell you something, Wheeler. The Commissioner spoke to me last night. He told me he was transferring you here. There were no strings attached, he said. Either you conformed to the discipline of the Precinct or I reported to him that you didn't, and he would take it from there. I had the impression, Wheeler, that he doesn't much care for you at the moment. I don't have to labor the point, do I?"

"No, sir," I said.

He nodded. "Then sit down."

"Yes, sir." I sat down in an uncomfortable chair and thought about a cigarette and decided against it.

"I expect a written report at the end of each day on precisely how you have spent your day," he said. "And that report gets written before you go home."

"Yes, sir."

"At all times you will conduct yourself as befits an officer of the rank of Lieutenant," he went on. "I don't like to see my men slovenly dressed, or smoking or chewing gum on duty."

"I get the picture," I said.

Captain Bligh shuffled some papers on his desk. "I have your first assignment right here, Wheeler. Missing Persons report. A girl who disappeared about a week ago. From what I can make out, it looks like a kidnapping."

He tossed a thin folder across to me. "The details are there. You can take the folder with you to the detectives' room and study it. Then I want you to commence an investigation. You are free to discuss the case with me at any time, if you feel you need advice or help. If you want any men or an extra man, then apply to me and if I consider it really necessary, I will grant it. Otherwise, of course, I shall refuse. I believe in results in this Precinct, Wheeler. I think that's all."

He glanced at his watch. "I suggest you start work right away as you have already lost fifteen minutes this morning by being late."

I took the folder from his desk and started toward the door.

"Just one thing more," he said. "You won't forget that written report at the end of the day, will you?"

"No, sir," I said.

"That will be all, Wheeler."

I went down the hall and found the detectives' room. There were a couple of guys inside I had never met. They introduced themselves—Lieutenant Ray and Sergeant Bannister.

"How come you aren't the Commissioner's white-haired little boy anymore?" Ray asked.

"It came as a surprise to me, too," I said. "And from a surprise it degenerated into a nightmare. A nightmare that masquerades as a cop under the name of Bligh."

Sergeant Bannister grinned. "That guy's a ghoul—and that's for sure."

"He give you some work?" Ray asked.

"Vital stuff," I said. "Missing Persons dame. She probably ran off with her music teacher and they're happily married now in Rio, busy raising a symphony orchestra."

They looked at each other and then back at me.

"What's the name of the girl, if you don't mind me asking?" Ray said casually.

"I'll find out," I said, then opened the folder. "Lili Hertz," I said after a while.

Then I looked up and saw them both grinning at each other.

"Is there something I should know?" I asked them politely. "Something that my best friends won't tell me?"

"Why, no," Bannister said quickly. "We were just curious, that's all."

I thought I might as well let it ride.

"Where do you get hot coffee in this joint?" I asked them.

"You mean when, not where," Ray said. "Ten forty-five is coffee break and you're allowed ten minutes. And when Bligh says ten minutes ..."

"He means five," I nodded. "I'm with that impression already."

I sat down at the nearest desk and opened the folder. The girl, Lili Hertz, had disappeared without trace a week ago. She had left the apartment she shared with her sister on a Saturday night to go down to the local drugstore and she had never come back.

Her description was interesting: Blonde, five feet five inches tall, weighed one hundred and twenty pounds. Wearing a red sweater and a pair of black slacks. Fair complexion. The only identification mark was a small scar on the inside of the right knee. Sister's name was Lois Hertz and the address was 1058A Lime Street, Calton, which was the suburb next to Cone Hill, but a million miles away all the same.

There had been the routine check with the Missing Persons Bureau, the hospitals, the morgue, with no result. According to the report, the sister had stated that Lili had no enemies she knew of and had not been under any emotional strain when she left the apartment. She could think of no reason why her sister should not return.

The drugstore had been checked, of course. Sure, the druggist remembered Miss Hertz coming in about ten-thirty and buying some aspirin and some tranquilizers—had a migraine, she'd told him. He had served her and she had left the drugstore.

I finished reading the folder and looked up, seeing the two of them still watching me intently.

"Who handled the questioning?" I asked.

"It so happened that I did, Lieutenant," Bannister said.

"This sister, Lois Hertz—what's she like?"

"Nice girl. Nice looker, too. Sincere type, I'd say."

"You think she was telling the truth about having no idea why her sister should disappear?"

"Sure," he nodded, "I think she was on the level. You can see from that folder, we just couldn't get a lead anyplace."

"If there are no leads," I said, "I wonder why Bligh should toss it back at me?"

"Could be a number of reasons, Wheeler," Ray said with a grin on his face. "The Captain doesn't like any unfinished business on his books—that's for one. Or maybe he knows this one is never going to work out and he wants you to boob on it, so it'll put you in the right frame of mind for future assignments."

"The more I get to know Bligh," I said, "the more I admire his character—in a macabre sort of way."

"What are you going to do, Lieutenant?" Bannister asked.

"I think I'll go talk to the sister," I said. "What do I do about transport?" Ray opened his mouth to answer. "Don't tell me," I said. "Let me guess. I see the Captain."

"After knocking on the door first," he agreed.

So I went back to Captain Bligh's office and I knocked on the door.

"Wait," his voice said curtly. So I waited five minutes and then the door opened and a cop came out.

"The Captain will see you now, Lieutenant," he told me.

I walked into the office and Bligh looked up.

"You read the report, Lieutenant?"

"Yeah," I nodded.

"Sir."

"Sir," I said.

He grunted. "What did you think of it?"

"There wasn't enough to think about—sir."

"What do you intend to do?"

"Go and see the sister," I said.

"Sergeant Bannister has already done that."

The Pine City administration retires its cops at sixty-three, if they live that long. My pension was thirty years away, not really close enough to worry about.

"Look, Captain," I said slowly. "You run this Precinct and I'll go along with the way you run it. You're entitled to that. But if you assign me to a case, then I'll handle it my way or not at all. I don't really care if Sergeant Bannister, Sherlock Holmes and Perry Mason all talked to that sister, I'm still going to talk to her. Is that clear?"

Bligh swallowed a couple of times and looked like he didn't believe his ears. "Very well," he said finally. "I shall expect you to make something of this, Wheeler. I'm sure the Commissioner will be most interested in what happens. So you can handle it your way—I'll give you all the rope you want."

"Thank you, sir. What do I do about transport?"

"Sergeant Finlay is in charge of all transport," he said. "Anyone requiring transport makes out his request in writing and gives it to the Sergeant. When he has my approval, he tells the officer concerned and allocates a unit."

"Thank you, sir," I said. "I'll provide my own transport—it will save me from getting writer's cramp."

CHAPTER 2

I pressed the buzzer outside the apartment and waited. After a minute or so, the door opened slowly and a dame looked out.

She was Titian-blonde, her hair cropped close in tight curls around her head. She had full red lips that made a firm mouth, but not so firm it didn't look as if it could weaken under emotional stress. She was wearing a sweater and skirt, and the sweater gave her that twin triangles look which used to delight the heart of Isosceles.

Her look wasn't exactly friendly. "What is it?" she asked.

"Lieutenant Wheeler," I said, and held out my shield so she could see it. "Eighth Precinct. I'd like to talk to you about your sister."

"I've already talked about my sister to somebody from the police."

"Let's talk some more, huh?"

"I don't have anything else to say."

"Don't let's make it difficult," I said. "I'd like to hear it from you."

She shrugged her shoulders. "OK," she said. "But make it fast, will you?"

"I'll make it fast," I said, and followed her into the apartment.

The living room was quite nicely furnished. She told me to sit down, which I did, and she sat opposite me and lit a cigarette.

"I read Sergeant Bannister's report," I said. "Your sister Lili walked out of here one Saturday night to go to the druggist. When she got there, she bought some aspirin and tranquilizers, said she had a migraine. She left. And that's the story—right?"

"That's the story," she agreed.

"It stinks," I said.

Her head came up. "What did you say?"

"I said it stinks. People just don't do things like that. She had a reason. People just don't vanish off the streets, unless you're going to swear that flying saucers are for real and little men from Mars swoop down with butterfly nets and pick up odd citizens here and there. She must have had a reason for disappearing. Either you know and you're lying for some reason, or you don't know and she was lying to you. Which theory are you taking out a subscription for?"

She took a deep breath which fractured an uncountable number of wool fibres. "I think you're being insulting, Lieutenant."

"Could be," I agreed. "I don't know yet. You tell me."

"I don't know any more than I told Sergeant Bannister."

"So your sister must have been lying to you. She had a secret all to her-self—a boyfriend she never mentioned, a murder she never told you about—something."

"That's ridiculous."

I lit myself a cigarette. "Did she have a steady boyfriend?"

"No."

"She must have gone out with fellows—she looks like you, doesn't she?"

Lois Hertz blushed faintly. "She had dates, but never more than a couple of dates with the same guy. She didn't take any of them seriously."

"She went out with a guy who took her seriously, maybe?"

"I'm sure she didn't."

"She has no enemies?"

"None."

"Where did she work?"

"The same place as I do—Maison Basiloff."

"Fashion house?"

She shook her head. "I thought everybody knew Basiloff's Jewelry."

"Where is it?"

"Cone Hill. Market Street."

"Maybe Basiloff was sweet on her?"

"He's been dead for twenty years," she said. "And Lili didn't have a planchette board."

"Somebody else who works there, maybe?"

"No," she said.

"How do you know?"

"I also work there. I'm sure of it."

I was beginning to feel for Bannister. "And you don't have any idea why she would disappear? She had no emotional upset, no worries, no noth-ing?"

"I've already told you, Lieutenant—none."

"OK," I said. "Thanks."

I got onto my feet and walked toward the door. She walked with me.

"Do you think you'll find her, Lieutenant?"

"If she can be found," I said. "If she wants to be found."

"You don't think anything's happened to her?"

"Something's happened to her," I said. "Or why would she disappear? She could have got married, or gone to sleep in an all-night movie and not woken up yet. A million things."

She opened the door for me.

"How come you aren't selling jewelry today?" I asked her.

"It's my day off."

"I should have thought of that," I said. "Thank you for your time, Miss Hertz."

"A pleasure, Lieutenant."

"I wish I could say the same," I said. "Did you ever study geometry at school?"

"Of course," she said blankly. "Why?"

"You're the most interesting proof of a theorem I've ever seen. I think maybe you've given me an idea for advanced education which should make me a million. Good morning, Miss Hertz."

"Goodbye, Lieutenant," she said. "Have you had a look at your sanity lately?"

"No," I said. "Is it showing?"

I got back into the Healey and drove up into Market Street to be precise. I parked the car outside Basiloff's and walked across the sidewalk into the store. It was more like a pagan temple, coupled with the hushed atmosphere of a church. Trinkets worth anything up to fifty thousand dollars each lay on velvet upholstery in glass-lined cases and reflected light from the ceiling.

The assistants were all dressed in black and the vast majority of them were young, female and filled their black dresses very adequately.

A black-haired, boyish-looking character with a wisp of mustache across his upper lip headed toward me. He wore a morning coat, with a carnation in the buttonhole. He looked so fragile that a hard word could break him clean in half.

"Can I be of service, sir?" he asked politely. "You are looking for a gift, perhaps? For a lady?"

"It so happens I am," I said. "I'd like to give her her sister back."

He looked blank.

"I'm Lieutenant Wheeler," I told him. "I'm investigating the disappearance of Lili Hertz who worked here, understand?"

"Oh," his face cleared. "Of course, Lieutenant. You will wish to see Madame Basiloff. I shall tell her you are here."

He waltzed off behind a counter and then disappeared through a doorway behind it. I lit a cigarette and waited and filled in the time calculating how many years it would take me to pay for the diamond bracelet in the showcase immediately in front of me.

Then the character came back.

"Madame will see you right away, Lieutenant. If you will walk this way?"

He minced off ahead of me. I watched him for a couple of seconds and thought if I walked that way, they'd toss me out of the Police Department. I followed him and we ended up in an ornate office.

"Lieutenant Wheeler, Madame," the character said, then went out, closing the door behind him.

Madame Basiloff looked up from her desk and right away I started taking an interest in the case.

She was brunette and chic. She looked like a ballerina should and I thought she would look even better in tights. She had high cheekbones and finely arched eyebrows. Her eyes had a greenish tinge and if she had sprouted horns, she would have been the most bewitching female imp this side of hell. Come to think of it, she didn't really need the horns.

She smiled slowly at me. "I'm Greta Basiloff, Lieutenant. You wished to speak about Lili Hertz?"

"That's right," I said.

"Won't you sit down, Lieutenant?"

"Thanks," I said.

I sat down carefully on what was either an antique chair or had cost more than an antique to reproduce.

"What did you want to know, Lieutenant?"

She wore a black dress that probably had a Dior label. The label would have been at the back because there wasn't room in the front. The neckline in front was a plunge nothing short of suicidal. Around her slim ivory neck a diamond necklace sparkled happily. In the same position, I'd have sparkled just as brightly.

"Does something bother you, Lieutenant?" she asked in a puzzled voice.

"I'll get used to it," I said. "I think."

"Oh?"

"Lili Hertz," I said, trying to fix my mind on business again.

"She worked here?"

"That's right, Lieutenant."

"You know she's disappeared?"

"Of course. I am deeply sympathetic for her sister, Lois. She also works here."

I lit myself a cigarette. "What did you know of Lili Hertz?"

She shrugged her slim shoulders. "What does one know of the people who work for you? She was a pretty girl. A good worker and a good salesgirl—but I don't employ those who are not."

"You know of no reason why she should disappear suddenly the way she did?"

"I'm afraid not, Lieutenant."

There are two ways to ask people questions—the nice and the nasty. The nice hadn't got me anyplace since I'd started.

"The sprightly character who showed me in here—what's his name?"

"You mean Basil," she said. "Basil Lupek. Such a charming boy."

"And all your girls," I said. "They all look charming, too."

"Thank you," she smiled.

"To sell the baubles you're selling," I said, "I imagine it would be an asset to have charming assistants. The girls to charm the male clientele and Basil to charm the female—the matronly in particular."

"You're delving into my trade secrets, Lieutenant." She seemed faintly amused. "Of course, you are right."

I sucked smoke into my lungs and began to wish I had eaten breakfast. There was a clamoring void where my stomach used to be.

"Maybe one of your clients became interested in Lili?" I suggested.

"I don't think so," she said quickly.

"Why?"

"Well," she shrugged her shoulders again and the neckline quivered from the top to way down past where it should have ended. "I just don't think that sort of thing happens in my establishment."

"You don't look a naive character, Madame Basiloff," I said. "Why the hell shouldn't it happen?"

"If it did," she said, the smile disappearing from her face, "I was not aware of it."

"No," I said. "You probably wouldn't see it. But somebody else would. Basil, maybe?"

"I shall ask him," she said.

"Wrong." I got up on my feet. "I shall ask him."

"Lieutenant. Do you presume to override my authority?"

I showed her my badge. "This allows me to override most things. I'm going to talk to Basil. I'll be right back."

I walked out of the office and through to the shop. Basil was fluttering around an elderly matron who was trying to make up her mind about a pair of earrings, which were a throwaway at four hundred and ninety-five dollars and seventy-five cents.

I waited until he'd clinched the sale and she had gone on her way rejoicing, or whatever it is women do after they've bought earrings. Then I tapped him on the shoulder and he jumped violently.

"I'd like to talk to you," I said.

He turned around and looked at me. "Of course, Lieutenant."

"You knew Lili Hertz?"

"Naturally. A charming girl, so natural, so ..."

"Sure," I interrupted. "She had a particular client who was particularly interested in her."

His eyes bulged slightly. "But ..."

"And now she's disappeared," I said. "We have a feeling the two events aren't unconnected. We'd like to know more about that client."

"But, but ..." he gurgled.

"I know," I said. "It's not the way Basiloff's usually treat a valued client. You assure them of discretion at all times. But being discreet this way could earn you five years in the State penitentiary. If you try and protect your client, you'll become an accessory after the fact, Basil, dear boy. And that is a felony. A compound felony if you'd care for me to be literal?"

He took a handkerchief from his top pocket and dabbed his face. The scent of eau de cologne wafted through the air.

"Lieutenant," he said in a quavering voice, "you've upset me."

"If I take you downtown," I said, "I could make a thorough job of it."

"There's no need to threaten me with physical violence," he said petulantly. "Naturally I shall be only too glad to co-operate with you, Lieutenant. I don't know how you found out, but ..."

"I think I'll do the co-operating with the Lieutenant, Basil," a cool voice said from behind me. "Go and have a cup of tea and calm your nerves."

"Yes, Madame," he said gratefully, and then scuttled off like a cockroach that's just come face to face with a poisoned bait.

I turned around and saw Madame Basiloff standing just behind me.

"I think we should go back to my office, Lieutenant," she said, then turned around and led the way. I followed. Some women walk like Marilyn Monroe and others just walk. Greta Basiloff walked like Greta Basiloff but it was reasonably close to Monroe. I was sorry when we reached her office again.

She sat down behind her desk and lit a cigarette. "You're smarter than I thought you were, Lieutenant."

"Do I get a pair of diamond earrings as the prize?" I asked.

"You're right, of course," she told me. "There was a client interested in Lili, but I'm sure he had nothing to do with her disappearance."

She hadn't offered me a cigarette, so I lit one of my own. "Tell me about it," I said.

"He comes in quite regularly," she said. "And he always asked for her to serve him."

"He has a name?"

"Clinton Walker."

"What does he do?"

She hesitated for a moment. "He is Absolem Kirch's private secretary."

"I begin to see a picture," I said.

"Would you like to go home now, Lieutenant?" she asked gently.

I got onto my feet. "I think I would. I might want to talk to you again, outside of office hours. Are you in the phone book?"

She shook her head. "Silent number. But you can have my address. It's Pine Trees, Horizon Street, Cone Hill."

"One of those thirty-bedroom shacks?"

"Only eight," she said. "I'm not married."

"I see," I said.

"The Madame is only used for professional reasons," she went on. "I am the daughter of the original Basiloff. He died twenty years ago and my mother died eight years ago."

"I see," I said. I didn't.

"I'd like you to call, Lieutenant," she said gently. "But not professionally."

Then I did see.

CHAPTER 3

The Commissioner's office looked just the same as it had on Friday afternoon. Now it was Monday afternoon and I didn't belong in it anymore. I knocked on his door and he yelled out to come in, so in I went.

He didn't give me the Prodigal Son routine.

"I'm busy, Wheeler," he said irritably. "And shouldn't you be working in the Eighth Precinct?"

"I should," I agreed. "I am. And no, it won't wait, and I don't give a damn how busy you are."

A look of interest showed in his eyes. "Are you talking to Captain Bligh the way you're talking to me?"

"I'm getting around to it fast. I want to ask you a question."

"All right," he said cautiously. "Make it brief."

"Sure," I said. "Three words—what's the gag?"

His eyebrows met in head-on collision. "What are you talking about?"

"The Lili Hertz—Absolem Kirch deal."

He shook his head. "I don't know what you're talking about."

"Let's stop playing games," I said. "You suddenly toss me out into the Eighth Precinct. Bligh suddenly tosses me a Missing Persons deal. All the other cops out there are leering at me and laughing up or down their sleeves every time they look my way. I spend one morning in checking facts the way a rookie cop can check facts and come up with a suspect—one Clinton Walker, personal secretary to Absolem Kirch. And this is coincidental?"

He started to fill his pipe. "You'd better sit down," he said. "It took the Precinct boys four days to come up with Walker and the Kirch tie-up. I hoped it would take you as long and by that time you'd be so mad with

Bligh you'd just go on with the thing."

"Why?"

He lit his pipe just as carefully as he'd filled it. "You know who Absolem Kirch is?"

"Owns a newspaper empire," I said. "Built himself a palace out on Cone Hill, with high walls around the place and uniformed guards on the gate. Probably has a personal fortune that runs into eight figures. Owns some television and radio networks. His reputation stinks vaguely, but I've never heard anybody put their finger on why."

Lavers nodded. "That's an average picture of Kirch. He makes people and he breaks them. He makes fortunes and he ruins people who had fortunes too, if he feels like it. He doesn't even need a reason."

"So here comes the bogeyman," I said. "Where does that leave Al Wheeler?"

His face was sober as he puffed his pipe. "I'm not sure, except that it will be out on a limb."

"Please, Commissioner," I said, "I'm all grown up. I understand plain English."

"It took them four days to arrive at the point you have arrived at," he said. "The tie-up between the disappearance of the girl and Walker. There was the tie-up, vaguely, and nothing more. Because of Kirch's name and influence, Captain Bligh decided to be a little cautious, so he sent Lieutenant Ray out to see Walker, instead of letting the Sergeant, who had handled the case up to then, go out and interview Walker.

"Ray arrived at Kirch's house and told the man on the gate who he was and that he wanted to see Walker. The man rang through to the house, then told Ray that Walker was out and wouldn't be back for a couple of days— was in New York, he said. So Ray never got past the gate. He went back and reported to Bligh."

I leaned back in the visitor's chair. "Then what?"

"The following day I was told," his face wrinkled in disgust. "I was ordered to lay off the case and was assured that the girl was quite all right. I was to close the case. Just another of the thousand-odd people reported missing in California every year—most of them are never found as you know, because they don't want to be found."

I was beginning to see a picture, as Rembrandt said to the lady when he found her stepping out of her bath.

"I couldn't ignore the source from where the instructions to leave the case alone came from," he said. "But on the other hand, we have an honest Police Department in Pine City. I even flatter myself that I, too, am fundamentally honest. So if I couldn't pursue the case officially, I could try it some other way."

"I don't know where this leaves me," I said. "But I have an uncomfortable feeling that it's right behind the eight ball."

"That is probably true," Lavers said. "I transferred you to the Eighth Precinct, giving my reasons officially to Captain Bligh in writing. I thought you had been attached to my office too long without a break and needed the routine of Precinct work to help you keep your hand in. Unofficially, I suggested to him that he could put you on this Missing Persons case and see how far you got. I—er, sort of intimated to him that I would be glad of the excuse to axe you, and this case might well provide me with the excuse."

I lit myself a cigarette. "You're going too fast for me," I said. "Can you tell me who gave you the instructions in the first place, so I can start from the beginning?"

"No," he said.

"Can I make a guess?"

"No."

"The D.A.?"

Lavers grinned. "Officially, I should deny it."

"How about Bligh? Does he know this?"

"I told him that the case was to rest in abeyance. I muttered something about politics and that the girl was all right. Bligh didn't like it, but what could he do? I'm the Commissioner and I was giving him a direct order."

"I'm still not sure why you bounced me out there, without tipping me off in the first place?"

"Al," he said quietly. "What I'm going to tell you now is in absolute confidence. The politics of this city have been getting dirtier and dirtier for a long time. There's a move afoot to have a Grand Jury investigate. Kirch is behind a lot of the dirty politics and if we could pin something on him, some evidence to put before the Grand Jury, then we would have won before they started their first sitting. But if Kirch or any of his friends, like the District Attorney for example, get wind of what we're trying to do, then we shall be finished smartly. My appointment, as you know, is a political one. When the party was clean, they put me in office—and now they're dirty, they'll let me stay in office just so long as I don't worry them. They figure an honest Police Department is a great thing so long as it doesn't interfere with them."

Like Rembrandt, I was seeing more with each passing second.

"So if anybody wants to look·at the records," I said, "you'll stick to your story that you canned the investigation. My being tossed out to the Eighth Precinct was a coincidence?"

"That's right. I have a tape recording of my conversation with Bligh telling him to drop it. If he disobeyed my instructions and put you on the case, it was without my knowledge.”

"Are you being friendly to Captain Bligh?”

"You mightn’t like his ideas or being punctual,” he said, “but he’s an honest cop. I talked to him a second time without making a recording. He knows what he’s doing.”

"If I continue the investigation,” I said, “I shall talk to Walker. Once that happens, the D.A. will be around to talk to you again. What then?”

"I shall be furious that my instructions have been disobeyed,” he said. “I shall immediately see Bligh and demand to know why. He will tell me that he only put you on the case to give you something to do, and he had no idea that you would trace the connection to Walker. He was firmly convinced that the people concerned, like the girl’s sister and the people where she worked, would never tell you about Walker. Bligh will be worried and apologetic, and then I shall tell him that something must happen to you. Something drastic and quick. And it will.”

"Nothing permanent, I hope. If I get shot by a cop, I shall be offended.”

"No,” he said. “But it could happen that we’ll have an excuse to toss you out of the department on your ear. And if you’re so mad about it that you go right on investigating the case as a private citizen and maybe come up with something of value for the Grand Jury ... can I help it?”

I didn’t answer his smile. “This is all taped, isn’t it?” I said. “This is the way you had it planned from last Friday?”

"That’s the way I had it planned,” he agreed. “You’re the fall guy, Al.”

"And everybody else is covered, except me?”

"That’s right.”

"If I hadn’t come up here this afternoon, when would you have told me about it?”

"After you’d been bounced.”

"When I wouldn’t have had the option to agree or not?”

"That’s right.”

I stubbed my cigarette out in his ashtray. “For the first time in my life,” I said, “I’m wondering whether I can trust you, Mr. Commissioner.”

"You have every right to wonder that,” he said. “It’s not a nice setup for you. I wish I could think of a better way, but I can’t.”

"I never did think I’d survive that long to enjoy my pension,” I said. “Looks like I was right.”

"You’ll go through with it?”

"I’ll go through with it,” I said. “But I’m not sure why.”

"I knew you would, Al,” he said. “If we’re going to have any hope of beating them at all, we’ve got to play it their way, which is dirty. I wish it wasn’t that way, but it is.”

I got onto my feet. “I’d better get back to the Precinct and put in my written report on the day's work."

"You do that, Al," he said. "And don't come near this office again. You're going to be too hot to be seen around here."

"OK," I said. "Tell Mrs. Lavers hello for me."

"I'll do that," he said. "For your information, a man called Bryan—Judge Bryan—is the man who will probably head the Grand Jury if it's convened. You might want to talk to him later. He doesn't know anything of what I've told you and he wouldn't believe it if he heard it without proof. But he just could be of some use to you."

"I'll remember the name," I assured him. "Good afternoon, Commissioner."

"So long, Al," he said. "Take care of yourself."

I drove back to the Precinct and arrived around four-thirty in the detectives' room. Bannister was out, but Ray was there. He looked at me interestedly as I came in.

"How did you make out?" he asked.

"A little here, a little there," I said. "Whether any of it means anything, I don't know."

I sat down at a typewriter and typed out my report.

"I have to give this to His Majesty before I go home?" I said when I'd finished it.

"I've got to see the Captain myself," he said casually. "I'll drop it in for you if you like."

"Thanks, Ray," said, and handed him the typewritten sheet. "That way I might catch up on a cup of coffee."

He took it and went out of the room. I wandered out and the desk sergeant said the diner across the street would send coffee over and he'd ring them for me. I went back to the detectives' room and waited. A couple of minutes later the coffee arrived, and five minutes after that Ray came back.

"The Captain wants to see you right away," he said.

"What's the matter?" I asked him as I stood up. "Did I make a couple of spelling mistakes?"

I went down the corridor and knocked on the door and Bligh yelled for me to come in. I went in, closed the door behind me and walked up to his desk.

"Sit down, Wheeler," he said.

I sat down and waited. He looked at me with an expressionless face. "I see you've been busy today," he said.

"Yes, sir."

"You think there may be a definite connection between the girl's disappearance and this man, Walker?"

"I think it's a lead worth following," I said. "The only lead I've got."

He nodded. "Perhaps you're right. What are you going to do about it?"

"I thought I'd go out and talk to him tomorrow. I understand he'll be at Kirch's house."

"Where did you hear that?"

"I didn't. If he's Kirch's personal secretary, where else would he be?"

"I suppose you're right," he said. "Just handle him carefully if you do see him. He's an important man in this city."

"He has a citizen's rights, no more and no less," I said. "I don't care much who he is otherwise."

"That's the way you think, is it, Wheeler?"

"Anything wrong with that—sir?"

Bligh's face reddened. "I'm not sure. Not in the words, but in your own attitude perhaps, Wheeler. I'm telling you now—handle the interview with him carefully. I shan't take kindly to any complaints from Walker about rough-necked lieutenants of police."

"Will that be all—sir?"

"I think so," he said curtly. "If you see him tomorrow, I want you to come straight back here afterward and type out a report of the whole interview. Wait a minute, I think you'd better take somebody along with you as well. Sergeant Bannister would be the best man."

"I don't need anybody along with me," I objected.

"I don't care what you think you need or don't need. I'm giving you an order. Bannister goes with you."

"Yes, sir. Can I go home now?"

He looked at his watch. "It is now ten to five, Wheeler. Your time to finish this shift is five o'clock. At one minute past five, your time is your own. Right now, it belongs to me. I'd like this report retyped before you go—there are a number of typographical errors."

"Would you like it tied with pink ribbon as well?"

He examined his fingernails carefully. "Wheeler," he said in a flat voice. "You are here on sufferance. I was prepared to be patient with you, but after one day my patience is nearly exhausted. Just remember that."

CHAPTER 4

It was a lousy morning, with rain beating down and all the world looking like it should go to the dry cleaner's and then have a fortnight in Miami.

Bannister sat beside me in the Healey and smoked a cigarette without saying anything. I drove up into Cone Hill where only the delivery boys drove last year's model Cadillac, and wondered if it would be nice to have a million dollars—a mansion and an ulcer on the same scale.

It took us fifteen minutes to reach Kirch's house. Or the gates that led to his house. The gates were massive, some twelve feet high and made of solid wrought iron. I stopped the Healey with the bonnet a couple of inches away from the gates and pounded the horn.

A guy in a peaked cap and a slicker came out through a side gate, locking it carefully behind him, and walked over to the car. He looked in at me.

"What do you want?" he asked.

"To see Mr. Walker," I said.

"Got an appointment?"

I showed him my shield. "Lieutenant Wheeler, of the Eighth Precinct," I said.

"I don't know whether he'll see you," he said.

"The choice is not his," I said. "Open up those gates."

"I'll find out if he'll see you," he said.

I looked at him coldly.

"Sergeant," I said.

"Yes, Lieutenant?" Bannister answered.

"I shall give him twenty seconds to open those gates," I said clearly. "If he doesn't, then I'm afraid we'll have to take him downtown and book him for aggravated assault. Assaulting a cop is a serious business, isn't it, Sergeant?"

"Yes, sir," Bannister muttered.

"Always gets the boys so mad they can't wait to show a guy the error of his ways," I went on. "You remember that character who went chicken on a nightstick just because it busted a blood vessel in his heart? He died, didn't he, Sergeant?"

The guard wasn't listening anymore. He was hurrying back to the side gate. A few seconds later the main gates swung open. I rammed the Healey forward and a couple of seconds later we were heading down the long drive toward the house.

"If that guy reports what you said, Lieutenant," Bannister said uneasily, "it won't look good."

"He won't," I said. "Is that really a house up there, or did Disney throw it up for Snow White and forget to pull it down again?"

It wasn't a house at all, it was a castle. It had towers and ramparts and sprawled all over the place. If a couple of dozen knights in shining armor had ridden out, I wouldn't even have been surprised.

We reached the front of the house which was more a paved courtyard, and I stopped the Healey and climbed out. Bannister followed me up the dozen marble steps that led to the front door.

I pushed the bell and we waited. Some twenty seconds went by, then a butler opened the door. If you couldn't afford a butler in Cone Hill, you either moved or committed suicide.

"Sir?" His accent was impeccably English.

"Lieutenant Wheeler," I said, "and Sergeant Bannister. To see Mr. Walker."

"If you'll come inside, gentlemen?"

So we came inside. He took our hats and deposited them in a small anteroom, then led the way majestically down the wide hall.

He stopped and threw open a pair of doors and announced us in ringing tones, then departed. The room was being used as an office—there was a wide desk, a couple of filing cabinets, and a heavy safe. There was a man standing with his back toward us, looking out of the window. He turned slowly and looked at us.

He was big and powerfully built, broad across the back like a wrestler. He had thick, black hair streaked with gray, and cold gray eyes. His top lip was thin, the lower lip full and protruding slightly. He was wearing an immaculate gray suit, a white shirt and a plain silk tie.

"Yes?" he said in a clipped voice.

"I'm Lieutenant Wheeler," I said. "This is Sergeant Bannister. We're from the Eighth Precinct. We would like to ask you some questions, Mr. Walker."

"There must be some mistake," he said evenly. "My name isn't Walker. I am Absolem Kirch."

I felt disappointed. Talking to ten million dollars didn't seem any different from talking to ten dollars.

"I wanted to see Mr. Walker," I said. "Your butler should start saving for a hearing aid."

"I told him to bring you in here," he said. "Walker is still in New York. Perhaps I may be able to answer your questions for you, Lieutenant?"

"I doubt it," I said.

His lips tightened a little. "I find your manner only just short of rudeness, Lieutenant," he said. "I don't care for it."

"You worry me," I told him. "Now I shan't sleep nights."

"Walker is my personal secretary," he said. "You'd better tell me what this is about."

I lit a cigarette. "It's about a girl," I said. "A girl named Lili Hertz. She's disappeared."

"A friend of Walker's?"

"I think so," I said. "She worked in Basiloff's and I understand that Mr. Walker was an admirer of hers. He always asked that she should serve him whenever he went into the shop."

Kirch smiled. "That seems a slender premise, Lieutenant? Just because

Walker had a preference for a salesgirl to serve him, he should have had something to do with her disappearance?"

"I'm not saying that," I said. "I thought he might be able to help us, that's all."

"I'm quite sure he couldn't," Kirch said. "If you'll forgive me saying so, Lieutenant, I think you're wasting your—"

The door swung open abruptly and a man came in.

"Absolem," he said hurriedly. "This steel merger. You must sign ..."

"Mr. Walker?" I said quickly.

"Yes," he said. "Who are you?"

"Lieutenant Wheeler, Police Department," I said. "Congratulations."

"What for?" he asked blankly.

"Making the fastest time from New York I've ever heard of."

He still stared blankly at me.

"Most amusing, Lieutenant," Kirch said coldly. "It so happens my secretary is busy with some most important work for me and I didn't want him interrupted. Apparently the butler missed you, Clinton?"

Walker looked slightly sick. "I didn't see him, Absolem. I'm sorry, I had no idea."

"It doesn't matter," Kirch said easily. "Now you're here you might as well stay. Apparently some shopgirl from Basiloff's has disappeared. The Lieutenant seems to think you might know something about it."

"Me." Walker shook his head. "Why should I know anything about it?"

I didn't seem to be getting my share of the dialogue. I thought that should be rectified.

"The girl's name is Lili Hertz, Mr. Walker," I said. "The girl you always asked for to attend to you whenever you bought anything at Basiloff's."

"Oh—Lili," he said. "I hope nothing has happened to her. She disappeared, you say?"

"Just over a week ago," I said. "I thought perhaps you might have seen something of her outside the shop, Mr. Walker?"

"Certainly not," he said. "Whatever makes you think that?"

"It's not uncommon," I said, "and there's no law against it. You could have taken her out once or twice?"

"It's unthinkable," he said.

"You only spoke to her while she served you in the shop?"

"Of course. I liked her manner—she was efficient. That's why I asked for her to serve me. She knew the sort of thing I would want, that was all."

"I see," I said.

Kirch moved his shoulders impatiently. "Does that satisfy you, Lieutenant?"

"Just a few more questions," I said. "Where were you last Saturday week,

Mr. Walker? In the evening—say between ten and eleven?"

"Really, Lieutenant. Are you asking me for an alibi?"

"For what?"

"I take it that was the time the girl disappeared," he said. "This is monstrous."

"I shall take this up with the District Attorney," Kirch said. "It's fantastic."

"You still haven't answered my question, Mr. Walker," I said. "Where were you?"

"I was right here."

"Can anybody substantiate that?"

"I can," Kirch said. "But you may doubt my word, of course, Lieutenant?"

"After you lied about Mr. Walker's whereabouts just a few minutes ago, you can't blame me, can you?" I said gently. "I'd prefer other corroboration than yours, Mr. Kirch."

"Get out," he shouted.

I looked at him. "What?"

"Get out." The veins stood out in his neck and his face was purple. "Get out or I'll have you thrown out. I won't be insulted by an oaf with a dimestore badge. If you want to ask any more questions of Mr. Walker or myself, you can ask my lawyers. Come back here with a warrant for arrest, Lieutenant. Then we will see."

"I was talking to Mr. Walker," I said curtly. "You speak when you're spoken to, Kirch."

He looked at me speechless for a moment, then strode across to a button on the desk and jabbed down on it. The butler appeared a couple of seconds later.

"Jones," Kirch said tightly. "The police officers are leaving. If they refuse to leave, call two of the guards and throw them out. I take full responsibility for your actions."

"Yes, sir," the butler said calmly. "Shall I get your hats now, gentlemen?" he asked politely.

"OK," I said. "You'll hear more of this, Kirch."

Then I strode past the butler out into the hall, with Bannister tagging along close behind me.

Bannister didn't say a word all the way back from Cone Hill to the Precinct. We got into the detectives' room and I looked at him.

"I'm not submitting a written report to the Captain on what happened up there," I said.

He shook his head dubiously. "I don't think you played it very smart, Lieutenant. That Kirch is a big man in this city—a big man."

"No bigger than the law, Sergeant," I said. "No man is that big."

Bannister still shook his head. "I don't think you handled it right, Lieutenant."

"The hell with it," I said. "I'm going out to have a drink and some lunch. If the Captain is looking for me, I'll be back around two."

I went out and walked a couple of blocks to a restaurant and had lunch. I had a couple of drinks on the way back at a bar, and got into the Precinct again at a quarter after two.

"The Captain is shouting from the hilltops," the desk sergeant said. "And he's shouting one word—Wheeler."

"Thank you, O Sage," I told him.

I walked down and knocked on the door and then went in. Captain Bligh dropped his pen onto the desk. "I had Sergeant Bannister in here before lunch. He told me how you conducted the interview this morning."

"Don't you usually ask lieutenants first before sergeants?"

"I would have done," he said, "but the Lieutenant had gone out to lunch at twelve-fifteen, and arrived back at two-fifteen. But that doesn't matter now. What does matter is the way you handled that interview. You threatened the man at the gate with false arrest on a trumped-up charge and a beating when you got him to the Precinct. You know how that would look in one of Kirch's papers. And then you try and browbeat Kirch himself."

Bligh's fist pounded the desk. "I told you to be discreet. To handle the thing gently. Are you a fool or an idiot, Wheeler?"

"I'm trying to work out which one I work for right now," I said. "Kirch lied to me about Walker being in New York when he was inside the house the whole time. Lied blatantly. Was I supposed to be polite and discreet about that?"

"You were only there to ask questions," he said. "You haven't one shred of proof that Walker was connected with the girl's disappearance in any way. And you leave the whole department, let alone this Precinct, open to all sorts of vicious attacks by the Kirch newspapers. I'm going to take this further, Wheeler—a whole lot further. I'm taking it straight to the Commissioner, and until I have further instructions from him, I don't want you around my Precinct. Go home and stay there till you hear from me."

"When I first met you yesterday morning, Bligh," I told him, "I thought you were a moron—but an honest one. Now I'm beginning to have my doubts."

"Get out," he said softly. "Get out before I kick you in the face."

So I got out. I didn't think he'd really kick me in the face, but then you never know and I like my face as it is. It's repulsive, but I've shaved it for so many years now I'm used to it. A violent change would frighten me.

I drove the Healey home and when I got inside the house, I put a stack of discs on the hi-fi and let them run. I'd just got Ellington's interpretation of Shakespeare, and I settled in an armchair with a full glass, to listen. Man. That Ellington is genius, pure and simple. Nobody ever has played blues the way that man can play blues. I can be progressive in jazz and string along with Kenton and Brubeck, but when the Old Duke gets into the groove I'm strictly a downbeat boy.

Around six I stopped drinking and listening and made myself a meal. And around eight I had another drink. I'd been drinking very sparingly all afternoon because I had a feeling the night was going to be a busy one.

At nine the phone rang and I answered it.

"Lieutenant Wheeler?" The voice was female and urgent.

"Sure," I said. "Who's this?"

"Lois Hertz," she told me. "Lieutenant, I can give you some information about my sister."

"You've heard from her?"

"No." Her voice quavered. "I've known it for days, but they threatened me if I told ... but I don't care anymore."

"All right," I said. "Give."

"I can't talk over the phone," she said. "Would you come to my apartment—now?"

"Sure," I said. "Take me about half an hour and I'll be there."

"Hurry," she said, then hung up.

I finished my drink and then got the Healey out and drove over to Calton, and it was near enough to the half-hour when I arrived there.

She opened the door almost as soon as I pressed the buzzer.

"Come in quickly," she said. "Did you see anybody outside?"

"Nobody," I said.

I followed her into the living room. She was wearing a robe belted tightly around her waist and she didn't look any different from the first time I'd seen her.

"Wait a minute," she said.

She crossed to the window that looked out onto the street and pulled down the blind.

"I feel they're watching me all the time," she said nervously.

"Who?" I asked her.

"I'll tell you," she said. "You don't know what a strain I've been under, Lieutenant. I thought I'd go mad."

"Just tell me what it's all about and I'll help you," I said.

"I will," she said. "Just give me a moment and I'll try and compose myself."

"Take your time, honey," I said. "I've got all night."

The buzzer sounded suddenly, harsh in my ears, and at the same time Lois

Hertz started to scream. She sprang forward and ripped her nails down the side of my face, screaming the whole time. Then she tore off her robe and trampled it on the floor. She knocked over an armchair and still kept on screaming.

I watched her, fascinated.

With the robe gone, she wasn't wearing much. A bra and a pair of blue satin panties. She grabbed hold of the bra and ripped at it so the straps broke. I looked away at the window so that I wouldn't offend her maidenly modesty, and at that juncture somebody shoulder-charged the door and a horde of cops came streaming into the room.

Lois Hertz was still screaming at the top of her voice and clothes-wise, as the man in Oklahoma says, she'd gone about as far as she could go.

Captain Bligh was the first one to reach me.

"Sex maniac, huh?" he grated, and the next moment a fist like a sledge-hammer caught me flush under the jaw, lifting me off my feet and sending me flying across the room.

My back jarred against the wall and then I slid down it into a sitting position on the floor. Rough hands grabbed me and hoisted me onto my feet. My hands were dragged behind my back and a pair of handcuffs snapped onto my wrists. Then they hustled me out of the apartment and down to the waiting prowl car.

It looked as if I was going to work the night shift down at the Precinct as well as the day.

CHAPTER 5

There was quite a crowd in Commissioner Lavers' office the next morning. There was Lavers himself, the D.A., Captain Bligh, Lieutenant Ray and Sergeant Bannister, Captain Hogarth, the senior Captain of Homicide and the senior Captain of the Police Department, and a male stenographer.

It was brief and to the point. Captain Bligh had gone through his routine. Lois Hertz had rung the Precinct the preceding night just after nine and told them she was frightened. That I had seen her earlier in the evening and told her unless she was nice to me I'd see she got into trouble over her sister's disappearance, and I would come back at nine-thirty that night to see her.

The Lieutenant on duty, Ray, had rung Bligh at his home. Bligh had rung the girl and told her to use the window blind as a signal when I arrived. He had taken four men with him in a prowl car and watched the apartment. They had heard the girl scream as they came up the stairs after seeing her signal. They had forced their way into the apartment, then he gave a lengthy description of how the girl looked when they arrived.

Bligh's evidence was corroborated by Ray, Bannister and the other two uniformed cops.

Lavers asked me had I anything to say.

"I have," I said. "I was framed. It was a put-up job. The girl rang me and said she had vital information concerning her sister, but she wouldn't give it to me over the phone. So I went over to see her. When I got inside the apartment she stalled until she heard the others outside the door. Then she started screaming, scratched me and started ripping off her clothing."

The Commissioner looked bored. "Why would she do that, Wheeler?"

"Because Kirch got at her," I shouted. "That's why. He and that personal secretary of his, Walker. They're behind it. They had something to do with the girl disappearing. They didn't like me getting so close to them. They organized the whole thing—had me framed by the sister."

Lavers shook his head sorrowfully. "That is absurd," he said. "And you know it, Wheeler."

"Pure fantasy," the D.A. said coldly. "The man should see a psychiatrist."

"I was framed, I tell you," I said passionately.

Lavers scowled at me. "Be quiet, Wheeler. There is no room for any doubt in my mind as to what happened in the girl's apartment. There is no reason to doubt that she is telling the truth and it is substantiated by officers of the caliber of Captain Bligh and Lieutenant Ray. The charge has been proved."

He shook his head as he looked at me. "The girl won't press charges. She's frightened of the publicity and I can't say I blame her. In view of your previous excellent record, Wheeler, and also bearing in mind that this sort of sordid story, should it be made public, will do us tremendous damage, I don't intend that the Police Department should proceed with a criminal charge. You are instantly dismissed from the Police Department and you forfeit all rights to superannuation and any other benefits that may have accrued to you. I can only offer you one word of advice, and that is get out of Pine City and stay out. We don't want you here. And if you even so much as dare to speak to that girl again, your life won't be worth living."

He turned his back on me. "Now get out of here, Wheeler. I'd like to get some fresh air into my office."

"All right," I said. "I'll go. But I know who fixed this frame for me. Kirch. And I'll get him if it's the last thing I ever do. You tell him that."

I walked out of the office and slammed the door behind me. I went out of City Hall, down the steps, and was just going to get into the Healey when somebody tapped my shoulder. I turned around and saw Bligh standing there, looking at me.

"The Commissioner said to collect your shield," he said. "You don't own it anymore."

I shrugged my shoulders and took the shield out of my pocket and gave it to him. He gave me an envelope.

"He said to give you this. It's your paycheck, up to date." Then he turned around and walked up the steps again.

I put the envelope into my pocket and drove home. I poured myself a drink because I thought if ever a guy had an excuse for a drink, it was me that morning. Then I opened the envelope. It contained the paycheck all right, and a note from Lavers.

The note said to watch my step and congratulated me on a good performance. Well, it wasn't every day a guy got tossed out of the Police Department—it was my big chance to ham it up and I'd made the most of it. Just so long as I hadn't overdone it.

I spent the afternoon listening to some discs, and then came early evening. I showered, shaved and changed into the new suit I hadn't paid for yet. I took the Healey and drove into town. I had a meal in a restaurant and then drove out to Cone Hill.

This house didn't have high walls and it didn't look like a castle. It was a small place for the district, around thirty squares. I left the car on the driveway and rang the buzzer.

Greta Basiloff answered the door to me. She was wearing a white jersey sweater off both shoulders, and a pair of black velveteen matador pants that fitted her without a wrinkle.

"Lieutenant Wheeler," she said. "This is a pleasant surprise."

"I hoped it would be," I said.

"Come on in," she said. "I was wondering what I would do tonight. I get bored living by myself."

"I know how you feel," I said. "You have a choice—cultivate friends or a hi-fi setup."

"Which do you recommend?"

"The hi-fi. You can turn it off whenever you want."

I followed her into the living room. It was strictly modern, with abstract chairs and free-form things made of wire which I presumed were for decoration. The only old-fashioned touch was the Picasso on one wall and the Salvador Dalí on the other facing it.

"What will you drink, Lieutenant?"

"Scotch," I said. "On the rocks."

She pressed a concealed button and a section of the wall revolved around, revealing a well-stocked bar. She disappeared for a few moments and came back with a bowl of ice cubes. She mixed the drinks, then brought them with her.

"Let's sit on the divan," she said. "It's more functional than it looks."

So we sat on the divan and I had to admit it was comfortable, just so long as it didn't change its shape when I wasn't looking.

"Let's drink to our meeting, Lieutenant," she said, and raised her glass.

So we drank. I'll drink to anything just so long as it's Scotch.

"How is the case progressing?" she asked. "Have you found any trace of Lili yet?"

"Not exactly," I said.

"What about Mr. Walker? Did he know anything?"

"I don't know," I said. "Life has moved swiftly since I last saw you. I am no longer Lieutenant Wheeler, just plain Al Wheeler on the skids and going down fast."

"You're joking."

"I wish I was."

I told her briefly about my visit to Kirch's house, and then how Lois Hertz had framed me and how I had been tossed out of the Police Department that morning.

"That's terrible," she said when I'd finished. "Can't you do something about it?"

"I'm working on it," I said. "Kirch had me framed for sure. So either he's got a guilty conscience or his secretary has."

"But Lois doing a thing like that," she said. "I can't believe it."

"I think she had good reason," I said. "I think they told her that her sister was safe, but something unpleasant would happen to her if Lois didn't co-operate."

She shook her head wonderingly. "I still can't believe it."

"You don't have to," I told her. "You could believe what the Commissioner and the rest of the Police Department believe."

"No." She shook her head. "I flatter myself I know people. I won't believe I could be wrong in judging a person."

I finished my drink. "Well, there it is—the sad story of my life."

"Would you like to help yourself to another drink?" she said.

"I would like that very much," I told her, and did it.

When I got back to the divan, she looked up at me. "Why did you call on me tonight?"

"You invited me," I said.

"But after what happened last night and this morning, I would have thought that you'd be too bitter to think of making any social calls."

"I would have," I said, "if you had a face like a mud fence and non-vital statistics."

"Thank you." Her mouth curved upward at the corners. "I'm flattered. I can't call you Lieutenant anymore, can I?"

"Al will do."

"Short for what?"

"Never you mind," I said hastily. "Just Al."

"You had better call me Greta."

"So now we're cozy."

"Light me a cigarette, Al."

I lit two cigarettes and gave her one.

"How are you going to get back at Kirch?" she asked.

"I don't know," I said. "I'm only just simmering down enough to think coherently about it."

"Any theories?"

"One," I said. "The way Kirch and Walker have reacted, they have something to hide. They know about the girl—they know what happened to her. If they could blackmail Lois Hertz into pulling that act last night, then they must have proved to her that her sister was still alive and well."

She nodded. "That sounds like sense."

"If that's so," I said. "Where would Lili Hertz be? Answer—inside that house of Kirch's."

"Also sounds like sense."

"Course of action—get inside the house and find girl."

"You're doing wonderfully." She clapped her hands together enthusiastically.

"How to get inside the house?" I went on. "I don't have the faintest clue."

She stopped clapping. "There must be a way, Al. Think."

"I don't know the answer to that one," I said. "I'm poison as far as they're concerned. You can't get over the walls—I'll bet they are wired with alarms if not high voltage—and they have armed guards on the gate. If they caught me and shot me trying to break into the place, the Commissioner would probably give them a medal."

"There must be a way," she said.

"Maybe if I disguised myself as an attractive blonde, they'd kidnap me."

She looked at me moodily. "We need another drink."

"Your turn to get it," I said.

"But it's such a walk across to the bar."

"Who's the hostess around here—you or me?"

"All right," she said. "I'll make you a deal. You get the drinks and you get to kiss me as a reward. How about that?"

"It's a deal," I said, and put my arms around her.

She pushed them away. "The drinks first, Al. I don't trust you to keep your part of the bargain."

"OK." I got the two fastest poured drinks this side of the Boston Tea Party and was back on the divan with them in about ten seconds flat.

"You are an eager beaver," she said.

"Consider it a compliment," I said, and put the drinks down carefully. Then I took her into my arms and kissed her. This was a business in which I considered myself a professional. I was wrong—I was strictly an amateur. Greta Basiloff was the professional.

Some ten minutes later I picked up the drinks and handed her one. "I thought I had experience," I said humbly. "I can see I haven't lived."

"You'll get by in a crowd," she said patronisingly. "I think it's something to do with the Russian blood in me, and how I spent my childhood in a hot climate. I matured early."

"That I'll go along with," I said.

She leaned back and stared at her glass reflectively. "There must be a way into that house, Al."

"Sure—through the front door. The trick is to get yourself invited."

She sat up very straight suddenly. "I've got it."

"What?"

"The way into the house."

"How?"

Her eyes sparkled like some of her diamonds. "Walker buys for Kirch, of course. And quite a lot of the stuff he buys, he takes out on approval for Kirch to see. I could ring him and tell him I've got something very special, but I can't let it out of my sight because the seller insists on that. I'll suggest to him that I bring it over and let him see it."

"He'll fall for that?"

"If the bauble is special enough. You can always stampede a diamond buyer by telling him someone else is after it. Let me think." She tapped her chin with the rim of her glass. "I know. The Emerson necklace."

"What's that?"

Greta looked at me, horrified. "You've never heard of it? It's famous. My father bought it twenty-five years ago and he paid fifty thousand dollars for it then. His will said it was never to leave the family."

"You mean you've got it right here?"

"Of course I have—in the safe."

"Aren't you taking an awful chance?"

She shook her head. "My safe is a very special one. No one could follow the combination and as soon as anybody tampers with it, it sets off alarms all over the city in different places—the police, the insurance office, a firm of private detectives. I'll go get it."

She got up from the divan and walked out of the room. I helped myself to another drink and then lit a cigarette. I had smoked it halfway down when she came back, carrying a thin jewel case. She sat down and handed me the case. I opened it and was nearly blinded.

The necklace had three diamonds, each in its own setting. Two of them were the size of my thumbnail and the third was half as large again.

I gaped at it for a while. "It must be priceless," I said.

"It is," she agreed casually. "Particularly to a collector."

"Will they believe you when you say you want to sell it?"

"Of course they will. A collector will believe anything that gives him a chance to lay his hands on something like the Emerson necklace."

"Well, that's fine," I said. "That gets you into the house—but how about me?"

"That's easy," she told me. "You ride in the boot of my car. I leave the car outside the house and once I'm inside, you can get out and then you're on your own."

"That sounds OK," I said. "But I don't go much on the idea of being locked in your boot. How do I get out?"

"I'll open it before I go inside the house," she said.

"I'll try anything once," I said.

She glanced at the clock on the wall, which consisted of two delicate hands of crystal. "It's not late now," she said. "I'll ring them right away."

She moved over to the phone, picked it up and then dialed a number. "Mr. Walker, please," she said briskly. "This is Madame Basiloff and please tell him it's urgent."

She winked at me solemnly as she waited. "Mr. Walker?" she said. "This is Madame Basiloff. I'm sorry to call you at this hour, but something has come up and I thought you'd be interested to know the Emerson neck-lace—Yes, I said the Emerson necklace. Without going into details, Mr. Walker, I have an urgent need for money, a great deal of money. So I'm go-ing to sell the necklace—there's no point in being sentimental about it. Di-amonds in a safe are of no use to me. Yes, I said I was going to sell it, and of course I thought of you first. You know I could sell it a hundred times with no difficulty. Yes, I have it here. I was going to suggest that I might drive over with it right away, then Kirch could see it and perhaps make an offer if he's interested? No, I'll be quite safe. No one would dream I'd be carrying that around with me. Yes, all right, Mr. Walker. I'll be there in half an hour."

She put the phone down and grinned at me. "You see? No trouble at all. I could hear him drooling down the phone."

"You aren't really going to sell?"

"Of course not," she said. "I shall refuse his offer finally but tonight I shall tell him I need twenty-four hours to think it over."

"Greta," I said, "you're great."

"For that," she curtsied, "you may kiss me again."

That took up another ten minutes of our time. Then she put on a short jacket and tucked the jewel case into the pocket.

"We'd better start, Al," she said softly. "Or we never will."

"I guess you're right," I agreed reluctantly. "Why does crime have to interfere with romance?"

"All romance and no crime would be a bore," she said.

I stared at her, open-mouthed. "Are you kidding?"

CHAPTER 6

Greta stopped the car—Cadillac, this year's model, of course—about a quarter of a mile away from the Big House. I got out and into the boot. The boot of a Cadillac is built with generous proportions—I could have piled in three other guys and played poker without being cramped. Greta slammed it shut.

The Caddy started again and then stopped after a short while. I could vaguely hear voices—a man's voice and Greta's husky contralto answering him—then the car went forward again.

It stopped and I guessed it must be outside the house. I heard the door slam and then her footsteps along the side of the car. There was a click and the boot lid sprung open an inch.

"All right?" she whispered.

"Fine," I said.

"Good luck, Al," she whispered. "I'd better start up the steps in case somebody's watching from the house."

"Sure," I said.

The sound of her footsteps receded and I heard her high heels clicking against the marble. I had my ear to the gap the boot lid had left when she sprang it. I heard the sound of the butler's voice faintly and then the sound of the door shutting again.

I counted up to thirty slowly, then got my fingers underneath the boot lid and pushed. It sprang up the full way smoothly and left me feeling more naked than Lady Godiva when the breeze sent her hair streaming out behind.

I climbed out of the boot and crouched down behind the car. I couldn't hear anything. I straightened up a little and eased the boot lid down until it shut with a click. Then I had a cautious look around. Nobody shouted. That was something—if they had I would have died of heart failure right there.

I scuttled across from the back of the car to a large shrub that grew in front of the house beside the front steps. I reached it and crouched down behind that. Then I flitted from shrub to shrub until I got around the corner of the house and down the side.

It took me five minutes to reach the back of the house. I wasn't kidding when I said it was a castle. I went past windows which all had one thing in common—bars on the outside. I came around the last corner, which led to the back of the house, and froze. There was a guard walking up and down and fortunately he had his back to me and was walking in the opposite direction.

I hit the ground behind another shrub and waited. He walked down to the far corner, then turned around and started on his way back.

I moved around slowly until I had the shrub between him and me when he came past—I hoped. I heard his footsteps coming closer and closer and then he went past the shrub. Four paces past and stopped.

My nerves twanged like a guitar being played by Les Paul. Then they eased down gradually when I saw him take a pack of cigarettes out of his pocket. He stuck a cigarette into his mouth and then fumbled for a match. Now was the time.

I got to my feet and jumped him, swinging my arm over my head, down in a rabbit punch that jarred my whole body when it connected. He collapsed onto the ground and just lay there. I knelt down beside him. He was still breathing and I hoped I hadn't broken his neck.

I went through his pockets and found a bunch of keys which I stuck into my own pocket. I lifted his gun out of its holster and then I had a better idea. I stripped off his uniform and hoped he didn't catch cold in his union suit. Then I took off my own suit and put on the uniform. I buckled the gunbelt around my waist and put the gun into the holster. I put on the cap and jammed it well down on my head so that the peak came low over my eyes. Then I was left with the problem of what to do with him.

I wished I knew how to do the Indian rope trick, because if I did I would probably always carry a rope around with me to surprise people whenever the party got dull. But I didn't. I had to settle for my suit instead of a rope.

I pulled his arms around behind his back and tied them at the elbows with the jacket. I tied his ankles with the pants, then pulled them right behind him and tied the pants to the jacket. I used my pocket handkerchief to gag him, then dragged him behind the shrub and left him there.

I walked down slowly along the length of the rear of the house, reached the corner and turned back again. There was a door I'd noticed on my way down which was half open and there was a light in the room behind.

I went past it for the second time and was maybe five yards past it when a voice called out, "Hey, Johnny."

I nearly jumped out of the uniform. "Yeah?" I growled, without turning around.

"I've left some coffee on the stove for you." The voice was feminine and unglamorous. The cook, I guessed. "You can have it anytime you want. I'm going to bed now."

"OK," I growled, and kept on walking.

I reached the shrub and had a look. The guard in the union suit and my new suit was still sleeping peacefully and still breathing. Maybe a rest would do him good.

I turned and walked back. I walked up to the door. I pushed it open a little further and took a cautious look inside. The room was unoccupied. It was the kitchen, about twice the size of my whole house. Sure enough, on top of the vast stove stood a lone percolator, bubbling happily.

I walked quickly across the kitchen to the door at the other side, opened it gently and looked out. It led into a hallway which was empty. I stepped out into the hallway and wondered which way I should go next. I thought I'd go left because nothing I did lately had turned out right. I followed the hallway for what seemed like half a mile and then came to a door at the end of it. I tried the handle gently and found it was locked. I took the bunch of keys out of the jacket and tried them one by one. The fifth one turned the lock. I pushed the door open and stepped inside.

It was a small room—you could have called it a cell more accurately. There was one high window with bars on the inside. There was a carpet on the floor, a bed to one side and a dressing table. Sitting on the bed was a hollow-eyed brunette in a pair of silk pyjamas.

She glowered at me. "What the hell do you want?"

"Wrong room," I said. "Where's the blonde—Lili?"

"How the hell would I know?" she said. "If I stay locked up in here much longer, I'll go crazy."

"I'm sorry," I said. "I'm new around here."

"Then you'd better get out of here," she said. "Absolem takes a dim view of anybody else roaming around his preserves."

"I don't get it," I said.

She shrugged her shoulders impatiently. "Look, he's mad with me because I swore at him, so he put me in here for twenty-four hours to cool off."

"You mean, he's got you a prisoner in the house?"

She laughed with a brittle sound. "I don't complain, soldier. I like it here— lot easier than making a living. He had a right to get mad at me—he'll cool off."

"Yeah," I said feebly. "I was told to get the blonde one—Lili. I must have got the rooms crossed up."

"You want to try downstairs," she said. "Go back to the end of this hall and down the stairs there. Probably in one of those rooms."

"Thanks," I said. "Sorry I disturbed you."

"That's OK," she told me. "Just don't let Absolem catch you making a mistake about rooms—he just won't believe it."

"Sure," I said.

I stepped outside and locked the door again. I went down the hall to the other end. The brunette had been right about the stairway, anyway. I went down it quickly and found myself in another hallway, but this one was smaller. There were three doors leading off. I was beginning to feel like Alice in Wonderland. Anytime now a bar of chocolate would nudge up against my leg and say, "Eat me."

I stopped at the first door and tried my keys. The second one opened it. The room was empty. I tried the second and that was empty and I crossed my fingers as I tried the third. The last key on the chain opened it and I hoped that was significant.

The room was occupied. By a blonde. For one awful moment I thought I had opened a time-door instead of an ordinary door.

Looking blandly at me was Cleopatra. There couldn't be any mistake.

She wore a two-piece outfit which glittered and sparkled in the light. It seemed to be covered with glittering stones. On her wrists and ankles were slave bangles which looked like gold to me. And on her head was a soft diamond tiara that blinded you just to look at it.

"What do you want?" she asked me.

I blinked and took another look at her. She would be around five feet five inches and would weigh somewhere close to one hundred and twenty. She was blonde and had a fair complexion. I took a couple of steps closer and saw the faint scar on the inside of her knee.

"Don't you dare touch me," she said in a high-pitched voice.

"Take it easy," I croaked. "You're Lili Hertz?"

"What of it?"

"I'm Al Wheeler," I said. "Lieutenant Wheeler." I didn't think then was the time to tell her I was ex-Lieutenant Wheeler.

"You've come to take me out of here?" she asked breathlessly. "Help me escape?"

"That's the general idea," I agreed. "Only it's not going to be easy and we'll have to hurry."

"All right," she said.

She followed me down the hall to the stairway. We went up the stairs into the hall above and then along to the kitchen, and met no one on the way.

The kitchen was deserted. The percolator was still bubbling but it had a slightly depressed sound—maybe it was beginning to feel unwanted.

The guard behind the shrub was squirming violently as we went past. I thought maybe I'd left him on top of an ants' nest, but I couldn't stop to find out.

We came eventually to the front of the house and everything looked just the same. I saw Greta's Cadillac standing there and offered a short prayer that she'd left the keys in it. I told Lili to wait behind the shrub I'd first taken cover behind, and I dived across to the car. The keys were there. I beckoned frantically and Lili ran across and got into the car.

I took the gun out of the holster and put it in my lap, then started the motor. I swung the car in a screaming U-turn and headed fast down the driveway toward the gates.

I jammed on the brakes at the last moment and the bonnet dipped and stopped a few feet from the gates. A guard sauntered out from beside the gates.

"Won't keep you a minute, Madame Basiloff," he said. "I have to get a clearance from the house before I ..."

Then he realized it wasn't Madame Basiloff. By that time I was out of the car and had the gun rammed into his ribs.

"Open the gates, buster," I told him. "Or I'll blow a hole clean through you."

He gurgled something and got a key out of his pocket and opened the gates. I reversed the gun in my hand and brought the butt down on top of his skull, then dragged him into the grass at the side of the driveway and left him there.

Lili Hertz was shivering when I got back into the car.

"Why did you come on your own?" she asked. "Why didn't you bring a lot of policemen with you?"

"It's a long story, honey," I said as I swung the Cadillac out onto the road and headed toward home. "But briefly, I was the only policeman who believed you were inside that place."

Twenty minutes later we stopped outside my house and I took her inside. I gave her a topcoat of mine to put on to keep her warm, and I mixed a drink to keep us both warm. I stripped off the guard's uniform and put on a pair of slacks and a sweater, and began to feel more like myself.

Then I went back into the living room. She was sitting in an armchair, sipping her drink.

"I'd like to go home," she said. "I want to let my sister know I'm all right."

"Sure," I said. "But I want you to speak to somebody first. I'll ring them now and have them come over—it won't take long."

"Well, please hurry, Lieutenant," she said.

I thumbed through the phone directory and finally found the number listed, then dialed it. After it had rung for a while, a courteous voice answered.

"Judge Bryan?" I asked.

"Yes," he said. "Who is that?"

"My name is Al Wheeler," I said. "Formerly a lieutenant of police, Judge. You may have heard of me?"

"Perhaps I have," he said. "What do you want, Wheeler?"

"I'd like you to come over to my house right away, Judge," I said. "I just got back from Kirch's house on Cone Hill. I brought one of his guests with me—a girl by the name of Lili Hertz."

I heard his sharp intake of breath. "She was being held a prisoner there?"

"She surely was," I agreed. "I'd like you to talk to her first, Judge, before anybody else does."

"I'll come straight away," he said. "Where is your house?"

I told him the address and then he hung up.

I put the phone back on the cradle and walked over to where I'd left my drink.

"Will he be very long?" the blonde asked.

"He's coming over right away," I said. "Once you've talked to him, you can go and see your sister."

"She must be half crazy with worry over what happened to me," she said.

"What happened that Saturday night after you left the drugstore and started for home?" I asked.

She shivered. "I had only gone about a hundred yards when a car pulled in at the curb beside me. The door opened and a couple of men got out. They grabbed me and hustled me into the rear—one of them had his hand over my mouth so I couldn't cry out. They took me back to that place and put me in a room. I was left alone for about half an hour, then Mr. Walker came in. I demanded that he let me go and he just smiled at me. He told me I was a lucky girl because Mr. Kirch was interested in me, and if I stayed at the house for a while he would pay me a lot of money.

"I told him he was crazy and if he didn't let me go straight away I would go straight to the police when I got out of the house. And he just laughed at that and said I'd never leave the house, unless Mr. Kirch wanted me to go. Then he went away and after a while a woman came in."

She shuddered. "A horrible woman, dressed in black. She brought in this outfit I'm wearing now. She told me to get dressed in it and then Mr. Kirch would see me. I told her I wouldn't and she threatened me. I still refused and she grabbed hold of me. She was terribly strong. She beat me and then forced me to get out of my own clothes and into this crazy outfit."

I took the empty glass out of her hand and refilled it for her. The phone rang suddenly. I debated whether to answer it and finally decided I would.

"Al?" a husky voice said, with a hint of laughter in it. "When can I have my car back?"

"Greta."

"You caused a riot when they found out what had happened. They couldn't get rid of me quickly enough—one of their men drove me home. Did you have any success?"

"A hundred percent."

"That's wonderful. Is she all right? Lili, I mean?"

"She's OK."

"I'm thrilled to hear it. You must be busy, so I won't waste your time anymore. Call me when you have a minute, Al. And don't worry about my car—I can always use your midget you left here." Then she hung up.

I went back to Lili Hertz. "What then?" I asked.

"After that it was a nightmare," she said. "That man Kirch is crazy. He thinks he's an Egyptian king or a Roman Emperor or something. He's got about four girls in that house—the others are there of their own free will, I think. I don't know if any of them were kidnapped first and then decided to make the best of it or what. I couldn't believe it could happen now. That sort of thing belongs in fairy tales."

"But not the sort kids read," I said. "I think we'll soon have Mr. Kirch where we want him."

I heard a car stop outside and footsteps hurrying up the path to the front door. A moment later the buzzer went.

"That will be Judge Bryan," I said. "I'll go let him in."

I went out into the hallway and along to the front door. I opened it and the sky fell in on my head.

CHAPTER 7

It sounded like a bookmakers' convention. A babble of voices all talking at once. I opened my eyes and winced as the light hit them. A gnawing pain spread around the back of my head, found it liked the territory and pitched camp for the night.

I closed my eyes for a long moment, then opened them again cautiously. This time it wasn't quite so bad. I sat up slowly and saw the place was full of cops.

Bligh was standing there looking down at me. "What did you do, Wheeler?" he asked. "Hit your head on something?"

"Something somebody had in their hand," I grunted. I levered myself onto my feet, grabbing the edge of a chair to help me up.

"You'd better come into the living room," he said.

"Sure," I nodded. I followed him unsteadily along the hall and into the living room. The other cops just stared at me without saying anything.

The living room looked much the same as when I had left it. Lili Hertz was sprawled out in the armchair and for a moment I thought she was sleeping. Then I took a closer look and saw that the bodice of the Cleopatra outfit was stained red. Her eyes were staring wide and her mouth was open as if she'd been going to scream.

"Who did it?" I asked thickly.

"Wheeler," Bligh said in a tired voice. "You aren't going to plead amnesia, are you?"

I stared at him. "What the hell are you talking about?"

He looked at Bannister. "Show him, Sergeant," he said curtly.

Sergeant Bannister carefully unwrapped a table napkin which I recognized as one of the set I keep for when I play formal dinners—which is maybe once a year. Inside the napkin was a gun.

"Ever seen that gun before?" Bligh asked me.

"Sure," I said. "It's the gun I took from one of the guards at Kirch's place."

"Always got an answer," he sighed. "OK, Sergeant." Bannister wrapped up the gun again carefully.

"What is this?" I asked.

"It's your gun," Bligh said. "It's the murder weapon—the one that killed her. My bet is that it will have your fingerprints on it—the lab will find that out soon enough."

He shook his head slowly. "You had her here all the time."

"Are you crazy?" I said. "I rescued her from Kirch's place tonight."

"Don't keep talking about Kirch," he said impatiently. "Tell us the truth for a change, Wheeler. I think you're going to get away with an insanity plea, dressing her up like that. And you had that blue uniform to wear as well, eh?"

He shook his head again. "Crazy like a fox. Trying to pin it on Kirch of all people. Then trying to take her sister. Wasn't one girl enough for you, Wheeler?"

"Look," I said. "I ..."

And then I stopped suddenly.

"Go on," he said. "Tell us the truth."

"I shot her," I said. "Then I hit myself on the back of the head to make sure I'd lay myself out long enough for the cops to get here. Is that what you want me to say?"

"You slipped in the hallway and banged your head," he said indifferently. "People do that all the time."

"How did you get here?" I asked him.

"Tip-off on the phone," he said.

"Who from?"

"They didn't say any name. Too scared, I guess. Maybe one of your neighbors got curious and peeked through a window."

"And maybe the real murderer tipped you off after slugging me, to make sure you got here before I recovered," I snarled.

"Save it for your lawyer, Wheeler," Bligh said tightly. "I'm booking you on a first-degree homicide. The sister's testimony on its own is enough to send you to the gas chamber."

"But ..." I started.

"Take him out to the car," Bligh said impatiently. "Let's get back to the Precinct and get him into a cell and out of my sight."

"The Precinct," I said. "Isn't this one for Homicide? How come you're handling it?"

"Commissioner's orders," he said curtly. "Let's move, men."

They moved. Half an hour later I was locked in a cell inside the Precinct. I sat down on the bunk and lit myself a cigarette. I wondered as I sat there—wondered a hell of a lot of things.

I wondered who had slugged me and then murdered Lili Hertz. I wondered what had happened to Judge Bryan. I wondered if I cited Greta Basiloff as an alibi, whether she'd tell the truth or be too scared and deny it.

I got tired of sitting down, so I got onto my feet and paced up and down the cell. I found a cigarette and lit it. I smoked it down and then another after it. Then I heard somebody coming.

A few seconds later the door of the cell was unlocked and Commissioner Lavers came in. Then the overweight cop outside locked the door again carefully and moved away.

Lavers looked at me. "Not so good, Al?" he said softly.

"Not so good," I agreed.

"What happened?"

I told him the story. He nodded when I'd finished.

"It makes it hard," he said.

"That's a sentiment I agree with," I said. "What the hell goes on with Bligh? I thought he was in on this."

"I'm sorry if I gave you that impression," Lavers said blandly.

I stared at him. "What. You mean he doesn't know?"

"No," he said. "I can't afford to trust anyone while this thing is going on. I only told you he was in on it so you wouldn't blow your top with him while you were working from the Precinct. I had to—you caught me out coming into my office, Al. I was a little bit flustered—I wanted to put it to you the best way I could."

"That's fine," I said. "So Bligh genuinely believes that I'm a homicidal maniac, and a sexual maniac as well."

"It doesn't much matter what he believes," Lavers said shortly. "The problem is, what happens to you now?"

"You don't have to worry about that," I said bitterly. "It's all arranged. I'm going to the gas chamber. Bligh has everything organized."

"Let us try and be reasonable," he said wearily.

"Sure," I said. "Why should I worry? I'm only facing a first-degree homicide rap, after all. And like Bligh said, the testimony of the other Hertz girl is enough to convict me on its own. I don't have a care in the world. I like this cell—it's comfortable."

He shook his head. "Stop it, Al. It doesn't get either of us anyplace. Try and think constructively."

"OK," I said. "What happened to Judge Bryan?"

"Judge Bryan?" he said quickly. "What about him?"

"As soon as I got the girl back into my house I rang him," I said. "I told him what had happened and he said he'd be right over. When the door buzzer went I thought it was him."

"I don't know," Lavers said heavily. "Maybe he arrived after Bligh and his men got there, and saw what was happening and left. He couldn't afford to reveal his hand at this stage."

"Why don't you call him and find out what happened?"

"I can't," he said bluntly. "Not without any proof. You had the proof, but now she's dead."

"That's fine," I said. "And it still leaves me with that homicide rap."

Lavers took out his pipe and started to fill it. "We'll have to think of something," he said.

"Like what?" I asked bitterly.

"I know I got you into this mess," he said. "But they've been damned clever about this, Wheeler. They've picked up so much damning evidence against you that ..."

"I can see those pellets dropping into the tank right now," I said, "and the gas vapors rising. If all you can do is stand here and write my obituary, I'd as soon you got the hell out of it. I can write my own obituary."

"Now, Al," he said placatingly. "Take it easy."

"You say that just once more," I threatened him, "and I shall scream right in your ear."

Heavy footsteps sounded down the corridor outside and then Captain Bligh came into view.

"What the hell does he want?" I snarled. "To order another flogging for Mr. Christian."

The overweight cop led Bligh into the cell and he stood there looking at us, an almost embarrassed expression on his face.

"Well?" Lavers said irritably. "What is it?"

"Something I thought you should know, sir," Captain Bligh said awkwardly. "Do you mind if I ask Wheeler a question first before I tell you?"

"No," Lavers said. "But hurry up."

Bligh looked at me. "Do you own any gloves?"

"Gloves?" I stared at him. Maybe he was losing his mind as well. It was a consolation to know I wasn't the only one going crazy.

"No," I said. "I don't wear gloves—I don't like them. If I want something to keep my hands warm, I'll ..."

"Your reputation is well known, Wheeler," Lavers said, his lips twitching into a grin. He looked at Bligh. "Tell me more, Mr. Holmes," he said. "Is this a parallel to the case of the dog that didn't bark?"

Bligh reddened. "It's the gun, sir. The murder weapon."

Lavers winced. "Stop talking like one of Kirch's tabloids. Gun is a good enough word."

"Yes, sir," Bligh said unhappily. "The gun. It didn't show any fingerprints at all. Obviously, whoever used it wore gloves. If Wheeler wore gloves, they disappeared between the time he shot the girl and the time he slipped and hit his head. And that must have been within seconds of his shooting her, if it happened that way."

"So?" Lavers said, his face brightening. "Go on."

"There's another thing, sir," Bligh said. "The license for the gun. It's registered in the name of John Lawson. And Lawson is employed by Absolem Kirch as watchman on his estate."

Lavers let out his breath slowly. "Well," he said. "Well, well, well. And what do you deduce from these new facts, Captain?"

He flushed but held his ground. "That Wheeler's story doesn't sound quite so fantastic as I first thought, sir. If he didn't fire the gun, he didn't murder the girl—and that presumes someone else did. And if someone else did, then it becomes logical to assume that Wheeler was hit on the head by that person and didn't knock himself out in a fall. And as the gun belongs to this man Lawson, who is employed by Absolem Kirch, his story about rescuing the girl from Kirch's house seems to be substantiated to a degree."

"Captain Bligh," I said emotionally. "I'll sail the Seven Seas with you anytime you ask. And never another mutiny."

"The kids I went to school with used to say that," he said, a pained expression on his face. "They thought it was original, too."

Lavers lit his pipe and puffed contentedly.

"Sir?" Bligh looked at him. "In the light of these findings, I feel we should investigate further into Kirch's estate."

"What about Wheeler?" Lavers asked.

"I don't see we can hold him, sir. The homicide charge hasn't formally been made, so it doesn't exist in any case."

"I think you're quite right about releasing Wheeler," Lavers said. "But don't do anything about Kirch yet. You know how much political power the man wields. We shall have to proceed carefully."

A look of distaste appeared on Bligh's face for a moment, then vanished again. "Yes, sir," he said tonelessly, then beckoned for the cop to unlock the cell door.

Lavers looked at me and grinned. "Poor Bligh. He's worrying now—he thinks he might have a dishonest Commissioner who is frightened to death of Kirch."

"The hell with poor Bligh," I said. "He's taken five years off my life in the last forty-eight hours. Just let me out of this cell."

"A pleasure," Lavers said. "Then there's something you should do right away."

"I know," I said.

"Good," he said. "Get over to Judge Bryan's place and tell him the whole story—only leave me out of it at this juncture."

"I was thinking of doing something else first," I said. "But I'll go and see the Judge before the night's out."

A prowl car ran me home. It was just on midnight when I got there. I had a drink to see me through the small dark hours and then l put a jacket on over the sweater I was still wearing and went out again. Greta's Cadillac was still parked at the curb and I thought she wouldn't mind me using it. She had my Healey, didn't she?

I drove over to Calton and got there a little before twelve-thirty. I left the car outside the apartment house and went up to number four. I pressed the buzzer half a dozen times, then waited.

Eventually the door opened a couple of inches. "Who's that?" Lois Hertz asked.

"Al Wheeler," I said. I saw she had the door on the chain.

"What do you want?"

"Just to talk to you, Lois."

"I've got nothing to say to you. Go away. I'll call the police again."

"Take it easy, honey," I said. "I know you were put up to the assault story. They told you if you didn't do it, your sister would be hurt. I've got news of your sister."

"You have?" she said in a low voice.

The chain scraped as she undid it, then opened the door wide. I followed her into the apartment. She turned around to face me, her eyes eager.

"What about Lili? Where is she?"

"Sit down, Lois," I said. "This is bad news, I'm afraid."

"Bad news?" Her eyes widened. "Is she hurt? Where is she? I want to see her now. You must take me to her—you must."

"Take it easy," I said gently. "It's too late, Lois. She's dead."

"Dead," she said numbly.

She sank slowly into the chair and looked at me. "Dead? She can't be. I don't believe it. It's some sort of a trick."

"No trick," I said. "She's dead. She was murdered tonight—a couple of hours ago."

Tears started to trickle down her face. "Lili," she whispered. "Poor Lili."

"Will I tell you how it happened?" I asked her.

"Yes," she nodded. "Yes, tell me."

So I told her the story of how I'd gone to Kirch's house and found Lili, then taken her back to my place. And how someone had knocked me out and then shot her sister.

"They told you to frame me," I said. "They said she would be all right if you did as you were told. And all the time they were keeping her a prisoner in that house against her will. And tonight when they knew she would expose them, they killed her. They murdered her in cold blood, Lois."

She lifted her head slowly and I saw the naked hatred staring out of her eyes. "What can I do?" she said slowly. "What can I do to revenge my sister?"

"I'll tell you what you can do, Lois," I said. "It will be a risk. You'll risk your own life to do it."

"That doesn't matter," she said contemptuously. "Just tell me what I can do."

I took a deep breath. "There's a chance a Grand Jury will be called," I said, "to investigate Kirch and all his affairs. They're hesitating to call it because they don't have anything definite against him—no concrete evidence. If you were to agree to testify at that Grand Jury hearing, it would give them the definite evidence they need. The jury would be convened and you would be the prime mover in bringing about the downfall of Absolem Kirch."

"I'd like that," she said softly. "Nothing I can do will repay him for my sister's murder. But anything I could do to revenge her even just a little would be nice. Where is this Grand Jury?"

"I can take you to the man who will head it," I said. "If you tell him what they did to you, it will clear me of the assault charge. That means I'm a clean witness again and I can testify to rescuing Lili from the house and how she told me she had been kidnapped and forcibly taken there in the first place."

"What are we waiting for?" she said fiercely.

She got up from the chair and disappeared into the bedroom. I lit a cigarette and waited for her. She came back ten minutes later, fully dressed. She had put on fresh make-up and her eyes were dry.

"I'm ready," she said quietly.

I checked Judge Bryan's address in the phone directory before we left, then took her down to the Cadillac. On the way across town she didn't say a word. I didn't try and make conversation with her. I could only respect her grief and leave her with it.

I parked the Cadillac outside the Judge's house and helped Lois out. We walked up to the front door and I pushed the buzzer. I pushed it twice more before lights went on inside the house and I heard feet walking down the hallway toward the front door.

The door swung open and a tall, gray-headed man stood there. He looked at me keenly. "What is it?" he asked.

"Judge Bryan?"

"That's correct."

"My name is Al Wheeler."

"Oh," he said softly. "I was about to call on you earlier on, but I saw you had visitors so I came home."

"It's quite a story, Judge," I said. "I'd like to talk to you about it. The girl, Lili Hertz, was murdered at my house tonight. That was why I had the company you saw."

"Yes?" His voice was brittle.

"This is Miss Lois Hertz," I said. "Her sister."

"Miss Hertz," he bowed stiffly.

"She has a story which should interest you as well, Judge," I said. "A story she's prepared to tell anywhere on oath—even in front of a Grand Jury."

CHAPTER 8

Judge Bryan smashed his clenched fist into the open palm of his other hand. "This is what I've been waiting for," he said. "With Miss Hertz willing to testify, then I can get the Grand Jury convened. You know what you're doing, Miss Hertz?"

"I do," Lois said tonelessly. "They murdered my sister. The only thing I have to live for now is revenge."

"It will be dangerous for you," he said. "I shall have to quote you by name. They will know of it. They will do anything they can to stop you testifying against them."

"I guess Lieutenant Wheeler is in the same boat," she said. "He doesn't seem to be worried."

Bryan shook his head. "He isn't in the same boat. Until your sworn testimony clears him of the assault charge, he is valueless as a witness. Only your word can clear him and if they remove you before you can testify, then Wheeler's testimony will be useless."

She didn't seem impressed. "It makes no difference," she said. "I'll testify. I want to. You can understand that, can't you?"

"Yes," he said softly. "I can understand that."

"What happens now, Judge?" I asked.

"We'll have to spirit Miss Hertz away somewhere," he said. "Guard her until the Jury is ready to hear her testimony."

"The police ..." I started.

He shook his head violently. "No. I can't afford to have her where the District Attorney has access to her, or knows where she is. The police are useless at this juncture to protect her. We will have to hire men to do it. Guards twenty-four hours a day. We'll have to find an empty house somewhere—a lonely place where people don't go. And we'll have guards around it every minute of the day. I don't care how much it costs—if it costs a thousand dollars a day, it will be cheap at the price. That's nothing for the city to pay to have scoundrels like Kirch swept from positions of power and their corruption cleaned away."

Then he stopped suddenly and grinned at me. "I should have a soapbox, shouldn't I?"

"How long will it take you to find a house and hire the guards, Judge?" I asked.

"Twenty-four hours, perhaps less. I have to get the machinery moving to convene the Jury as well. I shall have to name names to get the Jury convened. As soon as I do that, the press will have the story and Miss Hertz's name will be a headline in the city. So we must have her tucked away safely before that happens."

"What about the rest of tonight?" I asked him.

"I suggest Miss Hertz stays here," he said. "My wife will look after her. And perhaps you would care to sleep on the sofa here tonight, Lieutenant? Just in case?"

"I would," I said.

It was organized in the next twenty minutes. Mrs. Bryan, a gray-haired woman with a kindly face, took care of Lois like a mother and spirited her away upstairs.

The Judge finally went back to bed and I took the sofa. I slept like a log and was about as good a bodyguard as a girdle is to a catcher.

Next morning the Judge left the house before eight and came back at twelve.

"I've got the place," he said. "A shack in the hills, owned by one of the City Fathers—Owen Wainright. It is miles off the beaten track and nobody ever comes near the place."

"That's fine, Judge," I said. "How about the guards?"

"They're hired," he said. "Four men to stay up there all the time. Two men on guard the whole time. I hired them from Samson Security Services and they're men who know their job. I don't think we'll have to worry about Miss Hertz's safety."

I lit myself a cigarette. "What about the Grand Jury?"

"I state my case this afternoon," he said. "At three o'clock. I want Miss Hertz out of here and on her way up to the shack at least by then."

"Supposing I drive her up there now?" I suggested.

"Excellent idea, Lieutenant. I'll have my wife make us a quick lunch before you go."

We had the quick lunch and left his house at one o'clock. Lois sat beside me without saying anything, then as we came near to Calton, she said, "Could I stop and pick up my clothes and a few things, Lieutenant? I might be up there for a while and I've only got the things I'm wearing at the moment."

"I guess so," I said.

"Thanks," she said, and settled back again. I thought about it as I drove.

"I think it might be better if you didn't go back to your apartment, Lois," I said. "They'll know by now that they didn't pin the murder rap on me. It won't take them long to realize the potential danger you are to them. I think we'll stop somewhere on the way and buy you the clothes you need for a couple of days, and when we get up to the cabin you can write out a list and I'll have Mrs. Bryan pick the things up for you."

"All right, Lieutenant," she said listlessly.

We stopped in a shopping suburb the other side of the city and she spent half an hour buying the stuff she urgently needed, and then we drove on. We reached the shack about four in the afternoon. Bryan's description of it had been an accurate one. It was miles away from anywhere. I nearly lost my way twice and I had been told how to get there.

The four men from Samson's were already there. A capable-looking bunch of men. Samson's only employed ex-servicemen or ex-cops. I thought I wouldn't have to worry about Lois so long as they were around. I said goodbye to her and that I would probably see her within the next few days, then turned the car around and drove back to the city.

Six o'clock when I got back within the city limits. I stopped outside the nearest drugstore and went in to the phone. I rang Lavers' direct line and he answered immediately.

"Al Wheeler," I said.

"You've done very nicely," he said. "Bryan stated his case this afternoon and the Grand Jury convenes a week from today."

"I just left Lois Hertz," I said. "She's in a safe place with four professional bodyguards looking after her. If it cost a thousand a day to make sure she's there to testify, the Judge said, it would be cheap at the price."

"I should have thought of her straight away," he said. "I'm glad you did. I need my head read."

"You've needed that for years, Commissioner," I said happily. "What do you want me to do now?"

"Nothing," he said. "Take things easy and stay out of the way until the Jury convenes. Remember, once that girl has testified, Al, yours is the testimony that is really going to start things humming."

"Yes, sir," I said. "When I'm reinstated in the department, can I have a brass band playing? There was a horrible silence all the time I was being kicked out."

"I'll consider it," he said generously. "And who said anything about reinstating you, anyway?" He guffawed loudly and hung up before I had a chance to reply.

I went back to the car and drove leisurely through the city. I stopped off for a meal and wondered what I should do with the rest of the evening, and then I had a happy thought. My Healey was probably pining its twin carburetors away for me and I was still driving Greta's car. I should return it. What better way to spend an evening?

I pointed the Cadillac in the direction of Cone Hill and pushed on the gas pedal. Some fifteen minutes later I swung the Cadillac into her driveway and parked it behind my Healey which didn't have any dents, I was glad to see.

I got out and walked up to the porch and pressed the buzzer.

I heard light footsteps hurrying along the hallway and I grinned.

"You're the most beautiful thing I've seen in forty-eight hours straight," I said as the door swung open.

"Who—me?" Basil asked nervously.

I looked him up and down. He was wearing a mauve dressing gown, with a scarlet silk scarf knotted around his neck. He looked like an impressionist's interpretation of dementia praecox.

"You," I said. "Where's Greta?"

"If you mean Madame Basiloff," he said coldly, "she is here. I shall tell her you're calling."

"Don't bother," I said. "I'll tell her myself."

"Oh, very well," he said. "I'm sure I don't care one way or the other." He turned his back on me and flounced off down the hallway.

"Basil, dear boy," I said. "Where did you get that old blanket from you're wearing? It's tatty."

He swung around and glared at me, his eyes bright with hate.

"You ..." he nearly choked himself. "You—you philistine."

Then he turned around again and practically ran down the hall and disappeared into a room at the other end.

"You're cruel," a husky voice said.

I looked and saw Greta standing in the doorway of the living room.

"I brought you back one car," I said. "More or less intact."

"I'm glad to hear it," she said. "I only drove that horrible little thing of yours once—it has a gearshift."

"The horrors of primitive automobiles," I said.

"And every time you touch the gas pedal it goes like crazy," she said. "Just as well it only has two gears."

"It has four," I said and closed my eyes.

"Well, I can only say I'm glad I never found the other two," she said. "Goodness knows what might have happened."

"I need a drink," I said faintly. "Lead me to it."

She turned around and walked back into the living room with me following her.

"I'll give you a drink," she said. "But you don't deserve it, leaving me in suspense all this time. There I was, risking life and limb, and a fate worse than death. And for what? For you, that's all. And you don't even bother to ring me and tell me what happened."

"Life has been hectic," I said. "I come to make amends."

She turned around and handed me a drink. "Anyway," she smiled. "It's good to see you, Al."

I really looked at her for the first time. She was wearing a halter bra which must have been the top half of a bikini in its normal use and another pair of velveteen matador pants, this time a burgundy colour.

"It's good to see you, Greta," I said. "I haven't seen quite so much of you in a while."

She grinned. "I hate clothes."

"I hate your clothes, too," I said.

"I think," she said cautiously, "you had better sit down quietly and have your drink, Al. There's a gleam in your eye that needs diluting."

So I sat down on the divan and so did she, but she took good care to sit the other end, leaving a gap between us.

"I read about poor Lili being murdered in the newspapers this morning," she said soberly. "It was horrible. How did it happen, Al?"

I told her how it happened and how I'd been almost indicted for Lili's murder, and then the lab evidence coupled with the ownership of the gun had cleared me.

"Where's Lois now?" she asked.

"She's safe," I said. "With four bodyguards looking after her in a shack up in the hills. There she'll stay until she testifies to the Grand Jury."

"And that means the end of Kirch?" she said. "I didn't know I could hate anybody so much until I read about poor Lili being murdered. I hope they send him to the gas chamber."

"Could be," I said. "When the pressure gets really tough, he'll find his hired help will talk so fast and so loud to clear themselves that he'll be left holding all the cans."

"Serves him right," she said.

I finished my drink and handed her my empty glass.

"You get them," she said.

"I'll make a deal," I said hopefully.

"I think I'll get the drinks," she said thoughtfully. "I don't feel you're diluted enough yet."

She walked over to the bar and refilled the glasses, and then brought them back.

"Thanks," I said. "Something I meant to ask you and I nearly forgot. What's Basil doing here? And in that screaming robe, too."

"Basil?" she said casually. "He lives here."

"He ... what?"

"He didn't have anywhere to live, so I let him have a couple of rooms at the back—this house is much too big for me, but I don't like apartments. Why?"

"A fine thing," I said coldly. "He lives here—just like that. I suppose he was here the other evening when I was here?"

"Of course."

I was so shocked I lowered my glass instead of raising it.

"You just sit there," I said indignantly, "and casually admit you've got a man living with you."

"Oh." She gurgled with laughter. "That's what you're worrying about. You don't have to worry, Al. To Basil, all women are mothers and remind him of his own. He just doesn't see them in any other way. I'm as safe living with Basil as I would be living with a maiden aunt."

I thought about that and what I knew of Basil. And it seemed logical.

"I suppose you're right," I said. "It just sort of came as a surprise when he opened the door, that's all."

"Don't let it worry you, Al," she said. "Just drink your drink and relax."

"I'll drink my drink, anyway," I said.

Which I did. I then had a brilliant idea.

"Why don't we go to my place?" I suggested. "You could hear my hi-fi setup, which I tell you in all modesty is colossal. Reproduction like you've never heard."

She thought about it. "I'll have to put on some clothes."

"I'll keep the hood up on the Healey," I said. "Just throw a scarf around your neck. Borrow Basil's if the going is tough."

"Well, all right," she said, without sounding enthusiastic. "But I thought we could stay here tonight."

"There's nothing like hi-fi," I said firmly. "Music to soothe the savage breast. Wings of song and ... what did you say?"

"I said I thought we could stay here."

"You said more than that. Something else at the end of that?"

"I said," Greta thought for a moment, "we could stay here tonight."

"I couldn't agree more," I said heartily. "Who the hell wants to sit around and hear discs scraping on a turntable. *Yack-yack-yack* all night so it gets you can't hear a word you say. You're a genius, Greta. Let's stay here tonight. Right here." I patted the divan seat beside me to lend gentle emphasis to my words.

Her eyebrows arched upward. "Did I say tonight? I meant this evening, of course. How stupid of me."

"The beauty of music," I said icily, "reproduced with true fidelity."

"All right, Romeo," she said wearily. "I'll go along with my original version."

CHAPTER 9

Three days went by. Three nice lazy days with nothing to do and Greta to do it with. In the evening of the second day I introduced her to my hi-fi setup and they became friends. So much so that the hi-fi always got four discs further with her than I had intended it. In time that represents something like an hour and a half of frustration. It got to where I was seriously considering doing something brutal to the hi-fi and putting it out of action for a few days.

On the afternoon of the third day I had a ring from Judge Bryan.

"Are you going to be very busy tomorrow?" he asked.

"It depends, Judge," I said cagily. "What's on your mind?"

"I was wondering if you'd go out and see Miss Hertz for a little while?" he said. "She's very lonely out there, I think. I saw her yesterday. She's still grieving for her sister, of course, which adds to it. I think a visit would cheer her up."

"Sure," I said. "Maybe I could take her something?"

"I think she has everything she might want," he said. "I took a portable television set out with me yesterday. But she's sunk within herself and only talking to people who will make her fight it. The guards keep to themselves, of course, and in that sense they aren't any help."

"Be a pleasure, Judge," I said. "I'll go out there tomorrow afternoon."

I was having dinner with Greta that night. I showered and shaved carefully and got dressed in a one-year-old, seventy-five-dollar suit and thought wistfully of the new one I'd left trussed around one John Lawson. His uniform was no fair exchange.

I arrived at Greta's place around seven. She met me on the driveway. She was wearing a simple little number which seemed more revealing than a bikini and probably cost upward of five hundred bucks.

"Darling," she said. "I've got a wonderful surprise for you."

"You're going to give me all your beautiful money?" I asked hopefully.

She pouted. "Don't be so sordid. Come on in," she tugged my arm. "It's in the living room."

She pushed me into the house. I opened the door and stepped into the living room and saw Basil sitting on the floor, wearing his dementia praecox in mauve, with a dreamy look on his face.

"You call that a surprise," I yelped. "I wouldn't want Basil if he came on top of a Christmas tree loaded down with goodies."

Basil looked up at me scornfully. "Philistine," he said. "Does music mean nothing to you?"

Then I realized what he meant. There was music in the air. And in one corner stood a hi-fi setup that made mine look like the original Edison–Bell phonograph.

"I bought it," Greta said proudly.

"Well," I said. "Well, well, well. Does Basil come with the hi-fi?"

"I am merely listening to a recording of my favorite piece of music," he said. "As soon as it is finished, I shall depart."

"Oh," I said. "What's it called?"

"It's ..."

"*Tales of Hoffman?*" I asked him. "You know—the fairy tales."

"It's *Night on the Bare Mountain,*" he said. "I wouldn't expect you to know it, of course."

"But I do, Basil, dear boy," I said. "I once had a case where that had quite a lot of meaning. It was the theme song of a lot of people mixed up in it."

"You shatter me, Lieutenant," he said, and closed his eyes to concentrate on the music.

I walked over and took a closer look at the setup. I could feel my face turning green.

"You think it's all right?" Greta asked anxiously.

"I think it's all right the way Rolls-Royce think their auto is all right," I said in a hushed voice. "How much did this set you back?"

"I can't remember, exactly," she said carelessly. "Somewhere around fifteen thousand, as I remember."

I shuddered. "You having as much money as that," I said, "it's practically immoral."

"I am never impractical about anything," she said calmly. "Be it morals or hi-fi."

The disc finished and Basil got onto his feet.

"Thank you, Madame," he said. "It was a privilege. I shall now leave you to your more pedestrian pursuits."

He looked at me and pursed his lips. "Flat-footed pedestrian pursuits, naturally."

He wafted out of the room and closed the door gently behind him.

I said something softly under my breath and looked up to see Greta giggling helplessly. "Pour me a drink, flat-foot," she said.

"OK," I said. "So that's a point to Basil."

"The poor lamb," she said. "He has probably been sitting up nights for a week, thinking up cutting repartee. You aren't very kind to him, you know, Al."

"I don't like him," I said. "That doesn't have anything to do with his mother complex or anything else. I just don't like Basil."

"You're prejudiced, Al," she said. "Ever since you found out he lived here. You're frightened that underneath Basil's exterior lurks a Ferdinand you haven't seen yet."

"Psychiatry yet," I said. "I shall pour us a drink."

We sat on the divan, which was beginning to sag a little in the centre, and sipped our drinks.

"I thought that tomorrow we should have a picnic," she said. "Let us go gay and rustic. Take a simple meal—lobster and a couple of bottles of champagne—out into the country and sit beneath a greenwood tree, whatever that is."

"It's the thing that Robin Hood used to sit beneath," I said. "Don't you ever watch television?"

She sipped some more of her drink. "Well, you get the general idea, Al."

"It sounds attractive," I said. "But I can't make it."

"Why not?"

"I have to go someplace else."

"Oh," she said frigidly.

I finished my drink and offered her the glass.

"Get it yourself," she said.

"I'll make you a deal," I said, following the routine. "If I get the ..."

"Drop dead, comrade," she said. "If you want another drink, you get it."

The atmosphere seemed to have deteriorated suddenly. It was time I made with explanations, I realized.

"Seriously, honey," I said. "I promised to go see Lois Hertz. She's pining away in her cabin, I'm told, and she needs people to cheer her up."

"Oh." Greta thawed appreciatively. "Well, that's different."

"I'll be back around eight at night," I said.

She moved closer to me. "Al, I've got a wonderful idea. Why don't we just put the picnic basket in the car and invite Lois to join us?"

"It would be a wonderful idea," I admitted. "But I can't take you up there with me."

"You think I'm working hand in glove with Kirch?" she asked and as she asked, the temperature soared downward again.

"You know it's not that," I said. "Only the whole success of the Grand Jury depends on her testimony. We just can't take a chance, that's all."

She snuggled closer still to me. "Darling, seriously. Lois works for me—or she worked for me. I'd like to see her again, be able to do something for her. And without being rude to you, we'd have much more in common to talk about than you would alone with her."

"True," I agreed. "But—"

"Look, Al. Blindfold me—put a bag over my head. I don't mind. If I don't know how I got there, I couldn't find my way back or tell anyone else the way, could I?"

I grinned at her. "Well, OK. I guess you would do Lois a hell of a lot more good than I will. You can come. You won't need a blindfold—just close your eyes when I tell you to."

"Like this?" Greta closed her eyes and pouted her lips about three inches away from mine.

"Not like that, honey," I said five minutes later. "I'll run off the road."

"Is it a bumpy road?"

"In places."

"Then can we please take the Cadillac, darling? I know your little monster is awfully fast, but over a bumpy road I get bruises and even if they don't show, they're painful."

"OK," I said. "We'll take the Cadillac."

"That's my boy," she said. "We'll have the most wonderful picnic anybody ever had."

"It will take us about three hours to get up there," I told her. "We should leave no later than twelve if we're going to have a picnic."

"I'll have everything ready, darling," she promised. "Including myself."

"That I'll believe when I see it," I said.

She took the glasses and poured us another drink.

"You hungry, Al?"

"No."

"Don't you ever eat?"

"Only when there's nothing better to do."

"There's a chicken in the icebox. Yell when you feel hungry."

"I will," I said.

She brought the drinks back with her to the divan.

"Have you heard anything more about the Grand Jury or Kirch or anything?"

"Nothing much is happening yet," I said. "From what I hear, Kirch has a squad of lawyers out at his house. The Grand Jury will be ready to start three days from now on schedule and quite a number of interesting people that nobody had ever heard of before are offering to testify."

"So we've got nothing to worry about?" she asked. "We can really enjoy that picnic?"

I nodded. "How do I look?" I asked. "Dressed for a picnic?"

"You'd pass in a crowd," she said. "Why?"

"Saves me the trouble of going home to change before we leave," I said casually.

She looked me up and down slowly. "Al Wheeler. Are you presuming that you will stay here until noon tomorrow?"

"Sure I am," I said. "You think I'm a dope or something?"

"Of course I do," she said. "But what's that got to do with it?"

"Come a little closer," I told her, "and I will demonstrate."

We ate the cold chicken for breakfast, packed up the food for the picnic and put it into the Cadillac ready. From where I sat, there was enough food to feed the Grand Jury and everybody who testified before it for a month. But Greta said the country air made everybody hungry and maybe she knew what she was talking about.

It was five after twelve when we left. It was a nice sunny day, just right for a picnic. We made the journey there in just under the three hours. We came over a rise in the road that wasn't any more than a couple of tire tracks, then saw the cabin straight ahead of us.

"It looks beautiful," Greta said. "Like something out of one of those books you read when you were a kid."

"And it has all the modern comforts," I said. "Cold water that runs sometimes, mosquitoes the size of elephants, owls that hoot in the night and coyotes that yowl the whole twenty-four hours through."

"Coyotes." She looked at me.

"Well, maybe not," I said.

"Don't spoil my picture story," she said.

I braked sharply and she nearly bounced off the windscreen.

"What the ..." she started.

"Here's something to spoil your story," I said, and pointed. Two of the

Samson's men came toward us, carrying rifles. One of them recognized me and nodded.

"Hi, Lieutenant."

"Hi," I said.

"Judge said you'd probably be up today." He looked at Greta. "Who's the lady?"

"A friend of mine, and of Miss Hertz," I said. "I'll vouch for her."

He nodded. "I guess that's OK. Go on in. She ain't very happy, I guess. Got no reason to be, either. Just sits there, won't talk, won't do anything ..."

"We thought of taking her out on a picnic," I said. "We've got everything with us."

He shook his head dubiously. "Sorry, Lieutenant. I don't think it can be done. We got orders from Judge Bryan, and they're pretty solid."

Greta leaned forward eagerly. "Look, why don't you all come with us? Then you'll still be with Lois and be able to keep her safe."

"That's an idea, you know," I said. "I wasn't thinking of going very far—maybe a couple of miles further into the hills or until the tracks run out. There's cold lobster in there and champagne, iced."

He grinned slowly. "Guess that does sound like a good idea, Lieutenant, at that. Our orders are not to let her out of our sight for a minute. This way we're carrying out orders. Iced champagne and lobster." He smacked his lips. "We been eating hamburgers the last couple of days and every one of us is a lousy cook."

"Get the boys together and we'll organize Miss Hertz," I said.

We got out of the car and walked over to the cabin. We found Lois Hertz rocking listlessly in a rocking chair in the small living room. She didn't even bother to look up as we came in.

"Hello, Lieutenant," she said listlessly.

"Hi," I said.

"Hi there, Lois," Greta said.

Lois looked up then in surprise. "Why—Madame. I never expected to see you here."

"Surprise," Greta said. "And don't call me Madame. Call me Greta."

"All right," she smiled shyly. "How's everything at Basiloff's? I miss it so much, I wouldn't have believed it myself."

"Everything's fine," Greta said. "I'll tell you all in about a minute, but let's go out to the car first—we're going to have a picnic."

"A picnic," Lois said. "You're kidding."

"It's for real," I said. "Your bodyguards are coming with us."

A spark flickered in her eyes. "I'd like that—to get away from this cabin for a couple of hours."

"Then come on," Greta said. "Let's go."

We walked with her to the car. The four bodyguards were already in the back. The three of us got into the front seat and I drove off.

We followed the tracks for maybe another mile and then they petered out. There was a long stretch of tall grass and then outcrops of rock showed beyond it. The grass was part of a plateau set high with a magnificent view of undulating hills and valleys all around.

I stopped the car and switched off the motor. "This looks like it," I said.

"It's wonderful," Lois said. "Simply wonderful."

"You haven't seen anything yet," Greta said. "Wait until we open up the lobster."

CHAPTER 10

We sat around in the grass beside the Cadillac with the remains of the lobster, the chicken, the salad, the dozen other things spread around us. Four empty champagne bottles lay forlornly in the grass. I popped the cork of the last bottle and both girls shook their heads in unison.

"I should float away," Lois said dreamily. "In spite of my over-stuffed stomach, I should just rise from the ground like a piece of thistledown and float away."

"That's poetry," Greta said solemnly. "Well, almost. Matter of fact, I like it better than poetry. You don't have those stupid rhymes cluttering up the words."

I filled the glasses of the four bodyguards, who drank them down in one long steady draft. I would have had some more myself, but the bottle was empty.

"The perfect picnic," I sighed, and stretched out on my back. The next thing I knew, someone was shaking my shoulder roughly.

"Honey," I said sleepily, "there are times when a man must have his rest."

"Wake up, you pig," a voice said.

I opened one eye and saw Greta on her knees beside me, looking down at my face.

"What do I want to wake up for?" I asked her.

"Because you were snoring. That's why. Sit up."

She got hold of my arms and hauled me into a sitting position. I gave up all hope of sleep and fumbled around until I found a cigarette and lit it.

"It's disgusting," Greta said. "A lovely day in the country and just look at them." She made a wide, embracing gesture with her arms.

Lois lay with her head cradled on her arm, breathing gently, a half-smile on her lips. Three of the Samson's men were flat on their backs, snoring steadily. The fourth one sat on the running board of the car, a rifle cradled in his arms, very wide awake. He grinned at me and winked.

I winked back at him, then turned to look at Greta.

"I don't see anything wrong with it," I said. "They're just being sensible, that's all. What's wrong with sleep?"

"On a beautiful afternoon like this," she said. "I'm not going to waste it—I'm going for a walk. There's a stream down there on the other side."

"Just happy minding its own business," I said. "And I for one will follow its example."

She got onto her feet as I stretched out on my back again.

"Oh, no, you don't," she said, then put the sharp heel of her shoe into my solar plexus and let her weight come down on it. Too much lobster mixed with too much champagne suddenly and violently protested. I sat up quickly, gurgling.

"We are going for a walk, lover," she said firmly. "If I have to carry you."

What was the use? I grunted miserably and got onto my feet. "You're just a slave driver," I growled, "I should never have let you come in the first place."

"You're getting lazy," she said. "And that's bad when you're getting old as well. Getting fat and bald and lazy—ugh."

"I am neither fat nor bald," I protested indignantly. "Lazy I may be, but then I was born of lazy parents. My father was so lazy he used to sit in front of the fire and cry when it got too hot and was burning him."

She gave me a pitying look. "I can remember laughing at that the first time I heard it," she said. "When I was at school."

"They had school right through the Civil War?" I asked her interestedly.

Then I yelped and limped the next twenty yards after she'd kicked my shin.

"We are here to enjoy the beauties of nature," she said.

"That's what I told you last night and ..."

"Al." I saw the glint in her eye and the raised foot.

"OK," I said hastily. "Skip it."

We walked a little further and Greta was right. There it was two hundred feet below us, the stream which gurgled its way down over its rockbed to the bottom of the valley a couple of miles away from where we stood.

"There," Greta said. "Isn't that something?"

"It certainly is," I agreed. "Now let's go back to the car."

"Don't be stupid," she said. "You think I walked all this way just to look at it? I'm going down there to bathe my feet in that mountain stream."

"So long," I said.

"Are you coming with me or going home early tonight?" she asked sweetly.

"I guess I'm coming with you," I grinned.

"Well, hold my hand."

I held her hand and the next moment she ran forward, her grip on my hand nearly jerking my arm out of its socket.

The next moment we were running madly down the side of the steep slope toward the stream. I jumped frantically to avoid tripping over a large lump of rock and found I was taking giant strides like the first man on the moon. I heard Greta laughing helplessly, but I couldn't afford the time to look at her—I might have hit another rock.

The last twenty feet of the slope was nothing but soft grass, I observed thankfully, as we approached it at something close to the speed of light. Greta gave a piercing scream and her grip on my hand suddenly relaxed.

I leaned backward and tried to dig my feet in heel first, and gradually slowed down. I saw Greta tumbling helplessly head over heels down the grass to the water's edge.

Two long, slender, delectable suntanned legs stood stark against the sky, and waved gently in mute appeal. Flush with the edge of the bank, delicate lace edging showed at the tops of her legs. And that was all I could see of Greta. The rest of her was underwater. She'd rolled up to the edge of the stream and then gone headfirst into it.

As I watched the legs waved more wildly, then disappeared into the water. A moment later a bedraggled, wild-eyed mermaid emerged from the stream.

I made moaning noises and rolled over onto my stomach and thumped my fist onto the ground. She scrambled awkwardly up the bank and stood there just looking at me.

Her fresh print cotton frock was plastered to her from neck to knee, her hair hung limply around her like a tattered fishing net, and water streamed steadily from her the way it does from a punctured water barrel.

"Very funny," she said in a strangled voice.

"Honey," I gurgled helplessly, "you have the most unique way of bathing your feet in a mountain stream that I ever did see."

I screamed out laughing again and thumped the earth until my fist hurt. The next moment a rainstorm hit me. The skies opened up and I was deluged with water.

I stopped laughing suddenly and scrambled hastily onto my feet. Greta stood there, the skirt of her frock bunched in her hands.

"I'm so sorry," she said acidly. "I was just wringing out my dress. I hope all of it landed on your face?"

I looked at her and dissolved into laughter again. She scowled for a moment, then suddenly she started to laugh. We held onto each other and howled with mirth.

And then it happened.

It sounded as if the earth had been rent in two. A noise that sounded the way a blockbuster must have sounded when it exploded in a Berlin street in the latter days of World War II. I thought for a moment that my eardrums had been punctured, but then I heard the other sounds. The thin whistling noises that grew louder and louder and then the plunking noises of bits of steel dropping around us.

I pushed Greta over backward onto the ground, then flung myself on top of her. I put my hands over the back of my head and waited while Greta squirmed frantically beneath me, until the noises had stopped. Then I got onto my feet and helped her up onto hers.

Her face was white. "What was it, Al?"

"I don't know," I said. "Let's go and find out."

"It sounded like a bomb going off," she said.

"Maybe World War III has just started," I told her. "But we won't find out till we get to the top of this slope."

I started up the slope, my feet slipping on the grass, and with Greta coming up just behind me. It had been two hundred feet from top to bottom coming down—it seemed like six miles going up. For every two yards further up you got, you slipped back a yard.

When I finally reached the plateau I was covered in sweat. I looked back to see Greta twenty feet below me, still struggling. Then I looked across the plateau to make sure they were all right around the car.

And then I just looked.

Greta made it to the top and hauled herself up beside me. She straightened up, her breath coming in tearing gasps.

"If I ever want to do that again," she gasped, "just keep on hitting me on the head till the feeling goes away."

I didn't answer her, I was still staring.

"Al," she said. "What's the matter? The others are all right, aren't they? They're still by the car?"

"Car?" I said. "What car?"

Then she looked and realized for the first time. Across the surface of the plateau, the tall grass waved smoothly in the late-afternoon breeze. There was no car. Instead, where it had been was a large blackened patch of bare earth, and around the edges, smoke still drifted from the burning grass.

Greta grabbed my arm and I felt her nails dig into my flesh. "Oh, no," she said in a low voice. "Please, Al. No."

"You said it sounded like a bomb," I said hoarsely.

I took hold of her wrist and pulled her hand away from my arm and pushed her so that she stumbled away from me, fighting to retain her balance.

I walked slowly toward the blackened patch of earth, looking intently at the ground in front of me as I walked. There were a few things. A blackened cork from one of the champagne bottles, a bent and twisted chrome strip which had once graced the bonnet of the Cadillac.

There were other things, too, which were more unpleasant. The finger, with a signet ring still clamped firmly around it. A twisted and broken shoe that was undeniably feminine, and a pipe that was untouched. A well-used briar with the teethmarks in the stem still showing quite clearly.

I stood in the centre of the patch and looked down at it. It could have been burned by a forest fire—and that was all you could say for it. A car and the five people with it might never have existed.

I felt those fingernails dig into my arm again.

"Al," she said. "Tell me it didn't happen. Tell me it didn't happen. It's some sort of joke—they moved the car away and then they let off a firecracker and ..."

I turned around to face her. "It was you," I said slowly. "You who wanted to come, who talked me into letting you come. It was you who insisted on the picnic. It was you who suggested that all the guards should come with us. It was you who said we must take the Cadillac. It was you—damn you. You who made me get up and go for a walk, and you who said we had to go down to the stream. Where you were sure we'd be safe, below the ground level of the explosion."

I put my hands around her throat and gripped hard. Terror showed in her eyes.

"No," she choked. "Al. It wasn't me. It wasn't."

I tightened my grip on her throat some more and then she couldn't speak at all. She writhed helplessly, trying to kick me, her fists pummeling my chest wildly. Her eyes started to bulge and her tongue protruded from between her teeth. I felt my fingers lock around her throat, and I thought that all I had to do was squeeze a little tighter for a few seconds and it would be finished.

Then suddenly I realized what I was doing. I let go of her throat and she fell to the ground in a limp heap.

CHAPTER 11

It was dark when we got back to the cabin. For the last mile I had my arms around her shoulders, half carrying her with her feet trailing on the ground.

I pushed open the door of the cabin and felt my way across the room to the rocking chair and let her slide into it. It creaked with a rhythmic steadiness. I straightened up painfully and felt around in my pockets until I found a box of matches. I struck one and saw the oil lamp on the table. I went across to it and turned up the wick, then lit it.

The wick caught and burned steadily. I snapped the glass back down over it and the light grew until it illuminated the whole room with a soft glow.

The chair still creaked. Greta hadn't the will or energy to stop it rocking. Her eyes looked cavernous as she stared at me. Her face was chalkwhite and on her neck livid bruises were starting to show where my fingers had tried to strangle the life out of her.

I walked out into the kitchen and found another lamp there and lit it. There was a good kerosene stove out there and it was easy to get going. I made some coffee, strong and steaming hot, and tried not to think about what I'd give for a glass of Scotch.

I poured the coffee black and heaped sugar into the cups, then took them back with me. The chair had stopped rocking but she still just lay in it, staring up at me.

"Coffee," I said. "Black and strong. You need it. Try and sit up and drink it."

She looked at me for a few seconds longer and then made an effort and straightened up in the chair. "I can hold it," she said, and held out her hands for the cup.

I leaned against the wall and sipped the scalding hot coffee, feeling it burn its way down inside me and doing me good. After I'd finished it, I lit a cigarette and then looked at her again. She was still staring at me.

"Cigarette?" I said.

"You were going to kill me," she said. "You nearly did. Only a few seconds more—that's all you needed, Al. What made you change your mind?"

"I got my sanity back," I said. "I knew what I was doing then—before I didn't."

"Somebody put a bomb in the car," she went on in a low voice. "It must have been a time bomb?"

I nodded. "You can make them in your garage if you can use your hands. They're crude but they work."

"You still think it was me, Al?"

I shook my head.

"You think it might be me?" she persisted.

"No," I said slowly. "I don't think it was you, Greta. I wasn't thinking at all when I said it was you. All those things were just coincidences. Nobody in their right mind would travel for three hours in a car, and then picnic beside it right up to ten minutes before they knew the bomb was due to go off. Nobody would have the nerve to take that sort of risk. Too many things could go wrong with it. The timing device could be fast or slow. A sudden bump might trigger it off. Nobody could sit that out without showing any strain—or probably without losing their mind and running screaming. You didn't do it, Greta."

She seemed to relax a little. "It's nice to hear you say that," she said. Her fingers touched the bruises on her throat gently. "Now I don't mind this. I can understand how you felt. I didn't know what I was doing or what I was saying. The shock was too great. One moment they were lying there beside the car asleep, with that one bodyguard sitting there, watching for any attempts on her life, and the next moment—nothing."

She started to cry and I saw the tears were coming easily and I didn't do anything about it. She'd feel better after it was over.

I took the cups to the kitchen and refilled them with coffee.

When I got back into the living room she was dabbing her eyes with a ridiculous miniature handkerchief.

"Thanks, Al," she said as she took the cup. "I think I will have a cigarette."

I lit two and put one between her lips. She puffed on it and sucked the smoke down into her lungs.

"What do we do now?" she asked.

"Stay the night," I said. "There's no transport here. We'll have to walk five miles back to the nearest road that might have any traffic on it, and we're in no shape to do that tonight. Anyway, we'd probably get lost and wander all night in the woods."

"And hear the owls hoot and the coyotes yowl," she smiled, then burst into tears again.

"Take it easy, honey," I said.

She shook her head impatiently. "I'm sorry, Al. But it was such a wonderfully happy day."

"Sure it was," I said. "Would you like some food?"

She shook her head again. "I don't think so. The coffee was wonderful, but I don't think I could eat."

I walked through into the bedroom. It had a decent-sized bed in it, in the centre of the room. I took the lamp from the kitchen with me and went out onto the back veranda. Another room led off at the end of the veranda and inside were four bunks in two tiers, where the Samson's men had slept.

I came back into the house and found a coarse white towel in the bathroom and took it with me into the living room. I saw that Greta was shivering and thought I could have remembered before that her clothes had never dried from when she'd fallen into the stream.

"Here's a towel," I said. "You'd better get out of those clothes and dry yourself, then into bed."

She smiled wanly. "I don't think I have the energy, Al," she said slowly. "Just leave me here in the chair, I'll be quite all ..." The words trailed away and her head dropped forward.

I shook her a few times, but she didn't even stir. She was exhausted. I carried her into the bedroom, taking the towel with me, then I lay her on the bed and stripped off her clothes and toweled her vigorously until her skin began to glow. Then I wrapped a blanket around her and tucked her under the bedclothes, and she lay there sleeping peacefully like a child.

I took her damp clothes out with me and thought I should light a fire and dry them, but the thought of the energy needed to light a fire made my shoulder muscles jerk. I took her clothes out onto the veranda and draped them along the rail. The sun got up early and they should be dry by the time she wanted to put them on again, I thought.

I put out the lamps, carrying one with me to the bunkhouse. I left it on the small wooden table in between the bunks and stripped off my clothes, leaving them where they fell. Then I wrapped a couple of blankets around me and rolled onto the bottom bunk nearest me. I had been going to put out the lamp, but the thought of expending the enormous amount of energy required to sit up again just to blow out a lamp seemed too ridiculous to even think about.

I felt somebody shaking my shoulder and was conscious that they were shining a bright light onto my face. I buried my head under the blanket and tried to wriggle away from the hand that shook my shoulder, but it was no use.

Finally I had to stick my head above the blanket and open my eyes. The strong light was sunlight streaming in through the windows of the bunkhouse. The lamp stood on the table, its glass blackened and soot-streaked.

Greta stood there smiling down at me. "Aren't you ever going to wake up?" she said. "It's after eleven."

I sat up and rubbed my eyes. "Do I smell coffee?"

"And bacon—if you're quick," she said. "There's hot water in the bathroom, too."

Then she went out of the bunkhouse and I got off the bunk reluctantly and stood up. I found a razor belonging to one of the Samson's men and took it with me to the bathroom. Greta was right about the hot water. I had a shave and a shower and I felt a hell of a lot better. I got dressed, then went into the kitchen.

Greta kept on cooking and I kept on eating. When I really couldn't eat any more, I sat back and lit a cigarette. Then I took my first real look at her.

The pallor and gauntness of the night before had gone. The bruises on her throat still accused me with their dark-purple discoloration, but otherwise she looked as if she was back to normal.

The cotton dress had shrunk four inches above her knees and fitted her so tightly everywhere else that I expected to hear a ripping sound every time she breathed.

"Thank you for playing lady's maid last night," she said. "I couldn't have stood up to save my life."

"That's OK," I said. "I hope you feel like standing up this morning, honey, because we have to hike."

"I feel more like it this morning," she said. "As much as I'd ever feel like it."

We started walking just after noon and it was three o'clock when we reached the first road that had any right to the name. It was an hour after that when a battered farm truck stopped and gave us a lift into the nearest town.

The truck driver dropped us in the main street and Greta was surrounded by a group of disapproving women and approving men.

"Have you got any money with you?" she said desperately.

"I think so," I told her. I took out my billfold and opened it. "How much do you want?"

"Enough to buy a dress," she said. She snatched the billfold out of my hand. "I'll give you back what I don't spend." Then she disappeared up the street at a fast trot.

The group of people gradually dispersed, the women's faces brightening as they went and the men's tinged with regret. I lit a cigarette and waited. Fifteen long minutes went by and then she reappeared wearing a white cotton sweater and a full denim skirt.

I closed my eyes and shuddered as she came up to me. "Do they look that bad?" she asked.

"They look that good," I said. "Do we have any money left?"

"I got them in the five and ten," she said. "Ten dollars and thirty-five cents the lot."

"You're a genius," I said happily, and took my billfold back.

I found a pay booth a block down and rang Judge Bryan. I told him what had happened and it took five minutes after that to get him to believe it.

"Then it's the end of everything," he said in a stunned voice. "The five of them dead. The Grand Jury will be a farce. Without that opening testimony of hers, you cannot testify. Kirch's lawyers would tear you to ribbons. And none of the other people who have volunteered will testify once they know she won't appear."

"Hold your horses, Judge," I said. "We've got a couple of days yet to do something."

"I am not being blasphemous," he said softly. "But can you resurrect the dead?" There was a gentle click in my ear as he hung up.

I rang Lavers and got him at his office. I told him the story and he was with it in about ten seconds flat.

"We'll talk about it later, Al," he said. "Not over the phone. Have you told the Judge?"

"I rang him before I rang you," I said. "I figured it was his right."

"Sure," he said. "How did he take it?"

"Bad," I said. "He's despaired."

"Couple of days early to do that," the Commissioner grunted. "First thing to do is get you back to town, Al. Where are you calling from?"

I told him the name of the one-horse town.

"I'll drive out myself and pick you up," he said. "Take me a couple of hours at least. Where will I find you?"

"Outside the five and ten," I said, "in the main street."

"OK—I'll park there."

I rejoined Greta and told her that Lavers was coming out to pick us up.

"That's a break," she said. "I was frightened we might have to walk the rest of the way."

We walked around for an hour, then had a meal in a diner and that took the time to six-fifteen. We went down the street and stood outside the five and ten, and ten minutes later Lavers' car pulled into the curb.

We got into the front seat beside him and he swung the car in a U-turn and headed back for Pine City.

"You don't know Greta, Commissioner," I said. "Alias Madame Basiloff?"

"How do you do," he said. "You've had quite an experience."

Greta's fingers touched her throat unconsciously. "Quite an experience, Commissioner," she agreed.

"Greta knows what's what," I said. "So you don't have to be discreet in front of her, Commissioner."

"That's something," he said. "I talked to Judge Bryan after I finished talking to you. Your phone call made an old man out of him. But I talked him into not doing anything or saying anything until we get there, anyway."

"That's something," I said.

He grunted. "Though what we're going to tell him when we get there, I wouldn't know. Without Lois Hertz to testify, let's face it—we're shot. We don't have even a peashooter to blow at Kirch."

"I know it," I said.

We rode in silence for most of the way in. It was a little after nine-thirty when we stopped outside Judge Bryan's home.

His wife, red-eyed and openly weeping, let us into the house. "The Judge is in the living room," she told us, and went up the stairs slowly.

Greta and I followed Lavers into the living room. The Judge was sitting in an armchair, reading a book. He put the book down as we came in and got slowly to his feet, taking off his horn-rimmed spectacles and tucking them into the top pocket of his jacket.

"Mr. Commissioner," he said formally. "Lieutenant."

"This is Miss Basiloff," I said. "Judge Bryan, Greta."

"How do you do," Bryan bowed slightly in her direction and then looked questioningly at me.

"She knows the story, Judge," I said. "She was with me in the car—we're the only two survivors. You can trust her discretion about this thing."

"Thank you," he bowed again.

Lavers became engrossed in filling his pipe.

"Well, Mr. Commissioner," Bryan said in a tired voice. "I have kept my word. I haven't told anyone of the dreadful happenings of yesterday afternoon, with the exception of my wife."

"Thank you, Judge," Lavers said, and still concentrated on him.

"Although what good it can do to keep it a secret is beyond me," Bryan went on. "Those four Samson's men—some of them must have wives, families."

"I appreciate that, Judge," Lavers said. "I only wanted a few hours. I thought if we had time to think, we might just hit on something."

Bryan shook his head. "I've wracked my brains," he said. "But it's useless. When Lois Hertz died so tragically, all our hopes of a Grand Jury toppling Kirch from his throne died with her."

I was standing there listening like you listen to the *Funeral March*, wishing it would be over quickly but still hearing every note. And then a thought got up in the back of my head and bent my cranium with an awful smack.

"Wait a minute," I said.

They turned and looked at me.

"Well?" Bryan grunted.

"Who knows that Lois Hertz is dead?" I said.

They looked at me pityingly and slowly shook their heads in unison.

"Well, Wheeler," Lavers said in a voice you use to humor a child. "We do, for a start."

"No, we don't," I said. "Greta and I do because we were there. We know they couldn't have survived that explosion. But you don't know—you're only taking our word for it."

"I suppose so," Bryan said impatiently. "But really, I don't see what point there is in ...”

"Whoever planted that bomb inside the car," I went on, "they don’t know, either. They weren’t there to see it go up. It was a gamble right from the beginning. It might have exploded when nobody was within a hundred yards of the car, or it might have exploded before we even reached the cabin, killing Greta and myself, but not harming Lois Hertz—the one person it was designed to kill."

The Judge shrugged his shoulders. "That’s all true, of course, Lieutenant. But I don’t see where it leaves us?"

"It’s simple," I said. "It’s like all strokes of genius—the wheel, electricity, harnessing the atom ... it’s simple." I took a deep breath and added slowly: "Lois Hertz did not die."

Lavers and the Judge looked at each other. "Strain," Lavers said. "Reaction. You know."

"Yes, of course," Bryan said sympathetically. "We should be getting them to a hospital, to ..."

"Stop driveling, both of you," I snarled.

They both stared at me, their jaws dropping open.

"That’s better," I said. "Now, concentrate. Lois Hertz did not die. You release the story to the press. The tragic story of four good men being blown to little pieces. Two people escaped intact—Greta and myself. A third person also escaped, but not completely. She has been badly injured in the head and the face, but she lives. She lives to testify before the Grand Jury."

I saw the dawn break in Lavers’ eyes.

"Sure," I said. "That’s right. You put somebody up before the Grand Jury with their head swathed in bandages and a nurse standing either side of them. Who’s to say it isn’t Lois Hertz."

Bryan looked at me with horror on his face. "But what you’re suggesting, Lieutenant," he said, "is nothing more or less than a conspiracy."

"That’s right, Judge," I said. "That’s just what I’m suggesting—a conspiracy. You weren’t there yesterday afternoon at that picnic, Judge. You didn’t see Lois Hertz happy for the first time since her sister died. You didn’t see her asleep on the grass. You didn’t hear that explosion, Judge. You didn’t see that patch of blackened earth where one car and five people had been a few seconds before. You didn’t pick up the bits, Judge, did you? The signet ring with the finger still attached."

I pulled Greta toward him. "I nearly went crazy—out of my mind," I said. "I thought for a few seconds Greta had planted that bomb."

I pushed her chin back so he could see the purple bruises on her throat. "I nearly strangled her, Judge, because I thought for a crazy moment that she had been responsible for their deaths. And now we’ve got a way to beat the men who blew them into eternity. A way to bring them at least a rough sort of justice. But you say we can't do it because it will be a conspiracy."

I suddenly realized I was shouting and I stopped abruptly. The silence seemed awfully loud for a while. Lavers glared at me and shook his head. I knew I hadn't handled the Judge right. The hell with handling people right—were Lois Hertz and the four Samson's men handled right?

Lavers coughed delicately. "Er—Judge Bryan, I'm sure that Lieutenant Wheeler didn't mean to be quite so violent in making a suggestion. If you can overlook the ..."

"Nonsense," Judge Bryan barked suddenly. "He meant every word of it—and quite right, too. Five innocent people have been slaughtered and I am mouthing platitudes out of a dusty book. You're right, Wheeler. And I'm thankful you had the guts to tell me I was wrong."

"That's fine, Judge," I said. "Then we do it?"

"There's only one snag that I can see," he said. "Who plays the part of Lois Hertz?"

I turned and looked at Greta. "Honey," I said, "you'll be a riot in bandages."

CHAPTER 12

I dropped Greta off at her house.

"You aren't coming in with me?" she asked.

"I have something to do, honey," I said. "Something I have to do—it won't take more than a couple of hours. You still need a good night's sleep. See you tomorrow, honey. I'll call you in the morning."

"All right, Al," she said. "Call early. I'll miss you."

"Miss you, too," I said.

And with that piece of brilliant dialogue, I gunned the motor of the Healey and went thataway.

Thataway was a little further north in Cone Hill. The place with the big walls and the guards on the gate. The Big House, they called it, after Alcatraz. And that's what it had been for Lili Hertz—a prison. And my guess was it performed the same function for Absolem Kirch, the owner.

I stopped the Healey facing the gates and leaned on the horn. A guard came across to me and I vaguely recognized his face.

"I hope you treated my suit right," I said. "It's not even paid for yet."

He reared back as if I'd suddenly grown horns.

"You," he said, and I was back with the brilliant dialogue.

"Sorry I couldn't return your uniform and gun," I apologized. "But they're exhibits with the Grand Jury starting the day after tomorrow. Open up the gates for me, buster, and tell Mr. Kirch that Al Wheeler is calling on him—again."

Maybe it was the mention of the Grand Jury or maybe he just wanted to get rid of me. He opened the gates and I drove up the drive, making like a Grand Prix driver—touching eighty in the middle and then working my way down through the gears to a grandstanding, broadsiding stop outside the front of the house.

So it was stupid. A man has a right to be stupid sometimes, doesn't he?

I got out of the car and went up the marble steps and hit the bell push beside the door. The butler opened it in five seconds flat and I calculated he must have been waiting for me the other side of the door.

"Lieutenant Wheeler, sir," he said warmly. "Mr. Kirch is waiting for you in the treasure room."

"Fine," I said. "He's the man I want to ... in the what?"

"The treasure room, sir," he replied gravely. "Allow me to show you the way."

So he showed me the way.

We climbed the broad, sweeping staircase and then walked along the gallery with the wall beside us literally plastered with paintings. Maybe they were priceless, maybe they came a dime a dozen, I wouldn't have known. But that gallery had something.

Then, at the end of the gallery, were two huge glass doors. The butler stopped and gestured toward them. "Mr. Kirch is waiting for you in the treasure room, Lieutenant," he said.

I looked at him for a moment, then I stepped forward and pushed one of the doors open with my hand. And there, seeming to stretch into eternity, was Aladdin's treasure house.

There were glass cases like the ones in Greta's shop, and the velvet plush inside formed a background for precious stones. For hundreds of precious stones, thousands of precious stones—for diamonds and rubies, emeralds and pearls, topaz and zircons.

There was period furniture littering the floor. The walls were covered with tapestries woven eight centuries before in medieval Europe. There were silks and damasks from the East, delicate carvings in ivory and jade. There were weapons from the boomerang of the Australian Aborigine to the broadsword of the English Roundhead.

Wherever you looked there was treasure. So much treasure that it overflowed, it crowded one upon the other. Rare porcelain was stacked in heaps on the pile of a fine Persian rug. An ivory Buddha sat cheek by jowl with a statue worked in pure gold.

And in the centre of it all stood a big, painfully built man in a gray suit. The lamps that lit the whole vast room picked out the silver streaks in his black hair and burnished them gently.

He looked up at me and smiled slowly. "Come in, Lieutenant," he said. "What do you think of my junkroom?"

I picked my way through the shambles until I got close to him.

"I left instructions at the gate that you were to be admitted straight away, Lieutenant," he said. "Should you deign to visit us a third time."

"We had Lois Hertz hidden away in a cabin in the country," I said. "With four men guarding her. I drove out with Madame Basiloff yesterday to see her, in Madame Basiloff's car. We had a picnic."

"How pleasant for you, Lieutenant," he said. "I remember as a child that I ..."

"Someone else made it a surprise picnic," I went on. "They attached a time bomb to the car, Mr. Kirch. It blew up. The four men were killed. Madame Basiloff and I were lucky—we were well clear of the car and unhurt by the explosion. Lois Hertz was not so lucky as us, but luckier than the men. She lives, Mr. Kirch. She will be disfigured for life, but she will live and give her evidence to the Grand Jury."

He took a cigarette from a platinum case and put it in his mouth, then lit it carefully with a lighter that matched the case.

"You came here specially tonight to tell me this, Lieutenant?"

"Sure," I said. "I thought you'd like to know."

"My weapon is more the mortgage than the time bomb," he smiled at me. "The yellow-press smear rather than the gun. I'm sorry if I disappoint you, but I have to plead not guilty."

"I don't believe you, Mr. Kirch," I said. "I can't be quite sure because there isn't enough proof yet, but there will be."

Kirch shrugged his shoulders. "I hope you find your proof, Lieutenant." He looked at me intently. "You have hounded me from the start of this thing—why?"

"Because I was told to," I said. "I know it sounds a little corny to talk about honest citizens and people who have pride in their cities—but they exist. They can be frightened by the power a man like you can wield, but when that power gets too corrupt, then the stench of it takes the fear out of their nostrils."

He laughed easily. "Why, Lieutenant—you should have been politician."

"It's a new thing with me." I grinned at him. "I don't know where I got it—from reading *Li'l Abner*, maybe? But it doesn't really make any difference, does it, Mr. Kirch? When the Grand Jury's finished with you, you might as well give up, because you won't have anything left to go on with."

He exhaled smoke gently through his nostrils. "All this ..." The negligent wave of his hand encompassed the contents of the whole room. "Would you care to put a price on it, Lieutenant?"

"I wouldn't know where to start," I said.

"Make it millions," he said easily. "Once you make it that, the actual figure doesn't mean very much, does it? Who cares if two million is twice one million, so long as you have one million? Let us say two million—I think it's conservative, but it will do.

"Two million dollars' worth of art, Lieutenant. Of priceless art, some of it. There are individual pieces here that many collectors would seriously give their eyes to possess. It all belongs to me. I would trade the lot for one person I could trust, or more so for one woman who loved me—just as a man, not as a millionaire."

He grinned again. "That's my line of corn, Lieutenant. Not much better than yours when you look at it, is it?"

"Not as good," I said indifferently. "The people I was talking about—those four men who died—were real men. They had real wives and real kids. And now they're really dead. But you were talking about a phantom, Kirch."

He nodded. "Perhaps you are right, Lieutenant. Was there anything else you wanted to tell me?"

"Only that there are an awful lot of people going to talk to the Grand Jury—after Lois Hertz and myself, of course. You'll be surprised, I could almost say amazed, Mr. Kirch, just how many there are, and at their names."

He tossed the butt of his cigarette onto the pile of a carpet and watched it burn a hole before he slowly ground it out with the heel of one shoe.

"If I tell you I shan't sleep tonight, or even tomorrow night, Lieutenant, will that satisfy you?"

"The only thing that will satisfy me is to find out who put that bomb in Madame Basiloff's car," I said. "When I know that, I'll be satisfied."

"And when you find him? You intend to make a spectacular arrest?"

"I intend to kill him," I said. "And now I'm sounding corny again, Mr. Kirch. It's a personal matter with me. I wanted you to know that."

"Thank you, Lieutenant," he said. "I didn't order any bomb to be put into that car—I didn't put it there myself. I have no idea who did. But you won't believe me, of course?"

"No," I said. "But I won't disbelieve you, either."

"You're very generous," he said.

"I'll go further, Kirch," I said. "I'll believe you that you didn't put it there yourself. You wouldn't. You wouldn't take the risk. You'd hire somebody to do it, the way you always have. You'd hire somebody to plant a bomb in the car, the way you hired Walker to find your women for you, and to kidnap those who wouldn't be bought. I think you're a louse, Kirch. A louse that other lice wouldn't feed with."

"I think that will be all, Lieutenant," he said softly, his face white. "You know your way out, I think?"

"I know my way out," I said.

I walked back slowly through the treasure house that might just as well have been stacked with sawdust so far as the owner was concerned, and came back to the glass doors. I walked along the gallery and down the broad, sweeping stairs into the lower hall.

Walker stood there, waiting for me, biting his lip nervously. "I'd like a word with you, Lieutenant," he said eagerly. "I ..."

"Why don't you save it for the Grand Jury, Mr. Walker?" I suggested. "It's too late to talk to me now. Think how you're going to explain to them why you kidnapped girls for your master and saw them kept in this barn against their will."

His eyes bulged. "But—but it's not true," he said. "Every girl who came here came of her own free will and was treated very generously, in the bargain."

"Like I said, Mr. Walker," I told him. "Save it for the Grand Jury."

I walked past him toward the front door. The butler appeared from nowhere with my hat in his hand. "Your hat, sir," he said.

"Thanks." I took it from him and put it on. Then I looked at him. "You know something?" I said. "You're lucky."

"Indeed, sir?" he said politely.

"Sure," I said. "You're about the one guy in this house who'll be able to get another job after the Grand Jury's finished with them."

He held the door open for me and bowed me out. I walked down the marble steps to the Healey and got in. I drove sedately down the drive and the guard had plenty of time to open the gates. I went through out onto the street again and then headed toward home, idling along at a gentle thirty.

I wasn't feeling exactly happy with myself. I was the knight in shining armor who was going to gallop in his little white Healey to the castle gates and beard the dragon in his den, or something.

So I'd bearded the dragon in his den and the dragon had been a reluctant one with a tear in his eye, and all he wanted was a friend to write poetry with and a girl to gaze into his eyes instead of his bank balance.

I didn't get it.

I got home and ran the Healey up under the carport and then went into the house. I thought I'd have some coffee just to prove to myself there was something else besides Scotch that I could drink.

I went through into the kitchen and put the percolator on, then came back into the living room and dropped a heap of discs onto the turntable and switched it on.

I didn't hear the music and I didn't even taste the coffee when I poured it and drank it. I lit a cigarette and looked at my watch.

Ten to midnight. There was a lot of the night left untouched, and Al Wheeler had a hunch that just might pay off.

I took my bunch of keys and headed for the Healey. I drove over to Calton. To apartment four, 1058A Lime Street.

I went into the apartment house quietly and up the stairs even more quietly because I didn't want to frighten the tenants—or have them scare the hell out of me, either.

I tried five keys in the lock and the sixth fitted. I let myself into the apartment and closed the door gently, then switched on the light.

It had that slightly musty smell an apartment gets when no one has lived in it for a week or more, and the windows have been shut the whole time. I stood in the center of the living room and wondered what I had come for. I didn't know, so I thought I might as well start looking for it.

The bedroom had two beds, two dressing tables and one big wardrobe. I started with the dressing tables. I didn't find anything interesting in the first one and the second one looked as if it would be about the same. The last drawer was full of junk. Empty lipstick cases, battered powder compacts, chewed-looking cardboard containers that had once held vitamin tablets, aspirin, tranquilizers, migraine powders.

I sifted through the heap and found a brown-paper-wrapped package. I tore it open and saw it contained an unopened packet of tranquilizers and an untouched packet of aspirin. A piece of cardboard fell out and I picked it up and looked at it. It was one of those receipts a cash register prints with the cost of each item and the total as the shop assistant rings them up. It had the name of a druggist on it, and a date.

I was going to flip it back into the drawer again when the alarm bells rang loud and clear. I took another long look at it and I remembered. The name of the druggist was the one who had served Lili, the night she had been kidnapped and taken to Kirch's Big House. And the date stamped on the receipt was the same date.

I put the piece of cardboard carefully into my pocket and put the aspirin and tranquilizers carefully into another pocket, then let myself out of the apartment.

The druggist was an all-night druggist, which made sense because Lili had bought the stuff at eleven-thirty at night. At one-fifteen that morning he was still open but business was lousy.

As soon as he saw me he came bustling out of a bedroom and walked quickly along behind the counter to greet me. "Yes, sir."

"Lieutenant Wheeler," I said, which was not strictly accurate but I didn't think he'd get around to checking my fingerprints or anything. "Eighth

Precinct. You might remember me?"

"Oh—sure, Lieutenant," he said with false heartiness. "What can I do for you?"

"You remember Lili Hertz?" I asked him.

"Do I ever," he said. "The girl who got kidnapped and taken into Kirch's house. The girl who got murdered with a bullet in her. Do I remember Lili Hertz? Why, she used to come into this very drugstore and stand right where you're standing now ..."

I held up my hand in self-defense. "Don't make a production out of it," I pleaded with him. "I just wanted to know if you remembered her and you obviously do." I added hastily: "I wonder just how good your memory is?"

"It's not good, it's perfect," he said modestly. "I can remember things over the years. Little tiny things that wouldn't seem of no account to anybody, I can remember 'em—just like that. Why, I remember once ..."

"Fine," I said. "I'll make you a sporting bet on your memory. I'll bet you five dollars to a dime on your memory."

"You got yourself a deal, Lieutenant," he said eagerly. "Try me."

I took the five out of my billfold and the covers sagged together forlornly. "You remember Lili Hertz—right?"

"Right."

"Now—which day was she kidnapped? This isn't the bet."

"A Saturday," he said promptly. "The seventeenth."

"Right. One more feeder question, then the jackpot. At what time did she come into your drugstore here that day?"

"Wasn't the day," he said promptly. "Was that night—eleven-thirty."

"Right again," I said. "You look like you just might take the jackpot, Pop. You ready?"

"Try me."

"When she came in at eleven-thirty that night, what did she buy?"

He chuckled. "Shucks. This is like taking candy from a kid. She bought some aspirin and tranquilizers, that's what. Do you want the brand names?"

I handed him the five. "I take off my hat to your memory, Pop. It's a hundred percent."

He chuckled gleefully. "You want to try me some more?"

"Yeah," I said. "But not for money this time, you're too good for me. But this is an important question. Did she come into your drugstore at any other time on that particular Saturday? In the morning, afternoon, early evening."

He shook his head. "No, sir. Stake my life on it. Only time I saw Lili Hertz that day was eleven-thirty that night."

"Would you say that on oath?"

"Sure would."

"Thanks, Pop," I said. "Thanks a lot."

"Me to thank you, Lieutenant," he chuckled. "Don't often pick up a five that way."

I went out onto the sidewalk and lit a cigarette and stood there looking at the Healey, thinking I should give the paintwork a shine some day soon, and thinking about Lili Hertz and her aspirin and tranquilizers, and thinking maybe it meant nothing or maybe it meant a hell of a lot and right then I couldn't tell either way.

CHAPTER 13

The day of the opening of the Grand Jury dawned like any other day— I guess. I didn't see it, I was asleep. But it wasn't an ordinary day for the citizens—nobody was going to do much work that day.

When I got to the courtroom where the Jury was in session, I had to admit it looked impressive. Impressive because there was nothing really grand about the Grand Jury. They were a group of honest, decent citizens who had spent a great deal of their lives in service to their fellow citizens.

Judge Bryan sat in the center of them and the others sat either side of him. Facing them, but to one side of the courtroom, sat Absolem Kirch, with Walker sitting beside him on one side and two New York lawyers on the other.

There was a sort of public bench reserved for prominent citizens, a witness stand which was just a table and a chair, and anyone testifying could sit down while they did it.

The public galleries were swamped and I was glad I was to be called to testify, because otherwise I would never have got into the courtroom.

Judge Bryan raised his gavel and pounded the table for silence and got it right away. Nobody was going to risk being thrown out and miss the show.

"Fellow citizens," he said evenly. "This Grand Jury has been convened to examine certain charges of graft and corruption in the City Administration, certain charges of collusion between some newspapers and holders of public office, and more seriously actual crimes alleged to have been committed by persons also alleged to have been associated in these other activities.

"The purpose of a Grand Jury is to seek the truth and then, if it thinks fit, recommend that a certain course of action be taken. This is not a criminal court in any sense of the word. No information vouchsafed in this room can be transcribed and used as evidence against the person vouchsafing this information in any other court."

He looked slowly around the packed courtroom. "I wish to make it clear," he said quietly, "that this is no modern form of inquisition. We are here to seek the truth, that is all."

He nodded to the proctor, who called Absolem Kirch as the first witness. That's one of the things about a Grand Jury—it will accept relevant testimony from anyone who cares to give it on a voluntary basis, but it is also empowered to call on who it thinks fit to testify and they must do so.

Kirch got to his feet and faced them.

"Thank you, Mr. Kirch," Bryan said. "You may remain seated while you testify."

Kirch sat down again.

"Mr. Kirch," Judge Bryan leaned forward slightly. "Is it true that at certain times in your house situated at Cone Hill, there have been as many as four young women living there?"

"Quite true," he said.

"And were they all living there of their own free will?"

"Certainly."

"Were any of them ever abducted by force and kept in your house and its grounds against their will?"

"Certainly not."

"Thank you," Bryan said calmly. "Call Miss Lois Hertz."

A buzz of excitement sounded from all sides of the courtroom and then it died away to a tense silence as a figure moved slowly toward the empty table standing in the center of the court. On either side of the girl was a nurse, holding her arm and guiding her.

Her whole face was completely swathed in bandages and there were slits cut in the white crepe for her eyes, nose and mouth.

"You are Lois Hertz?" Bryan asked gently.

"Yes," she said in an inaudible murmur.

"If you could speak up a little, Miss Hertz?" he said gently. "You had a sister, one Lili Hertz, now deceased?"

"Yes."

"Your sister disappeared. On Saturday, May 17, during the late evening?"

"Yes."

"Please tell us, in your own words, what happened?"

The swathed figure did. She told of them both working in Madame Basiloff's jewelry shop and how a Mr. Walker had always insisted on her sister serving him. How her sister had gone to the drugstore and never returned. Then she mentioned me. How I had questioned her about Madame Basiloff's and she had been too frightened to mention Mr. Walker, because she knew he worked for Mr. Kirch and he had a reputation of being a very powerful man in the city. It went on, every word that came from behind those bandages damning against Kirch.

She told them about a phone call from Mr. Walker, telling her that I must be stopped from proceeding any further with my investigation, and how she was to frame me on the assault charge.

When she had finished, there was a short silence. Then Judge Bryan looked inquiringly at Kirch's table. "Any questions of the witness, gentlemen?"

"Yes, sir." One of Kirch's lawyers got onto his feet. His voice was gentle. "You say this phone call you received concerning Lieutenant Wheeler came from Mr. Walker, Miss Hertz? How could you be sure of that? Did he say who he was?"

There was a long pause and I thought that was a curly one for Greta and she must be as hot as hell behind all those bandages, already.

"No," she said finally.

"Then how did you know it was Mr. Walker?"

"I recognized his voice."

"Over the telephone?" The lawyer's voice registered polite incredulity. "Many voices sound alike over the telephone, Miss Hertz. I put it to you that you thought you recognized Mr. Walker's voice?"

"I suppose so," she said.

"There is a world of difference," he said, and sat down with a satisfied air.

To you, pal, I thought—and, funnily enough, to me, too. But to everybody else in the room, that was Walker's voice all right and they won't hear any different.

I was the next witness called. I told them about the frame-up, how I'd been tossed out of the Police Department because of it. I told them how I had been convinced that Lili Hertz was being held prisoner inside the Big House and how I had broken in and found her. How I had taken her to my house and then rung the Judge. Then the buzzer had sounded and I had opened the door to be hit on the head and the next thing I knew was that she had been shot dead.

The New York lawyers took one look at me and declined to ask any questions.

I stood down and my place was taken by a fat woman in her fifties who had been employed as a cook at the Kirch house, but had left in disgust because of the number of young women who were living in the house and spent their time walking around with hardly any clothes on. She was everyone's witness of the year. Now the spectators thought they were really getting down to the dirt.

That afternoon and the second day there was a number of people who had volunteered to testify, and of course all of them testified against Kirch. They revealed his tie-up through his newspapers and his money with members of the City Council, with two State Judges, and three of them testified to his tie-up with the District Attorney.

Then the D.A. was put in the box and he was fighting for his political life and he knew it. He sounded almost convincing, but when he'd finished they put Lavers in the box who testified that his instructions to do nothing about the Lili Hertz case had come directly from the D.A. himself. And that was that for the D.A.

In the afternoon of the third day, they got back to Kirch himself. They asked him if this was true and if that was true.

They spent an hour and a half asking him and he kept on saying yes, it was true.

Then they asked him about Lili Hertz.

He got to his feet and looked at them—the Grand Jury first, then the spectators on the packed public benches.

"No," he said clearly. "It's a downright lie. She came to my house of her own free will. In fact, she wanted to come—she asked Walker if she could come. She knew that any girl in my house was treated generously. And treated very generously as far as money was concerned."

Bryan looked at him coldly and tapped his fingertips together. "This conflicts with all the other previous testimony concerning Lili Hertz, Mr. Kirch."

"It's part of a conspiracy," he said passionately. "A conspiracy to blacken my name and ruin me—to leave me open for criminal charges. I never abducted or had abducted a girl against her will in my whole life."

He looked around the room again with a trace of arrogance on his face. "All right," he said contemptuously. "So I bribed and blackmailed your City Officers. I had the District Attorney in my pocket. I used my newspapers to further my own ends. I did exactly as anyone else would have done with my wealth and power. I came close to having the whole city in my pocket. I'll admit it. You have beaten me, this Grand Jury has beaten me. I will never again be able to hold such power in this city. That I don't mind. Things like that have an era and the era comes to an end.

"The Kirch era in city politics is finished. But I will not have my name associated with the abducting of young women, or of being implicated in a plot to ruin the career of a lieutenant of police. I am innocent of these things. Lili Hertz, I say again, came to my house of her own free will and, in fact, begged to come. Why she lied to Lieutenant Wheeler when he broke into my house and talked to her, I shall never know."

He sat down again at his table and the two lawyers shook their heads at him vigorously, then a woman in the back row of the public benches jumped onto her feet and shouted out: "Liar. Murderer."

And that unleashed the whole feeling of the crowd. They got to their feet and howled abuse at him. Judge Bryan broke his gavel pounding on the table, but no one heard it. The ushers tried to clear the courtroom and no one moved for them.

For perhaps half a minute, Absolem Kirch sat and listened to what they thought of him, then he got up from his chair and walked from the court.

I managed to get close to Lavers and grabbed his arm.

"Well," he grinned at me. "That's that, Wheeler. Kirch is finished in this city and a lot of other people with him, including our respected District Attorney. I mustn't forget to reinstate you into the Police Department with no loss of seniority, salary, superannuation or ..."

"Later, Commissioner," I said. There's something that has to be done quickly—today."

Lavers frowned at me. "What the hell are you talking about, Wheeler?"

"Lois Hertz," I said. "She's got to have a sudden relapse early tonight and die."

"All right," he shrugged his shoulders. "But I don't see the need for hurry ..."

"I think I'm beginning to," I said. "Believe me, Commissioner, it's urgent. If she doesn't die within the next few hours, there's going to be trouble."

"You mean you're getting tired of a girlfriend covered in bandages?" he chuckled.

"No, sir," I said soberly. "I don't mean that at all. I mean I'm beginning to think that Kirch was speaking the truth about Lili Hertz, and he's just smart enough to wake up to who is behind those bandages."

He started to look worried. "Kirch speaking the truth about Lili Hertz? But that's impossible, Wheeler—and you know it. Why, the girl told you the story herself. And then she was murdered."

"I know it," I said. "But she could have been lying—I have a feeling she was lying. I can't figure out why. But Lois Hertz has got to die tonight."

"I'll arrange it," he said. "Don't worry about it anymore."

I watched him go, then I drifted with the crowd out of the courtroom. It was five-thirty in the afternoon. I had a couple of drinks in a nearby bar and then I had a meal, which took the time along to seven. I got into the Healey and drove out to Cone Hill again.

There was a mob of people pressed against the gates, staring into the grounds. The guard was one I hadn't seen before, and he looked nervous. He opened the gates for me when I told him who I was, and he closed them again hurriedly as soon as the car was through. Somebody in the crowd called out jeeringly and asked him what he was worried about, and somebody else threw a brick which landed near him. He scuttled back behind the cover of the wall and out of sight of the crowd pressing against the gates. I didn't like the look of it much.

I parked the Healey outside and walked up the marble steps. I turned around when I reached the top step and looked back down the drive. The gates were one dark mass and I could hear the roar of the crowd, muted by distance to a murmur.

The front door was open. I pressed the bell push and waited, but no one came. No butler, no one. I stepped inside and pushed the door shut behind me. I walked down the hall, my footsteps sounding loud in the silence. There was no one in the office, the living room, the library, the sunroom, the kitchen—no one at all on the ground floor so far as I could see.

I retraced my steps to the foot of the staircase, then climbed it to the gallery and walked along to the double glass doors. I stepped inside the treasure room and for a moment I thought it was empty, then I spotted him, standing in the far corner and looking out of the window.

I walked across to where he stood, my footsteps sounding loud once again in the stillness. He turned around to face me as I came up to him.

"Come to gloat, Lieutenant?" he asked.

"No," I said. "Where is everybody?"

"You've heard the story of the rats and the sinking ship," he said easily. "The lawyers have collected their fees and caught a plane back to New York. The domestic staff deserted in a hurry once the Grand Jury hearing started. And the young girls who would care to partake of my hospitality after the story of Lili Hertz are non-existent. And Walker, dear old Walker, suddenly remembered his poor old mother in Milwaukee or some such place and had to leave immediately."

"There's only you in the house?"

"Only me," he agreed.

He turned away and looked out of the window again.

"The crowd seems to have broken down the gates," he said casually.

"Where's your phone—the nearest phone?" I asked him. "I had a feeling something like this might happen."

"I wouldn't bother, Lieutenant," he said easily. "If they burn the place down it wouldn't matter to anyone, would it?"

"It wouldn't matter to you?"

He shook his head. "Not in the least, Lieutenant. The whole place is beginning to bore me considerably."

He opened the window and I heard the ugly shouts of the crowd coming closer.

"I'll still use a phone if you don't mind," I said.

"You can try," he said. "But the guard at the gates rang me ten minutes ago and the line went dead while he was talking. I think some enterprising member of the crowd must have cut the wires. All the phones are dead—I tried them."

I took hold of his arm. "Then you'd better get out of here. That crowd is in an ugly mood."

He shook my hold free, gently. "I am not going to run from them, Lieutenant," he said wearily. "If they hate me so much, I won't give them the satisfaction of seeing me a coward in the bargain."

There was the sound of breaking glass below us.

"They're smashing the windows," I said. "You must get away from here."

"I find your concern touching, Lieutenant," he said. "But I can't understand it."

"I came here to ask you a couple of questions," I said. "Just between ourselves, with no one else to overhear. When you spoke of Lili Hertz this afternoon in the courtroom, were you telling the truth—that she came here of her own free will and she lied to me that night I took her away from here?"

"I was telling the truth," he said quietly.

"I believe it," I said.

He looked surprised. "You do? But why?"

"Little thing here and there," I said. "They start to add up."

The sound of breaking glass from below us was a continual clamor.

"This is no time to talk about it," I said. "If you value your life, Kirch, you'll leave this house now."

He smiled and shook his head. "I don't value it particularly, Lieutenant. And I'm not going to run from a mob. Damn it," he added almost to himself, "I'm going to face them."

He walked past me toward the double glass doors. I followed him. "Kirch," I said. "Wait a minute."

He walked down the gallery quickly with long strides and I hurried to catch up with him. He reached the staircase and then started down the stairs.

At that moment the front door burst open and a group of shouting men burst into the hall. Kirch stood on the middle stair, looking down at them.

"What do you want in my house?" he asked contemptuously.

They made a wild, animal noise when they saw him and then slowly they began to walk toward the stairs. There was something menacing in the way they came. They'd stopped shouting and the silence was somehow worse than the noise had been.

I came down the stairs three at a time, pushing past Kirch, to meet them. They looked at me sullenly.

"A lot of you know me," I said. "Lieutenant Wheeler, Police Department. I'm telling you to break this up right now. Go on home. The riot squad is on its way and if they find anybody in this house, you'll really be ..."

A giant of a man stood not two feet away from me. He reached out and took my arm firmly and pulled me toward him. "Go on home, Lieutenant," he said. "Nobody's got any fight with you."

I couldn't fight against his strength. He pulled me to him and then turned, facing the rest of the crowd and swinging me with him. Somebody else grabbed my elbows and then I was passed through the crowd like a package, until suddenly I was behind them.

They still just stood, grouped together at the bottom of the staircase, looking up at Kirch. Even then, he could have been all right. They were respecting his courage then in facing them—at that moment they could have swung in any direction. If he had cracked a joke, they could have laughed with him.

For a few seconds I hoped that it could be all right, and then Kirch spoke and said the one thing that sealed his own fate. Maybe he said it deliberately, knowing the result could only be disastrous.

"What are you looking for?" he asked them contemptuously. "More girls? You won't find Lili Hertz here now. She's dead and buried."

The animal roar came again and they swarmed up the stairs, up to where he stood, and suddenly I couldn't see him anymore.

The crowd was thick on the stairs, right up to the gallery. I heard him scream once and that was it.

I walked out of the door and down the marble steps to where the Healey stood.

CHAPTER 14

The Big House burned down that night. The mob set fire to it before the riot squad arrived and by the time the fire trucks got there, there was no hope of saving the house. People stood in their thousands and watched it burn.

They stood silently while the flames licked hungrily through its massive beams and devoured the treasure room and its priceless pieces of art that Kirch had once told me some collectors would give their eyes for. They would have to have given their lives for it that night to try and save any of it.

The next day the city was quiet. The newspapers had carried the story in banner headlines. It was a story that made the front page of practically every newspaper throughout America. And it was a story that the citizens of Pine City were ashamed of in the cold light of day. It was the story of one man being lynched by a mob, and of arson being carried out by that same mob. And many a meek storekeeper or clerk had been one of that wild, shouting mob the night before.

In the afternoon, in Commissioner Lavers' office, a pleasant little ceremony was held to reinstate a certain Lieutenant Wheeler into the Police Department. I didn't get my brass band, but I suppose you can't have everything—and the paychecks would be useful.

Afterward, everyone congratulated me—even Captain Bligh smiled when I said he was bountiful, but I made a quick check with the Commissioner that he wasn't sending me back to the Eighth Precinct. I didn't think my nervous system would be able to cope with getting there every morning on the day shift at nine sharp, and sending in a written report on the day's work before I could go home nights.

An official announcement had been made the previous night that Miss Lois Hertz had unfortunately had a relapse and had died about nine that evening, but no one had taken much interest because of the news of Kirch's death and the burning of his house.

I was one character who had been particularly interested in that news item because it meant that tonight I had a dinner date with a girl by the name of Greta Basiloff, and I preferred to see a face on the opposite side of the table rather than a mass of bandages.

It was five o'clock when the rest of them had gone, leaving me and the Commissioner.

"You saw the item about Miss Hertz's unfortunate relapse?" he asked me.

"I did," I said. "It so happened that it wasn't vital, after all."

"Why was that?"

"Once Absolem Kirch was dead, it didn't matter," I said. "He was the only one who knew it mattered, because it mattered to him."

Lavers looked at me admiringly. "I don't know how you do it, Wheeler," he said. "But you talk for days on end sometimes and not one word of it makes any sense."

"It's a gift," I said. "Developed by long years of practice, and who knows? One day I might wish to enter politics."

"You're an unorthodox cop now," he growled. "You'd be an unscrupulous politician."

"You mean there's more than one kind of politician?" I asked.

"Go away," he said. "Give my blood pressure a break. Go and get lost somewhere until the weekend. Come back here on Monday and by that time I'll have thought of another Precinct I can foist you on."

"Yes, sir," I said. "But I would remind you that I've had all the experience of being an orthodox cop that I can use down in the Eighth Precinct already. A nice, solid, routine job—just like you said. Including getting framed for an assault, dismissed from the Police Department, bludgeoned over the head, corpses left in my own living room and ...”

“All right,” he said. “Maybe Dick Tracy needs some help.”

“I’ll practice wearing my wrist around a radio,” I said.

“You mean a radio around your wrist.”

“No, sir. That way the crooks can see the radio—wear it my way and they only see the wrist.”

“Maybe you’d better take Monday off as well,” he growled.

I got out of his office quick before he had a brilliant thought and told me not to come back at all.

Into the Healey, out to Cone Hill, park on the driveway and press the buzzer. Greta answered the door. She was wearing a gown with no visible means of support and it had a scoop neckline. They must have used one of those machines they make tunnels with to scoop out the neckline. If that was her neck I was seeing then I was going to take a course in anatomy because, brother, I was confused.

She smiled and her eyes had that look in them, and I thought the horns could sprout out of her head at any minute.

“Al,” she said.

“Lieutenant Wheeler to you, ma’am,” I said. “Official since this afternoon.”

“Does that mean you’re eating regularly again?”

“Depends how many times you ask me over to dinner,” I said.

We went into the living room. That sag in the middle of the divan hadn’t improved any, I noted.

“A drink,” she said. “We’ve earned it.”

“We surely have,” I agreed.

“I got some new discs,” she said. “They’re on the turntable. See what you think of them while I pour the drinks.”

I went over and had a look at them. She’d bought half a dozen new discs: two Liberace, two Frankie Laine and two Elvis Presley. I shuddered and put them down quickly. Everybody to their own taste, but if I had a taste like that I’d drown it, preferably in good Scotch.

I had another look at her new hi-fi outfit and became absorbed in it. I had a look down behind the cabinet and wondered how anybody could know where all the wires went to. She had seven speakers spread through the room, I knew. I counted the seven leads and then I saw an eighth.

“You get another speaker put in?” I asked her.

“No,” she said. “Aren’t seven enough?”

“They are for Carnegie Hall,” I said. “The Hollywood Bowl uses a few more, I understand."

"You started this conversation," she reminded me.

She gave me a drink and I took it absently, so absently that I didn't drink any of it.

"You have one more lead than you need," I said thoughtfully.

"That rhymes," she said.

I thought that we were developing the type of conversation I usually try and avoid. I concentrated on the eighth lead again and saw something interesting. It didn't hook into the amplifying circuit at all—it only vaguely looked as if it did, but actually it disappeared under the skirting board.

I tried the other end. I traced the wire away from the skirting board. It ran quite a way. Along the skirting boards parallel with a couple of speaker wires and then it became all independent and went off at a tangent. The tangent took it behind the Picasso and at the end of the tangent was a tiny, super-sensitive microphone.

I lowered the Picasso gently back into place and walked back to where the wire disappeared under the skirting board. It was quite a thin wire. I picked it up in both hands and bent a tight loop in it, then jerked my hands apart. It burned my hands a little, but the wire snapped cleanly.

"Are you wrecking something?" Greta asked interestedly. "It doesn't matter—the whole thing is still under guarantee."

"I'll show you something," I said, and took her arm and steered her over to the Picasso.

"Oh, that," she said. "I look at that at least once a week, mostly."

"Not the Picasso," I said. I lifted the painting so she could see the microphone concealed underneath.

"What is it?" she asked. "Part of the air-conditioning?"

I put the painting back into its place. "I just wondered if you knew," I said.

"I'm a pretty smart woman around the house," she told me, complacently. "I'm a do-it-yourself fan."

"Me, too," I agreed. "I'm seriously thinking of going into that market myself with a Build Yourself a Blonde kit. It should sell a million. Think of the advertising gimmicks. I quote: Why be content with your wife when for an outlay of four dollars, ninety-five cents and the use of a few simple tools, you can have a Monroe? Unquote."

"That's meant to be amusing, I suppose?" she said coldly, and patted her brunette hair into place.

There was a gentle tap on the door and then Basil walked into the room, with a disc under his arm.

"Madame," he said, "do you mind if I just play my ..." Then he saw me. "Oh," he said. "I'm sorry. I didn't know you had company."

"Don't mind me," I said. "We're just talking shop, my shop. You know, cops-and-robbers stuff. Go right ahead and play your disc, Basil."

"Well, thanks," he arched an eyebrow in my direction. "What happened to you, Lieutenant? You seem to have got human all of a sudden."

"There is a softer side to my nature," I told him. "Most people don't see it because usually I sleep on it, but last week I invested in a mattress for my bed and ..."

He shuddered. "I'll just play the disc, if you don't mind?"

"Go right ahead, Basil," I told him.

He walked over to the hi-fi and put his disc on the turntable. I turned and looked at Greta. "Where was I?" I said. "I know. I was just telling you about the little things. The aspirin and the tranquilizers Lili Hertz bought from the drugstore the night she disappeared turned up in the drawer of her dressing table later on. Now, her story was that she'd left the drugstore and walked a hundred yards down the street when a car stopped beside her and two men jumped out, bundled her into the car and took her to Kirch's house. But when the things she had bought from the drugstore turned up in her dressing table, it made things look different, didn't it?"

Greta was staring at me blankly. "Huh?" she said.

"It meant that either the kidnappers had been most obliging and stopped outside her apartment and waited while she dropped off her purchases, or else she had just walked home, put the stuff in the drawer then gone out again to keep an appointment with somebody who was going to take her to the Big House."

"Huh?" Greta repeated.

I sipped some of my drink. "The second theory seems more plausible," I said. "That she kept a voluntary appointment to go to Kirch's house. And that means her sister, Lois, must have seen her come home and go out again. Yet Lois rushes down to the Eighth Precinct the following morning and reports her sister as missing and says the last time she saw her was when she left to go down to the drugstore."

Greta closed her eyes and took a long pull on her drink. "Crazy," she muttered, and stared at me again.

"So you've got both of them lying," I said. "Why? That's an intriguing question, isn't it, honey?"

"The most," she said blankly.

I put my drink onto a freeform table and hoped it didn't fall through. Then I lit myself a cigarette.

"We'll leave the Hertz sisters for a moment," I went on, "both lying like crazy, and talk about Absolem Kirch. The guy with more millions than he could count, and no friends and nobody to love him for his very self. He wanted female company. So he got female company. Girls came and went. They were looked after financially on a generous scale and they were content.

"The last thing he'd want to do would be forcibly abduct a girl. He'd lay himself open to criminal charges which could land him with twenty years or more in the pen ... or he could lay himself open to blackmail. So he only took the girls into his Big House who were willing if not eager to come of their own free will."

I blew a stream of smoke across the room. "Kirch would be a fascinating problem to a blackmailer," I said. "He was obviously fond of women, but shrewd enough not to step out of line far enough to expose himself to danger. But a blackmailer with a subtle mind could figure out something like this ...

"You need a pair of girls—if they happened to be sisters, so much the better. And one of them pushes herself under Kirch's notice, or his agent's notice—Walker, in this case. She suggests breathlessly that the height of her ambition is to grace the ancestral home of Absolem Kirch. It's a deal—he'll send a car to pick her up, and he does.

"The girls organize between them the little drama of Lili going down to the drugstore, then never being seen again. The following morning, another little drama when Big Sister reports Little Sister has disappeared. So now you have a basis prepared for the blackmailer to move in.

"But the blackmailer miscalculated on one thing," I went on. "With the connections Kirch had, he heard about the girl being reported missing and he passed the word through his tame D.A. that the girl was quite OK, had arrived of her own free will and the Missing Persons report should be pigeonholed.

"That's very frustrating to the blackmailer. Meanwhile, one eager Lieutenant by the name of Wheeler starts an investigation and starts finding out much too much, so he's got to be disposed of—so our blackmailer sets up Big Sister to pull her assault act."

Greta's eyes bulged. "You mean that Lois was lying about it being Walker who rang and told her to do that, if she wanted her sister safe?"

"Sure," I said. "Just as much as Lili was lying when she told me about being abducted by Walker for Kirch's sake. She lied because she thought that the blackmailer must have somehow organized me into making a rescue, and that was her story.

"The blackmailer found out about the rescue and it presented him with a terrible problem. Kirch could call the girl a liar once he realized what was happening, and the girl would then spill the whole beans. He had to prevent that at all costs and he or she did, by putting a bullet into Lili.

"Let's go back to Lois. She hears I have rescued her sister from Kirch. Then she hears that her sister has been murdered. It never occurs to her that their partner, the blackmailer, would have murdered Lili, so she thinks it must be Kirch. So she decides to lie all she can in testifying against Kirch before the Grand Jury.

"Our blackmailer by this time is gibbering. Lois is in exactly the same position that Lili was. Once she finds out the whole truth, she'll spill the beans. So the blackmailer hopes to dispose of Lois with a homemade time bomb attached to your car. And anybody else who goes up with it is coincidental."

Greta drained her glass. "Where did all this start?"

"A good question, honey," I said. "It started in a place where the blackmailer had regular contact with one of Kirch's men. Regular contact with Kirch himself would have been impossible, because he always employed people to shop for him—do everything that involved contact with the world outside his high walls. The name of the place was Maison Basiloff, of course."

She stared at me, the color draining from her face. "Al. You don't think that I ..."

"When I took Lili to my place after getting her out of the Big House," I said, "I only told two people she was there. One was Judge Bryan and the other was you. And the murderer arrived before the Judge, slugged me over the head and shot Lili. You were the only person I told of Lois's whereabouts when she was at the cabin. I told you it was three hours' run by car. I agreed with you to take the Cadillac. I agreed we should take Lois out for a picnic.

"Anybody knowing those facts and being a do-it-yourself fan could have manufactured the bomb and fitted it to the Cadillac, knowing that was the car to be used, and timed it to explode four hours after the Cadillac was due to leave—which was noon as I'd already told Lili. They couldn't be certain that the bomb would finish Lois, but there was a good chance that it would. The sort of chance that an amateur would take ..."

Greta backed off a pace, her hand to her mouth. "Al. You're saying that I'm the blackmailer. That I killed Lili and then put the bomb inside the car and killed Lois and those four men."

"You were the only one who had all the necessary information from me," I said.

I turned and walked down to the Picasso and lifted it up. "You," I added slowly, "and whoever was listening to every conversation and phone call that you and I ever had."

She closed her eyes and swayed on her toes for a moment. "Don't do things like that to me, Al," she told me. Then she registered. "That thing's a microphone. I thought it part of the air-conditioning. You mean that somebody heard everything we said?"

"Every single word," I agreed.

She just stood there and a deep blush started from her forehead and spread down over her face and then finally disappeared under the scoop neckline.

"Oh," she said faintly.

"You aren't playing your disc, Basil," I said. "I thought that *Night on the Bare Mountain* was your favorite piece of music?"

"I couldn't help listening to your conversation, Lieutenant," he said. "I found it fascinating."

"Blackmail could only appeal to a nasty little mind," I said. "A time bomb that would kill a number of other people besides the person it was meant to kill is the sort of murder weapon that needs a very special type of nasty little mind. The sort of nasty little mind that would enjoy *Night on the Bare Mountain*, not for the music itself, but for its associations. The sort of nasty little mind, in fact," I grinned at him, "that would wear a dressing gown in public, dear boy."

His lips curled back from his teeth in a snarl and it made him look the diseased rat that he was. I walked toward him slowly and he backed away a couple of paces, until he was against the wall and couldn't go any further.

"You can ask Greta about this," I said conversationally. "That afternoon when the car exploded and five people were killed, I swore that I would catch up with whoever put the bomb there. And when I caught up with them, I would strangle them with my own hands."

I stretched out my hands in front of me, the fingers crooked. They reached out slowly, drawing steadily closer to his throat. The pupils of his eyes dilated.

"No," he said. "You can't. You wouldn't. I'm only half your weight— half your size. It's just murder. I can't fight with my hand ... I don't know how. I haven't got the physical strength. It's just murder, that's what it is— murder." His voice broke hysterically on the last word.

"Basil, dear boy," I said as my fingers found his throat. "All you say is true. But even so, you've got much more of a chance than those five people sitting beside the Cadillac ever had."

My fingers tightened, choking his scream into a gurgle. I bent my arms so that I lifted him off the floor and his legs thrashed desperately, thumping against the wall in a tattoo of terror.

I gradually increased my grip on his throat and I saw his eyes bulge. His face was a mottled red and he looked as if he was going to explode at any moment.

"Al," Greta said desperately from behind me. "Don't."

"Stay out of this," I said thickly.

The tattoo on the wall was becoming spasmodic and each kick had less strength than the one before. It was only a matter of seconds.

I saw it swinging through the air out of the corner of my eye and l tried to duck, but it was too late. A full bottle of Scotch smashed against the side of my head, sending me crashing onto the floor in a haze of exploding fireworks. Somewhere along the line I'd lost my grip on Basil and I couldn't see him at all.

I lay there on the floor while the ceiling revolved crazily and then gradually it steadied down and I saw Greta standing there, the bottle still in her hand.

"You're a cop, Al Wheeler," she said passionately. "You could have lost your life trying to save Kirch's, when you faced that mob in his house last night. If you killed Basil, you aren't any better than those men who lynched Kirch. You're no better than Basil. You were murdering him—you understand? Murdering him. You—a lieutenant of police, sworn to uphold the law—and you take it into your own hands. Does murdering a murderer make you any less of a murderer?"

I rubbed the side of my head gently.

"Does it?" she demanded fiercely.

"I guess not," I said humbly. "You're right, Greta." I stumbled onto my feet. "Only next time, honey, use an empty bottle, will you? Maybe it won't hurt so much."

I heard a shuddering intake of breath beside me and then I remembered Basil. He was leaning against the wall, gulping great drafts of air into his lungs. Gradually he started to breathe normally again and his face lost the violent purple hue, but the look of horror was fixed in his eyes.

He shuddered suddenly. "I can't stand any sort of physical violence," he said jerkily. "My heart—it's ..."

He jerked upright almost onto his toes. Sudden pain distorted his features into a blur of writhing outlines.

"The pain," he whimpered. "In my side. Please. Don't let me have to ..." Then he groaned piteously and suddenly relaxed.

He hit the floor limp and lay there without moving.

"I'll get a doctor," Greta said quickly.

I knelt down beside him and felt for a heartbeat.

"Don't bother about a doctor, honey," I told her. "He needs a hearse."

THE END

Chorine Makes a Killing

— — — —

Carter Brown

CHAPTER 1

I was having a quiet evening at home. It was quiet because I'd mislaid my blonde date—she'd gone out with another guy just because he wanted to marry her. I'll never understand women.

So there I was, with some muted Kostelanetz strings playing on the hi-fi, a tall glass by my right elbow, and the latest copy of *Sports Cars Unlimited* in front of me.

I was reading about the new Jaguar XK-SS—a 170 m.p.h. car developed from the 0-type. As far as I could see there was only one thing wrong with it from my point of view and that was the price ... six thousand nine hundred dollars.

I made that sort of money, but it took me twelve months to do it. That's the trouble with being in a legitimate business like being a cop—it's a healthy life but you don't make much money. And when you have a hi-fi set-up and an untold number of blondes, brunettes and redheads to support, the price of the Jag looked as obtainable as the price of the moon.

The buzzer sounded and I stopped thinking about sports cars and started thinking that maybe my blonde date had stopped thinking about marriage and started thinking about Al Wheeler. That thought put enough adrenalin through my veins to take me to the front door in two seconds flat.

I swung open the door and said, "Honey! It's wonderful to see you!"

"It's wonderful to see you too, sugar," replied a short, bald-headed guy with an over-large paunch.

"Well," I said. "As I lie and feel sick. If it isn't Mr. Moss, the eager beaver from United Insurance."

"Hello, Wheeler," he grunted. "Like you to meet Mr. Irvine, of Hammond, Irvine and Snooks."

I looked at the tall guy in the grey homburg and dark topcoat standing beside Moss. "Hello, Mr. Irvine of Hammond, Irvine and Snooks."

"I wondered if I could have a talk with you, Mr. Wheeler," he said in a courteous voice. "It's rather urgent."

"Why not?" I said. "Only it's Lieutenant, not Mister."

"That's what I wanted to talk to you about," he said.

"Come on in," I said.

Moss cleared his throat. "If you don't mind, Al, I won't come in. I only tagged along to introduce Mr. Irvine to you and let you know he's okay."

"The only thing I know from your introducing him is he's a good insurance risk," I replied. "How's that psychic stomach of yours—getting any rumbles lately?"

Moss laughed half-heartedly. "He's a funny guy, Mr. Irvine, or he thinks he is, anyway."

"Quite," Irvine said cautiously.

"Be seeing you, Al," Moss said. "Just don't make any insurance claims."

I took Irvine into the living-room and poured him a drink.

"I'm sorry to disturb you at home, Lieutenant," he said. "But the matter I wished to discuss with you is of vital importance and urgency."

"You're a lawyer?" I said cleverly.

"Correct."

"I deny it!" I said firmly. "I don't even know the girl!"

"I beg your pardon?"

"And I certainly never mentioned marriage," I went on. "And in any case, on what a cop makes a year, it isn't worth your while to sue for breach of promise."

"I think there must be some misunderstanding," Irvine said. "I came to see you in the hope of a confidential talk with you, that's all."

I relaxed a little. "In that case," I said, "why don't you sit down?"

"Thank you," he replied, and sat on the edge of an armchair. "I think I should tell you a little about Hammond, Irvine and Snooks, Lieutenant. We are attorneys-at-law, with quite a good practice. We handle mainly criminal cases—we have built up a certain reputation in that field."

"Bully for you, Mr. Irvine," I said brightly.

He took a cautious sip of his drink and smiled uncertainly. "Well, thank you, Lieutenant. Of late, my other two partners and myself have felt there is something lacking in our organisation. There is a definite need for someone to handle the minor investigations we often require on behalf of a client."

"You want the name of a good private detective?" I suggested.

He shook his head decisively. "No, Lieutenant. We feel that anyone so employed by us would be handling detail of a most confidential nature … and that person should be in our employ. You can appreciate he would have to be experienced, capable of making his own decisions and entirely trustworthy."

"I'm sorry," I said. "I don't know anybody like that."

Irvine permitted himself a fleeting smile. "We think we do, Lieutenant."

"In that case," I said. "Why don't you go talk to him?"

"I am," he said.

I poured myself another drink. "Well, what the hell are you doing here then? Why waste your time talking to …" I stopped pouring and stared at him. "Me?"

"Precisely," he nodded. "You, Lieutenant. You have quite a high reputation in some quarters, you know. A reputation for being unorthodox, but also for getting things done."

"But I'm a cop."

"It's possible for even policemen to resign," he said. "We feel we could make you a worthwhile offer."

I finished pouring the drink, drank it straight down and started to refill the glass again.

"It's an idea that will take some getting used to," I said finally. "I never thought anyone but Commissioner Lavers could tolerate me for any length of time."

"Your salary is seven thousand dollars per annum, I understand, Lieutenant," he said. "We are prepared to offer you twice that. And a reasonable expense account, of course."

I closed my eyes and saw a brand new XK-SS standing in the driveway. An XK-SS with the most beautiful blonde you ever did see sitting inside it. And me, in a custom-made suit, dropping a diamond necklace into her lovely lap and saying casually, "It's nothing, honey. Just an item on my expense account."

I opened my eyes again and the dream faded a little. "What would I have to do?" I asked him.

"Well," he said. "Perhaps the best way to answer that would be to give you a hypothetical case."

"I already have a briefcase," I said. "But I suppose another one would come in handy."

"Suppose, just for the sake of an example," he said carefully. "We had a client—Smith, we'll call him—who was innocently involved in a murder."

"It's always a guy named Smith who gets innocently involved in a murder," I said. "If his name is Hackenbush, the jury know right away he's guilty."

Irvine sighed gently. "Smith is a man of some standing in the community, a man with a solid reputation for integrity and so on. A family—wife and daughter. But unfortunately, like a number of other middle-aged men, he forms an illicit liaison with a chorus-girl—a chorine."

"And the chorus-girl gets herself murdered in the apartment he rented for her," I said. "And when the police arrive they find Smith there with the corpse. And the gun that killed her is on the floor and it shows Smith's fingerprints under test. Smith himself appears dazed, claims he doesn't know what happened but claims he didn't shoot her."

Irvine raised his eyebrows a fraction. "Go on, Lieutenant—tell me more."

"Sure," I said. "In Smith's office, the police find a letter from the girl threatening to tell his wife and his co-directors in the steel organisation he is president of. She says in the letter she is sick and tired of him and he either pays her twenty thousand dollars to keep quiet or else. So it looks like the most open and shut of this year's open and shut cases. The cops charge him with first-degree murder and there's no bail allowed.

"There are a couple of points more—Smith's name is Walter J. Byrne, president of United Steel, and the murdered girl's name was Wendy Martin. And it happened three days ago."

Irvine pursed his lips and nodded slowly. "Will you consider our proposition, Lieutenant?"

"Byrne is your client?"

"That's correct, Lieutenant."

"Plead insanity," I said. "That's the only hope you've got."

"Mr. Byrne is not only our client," Irvine said. "He is also a personal friend of our senior partner, Mr. Hammond. And Mr. Hammond is convinced that Mr. Byrne is innocent."

"On what grounds?"

"Personal knowledge of our client. Mr. Hammond has known Mr. Byrne for a great number of years."

"Nobody knows anybody else well enough to know whether they'll commit a murder or not," I said. "Mr. Hammond may let sentiment cloud his judgment."

"Once you've met our Mr. Hammond," he smiled thinly, "you will realise that is an accusation that could never be made against him."

I lit myself a cigarette and noticed Peggy Lee had replaced Kostelanetz on the hi-fi. "If I accept your offer, Mr. Byrne will be my first job?"

"Precisely, Lieutenant. You might regard it in the nature of a challenge."

"I might," I said. "I might also regard it as hopeless!"

"The girl," he said, "Wendy Martin. She worked for club called the Due D'Or. A nightclub of dubious reputation with an illegal gaming-room in the back. The proprietress is a woman by the name of Isobel Lamont."

"Oh."

"Mr. Hammond feels that she may know more about the murder than she has said."

"Your Mr. Hammond seems to know all the answers," I said. "Why doesn't he hire himself to clear Mr. Byrne and save you fourteen thousand dollars a year?"

He shrugged his shoulders. "A qualified attorney cannot afford to jeopardise his professional standing, Lieutenant—but someone like yourself, with your *unorthodox* approach coupled with your professional experience as a lieutenant of detectives, could handle this assignment. You would be an invaluable addition to our staff. What do you say?"

I closed my eyes and saw that XK-SS again, and this time there was a magnificent brunette sitting inside it. I dropped a diamond pendant into her lovely lap and told her, "It's only a trinket, doll. An item on my expense account."

I opened my eyes again and forced myself back into reality. "If I did take it, how soon do you want me to start work?"

"Right away," he said. "With each day, the trail grows colder and our chances of uncovering new evidence to clear Mr. Byrne grow less."

"I would want your assurance I could work in my own way, without any interference from you or either of your partners."

"I think I could give you that assurance, Lieutenant."

"And fourteen thousand a year and expenses?"

"Precisely. We'd pay you monthly by cheque—in advance."

"I'll take it!" I said.

What else could I do? Lavers' term in office had two more years to run, and then he would retire. I wouldn't find another Commissioner of Police who would tolerate my methods for more than five minutes. I'd been lucky to last this long.

"I'm glad to hear you say that, Mr. Wheeler," Irvine said.

"Lieut …" I stopped. "That's right—Mister—I'll get used to it."

"You won't regret it," he said. "Will you get in touch with me and let me know as soon as you can start? And believe me, Mr. Wheeler, the sooner the better."

"I think I can organise that," I said. "I'll let you know."

"Then I look forward to a long and happy association," Irvine said, and shook my hand firmly.

I escorted him to the front door and then came back to the living-room after he'd gone. I picked up the phone and dialled Lavers' home number and he answered. I recognised his bark—like a mad dog that's just been prodded with a sharp spike.

"I would like to talk to a barrel of lard, commonly known as Lavers," I said. "To rhyme with Slavers. Slavers: to drool at the mouth or slave-drive. Both definitions are appropriate."

There was a choking noise at the other end of the line.

"I am sick and fired of playing cops and robbers with a greaseball playing Commissioner," I said. "I quit! As of now. If you want me to work out another fortnight, I have to warn you that I shall resent it. I shall pour ink over your desk, set fire to your wastepaper-bin and make violent love to your secretary whenever you wish to dictate correspondence. Should said correspondence accidentally be typed, I shall add it immediately to the flames of the wastepaper-bin!"

The volcano erupted at the other end of the line. "Wheeler, if you're even half-serious about this, I accept your resignation with pleasure! You don't have to work it out—we'll deduct a fortnight's pay from your final cheque in lieu!" There was a gloating tone in his snarl. "How would that suit you?"

"Fine!" I said.

There was a short silence the other end.

"All right," he said. "You've had your joke. Now tell me what it's all about!"

"I have," I said. "I quit. And you deduct a fortnight's pay instead of me working out the fortnight. Thanks, greaseball!"

"Are you drunk?"

"Sober as a Commissioner."

"You really mean this—you want to resign?"

"You got it."

"And this isn't a gag?"

"No!"

The silence started to grow man-sized again. "What are you going to do?"

"I've got another job."

"Well," Lavers heaved a sigh. "You can offer my condolences to your new employers. Only please make it quite clear to them, Wheeler, that under no circumstances will the Police Department take you back." Then his voice rose an octave. "Not even to put you where you belong … scrubbing floors!"

A moment later the receiver smashed down, the noise exploding inside my eardrum.

CHAPTER 2

It was a neat, efficient-looking office with a neat desk, a comfortable chair, two filing cabinets and a door with a frosted glass panel. On the door was stencilled Mr. A. Wheeler. From where I sat behind the desk it read releehW .A .rM. I resolved never to look at it when suffering from a hangover.

I had been there precisely one hour. The offices of Hammond, Irvine and Snooks were vast and palatial. Irvine had shown me into the office, told me it was mine, then disappeared, saying he would be back. So far he hadn't been back.

I lit myself a cigarette and shifted uneasily in the chair. I was getting tired of the office. An office is for cornering a secretary and I didn't have a secretary—only four corners. I was getting bored and already getting nostalgic for the Commissioner's office where at least there would be the Commissioner's secretary to look at, if not corner.

The door opened suddenly and a refugee from a tailor's shop came in. I took a second look at him and revised my opinion. He was a refugee from the Moravian Desert. He had a completely bald head, a hooked nose and sagging bags under his eyes. He looked like a dissipated vulture wanting somewhere he could die quietly without any fuss. I didn't blame him—if I looked like that I'd feel the same way.

He stood in front of the desk and glared at me from beneath hooded lids. His suit was shapeless and hung around him in folds. It looked as if he had slept in it for the past twenty years.

"If you've come to empty the wastepaper bin," I said, "you're too early. I haven't even started to fill it yet."

"Wheeler?" he asked. His voice was high-pitched and metallic, off-key and grated like a hacksaw blade against glass.

"That's me," I said. "But the wastepaper bin is still clean."

"My name is Hammond!" he said.

I digested that fact. "Will you give me a reference?"

He came a couple of steps nearer to the desk. "I might add, Wheeler, that your being here was not my idea—but my two partners' idea. I consider it a waste of money. But since you are here, I feel it necessary to point out to you that we are not paying you a fantastic sum of money for you to sit on your chair, doing nothing!"

"I think I see what you mean," I said cautiously.

"You had better start your investigations into the Byrne case right away," he went on. "What is the first thing you propose doing?"

"Getting away from you, Mr. Hammond," I said promptly.

He smiled, giving a perfect impersonation of a screaming skull. "In this organisation, Wheeler," he said slowly, "you will find that is impossible!"

"Impossible or not," I said, "I intend to try. Good morning, Mr. Hammond." I got up from behind the desk and beat it out of the office at a rapid rate.

Two floors lower down I slowed down to a walk, and came around a corner straight into Irvine.

"You're in a hurry, Mr. Wheeler?" he asked.

"I have just had a session with the living dead," I said. "Who says his name is Hammond!"

"Oh? And what did Mr. Hammond have to say?"

I gave it to him verbatim. When I had finished, Irvine smiled feebly, "Mr. Hammond likes his little jokes."

"That must be the only thing he does like," I said.

"Don't let him upset you," Irvine said. "He always adopts that attitude to the employees—even to myself and Mr. Snooks. It's just his way."

"In future I intend to stay away from his way," I said. "As far away as I can get!"

He nodded. "Did you have any immediate plans? Where will you start?"

"I think I'll start with Mrs. Byrne," I said. "A wife generally knows her husband better than he does."

"That sounds a good idea," he said. "If you like, I'll ring Mrs. Byrne and let her know you're coming out to see her."

"Fine," I said.

I took the elevator to the ground floor and walked out of the building and along the block to where my new pride and joy was parked against the kerb. There it stood—the brand-new XK-SS, its duco a flaming scarlet gleaming in the morning sunlight. The day before I'd traded in my other sports car as a down payment and in just another twelve months and five thousand dollars, the XK-SS would be all mine.

I slid into the driving seat and started the engine. It sounded like something from outer space and I moved it out into the line of traffic and at the first stop-light, three guys stalled their cars when they heard me coming.

Twenty minutes' driving brought me to the Byrne residence, which was one of those comfortable houses that anybody can afford ... providing they're in the fifty thousand dollars a year bracket. It had a nice winding driveway lined with poplars, and outside the front of the house this year's Cadillac and a near-new Porsche were parked.

A butler opened the door and by that very act Byrne had to be in the seventy thousand a year or up income bracket. Butlers, besides being hard to get, are most expensive this year.

"Wheeler," I told him. "To see Mrs. Byrne."

"Yes, sir," he nodded. "You're expected. Mrs. Byrne is waiting for you in the sunroom."

I looked up at the cloud-ridden sky. "I'm glad she's not waiting for the sun!"

"Yes, indeed, sir," he said. "If you will follow me?"

I followed him down the hallway, the length of the house and then into the sunroom. You could tell it was a sunroom because three of the walls were glass and all the furniture was cane. I thought it was a little indecent of the sun not to appear after the obvious trouble the Byrnes had taken to prepare for it.

"Mr. Wheeler," the butler announced, then turned around and disappeared.

A woman got up from one of the cane chairs. Life is full of surprises, as the blonde said the first time she was shown an etching. Mrs. Byrne was brunette, beautiful and knew it. She wore a skirt and sweater which would have been conventional on a lesser figure. But Mrs. Byrne gave them curves and lines, light and shadow, that gave them almost a life of their own. And what a life!

I swallowed twice and got my voice back. "Good morning, Mrs. Byrne," I said.

"Good morning, Mr. Wheeler," she said. "Mr. Irvine rang to say you were coming out to see me. I'm afraid you're wasting your time. There is nothing more I can tell you."

"I'm new on this case," I said. "So I haven't heard anybody's story except the official one—the one the police have."

"Oh, yes," she said. "Mr. Irvine mentioned that you were an ex-policeman." She made it sound rather unclean.

"So anything you can tell me would help," I said.

"Why don't you sit down?" she suggested.

I sat down on a cane chair that was more comfortable than it looked.

"I don't know anything much about it," she said. "My husband apparently was running around with this chorus-girl." She sniffed delicately. "I always suspected he had a vulgar streak in him—and this proved it. Have you seen a photograph of the girl? Well, really!"

"Do you think he killed her?"

"It seems quite obvious that he did," she replied. "Walter has always been a moral coward. I could quite imagine him doing something as stupid as that, if he were faced with the threat of exposure."

"If he's convicted he'll go to the gas chamber," I said. "Doesn't that worry you at all, Mrs. Byrne?"

"I'm afraid I don't appreciate that question, Mr. Wheeler," she said.

I lit myself a cigarette. "The reason I asked it, Mrs. Byrne, was that if you don't care whether your husband is convicted of this murder or not, there isn't very much point in my asking you for help."

She crossed her legs and the movement was a poem in itself. "I don't want to see him die, of course," she said. "But if he did kill this girl and is convicted of the murder, there isn't much I can do about it, is there?"

"If you would answer some of my questions it might help."

"Very well," she said.

I drew smoke deep into my lungs. "What sort of relationship did you have with your husband? Were you friendly?"

"We have been married three years," she told me. "This is his second marriage. Walter, as you probably know, is considerably older than I am. He has a daughter by his first marriage, Lucrece. She lives here with us. After the first six months of our marriage, Walter seemed to lose interest in his home life. He spent a good deal of time away from the house. I thought it was pressure of work that kept him away—he's the president of United Steel, as you probably know. I didn't suspect another woman … I didn't think Walter was the type." She shrugged her shoulders. "It just goes to prove that you never really know another person—not even your husband."

"The night of the murder?" I asked her. "Did you see him at all that night?"

"He was here for dinner," she said. "Then he told me he had an appointment he had to keep and he left around eight-thirty. I didn't see him again until the police contacted me."

"And you had no idea of the existence of the girl—Wendy Martin—until the police told you what had happened?"

"None at all."

I stubbed out the cigarette and looked out through one of the glass walls. The sky looked even dirtier than it had when I'd first entered the house.

"Thanks, Mrs. Byrne," I told her. "I can't think of any other questions right now. If I do, may I call back and see you?"

"Of course," she said. "But I think you're wasting your time, Mr. Wheeler. I'm afraid Walter killed the girl and there is just nothing that anybody can do that will alter the fact."

I left the sunroom and walked down the hallway. The butler appeared with my hat.

"Thanks," I said as I took it. "Have you been here long?"

"Twelve months, sir," he said.

"I'm from the lawyers—Hammond, Irvine and Snooks," I said.

"So I understand, sir. Mrs. Byrne was good enough to inform me of the nature of your call."

"Then you don't mind if I ask you some questions?"

"Not at all, sir."

"What's your name?"

"Billings, sir. Cedric Billings."

I took another look at him. When you really looked at him, you realised he wasn't a bad-looking guy at all. Somewhere in his middle thirties, tall, dark-haired. Impassive face, intelligent eyes.

"What did you think of Mr. Byrne, between the two of us?"

"Mr. Byrne is a very good employer, sir."

"Is that all?"

"Should there be anything else, sir?"

"How about Mrs. Byrne?"

"A very considerate lady."

"Okay," I stuck my hat on my head. "It sounds like a beautiful family. You tell the police the same story?"

"Of course, sir," he smiled momentarily. "It's the truth."

I gave up.

He opened the door for me and I went down the steps to the Jag. I had company—somebody was sitting in the passenger's seat. Somebody who was young, blonde and wearing a silk shirt tucked into a pair of shorts. I got closer and took a better look. Filling more than their share of the car were two long, suntanned legs.

"I meant to ask the dealer about a mascot to go with the car," I said. "This really is a nice thought on his part."

"Get in," the blonde said, "and you can drive me somewhere."

"Where?"

"Some place they'll sell us a drink," she said. "That Porsche up ahead is mine. I haven't ridden in one of these before. Now is my chance."

"Who am I to argue with, lady?" I said, and plunked down beside her.

"I'm not a lady," she said. "I'm Lucrece, but no Borgia!"

I started the engine and drove down the driveway towards the gates.

"Turn left and take the coast road," she said. "You can buy me a drink at the Cabana on the beach. It's five miles and you can let this out a little."

"I'm running it in," I told her. "Nothing over ninety."

"Piker!" she snorted.

We reached the Cabana four minutes later and I swung the car off the road into the parking lot.

"Let's sit under one of those striped umbrellas and get some more sun," she said.

"Okay," I said. I got out of the car and followed her across to an empty table. She walked with a lithe swing of her hips—a walk which would have been athletic except that her curves were much too feminine to make you think of anything athletic.

We sat down and a waiter appeared.

"What will you have?" I asked her.

"Vodka and lime juice," she said.

I winced. "And I'll have a Scotch on the rocks."

The waiter went away. I offered her a cigarette and lit it for her and one for myself.

"You're Lucrece?" I said. "Not one of the Borgias—the Boston Borgias?"

"I am Lucrece Byrne," she told me. "One of the Murdering Byrnes!"

I winced again. "You are the daughter?"

"Of the first part," she agreed. "And Myra is the party of the second part."

"Myra is the current Mrs. Byrne?"

"You're smart," she said. "You've been talking to her for the last fifteen minutes and right away you catch on when I mention her name."

The waiter came back with the drinks and I paid him.

She lifted her glass. "You are Mr. Wheeler," she said. "From the celebrated trio of attorneys—Hammond, Irvine and Snooks."

"Check."

"Mr. Al Wheeler," she said. "Formerly Lieutenant of Police Wheeler, known as the Unorthodox Cop. I read about you in the newspapers."

"I'm flattered."

"No need to be," she said coolly. "I always read the funnies."

I sipped some of my Scotch. "Having a drink at the Cabana with a blonde so well-shaped as you is nice. Is there a special reason?"

"I thought you might like me to talk about my father," she said calmly. "And I thought you might also like me to talk about my stepmother—who is at least six years older than I am. I thought you might like me to even talk about our butler—and my stepmother!"

"You're really a horror, aren't you?"

Lucrece nodded complacently. "That's what Myra calls me—a horror. Ever since I found her and Billings in what the magazines used to call 'an embarrassing situation'. But I thought I was quite generous about it. I didn't reproach her for it. I didn't even run straight to Father with the news. I just offered her a working arrangement."

"A working arrangement?"

"She pays my garage bills for the month," Lucrece said, "and I make like a clam. A very reasonable arrangement. But now that Father looks like he's heading for the gas-chamber, she's welshed on the deal."

I took another pull on my glass. I needed it.

"So I'd like to see Father cleared, if that's possible," she went on. "I can't afford to pay those bills out of my allowance. I'd like to see things come back to normal again."

"You must love him very deeply," I said. "I've never heard of a stronger emotional reason for wanting your father cleared of a murder indictment."

She finished her drink and waved her hand over her head until the waiter reappeared. "Two more," she told him. "And double the vodka in mine."

"Yes, Miss Byrne," the waiter said, and removed the glasses.

She smiled at me. "Where were we? Oh, yes, you were just about through with your cheap sarcasm. I thought that if you're investigating the murder, there are a couple of points you should know. Point one—the beautiful Myra married Father strictly for his money and social position. And the beautiful Myra got very bored with both after the first twelve months of the marriage and has been playing the field ever since. But over the last few months the field has narrowed down to one … Billings. Billings has a lot in his favour. He is tall, handsome and discreet. And being an employee, he is always available."

I paid for the second round of drinks and watched the waiter's receding back for a few moments.

"Are you trying to suggest that Myra may have had something to do with the chorine's murder?"

"Oh, no," she shook her head. "I'm sure she didn't. She was home at the time the murder was committed. But Billings wasn't. It was his night off."

"That's interesting," I said.

"I thought you might think it was," Lucrece smiled dreamily. "I must admit I never have liked Billings. He wouldn't even make a pass at me one time when I offered him active encouragement. No man ignores little Lucrece and gets away with it."

"I can imagine," I said. "I wonder you haven't introduced a little cyanide into his morning coffee."

"I did think of it," she admitted. "But I don't like obvious methods."

"Did you know about your father and Wendy Martin?"

"No," she said. "I wish I had—I could have got my allowance doubled, probably. But then I always miss out on the best dirt."

"You're a charming child."

"I'm not a child—I'm a full twenty-one," she said. She looked down at her shirt complacently. "And if I were a child, I'd be a little over-developed, don't you think?"

"I think!" I agreed.

"I'm glad of that," she said. "So few men do."

I lit another cigarette helplessly and watched even more helplessly while Lucrece took it out of my fingers and put it into her mouth.

"Where are your manners, Al?" she asked. "Don't you know it's polite to offer the lady a smoke?"

"I didn't realise you were a lady as well," I said. "My humble apologies."

"I thought I could help you with your investigation," she went on. "I'll keep my ears pinned back inside the house. I've got a natural genius for picking out anything somebody is trying to hide."

"I'll bet you have."

"So you'd better take me with you when you go to the Due D'Or," she said. "How about tonight? You'd better not pick me up at the house. I'll come around to your place around eight. You can have the drinks ready."

CHAPTER 3

It was fifteen minutes to eight. I had the drinks ready. I had even got in a bottle of vodka especially for the occasion. I'd set up the turntable of the hi-fi unit with "Danse Macabre" followed by "Night On Bare Mountain". It was the nearest I could get to suitable mood music for Lucrece Byrne.

She arrived at eight precisely. She wore a short evening gown that was shorter at the top than at the bottom. I looked at it and goggled.

"What did you put that on with—fish-glue?" I asked her.

"Liquid cement," she replied. "It's the latest thing in anti-wolf devices. Haven't you poured me a drink yet?"

"I didn't think punctuality would be one of your vices," I apologised. "I got a bottle of vodka special."

"Charge it to your expense account," she said. "In fact, you can charge the whole evening to your expense account. I'm going to drink nothing else but champagne the whole night at the Due D'Or, and I'm going to have at least three serves of pheasant under glass."

"The pheasant won't be the only bird under glass if that happens!" I said. "And I'm not at all sure I can charge this to expenses. Having met the senior partner this morning, I doubt if I could charge an aspirin to expenses."

"Don't worry about him," she said. "He's a friend of Father's. You only have to tell him you found a couple of valuable clues and he'll okay the account without even reading it."

"I wish I could believe you," I said.

I handed her a vodka and lime juice.

"Are you going to play me some music?" she asked, nodding towards the turntable.

"Sure." I went across and switched it on. "Your signature tune, honey." A moment later the opening bars of "Danse Macabre" flowed across the room.

"Very amusing," she said coldly.

"I'm glad your sense of humour is as well-developed as the rest of you," I said.

She finished her drink and helped herself to another, pouring almost exactly three times the quantity of vodka into the glass that I had.

"I'm still not quite sure why you're coming with me tonight," I said.

"I'm helping you in your investigation," she said. "I thought that was obvious. Wendy Martin kicked her legs up in the chorus at the nightclub. So obviously you must investigate the club and try and find out something of her background. I'm going to help you."

"You're very kind," I said.

"Warm-hearted, generous," she said airily. "That's me. The proverbial heart of gold."

"Encased in granite?"

"Come on," she said, and finished her drink. "We don't want to be late or we might miss that pheasant under glass."

We went out to the Jaguar. Her Porsche was parked next to it on the driveway. "You can drive," she said.

"Thanks very much."

We arrived at the Due D'Or some twenty minutes later and the head-waiter showed us to a table near the floor. Lucrece ordered two bottles of champagne as a starter, then got down to the serious business of ordering food which included the pheasant under glass. For the next hour she was too busy eating to talk very much. Finally when she had reached the cof-fee stage, she ordered two more bottles of champagne, then lit a cigarette and settled back in her chair with a contented sigh.

I looked at her bitterly. "I hope your girdle strangles you!"

She smiled contentedly. "I never wear one, don't need the things. Isn't it time the floorshow started?"

"If you like I'll make an offer for the club, then it could start whenever you want it to start!"

"That's an idea," she said interestedly.

Ten minutes later the floorshow did start. It wasn't exactly unique. It had a compere who told mildly risqué stories, a juggler who managed not to drop anything and a chorus-line who kicked up their heels almost as if they enjoyed doing it. When it was all over and the lights were turned full on again, I saw Lucrece had her chin in her hand and an air of intense con-centration on her face.

"If you're thinking of another serve of pheasant under glass," I told her, "it will only be over my dead body!"

"That wouldn't worry me," she replied. "I was thinking of helping you, but you wouldn't appreciate that."

"If you'd stop drinking champagne, I'd consider that a help."

"I was thinking that since Wendy Martin isn't with them any more, they're probably a girl short in the chorus-line," she said. "The poster out-side says eight beautiful girls and I counted them—there were only seven."

"So what?"

"So why don't I apply for a job in the chorus-line? That way I'd really be working on the inside. All those other girls would have known Wendy and they'd open up to another chorine, where they'd never open up to you."

"That's an idea that's just crazy enough to have some sense in it," I said.

"But you wouldn't be able to do the dance routines."

"Oh, yes I would," she said. "I took dancing lessons. When I was a child of nineteen, I had an ambition to go on the stage."

"How long ago was that?"

"All of three years," she said disdainfully. "I gave up the idea when I realised it would probably mean getting up early in the mornings. I hate getting up early in the mornings, don't you?"

"Yes," I admitted. "But you might have to get up early in this job."

"It's a nightclub," she said triumphantly. "It says so outside quite distinctly. I don't mind staying up late—even if it's only to kick my legs in the air. I've got a nice pair of legs—did you notice them this morning?"

"With those shorts you were wearing, how could I miss?"

"I'm glad you noticed," she said smugly. "That's why I wore those shorts—I wear those shorts for the same reason a fisherman baits a hook."

"You think you've got me hooked?"

"Not yet," she said. "But you're swimming around in an awfully tight circle right now."

I gave up. "Okay—go and get a job as a chorine."

"I think I will," she said. "Maybe it would be a good idea if we aren't seen together afterwards, don't you think?"

"I suppose so," I said slowly.

"I'll see you back at your house. I'll get a cab after I've got the job." She got to her feet. "Keep an upturned glass close to the vodka bottle for me till I arrive."

She sauntered across the floor and I watched her walk. Sister Kate couldn't have taught Lucrece one single thing. I finished my drink, had another and then called the waiter over. I got out one of the Hammond, Irvine and Snooks business cards that Irvine had given me and scribbled on the back: *Am investigating the death of Wendy Martin. Could you spare me a few minutes?*

Then I gave the waiter the card and a sawbuck and asked him to deliver it to Miss Lamont. He went on his way and I poured myself one more drink. Isobel Lamont, owner of the Due D'Or, had herself quite a reputation around the town, and that made interesting thinking to fill in the time. The waiter came back five minutes later and told me Miss Lamont would see me. I got up from the table and followed him across the floor and then down a corridor past some changing-rooms, until we came to a door marked, Office.

The waiter left me then. I knocked on the door and a feminine voice called out to come in, so I went in, closing the door behind me.

Miss Lamont sat behind a neat desk, looking neat herself. She wore a neat black suit with a neat nylon blouse underneath, and her black hair was pulled neatly back across her head. She wore a pair of heavy-framed, black tortoiseshell glasses—the only feminine touch was a pair of long pearl earrings that swayed gently with the movement of the air-conditioned air.

"Sit down, Mr. Wheeler," she said, and glanced at the square-faced wristwatch on her wrist. "I can give you five minutes of my time."

I sat down facing her and lit a cigarette.

"I don't really think I can tell you much," she said. "I told the police all I know."

"I'd like to hear it," I said.

"Wendy Martin had been in the chorus-line for perhaps six months," she said in a flat voice. "She kept herself to herself. She was hard-working, never missed a show, was never even late for a rehearsal. That's about all I can tell you."

"You didn't know that Mr. Byrne was paying the rent of her apartment?"

"No," she said crisply. "And even if I had, I wouldn't have considered it any of my business."

I thought about it for a few moments. "Did Mr. Byrne come here at all?"

"Yes," she nodded. "Quite a few times."

"Did he play the tables?"

"Yes."

"Lose much?"

"Not that I recall."

"Win much?"

"Not that I recall."

"Did he strike you as the sort of man who'd commit murder?"

"I don't know the sort of man who'd commit murder, Mr. Wheeler," she said. "So I'm afraid I can't answer that question."

I stubbed out my cigarette and she glanced at the square-faced wristwatch again. "You have three minutes left, Mr. Wheeler, are there any more questions?"

"I can't think of any in particular, Miss Lamont," I said. "If I do, I'll come back."

"I don't really think I can be of any help to you, Mr. Wheeler. I told you I don't know anything about it. Not one single thing."

"Well, thanks for your four and a half minutes," I told her.

I went back to the table, had one more drink, paid the bill and prayed Hammond would accept it as expenses, then left. I drove back to the house and saw the lights were on and heard some gravel voice Satchmo giving out on the hi-fi. I walked into the house, into the living-room and a long leg waved me a greeting from the depths of an armchair.

The vodka bottle was two-thirds empty and Lucrece Byrne sat comfortably curled up in the armchair, her shoes off and her gown hitched well above her knees.

"Hi!" she said brightly, if a little indistinctly. "You are now talking to one of the army of working-girls. I have a rehearsal at eleven a.m. tomorrow."

"You got the job?"

"It was a cinch." She tried snapping her fingers a couple of times, then gave up. "Easy! There's a character named Rogers and he said, 'Show me your legs, kid!' And I did. He just took one long look and said, 'You're hired!' And there I was—hired."

"Seeing that I have to be up early in the morning," I said, "supposing I take you home?"

"Got my own transport. That beautiful li'l Porsche—not to be confused with Bill Shakespeare's beautiful li'l Portia! So I've got all the time in the world to go home, Mister ex-Lieutenant Al Wheeler. And you haven't even kissed me yet!"

"That can wait," I said, "until you're sober."

"But, Al-honey," Lucrece looked surprised. "That's practically never!"

"That I can believe," I said. "Tell me about Mr. Hammond."

"That creep."

"That friend of your father's and my employer," I said. "That fount of human kindness who is going to okay my expense account in the morning. How come he worries so much about your father?"

She shook her head. "Don't ask me. I don't think he's human, except sometimes I see him watching me out of the corner of his eye and then I get his message!"

"I would as soon call a vulture my blood-brother as call Hammond my friend," I said. "What did he and your father have in common?"

"That is one of life's mysteries, Al ol' pal," she said solemnly. "I know what my dear stepmother and that charming butler have in common. I even have a shrewd idea of what you and I have in common—if you'd only relax a little. But what dear ol' Pa and Hammond have in common, I don't know."

I poured myself a Scotch and managed to accidentally knock the vodka bottle with my elbow, so that it fell to the floor and the remaining contents seeped into the carpet.

"Look what you've done!" she said in an agonised voice. "And I never drink anything else! What am I going to do?"

"I could cut a couple of squares out of the carpet and give you a vodka sandwich?" I suggested. She answered me in four sharp words that could have raised blisters on my skin.

I drank some of my Scotch and looked at her. "You know something?" I said. "I never met a case like this before—everybody knows nothing. Nobody knows anything. I even wonder that your father and Wendy Martin ever met each other."

"It's wheels within wheels within wheels, buster," Lucrece said drowsily. "And if you can't keep this damned room still for just a couple of seconds, I'm going to complain to the City Fathers!"

She staggered to her feet and stood there swaying gently for a moment. Then she turned around so that her back was towards me.

"I can't breathe, Wheeler," she said. "Unhook me."

"What happens if I do?"

"Why, Wheeler," she said dreamily, "just everything comes apart, that's what."

"Honey," I said, "you stay hooked."

She teetered around on the balls of her feet until she faced me again. "I think you're scared of me," she said.

"That's right," I agreed. "Are you ready to go home now?"

"Don't be ridic … ridi … abshurd!" she said coldly, then passed out gently at my feet.

I picked her up and carried her out to the Jag and put her in the front seat. I drove back to the Byrne residence and carried her in my arms up the front steps and pressed the buzzer. The butler opened the door a few seconds later and looked at me, impassively.

"I am returning Miss Byrne," I said. "Miss Byrne has had rather a full evening."

"Yes, sir," he said. "Miss Byrne often does have a rather full evening. If you would be so kind as to deposit her in that chair, I shall call the housekeeper whose duty it is to attend to such matters."

I lowered Lucrece into the chair and she still snored gently. I straightened up again. "Thank you, Billings," I said.

"Not at all, sir. If I may presume on behalf of Mrs. Byrne, I should thank you for seeing that Miss Byrne was returned home safely."

I went back to the Jag and drove home slowly. I thought that being a cop had had its advantages, and one of them was you didn't have to be so damned polite to people. But on the other hand, people were mostly damned polite to you. With which philosophical thought I went home to bed.

CHAPTER 4

It was a big, imposing room with expensive carpet, muted colours and the biggest desk I'd ever seen in the middle of it.

"This," Mr. Delmar said in a hushed voice, "is Mr. Byrne's office."

Delmar was the picture of the rising executive. Somewhere around thirty-five, with a toothbrush moustache and tooth-brushed gleaming teeth underneath it. He was Byrne's personal assistant and I had the impression he was worried in case United Steel might be thinking he assisted Byrne in the murder as well.

I looked around the office. It didn't look as if it held any secrets—not any secrets that might interest me, anyway. I walked over to the desk and looked down at it, running my hand across the smooth polished grain of the top.

"This was where the police found the threatening note from Wendy Martin?" I asked.

Delmar sighed and nodded. "That is correct, Mr. Wheeler, quite correct. Right here—in the top drawer of the left-hand side."

"When did they find that?"

"First thing next morning after the murder. They arrived with a search warrant and naturally I showed them in here. Then they started to go through the desk and that was the first thing they found."

"What was the officer's name who found the note?"

Delmar thought for a moment. "Lieutenant Hanlon, from the Homicide Bureau."

"And he just opened that top drawer and there it was?"

"Exactly, Mr. Wheeler," he flashed his teeth at me.

"Was there anything else? Being Mr. Byrne's personal assistant, I suppose you knew him pretty well."

He winced. "Not that well, Mr. Wheeler. Outside the office I hardly knew him at all."

"Then you didn't know about his liaison with this girl, Wendy Martin?"

He shook his head vigorously. "Certainly not."

"What sort of man is Byrne?"

"A very efficient businessman," he told me. "Very efficient indeed."

"What sort of man was he apart from his work?"

"As I said before, I really couldn't tell you. I just don't know. He never referred to his personal life at all. He was—is—a man who kept to himself, Mr. Wheeler. Not a man given to taking anyone else into his confidence."

"Well, thanks anyway," I said.

I left the offices of United Steel, drove down to the Homicide Bureau and got to see Hanlon. A uniformed cop showed me into his office and Hanlon looked up from his desk with a wide grin on his face as I walked in.

"Well, well, well," he said. "The wonder boy of copland. If you're looking for a job, Al, there are definitely no vacancies——by special order of the Commissioner."

"I was looking for some help, Pete," I said. "About the Byrne case."

"Open and shut, my boy," he said. "Open and shut."

I sat down and offered him a cigarette and lit it and one for myself.

"I'm working for Hammond, Irvine and Snooks," I explained. "Byrne is their client. I'm seeing if I can pick up any leads."

"Why, Al," he grinned. "You don't expect any help from the Bureau, do you?"

"I thought you might tell me about it," I said. "You picked him up at the dame's apartment, right?"

"Sure."

"Her body on the floor—the gun alongside it?"

"You got the picture."

"How did you get there so fast?"

"Phone call from somebody in the building—heard the shot and rang Homicide."

"What was the neighbour's name?"

"Anonymous call—said they didn't want to get into any trouble."

"Man or woman?"

"Woman."

"Convenient, her ringing like that."

Hanlon shrugged his shoulders. "It happens all the time—you know that, Al. A neighbour hears a shot or screams or something and they phone the police. But they won't leave a name because they don't want to get involved."

"Sure," I said. "And when you got there?"

"We knocked on the door," he said. "Byrne answered it. He appeared completely dazed. We found the dame's body on the floor and the gun lying there beside it. Byrne claimed he didn't know what had happened but that he didn't kill her. The doctor said he was suffering from traumatic shock. That isn't unusual either for a guy who has just murdered somebody. And that you also know, Al."

"What made you search his office the next morning?"

"Routine. We searched his house first and then went over to his office. The note from the girl we found in his desk was the clincher."

"Sure," I said.

He grinned at me. "You've picked a tough one, Al. You think he didn't do it?"

I was honest. "I don't know. I'm getting paid to try and prove he didn't do it. Right now, I don't know enough to make up my mind either way."

"Well, this is an open case that's really open and shut, Al," he said confidently. "Motive, opportunity—the lot. Byrne's prints on the gun … I'd look for an easier one."

"Maybe I will," I said. "Thanks anyway, Pete."

"Any time, Al," he said. "Any time at all. Only don't tell the Commissioner. He doesn't like you very much at the moment. I wouldn't go parking your car in front of a fire-hydrant. The way he feels right now, he'll probably get you three years for conspiracy to commit arson."

"Thanks, Pete," I said. "I'll watch it."

I went from the Bureau to the offices of Hammond, Irvine and Snooks and arrived in the neat cubicle with my name on the door just after eleven-thirty. Both Irvine and Hammond were there before me.

"So nice of you to drop in, Wheeler," Hammond said coldly. "I wonder you bothered to get in so early."

"I had an assurance from Mr. Irvine that if I took this job, I could handle it my own way," I said. "But if you'd like me to bring a note every morning I'm not here by nine o'clock, I'll talk to my mother about it."

Hammond sucked his teeth audibly. "Would it be asking too much to ask you just how much progress you have made? Or would that be violating a clause of your contract with us?"

"There's a simple answer," I said. "None!"

He glared at Irvine, then back at me. "Then I suggest you start getting some results, Wheeler. Even the goodwill of Mr. Irvine must have some financial limitations."

"I'd like to talk to Byrne," I said.

"It can be arranged," he said coldly. "Mr. Irvine can arrange to see him and take you with him."

"What are your thoughts on the case so far, Mr. Wheeler?" Irvine asked anxiously.

I thought I owed him that much to tell him something.

"I've talked to his wife, his daughter, his butler, his personal assistant, and the woman who runs the Due D'Or," I said. "I've talked to the Lieutenant in charge of the case at Homicide. And the only one of those people who gave me any facts was the Lieutenant in charge of the case. Nobody else knows anything. From the evidence he's got, I'd say Byrne was as guilty as hell."

Hammond snorted loudly. "That's an encouraging attitude for you to have towards our client!"

"I hadn't finished," I said evenly. "I also think it stinks."

"And what exactly does that mean?"

"Too many coincidences," I said. "Byrne shoots the dame. A neighbour hears the shot and rings up Homicide so fast that they arrive and find Byrne still inside the apartment and the girl still on the floor. The neighbour remains anonymous incidentally. Then the next morning the police search Byrne's office and right on top of everything in the first drawer of his desk that they open they find the letter from Wendy Martin threatening him.

"I wouldn't have thought that the President of United Steel would be that naive. If I had been going to murder Wendy, the first thing I would have done would be destroy that letter. And the second thing would have been to at least get rid of my prints on the gun, if not the gun itself."

Hammond grunted. "So you think that he's innocent?"

"I didn't say that. Byrne could have easily panicked. Also I just think there were too many coincidences about the case. And I think that if somebody framed him for the murder, they did too good a job. Most times, even if you see a guy commit murder right in front of your own eyes, you still have a fairly tough job proving it. But this case was filled with proof right from the start. It's too good!"

Hammond grunted again. "Well, I hope to hear something a little more positive soon from you, Wheeler. Something you can back up with proof and not just wild conjecture."

Then he stalked out of the office and Irvine looked at me with upraised eyebrows.

"Don't pay too much attention to him, Mr. Wheeler," he said. "He always acts that way."

"He doesn't really bother me," I said. "What does he have for lunch—a pint of human blood?"

Irvine smiled weakly. "Mr. Hammond always appears to be very bad-tempered. Actually, I think it's part of an act. How soon do you want to see Mr. Byrne?"

"As soon as you can arrange it," I said.

"I'll see if we can make it this afternoon," he said. "I'll call you back on it."

"Thanks," I told him.

He went out of the office and I sat down behind the desk, put my feet up on it and lit a cigarette. About five minutes later there was a soft tap on the door and a character shuffled in. He was small and bent in the middle. He had one large tuft of white hair in the centre of his head and the rest was completely bald. He looked like Davy Crockett back from the Alamo. He wore a pair of rimless glasses which had slipped halfway down his nose, a crumpled blue suit and a pair of carpet slippers.

"You're the new man?" he asked in a cracked voice.

"Check," I said. "If you've come to empty the wastepaper-bin, I haven't filled it yet."

"I'm the other partner," he told me. "They call me a sleeping partner because I sleep most of the time!" His chuckle had a dry rusty sound—I wished I had a can of oil with me so I could give him a drink.

"You're Snooks?"

"That's right," he said. "Past tense of the verb, to sneak. I sneak, he snuck, you snook!" He chuckled again.

"Why don't you get that oiled?" I suggested.

"But I do," he said. "A bottle of brandy every day. Do you drink, whateveryournameis?"

"Regularly."

"Ah!" He made a satisfied sound. "Then why don't you come up to my office and have one?"

"That's the most civilised suggestion I've heard this morning, Mr. Snooks," I told him.

The phone jangled at my elbow. "Excuse me," I picked up the receiver.

It was Irvine. "We can see Mr. Byrne at three this afternoon, Mr. Wheeler," he said. "Supposing you pick me up in my office at twelve-thirty? That'll give us plenty of time to get down there."

"Fine," I said, then hung up.

I followed Snooks down the corridor to the elevators, up two floors, then along to his office. He had a nice, comfortable office with a bar running the full length of one wall. He shuffled up to his desk and pressed a button. A few moments later the inside door opened and a woman came in. My eyes widened as I looked at her. She was a honey-blonde, wearing a black sheath that clung to her like a taxation official to my money.

"Yes, Mr. Snooks?" she smiled at him.

"This is Mr. Wheeer," he said. "Wheeler—this is Pauline."

"Well, hello," I said.

"Hello, Mr. Wheeler," she smiled brightly at me, then looked at Snooks. "Mr. Hammond was looking for you a few moments ago."

"Ah!" Snooks said. "I thought he might be. That's why I left the office." He rubbed his hands together. "I'm happy to say, Pauline, that Mr. Wheeler is a drinking man. What will you have?"

"Scotch, thanks."

"And I'll have a little brandy," he said. "Would you pour them for us, my dear?"

The blonde busied herself with bottles and glasses.

"Sit down, sit down," Snooks said, gesturing towards a deep, leather armchair.

I sat down and the blonde brought me over the drink. She bent forward to hand me the glass and I expected the sheath to split, but it didn't.

"Thank you," I said in a hushed voice. "I didn't know that an attorney's office could be like this."

"I've been working at it for a number of years now," Snooks said. "With some success, I must admit. Thank you, my dear." He took his drink from Pauline and she smiled again, then went out of the office.

"How do you get a secretary like that?" I asked interestedly.

"It takes a good deal of finesse," he said. "These things take a little organising, you know. But I wouldn't be foolish enough to offer to rent an apartment for her or something like that, eh?" He made the rusty noise again. "First thing you know and she would be dead, eh? And the gun would have my fingerprints on it, eh?" He chuckled some more.

"You're interested in the Byrne case, Mr. Snooks?" I asked.

"Oh, yes, very," he nodded. "He's a great friend of our senior partner. Did you know that?"

"Yes," I said. "I find it hard to believe."

"That our senior partner could have a friend?" he chuckled. "It's a quaint idea, isn't it, Wheeler. But I mustn't be too nasty. I'm quite sure that underneath that bloodless exterior there beats a passionate heart. Oh, yes, I'm quite sure about that—I've seen the way he looks at my secretary. He'd like a secretary who looks like that, but he's frightened what he might do, so he keeps a female vampire in his office to make sure he's safe!"

He downed his drink in one gulp and shuffled towards the bar, the empty glass in his hand. "But I do talk on, don't I, Wheeler? How are you finding things in the organisation?"

"I haven't had time to form any impressions yet," I said.

"Except about our senior partner, eh?"

"You could say that," I admitted.

He shuffled back to his chair, the refilled glass in his hand. "Friendship is a wonderful thing," he said. "I suppose in your investigation of the Byrne case, Wheeler, one point must have struck you forcibly—the strong friendship of our senior partner for Byrne, in the face of overwhelming evidence."

"They must have been friends for a long time," I said.

"Oh, yes," he nodded. "A long time. They reached the acme of friendship, you might say—they both had the same wife."

"Huh?"

That dry, rusty chuckle came again. "You must forgive me, Wheeler. I'm becoming careless in my phraseology—old age, I suppose. What I meant to say was that Mrs. Byrne was formerly married to our senior partner—Hammond. They were divorced and then she married Byrne."

CHAPTER 5

Walter Byrne was somewhere in his fifties, a rugged looking character with grey-streaked black hair and the beginnings of a paunch. Irvine introduced me, told him a little of my background and how I was investigating the case from his angle.

"If there's anything at all you can tell me that will help, Mr. Bryne," I said, "I'll follow it up."

He shrugged his shoulders. "I don't know that there is. I was having an affair with Wendy—sure. I was paying the rent of the apartment. The night she was killed I was there in the apartment, but I didn't kill her."

"What happened?"

A look of uncertainty crossed his face. "I don't know," he said slowly. "I can't remember. I remember sitting there, talking to her, then I remember nothing else until the police were there, talking to me."

"You have no memory of the shooting whatsoever?"

"None at all."

"What about the threatening note she wrote you—did you go to see her that night to talk about that?"

"I never saw that note," he said. "I can't believe she ever wrote it. It's—it's crazy! Wendy would never have dreamed of trying to blackmail me."

I looked at Irvine, whose face was blank. Then I looked at Byrne and tried again. "If you didn't kill her, Mr. Byrne, then you are obviously the victim of a conspiracy. Do you have any enemies who might go to that extent to hurt you?"

He shook his head miserably. "No, I can't say that I have-—none that I know of, anyway."

"What about Wendy Martin? Would she have any enemies that you know of who would want to kill her?"

Byrne shook his head again. "I knew very little of her background. She never talked about her past and I never enquired. We had a good relationship based on enjoyment of each other's company."

"You can't think of anything—anything at all, however slight, that might have some bearing on the case?"

"I'm sorry, Mr. Wheeler," he said miserably. "I can't."

Fifteen minutes later we were in Irvine's car, heading back to the office.

"What do you think, Al?" Irvine asked, breaking right down and using my Christian name for the first time.

"If I were still a cop, I'd say what Lieutenant Hanlon says—traumatic shock. He can't remember what happened because he doesn't want to remember what happened."

"I know," Irvine said unhappily. "He doesn't seem to want to help himself. I don't understand it."

"Could you think of anyone he might be protecting?"

"No," he said brusquely. "The only person who could want to murder Wendy Martin would be Mrs. Byrne, presumably, if she had learned of the liaison. But in the cold light of day, that supposition becomes ridiculous. Absolutely ridiculous. Because Mrs. Byrne is not the type to suffer from passionate jealousy. She and her husband lived their own lives with no interference from either side."

"Mrs. Byrne was formerly Mrs. Hammond, wasn't she?" I said casually.

Irvine looked sideways at me for a moment. "Yes, that's right."

"It's an unusual friendship between the two men," I said. "You don't normally see husbands number one and two being such buddies."

"I suppose not," he said. "But they are both broadminded men in their respective ways. And this is a civilised age we live in."

"Of course," I said. "The front pages of the newspapers prove that!"

There was more conversation after that. I left Irvine inside the office and went to my own office. I put my feet up on the desk again and lit a cigarette. A few minutes later the phone rang.

"Mr. Wheeler?" a very feminine voice asked.

"Check."

"This is Pauline Whitby here. Mr. Snooks has a file he asked me to deliver to you."

"Well, come right on down," I said.

"Thank you, Mr. Wheeler."

She came into the office five minutes later, with a slender file in her hand.

"Mr. Snooks insisted that I deliver this personally to you," she said. "He said to tell you that it is most private and confidential, for you only to read, and you mustn't leave it around your office. He'd like you to return it as soon as possible."

"What is it?" I said. "The blueprints of the Inter-Continental Ballistic Missile?"

She laughed. "I don't have any idea." She put the file on my desk. "He sealed it before he gave it to me."

"I can hardly wait to open it," I said.

"I should get you to sign for it in triplicate," she smiled. "But Mr. Snooks isn't a lawyer like that, thank heaven."

"Does he do any work?" I asked her. "Or just sit around his bar and drink brandy all day long?"

"You would be surprised at the amount of work he does get through," she said. She walked towards the door. "Goodbye for now, Mr. Wheeler."

"So long," I said.

She went out, closing the door gently behind her. I looked at my watch and saw it was a quarter of five. I thought I'd take the file home and read it in more comfortable surroundings. I wondered if Hammond would consider equipping my office with a hi-fi unit and thought perhaps he wouldn't.

It was five-thirty when I got home. I put some Kenton LP's on the turntable to keep my mind agile and poured myself a drink, then I settled down in an armchair and broke the seal on the file. At the same moment the door buzzer sounded. I got up and put the file in the bureau drawer and closed it, then I went to the front door.

A blonde in a turtle-necked sweater and a pair of tapering frontier pants stood there smiling at me. The evening began to look complicated.

"Hello," she said. "I've sworn off vodka."

"I'm glad to hear it."

"It's a good thing," she said, walking past me into the house. "Now I can drink anything at all and it doesn't matter if you knock a bottle over accidentally on purpose."

I caught up with her in the living-room where she had a glass in one hand and a Scotch bottle in the other.

"You remember the incident with the bottle?" I said respectfully.

"I always remember everything right up to the moment I pass out," she said. "Thanks for taking me home, Al. I dropped by to pick up the Porsche."

"Did you make the rehearsal this morning?"

"Of course," she said. "Mr. Rogers was most impressed with my possibilities."

"What did he think of your dancing?"

She poked out her tongue at me. "You're a riot, Mr. Wheeler, you really are."

"Did you get any dirt on Wendy Martin?"

"Give me a chance," she said. "I only had five minutes in the dressing-room with the other girls. I don't even know their names yet."

I helped myself to another drink. "You didn't tell me your stepmother was married to Hammond before she married your father."

"Didn't I?" She yawned elaborately. "I couldn't have thought it was important."

"Maybe it isn't," I said.

She yawned again. "Are you trying to make something out of it, by any chance?"

"No," I told her. "I just think it's odd that your father and Hammond should be such good friends under the circumstances."

"I don't see why," she said.

"Let's say it's not usual," I said.

Lucrece finished her drink and put down the glass. "I guess I should be going," she said. "I don't want to be late for my first night. You coming along to watch me?"

"Not tonight, honey," I said. "I'm tired—I've been up all day."

"I'm disappointed," she said. "I was going to dance just for you—like Salome!"

"Whose head were you thinking of offering on a platter?"

"Whose head would you like?"

"I'm easy—so long as it's female."

"And I thought I had you crazy over me!"

"You had it wrong," I said. "I think you're crazy. I even have an original phrase for it—a crazy, mixed-up kid!"

She poured herself another drink. "Maybe I'm early," she said. "There's time for another drink, anyway."

"There's always time for another drink," I said. "But just make sure you can stand up and dance. It would look stupid dancing while you were sitting down."

"You're positively brilliant tonight," she said. "You sound like an accounts clerk giving a monologue at the company's annual dinner."

That gave me grounds to pour myself another drink.

"If you're staying long enough I'll give you something to eat," I suggested. "I can offer you the finest salmon that ever came out of a can—genuine pink salmon!"

"You make it sound entrancing," she shuddered. "Thank you, I'll eat when I get to work. That's something else I get at the Due D'Or—free food."

"If I didn't have flat feet, I'd apply for a job there myself."

Lucrece finished the drink in one practised swallow. "How did your investigating go today?" she asked.

"I saw your father this afternoon."

"How is he?"

"All right—physically."

"Did he have anything interesting to say?"

"Only that he didn't kill her. Unfortunately, he can't help us find any proof to back his statement."

"What about when it happened—he was there, wasn't he? If he didn't kill her, then he must have seen who did."

I watched her closely. "That's a logical supposition. But he says he doesn't remember. His mind is a complete blank over the period of time the murder was committed. The police theory is traumatic shock—his subconscious mind doesn't want to remember that he killed her, so his conscious mind can't remember."

"Do you subscribe to that theory?"

"I don't know," I said. "There's only one other alternative I can think of—he's shielding someone else."

"Who?"

"You, for example."

Lucrece stared at me for a long moment. "That's an interesting theory. Why would he shield me?"

"It would have to be someone he cared for very much. His wife doesn't seem to fit that picture. You're his only family."

"Why would I have killed Wendy Martin?"

"I wouldn't know," I said. "But you seem to have developed blackmail to a fine art. You told me about Myra and the butler, Billings, and how you were making your garage bills out of that. There was the blackmail note Wendy sent your father. Maybe you put her up to it and were going to take a percentage—and maybe she backed out at the last moment and you lost your temper and killed her."

She laughed with a brittle sound. "In front of Father!"

"That might have appealed to your perverted sense of humour or something," I told her. "Or you could have been just blind drunk."

Her face coloured a deep red. "You must have a very high opinion of me."

"What sort of opinion would I have?" I smiled at her. "You boast about blackmailing your stepmother. You pass out cold in my house and I have to cart you home. Every time I see you, you have a glass in your hand and you're intent on getting as high as you can. I have to say frankly that when it comes to choosing the woman of the year, you won't get my vote!"

Lucrece picked up her empty glass; her other hand reaching automatically for the bottle, then she stopped suddenly and put down both the bottle and glass.

"Well," she said tautly. "You've expressed yourself only too clearly, Mr. Wheeler. I'm sure you won't mind if I leave now?"

"Not at all," I said. "Don't trip over the carpet on your way out."

She walked past me with her head held high in the air, and a few seconds later I heard the Porsche snarl into life. I listened until the sound of the engine died away in the distance, then I went over to the bureau drawer and took out the file Snooks had sent me and sat down with it again.

The file contained exactly two sheets. The first one was a photocopy of a legal agreement which nominated the four partners who owned and operated the Due D'Or. And the names read ... Isobel Lamont, Walter Byrne, Myra Byrne and James Hammond.

The second sheet had a newspaper clipping pasted onto it. The clipping was just over two years old. It reported the granting of a divorce to Myra Hammond on the grounds of gross cruelty and physical violence.

The divorce action had not been defended. I figured there was more to Mr. Hammond than had met my little blue eyes.

I lit a cigarette and re-read the legal agreement. Nobody had mentioned the owners of the nightclub before. Hammond hadn't mentioned his interest … neither had Byrne. Neither had Myra Byrne. Neither, for that matter, had Isobel Lamont. By her answers to my questions, she had led me to believe that Byrne was a comparative stranger to her, someone she hardly knew.

I thought about it a little more. The agreement must have been kept highly secret. I felt sure that Irvine couldn't have known of its existence otherwise he would have told me. I was still thinking about it when the phone rang.

I picked up the receiver and said originally, "Wheeler," into the mouthpiece.

"Mr. Wheeler, this is Myra Byrne." Her voice sounded tense. "Could you come over to the house right away? It's urgent."

"Sure," I said, "I'll come."

"Don't say anything about me ringing you or expecting you." Her voice sank to a whisper. "You understand? I don't know you're coming."

"If that's the way you want it," I said.

"Thank you," she breathed. "And please hurry."

CHAPTER 6

If ever there was the perfect answer to hurrying, the XK-SS was that very thing. I made the Byrne house in double time and felt glad I didn't meet any cops on the way. From what Hanlon had told me, Lavers would have probably seen to it that I did a five-to-ten if I was booked for speeding.

I pressed the buzzer and the butler opened the door.

"Good evening, Mr. Wheeler," he smiled. "I'm sorry, but Miss Byrne is out and she isn't expected home till very late."

"I didn't come to see Miss Byrne," I said. "I'm calling on Mrs. Byrne."

"She has a headache," he said, looking doubtful. "I don't know whether she will …"

"Look," I said coldly, "Mrs. Byrne has a headache … that's tough. Her husband has every chance of facing the gas-chamber and that's tougher still. I'm trying to collect evidence to clear him of a murder rap. I need to ask Mrs. Byrne some questions and they won't wait. You tell her that!"

"Yes, sir," he pursed his lips. "I'll tell her that."

He went off down the hallway and came back half a minute later. "Mrs. Byrne will see you in the sunroom, Mr. Wheeler."

"Thanks," I said. "You don't need to show me the way. I remember quite distinctly."

"Very good, sir." He took my hat between two fingers and stood there, looking at it dubiously.

"Handle that hat carefully," I told him. "I'm growing penicillin around the brim." I walked the length of the hall and into the sunroom, closing the door carefully behind me. Myra Byrne was standing, looking out into the darkness beyond one of the glass walls when I came into the room.

She turned around quickly as she heard the door close. "Thank goodness you got here," she said in a taut voice. She was wearing a simple number in white pique with a neck-line edged in Venetian lace. The sort of number you can pick up any time in Paris for around five hundred dollars and up.

"You've got trouble?" I asked her.

"I'm frightened, Mr. Wheeler," she said.

"Of whom?"

"You didn't say what but I can't be sure who it is. I think it's Billings, but I can't even be sure of that." She put both hands to her face and her voice rose sharply. "I think I'm going out of my mind!"

I stood there looking at her. There was a tap on the door and then it swung open and the butler stepped into the room.

"You called, Madame?" he said.

Myra Byrne took her hands away from her face and looked at him blankly.

"You made a mistake, Billings," I said. "Actually, Mrs. Byrne shrieked."

"Shrieked!" he repeated.

"Sure—with laughter," I said. "Though I say it myself I am, on occasion, a witty man. That was one of the occasions. Would you shut the door again on your way out, Billings? The draught is uncomfortable."

He looked at me bewilderedly for a couple of seconds, then he slowly retreated back into the hall, closing the door behind him.

I walked across the room to where Myra Byrne stood. "How about telling me the story?" I said.

"I have to get out of here," she said. "Anywhere, but away from this house for a while. Will you take me somewhere, Mr. Wheeler?"

"Okay," I said. "Let's go."

"I'll collect a purse and a wrap," she said. "I'll meet you in the hall." We walked out of the sunroom into the hall. I walked towards the front door while she ran up the stairs. Billings handed me my hat.

"There are a couple of things I want Mrs. Byrne to see," I said. "She may not be back until late."

"Very good, sir," Billings said formally.

Myra Byrne came down the stairs, a mink stole draped across her shoulders, carrying a diamante purse in one hand. She walked quickly up to me and Billings opened the door for us. We went down the steps to the Jag and I helped her into it, then walked around and got behind the wheel.

Five minutes later we were heading back to town.

"If you're not particular," I said, "I have a house."

"That would be fine," she said. Then she just sat there, staring through the windscreen without any more conversation.

We arrived and I took her into the house, into the living-room. She sat in an armchair and took off her stole.

"Would you like a drink?" I asked her.

"I think I would," she said.

I poured two drinks, handed her one and took the other with me to the chair opposite hers. "What's it all about?" I asked her.

She hesitated. "I don't know where to start, Mr. Wheeler."

"Call me Al," I said.

"All right," she said. "I'm still not sure whether I'm imagining things or not. Maybe I should fill in some of the background you should know—the things I haven't told you."

"I might be able to help," I suggested. "You were married to James Hammond and divorced him on the grounds of cruelty and physical violence. Then you married Walter Byrne. You and your husband, along with Hammond and Isobel Lamont, own the Due D'Or. Your relationship with your butler has been—well, indiscreet. So indiscreet in fact that your stepdaughter has been blackmailing you into paying her garage bills each month."

Her mouth dropped open for a moment. "Who told you all that? Lucrece! It must have been Lucrece! Why, the little …"

"She told me some of it," I said. "What's important is whether it's all true or not?"

She bit her lip. "Yes," she said in a low voice. "It's fundamentally all true."

"Is there any other background you think I should know?"

She shook her head. "You seem to have it all. It only leaves the thing that's driving me crazy right now."

"What's that?"

"I think someone is trying to kill me!"

I took a sip of Scotch. She meant it, all right. "How do you mean—think? Don't you know?"

"That's what's driving me crazy," she said. "I can't be sure."

"When did it start?"

"The day before yesterday," she said. "In the morning. I have a habit of running a bath, then drinking the coffee Mrs. Marsh, the housekeeper, brings me till the bath is ready, then going back to the bathroom and getting straight into the bath. I don't know what made me stop and look this particular morning. We have an oversized bath with the shower at one end of it, and plastic curtains cut off a portion of the bath. For some reason I pulled them aside and looked at the end of the bath. Someone had cut the lead to my husband's electric razor, plugged it into the wall plug, switched it on and left bare wires at the other end in the water." She shuddered. "I would have been electrocuted as soon as I put one foot into the bath, if I hadn't seen it."

"What did you do about it?"

"I switched off the wall plug and took the lead out, of course," she said. "I couldn't ask anyone in the house about it directly—how could you ask people if they had tried to murder you that morning? I did ask Mrs. Marsh if she had been into the bathroom that morning and she said she hadn't, and she hadn't seen anyone else go in."

"Who else was there in the house besides yourself and Mrs. Marsh?"

"Only Lucrece—and Billings."

She bit her lip again. "Then that night, just before I went to bed, I went out onto the balcony outside my bedroom, just to get some fresh air. I felt restless—you know how it is sometimes. I had been standing on the balcony for perhaps five minutes when someone outside in the grounds shot at me."

"You heard the noise of the gun?"

"It was very muffled—just a pop. But the bullet hit the wall beside me. I heard the noise of the ricochet. I ran into the room and locked the doors leading onto the balcony and the bedroom door. I lay awake nearly all night, too terrified to sleep till finally somewhere near dawn I fell asleep out of sheer exhaustion."

"Any more?"

She nodded, swallowing hard. "Yes—this evening. That's when I couldn't stand it any longer—when I rang you."

"What happened?"

"It was just after dinner … Lucrece was out, so I had dinner alone. Mrs. Marsh had prepared the meal and Billings served it. When it was over I went up to my room. I had a bad headache and I thought I would lie down for a little to see if it cleared. I hadn't switched on the lights. I lay there for about a quarter of an hour, I suppose. I was half asleep when suddenly two hands gripped my throat. Someone was trying to strangle me. I tried to fight—I couldn't make any sound because the grip was too tight."

She closed her eyes. "Then I heard Mrs. Marsh coming up the stairs, going to her room. Her tread is slow and heavy. Whoever was trying to strangle me heard it too. They relaxed their grip on my throat suddenly and the relief was too much for me … I fainted. When I came round the lights were on and Mrs. Marsh was there, looking worried. She said she'd heard me call out and thought I must be asleep and having a nightmare, so she'd come into the room and had a hard job to wake me. After that my nerves were shattered completely. That was when I rang you."

I got up and poured her another drink.

"You could have told the police," I said. "Why didn't you?"

"I—I thought …"

"You thought it was Billings?" I said. "And if you told the police, that they would question him and he might tell them his relationship to you was something more than a butler's?"

She nodded. "There was that … but that wasn't the entire reason. You see, Al," she looked at me and her eyes were haunted. "The next day after the incident with the bath, I looked in the cupboard and my husband's razor was there, the lead attached to it just the way it normally is. I had a look at the wall next to where I'd been standing when that bullet was fired. I'd heard it ricochet off the wall, but I couldn't see any mark on it anywhere. I spent one whole hour looking, going over each brick in detail, but there wasn't one mark. Then tonight. Mrs. Marsh said she heard me yell … I don't remember yelling. I could have, the moment before I fainted, I suppose. But then she said I must have been having a nightmare. Well, perhaps I was. Perhaps I'm just imagining the whole thing—suffering from delusions. That's the other part of why I didn't want to call the police. I was afraid they might turn me over to a psychiatrist—even put me into a hospital."

"Drink your drink," I told her.

I watched the hand that held her glass tremble as she raised it to her lips.

"I don't know," I said. "But I'd like to check on it. How about I go back to your house and take a look around—have a talk to Billings, anyway? He can't tell me anything about his association with you that I don't know. I used to be a cop—I can have him jumping through hoops inside of ten minutes. If he's been trying to murder you, I'll find out."

"At least I'd know then," she said. "That's the worst part of it—not being sure whether the things really happened or not. If you'd go out to the house as you said, I'd be awfully grateful."

"I'll do that then," I said. "You wait here. Help yourself when you feel like another drink—and play some discs if you feel like it."

"Thank you, Al," she smiled at me. "You're being very kind to me, for no reason at all."

"I shouldn't be long," I said. "Not more than an hour at the most."

"I'll be all right here," she said.

I went out of the house to the Jaguar and drove back to the Byrne house. Billings opened the door and looked more than vaguely surprised to see me back alone.

"I'd like to talk to you for a few minutes, Billings," I said.

"Yes, sir. Perhaps the kitchen?"

"Sounds a good place," I said.

I followed him through to the back of the house and into the kitchen, which was somewhat bigger than my living-room.

"Would you care to sit down, sir?" Billings gestured towards the table in the centre of the room. "There is some coffee made, if you would care for a cup?"

"That would be fine," I said.

I sat down at the table, lit a cigarette and watched him pour the coffee. Be brought the cups over to the table and sat down opposite me.

I stirred the coffee, added some cream and sugar and drank some of it. "That's good coffee," I said.

"Thank you, sir." He sat there, looking at me expectantly.

"Do you have any particular reason for trying to murder Mrs. Byrne?" I asked him.

"Is this a joke?" he said evenly.

"Not according to Mrs. Byrne," I said. "I know your relationship to her is somewhat intimate. She tells me that three attempts have been made on her life in the past forty-eight hours."

"I think she needs help, Mr. Wheeler. Professional help."

"She's getting help—from me," I said. "I'm an ex-professional cop."

"I didn't mean that sort of help, Mr. Wheeler. I was referring to medical assistance. I think she needs a doctor—a psychiatrist."

"You think she's imagined these things?"

"Certainly—if she imagines I have been trying to murder her."

"You have no reason to want to kill her?"

He shook his head. "None. Why should I?"

"I can think of two possible reasons. One would be emotional—you are emotionally involved with her. The second could be that someone was paying you to murder her."

"You're joking, Mr. Wheeler?"

I drank the rest of the coffee. "I'm not joking, Billings. Do you possess a gun?"

"No," he said. "Another cup of coffee, Mr. Wheeler?"

"Thanks," I told him.

He took my cup and refilled it, then came back to the table.

"Tonight," I said, "Mrs. Byrne retired to her room after dinner. What did you do then?"

"I cleared the table," he said evenly. "Then Mrs. Marsh—the house-keeper—and I had our dinner in here. I helped her with the dishes. Then she went up to her room. I was reading in here when you called."

"You never went upstairs to Mrs. Byrne's room at all?"

"No."

"Who else was in the house besides you and Mrs. Marsh—and Mrs. Byrne, of course."

"Nobody," he said. "Miss Byrne left the house before dinner."

I drank some of the second cup of coffee. "You know, Billings," I said softly. "You wouldn't have a prayer—with Byrne in gaol, you're the only man in the house. If we claimed you forced your attentions on Mrs. Byrne and because she rejected you, you tried to murder her. You don't have the sort of friends she has—friends like Hammond who's a smart criminal lawyer. We could put you in gaol and get you twenty years with no trouble at all."

His lips twisted for a moment. "Is this the way you worked as a professional policeman, Mr. Wheeler? Threatening people with false arrest and conviction?"

"It could be done," I said. "I'm just mean enough to do it, if you don't start levelling with me soon. You know more than you're saying. I want to hear it—now."

He thought about it for a moment, then got onto his feet. "I'd like you to come with me to my room, Mr. Wheeler," he said formally. "There is something I'd like you to see."

"Okay," I finished the coffee and got to my feet. "Lead on."

We went up the stairs and along to his room. He opened the door and switched on the light.

"Mrs. Marsh has the adjoining room," he said. "The other two rooms on this side of the house are empty. On the other side are Mr. Byrne's room, Mrs. Byrne's next to it, one empty room and then Miss Lucrece's room."

"Is that what you brought me up here to tell me?"

"I thought you might be interested," he said.

He walked over to a chest of drawers and pulled open the top drawer. He took a cup out of it and brought it back to me.

"What's this?" I asked him.

"A coffee cup," he said. "Mine. From breakfast this morning. Would you care to look at the contents?"

There was a plastic cover stretched across the top of the cup. I peeled it off and saw the cup was two parts full of black coffee.

"Coffee?" I said.

"Can you smell anything besides coffee, Mr. Wheeler?"

I sniffed cautiously and the tang of bitter almonds pierced my nostrils. "Cyanide?" I said.

"I think so," Billings said carefully. "I haven't tried to have it analysed, of course."

"How come?"

"I don't really know," he said. "I served breakfast this morning to Mrs. Byrne and Miss Lucrece. Afterwards, as usual, I had my own breakfast in the kitchen. Mrs. Marsh was upstairs tidying her room and I'd just poured this cup of coffee when the bell went. There's a system—a bell-push in practically every room of the house and an indicator board lights up in the kitchen showing which room when one of the bell-pushes is operated. The light showed Miss Lucrece's room. So I went upstairs—and she wasn't there. I didn't think too much about it because that's just the sort of thing she can do.

"I came downstairs again back into the kitchen, picked up my cup of coffee and was just going to drink it when I smelled that bitter almonds scent. I don't have to tell you I didn't drink any of it. I thought it might be interesting to keep the cup as proof."

I thought back over the two cups of coffee I'd just drunk, but I couldn't remember the smell of bitter almonds. At least I hoped.

I handed back the cup to him. "What does this prove?" I said.

"I think it proves that whoever is trying to murder Mrs. Byrne is trying to murder me as well," he said steadily.

CHAPTER 7

I looked at my watch as I walked back inside my house. It was a couple of minutes before midnight. I thought there wasn't much difference between the hours I had worked as a cop and the hours I worked for Hammond, Irvine and Snooks.

I walked into the living-room and Myra Byrne looked at me expectantly. "You've been gone quite a while, Al," she said. "I was beginning to think something must have happened to you."

"I was talking to Billings," I said.

"Yes?"

"He thinks someone is trying to murder him, too."

She shook her head slowly as if trying to clear her brain. "But that's ridiculous." she said.

"Billings doesn't think so—he even has a cup of coffee with some cyanide added, as proof.”

“Coffee—with cyanide?” She clenched her hands together in her lap. “Maybe we’re both crazy,” she muttered.

“Or crazy like a couple of foxes,” I said.

“What do you mean by that?”

“Maybe you’re both putting over a good story,” I said.

“You mean—you think we’re both making up the story that someone is trying to murder us? Why would we do that?”

“I don’t know,” I said. “I was sort of hoping you’d tell me. Billings didn’t.”

She got to her feet. “If you think that, I don’t imagine there is much point in staying here any longer.”

“I’ll drive you wherever you want to go,” I said.

“Please don’t bother.” She moved over to the phone. “I’ll call a cab.”

“As you wish,” I said.

I poured myself a drink while she made the call. I was halfway through it when the cab honked outside.

“Goodnight, Mr. Wheeler,” she said coldly. “I’m sorry to have wasted your evening.”

“Goodnight, Mrs. Byrne,” I said.

She went out of the house and I heard the cab pull away from the kerb. I finished my drink. Then I put a Peggy Lee disc on the turntable and let her voice soothe me for another twenty minutes. I was turning the disc when the phone rang. I answered it and it was Irvine on the other end of the line.

“Hate to phone you at this time of night, Wheeler,” he said. “Hope you weren’t asleep?”

“I wasn’t asleep,” I said.

“I just heard from the police.”

“Something exciting?”

“They’ve just found Delmar’s body—he’s been murdered!”

“Well,” I said slowly. “United Steel must have a staff shortage. The vice-president heading for the gas-chamber and his personal assistant renting space at the morgue.”

Irvine ignored the remark.

“I’m going down to the Bureau now and I’d like you to come with me. Can I pick you up in about ten minutes?”

“Sure,” I said.

“You know the police better than we do,” he said. “You realise what I’m going to do?”

“Sure,” I said. “Try and spring Byrne.”

“I’ll need your help.”

"Okay," I said. "See you in ten minutes."

I hung up and went and poured myself another drink. Things were moving fast, much too fast. I almost began to wish I was back in copland again. This working in the dark on your own wasn't exactly an easy way of making a living.

Irvine picked me up on schedule and I sat beside him as he drove into the city.

"Did you hear any details?" I asked him.

"About Delmar? Not very much, Al. A cleaner found him in United Steel's building—in Byrne's office to be precise. He had been shot twice through the back of the head. Been dead about two hours, the police surgeon said. That makes the time of the murder somewhere around nine this evening."

"No other details?"

"None," he said.

I lit a cigarette and by the time I'd smoked it we were stopping outside the Homicide Bureau. We went inside and were shown into Hanlon's office. He greeted us pleasantly enough though he looked tired.

"What brings you here at this time of the night, Mr. Irvine?"

"Delmar's murder," Irvine replied. "It's obviously the work of the person who murdered Wendy Martin. And equally obvious, Walter Byrne couldn't have got out of his cell to kill Delmar. Therefore Byrne is innocent and you have no reasonable grounds for detaining him any longer."

Hanlon smiled wearily and shook his head. "I don't quite agree with your reasoning, Mr. Irvine. Who says that whoever killed Delmar must have killed Wendy Martin? I don't see any obvious connection between the two."

"It's very obvious to me, Lieutenant," Irvine said. "I'm paying you the courtesy of speaking to you first before I speak to the District Attorney. But if you'd prefer ..."

He'd made a mistake—it wasn't the way to talk to Hanlon. For Hanlon's money the D.A. could drop dead any time he cared to, and Hanlon. knew he would be backed by Lavers.

He raised his eyebrows slightly. "I wouldn't like you to waste your time on a mere cop, Mr. Irvine. You go right ahead and talk to the D.A."

Irvine bit his lip, then glanced at me. It was an obvious cue to take over.

"Let's not get excited, Mr. Irvine," I said. "The only threat that would worry the Lieutenant right now would be promotion."

Hanlon grinned. "Al Wheeler, the peacemaker," he said. "This is a switch!"

I returned the grin—gift wrapped. "Look at it this way," I said, "Delmar was probably the guy who planted that blackmail note from Wendy Martin in Byrne's desk. That could leave the murderer with another problem—Delmar. Maybe he took care of it tonight?"

Hanlon grinned. "It sounds very nice, Al, but there still isn't any evidence to support it. You bring me proof that somebody else had motive both to kill the chorine and frame Byrne for it, and I'll go to the D.A. with a strong recommendation that Byrne be released."

"But …" Irvine started to protest.

I took him by the arm. "Come on, Mr. Irvine," I said. "You heard what the Lieutenant said."

Irvine allowed me to lead him out of the office, then he turned and looked at me coldly. "You're a great help, Wheeler, I must say."

"We won't get anywhere without proof, Mr. Irvine," I said patiently. "And the D.A. won't even listen to us as Hanlon did. And there is one other point."

"It probably escaped my notice," he said with heavy sarcasm. "Do tell me."

"If our supposition is right that somebody else killed Wendy Martin and tried to frame Byrne … and the same person used Delmar to help make the frame and then killed him to keep his mouth shut … maybe our client is better off in gaol. Safer, anyway."

Irvine opened and closed his mouth a couple of times. "You may be right," he said finally. "But Mr. Hammond was most insistent I get Mr. Byrne released tonight."

"Was he?" I said. "How did he come to hear about Delmar's murder?"

"I rang him as soon as I heard the news," Irvine said, thus destroying all my detecting instincts.

"I think we ought to go home," I said.

He dropped me off at the house and refused my offer of a drink. I watched him drive away, then I went inside the house.

My watch said it was now two a.m. I went into the bathroom, had a shower, then got into a pair of pyjamas and a robe.

I looked into the mirror to comb my hair and said, "Okay, Wheeler! Whodunit?"

My reflection looked back at me and shook his head hopelessly. "Your guess is as good as mine," he said.

"You guess first," I told him.

"Well," he said thoughtfully. "It could be Myra Byrne—then again it could be Lucrece Byrne."

"Aren't you forgetting the butler?" I said. "Just because it's the fashion nowadays for the butler never to have done it, you can't rule him out entirely."

"Then there's the senior partner—Hammond," my reflection reflected.

"Agreed," I said. "And don't forget Isobel Lamont!"

"I won't," my reflection said gratefully.

"Tell me honestly," I said. "Did you do it?"

"No," my reflection assured me. "I wouldn't forget a murder if I'd committed one, and I don't remember any murder."

"Well," I said. "That's something, anyway."

I went out into the living-room and tidied it up a little, then poured myself a drink. Suddenly I didn't feel tired any more. I thought I might play a couple of discs, drink a couple of drinks, and see if I felt tired after that.

I put some Sinatra on the turntable—"The Wee Small Hours of the Morning" followed by "Mood Indigo" seemed particularly appropriate.

We were halfway through "Mood Indigo"—Frankie handling the lyrics and Wheeler putting in some fancy background, when something snarled to a stop on the driveway. I recognised that sound from way back. Lucrece's Porsche.

I opened the door as her finger was poised a couple of inches from the buzzer.

"Good morning," I said. "Come right on in and make yourself comfortable. I know it won't make any difference if I say I'm asleep!"

She walked past me into the living-room. She was wearing a cute number in black taffeta with a heart-shaped neckline, and it rustled as she walked.

"I decided to ignore your nasty remarks you made earlier this evening," she said. "You don't even have to apologise."

"Well," thank you," I told her. "And how was the first show tonight?"

We sat down together on the divan.

"Fine," she said. "I had three notes sent to the dressing-room. All from men in their fifties who wanted to show me a time."

"Which one are you taking first?"

"I wrote them all a note," she said complacently. "Saying thank you very much, but I'd already seen the City Morgue."

"I just wondered," I said. "Did you find out anything about Wendy Martin?"

"You don't seriously imagine it was Al Wheeler's personality that dragged me back here?"

I shrugged my shoulders. "Well, let's hear the backroom gossip of the chorus-line."

I sank back on the divan to listen to Lucrece's spiel.

"Wendy Martin had been working at the Due D'Or for the last six months," she said. "And before that she'd been in a song and dance team with her brother."

"How was their act?"

"Sort of corny, the way I heard it. He used to wear a set of tails, top-hat, and carry a cane. She wore a top-hat, blouse and tights, and also carried a cane. I guess they did those original routines—you know, banging down the cane and raising their top-hats every second beat to the bar."

"Anything special at all about it?"

"Nothing really. They had a signature tune though, 'California, Here I Come!'"

"Sure, sure," I said. "Those acts always do. But what about her brother?"

"No one seemed to know."

"That's a lot of help, I don't think." I glared at Lucrece.

"Let me tell you, Al Wheeler, I worked hard for that information!"

"Weren't the girls in a chatty mood?"

"No," she said. "I got it straight from that character Rogers, who organises the chorus-line."

"Uh, huh," I nodded, grinning. "Are you going to continue working there?"

"I think so," Lucrece said. "You never know, I could learn something more."

"Well," I said, "I think you deserve a drink."

"No, thanks," she said.

I did a double-take. "You're joking—of course!"

"I just intend to prove to you that I can take a drink or leave it alone," she said. "But I'd like some coffee. I'll make some, shall I?"

"Sounds like a wonderful idea," I said. "Since when have you become domesticated?"

"You'd be surprised," she said. "One of these days I'll cook you a meal."

"I'll get somebody else to taste it first," I said. "If you don't mind?" But I was talking to myself—Lucrece was already in the kitchen.

Frankie and I vocalised through to the end of that side of the disc. Lucrece came back with the coffee and the rest of it on a tray, which she put down on the table carefully.

"Black?" she asked me.

"Fine," I said.

She poured the coffee and handed me my cup. I took it over to the divan with me and sat down. She brought her cup with her and sat down beside me.

I tasted the coffee again. It was good—good as Billings' coffee. "Who taught you to make coffee?" I asked her. "Billings?"

"I taught him!" she said. Then she looked at me. "What made you say that?"

"Billings made me some coffee earlier on tonight," I told her.

"You were over at the house?"

"That's right—at your stepmother's invitation."

"Is she getting tired of Billings?"

"Either that, or she thinks Billings is getting tired of her."

"Why did she want you over there?"

"Did you teach Billings to lace his coffee with cyanide?"

"Is this another gag?"

"Or did you lace it for him?"

"What the hell are you talking about, Wheeler!"

"Did you try and electrocute your stepmother in her bath, fire a shot at her from the grounds … or sneak back into the house tonight and try and strangle her?"

"You should drink less, Wheeler," she said. "Your sodden mind is coming unhinged!"

"Do you know Mr. Delmar, your father's assistant?" I asked, ignoring the last remark.

"That slob!" she said disgustedly. "Why Father ever keeps him around the office is something I've never worked out."

"What's wrong with him?"

"He could crawl under a snake without mussing up his hair!"

"You aren't giving him a nice epitaph," I said.

"Epitaph!" She stared at me. "You mean he's dead?"

"Somebody worked overtime at United Steel," I told her, "and shot him twice in the back of the head."

"Then that proves Father didn't do it," she said excitedly.

"I've already been through that routine with Irvine down at the Homicide Bureau," I said. "It proves your father didn't kill Delmar but as far as the police are concerned, it doesn't prove that your father didn't kill Wendy Martin."

"They're crazy!" she said.

I put the coffee cup down on the floor at my feet and lit a cigarette. "You don't believe your father killed the girl?"

"No!"

"Who do you think did?"

"I don't have any idea at all," she said. "I wish I did."

"Your stepmother told me tonight that someone was trying to kill her," I said. "I brought her over here for a while, then went back to the house and talked to Billings. He claimed someone was trying to kill him."

Lucrece looked at me wonderingly. "Are they both crazy?"

"I don't know," I said. "Have you been trying to kill either of them—or both?"

"So that's what you were babbling about a few minutes ago!" she said.

"Of course I haven't!"

"Do you think it's possible they may have been trying to kill each other?"

"It's ridiculous!"

I got up and walked across the room to pour myself another drink.

"Maybe one of them is going to kill somebody," I said. "It's not an original line of approach, but it has its points. You scream blue murder—somebody has already made attempts on your life. Then they make a further attempt, but fortunately you manage to forestall them—and you kill them instead. Your stepmother or Billings may have that sort of approach in mind. Or maybe it's a mutual project even."

She stared at me. "You mean, they tell the story that someone is trying to murder them so that they can murder somebody and claim it was self-defence?"

"That could be the general idea," I agreed.

"But who would they want to murder?"

"If it's not each other," I said, "I doubt if it's the housekeeper. Firing her would be an easier way of getting rid of her."

"But that leaves only …"

"I'd lock your door at nights," I said. "And don't go making a nice silhouette by your window."

CHAPTER 8

I slept in late. The phone woke me at ten-thirty. Lucrece had gone home around three-thirty. Seven hours, I thought as I staggered out to the phone. That's a healthy sleep—why the hell do I feel tired?

I picked up the phone and grunted, "Wheeler," into it.

"Mr. Wheeler," the voice was feminine and precise. "This is Isobel Lamont. I would like to talk to you urgently. Could you possibly come over to the club?"

"I guess so," I said. "When?"

"Eleven-thirty?"

"Okay," I said, then hung up.

I showered, shaved, cleaned my teeth, got dressed, drank some coffee, saw the morning newspaper carried the story of Delmar's murder but no details, then got into the Jag and drove myself to the Due D'Or.

There was a guy in a janitor's uniform on the door. I told him I was here to see Miss Lamont and I told him my name, and he didn't tell me his name but—told me I was expected.

I went through the main room on my way to Miss Lamont's office and saw the chorus-line was in rehearsal on the floor. A big, thick-set guy who I guessed must be Rogers was putting them through their paces.

Lucrece was third from the end of the line, wearing the littlest leotard I'd ever seen. My head swivelled on my neck as I walked past her and I felt a distinct twinge of regret when I got into the corridor and could no longer see her. I walked down to Isobel Lamont's office and knocked on the door. Her voice from inside told me crisply to come in.

I went in, closing the door behind me. Her eyes were vague behind the lens of her hornrims as she looked at me.

"Thank you for coming, Mr. Wheeler," she said. "Won't you sit down?"

"Thanks." I sat down facing her across the desk.

The tips of her fingers beat a tattoo on the desk-top for a few moments. "Mr. Wheeler," she said finally. "Are you interested in money?"

"That's a fair question," I said. "Who isn't?"

"I have a proposition," she said. "It involves money for you."

"It sounds interesting," I said.

"I may as well be frank," she said.

"I think Isobel sounds nicer," I murmured.

She sniffed. "I'm not in a mood for humour, Mr. Wheeler. This matter is too serious for levity."

"Okay," I said. "Let's all be serious."

"You know I have a gambling-room here," she said flatly. "It's common knowledge. No one has ever worried about it before——the games are honest and the house takes a percentage. It is a very profitable side of the business—in fact, the most profitable. Unfortunately, we have received a good deal of the wrong sort of publicity since the Martin girl was murdered. And one or two of the newspapers have been harping on the gambling that goes on here. So much so, that I understand the police intend forcibly closing me down—at least as far as the gambling is concerned."

"That's tough," I said.

"You are an ex-lieutenant of police," she said. "Undoubtedly you would still have some influence with them. If you could persuade them to change their minds, Mr. Wheeler, I should be very grateful."

"How grateful is your grateful?"

"I think I am prepared to be quite generous," she said. "As opposed to a lump sum of cash, I would be happy to pay you five per cent of the profit made each month from the tables. That would run into something like five hundred dollars a month, Mr. Wheeler."

I grinned at her. "And of course, that way I would have a perpetual interest in seeing that the police didn't close you down."

"Exactly," she agreed. "Whereas if I paid you a lump sum, I would have no guarantee the police wouldn't close me down in two months' time—

after I'd paid you."

I lit myself a cigarette. "It's quite an attractive offer, Miss Lamont."

"Then you'll accept?" she asked eagerly.

"I think you overestimate the influence I have with the police," I said. "I'd like to accept, but I don't think I could really help you."

"I think you're being unduly modest, Mr. Wheeler," she said sharply. "It would most probably run out to something like four thousand dollars a year."

"I'd have to think about it," I said. "Is this your own idea, Miss Lamont, or does it have the approval of your partners?"

"My partners?" she said blankly.

"Sure," I said. "Walter and Myra Byrne—and Hammond. Are they in agreement with this?"

"How did you know of my partners?"

"It's surprising what you hear around," I said.

"It's entirely my own idea," she said. "I run the club—they have no hand in the running of it at all."

"Do you think they would be in agreement with it?"

"I'm quite sure they would," she said. "Don't you trust me, Mr. Wheeler?"

"You told me you hardly knew Walter Byrne the last time I spoke to you," I reminded her. "Then I found out he was one of your partners. You haven't exactly built a basis for trust, Miss Lamont."

She smiled suddenly. "Is that why Byrne's daughter is working in my chorus?"

"That was strictly her own idea," I said. "She was hoping to find out something that would help clear her father."

"How noble of her," she said. "And how out of character for Lucrece to be noble. I wouldn't be too sure that's her only reason, Mr. Wheeler."

"You could be right," I told her. "Is there anything else you wanted to talk about?"

"No," she said. "But please consider my offer very carefully, Mr. Wheeler."

"I'll think about it very hard," I assured her.

"When will you let me know your answer?"

"Within the next couple of days," I said.

"I'll look forward to hearing from you, Mr. Wheeler."

I left her office and went through the club to the front, passing the chorus-line again on my way. I would have liked to stay and watch, but I had a couple of other things to do.

The first one was to see Hanlon. He looked even more cited than when I'd last seen him.

"You got it all wrapped up, Al?" he asked. "Brought the proof with you that whoever killed Wendy Martin killed Delmar?"

I grinned at him. "I'm just a humble citizen, pal, hoping for some information."

"Such as?" he grunted.

"Such as whose idea is it to close down the gambling at the Due D'Or, and when is it going to happen?"

He shrugged his shoulders. "It's all news to me, pal. I've got enough Homicide troubles without going looking for more."

"Do me a favour," I said. "Find out for me."

"I'm a sucker," he sighed. He picked up his phone and dialled a number, then waited. "Lieutenant Jorgens," he said. "Hanlon speaking … Mike? I hear you're going to close down the tables at the Due D'Or. Is that right? … Uh-huh … Huh-uh. Yeah, thanks, Mike."

He put the phone down and looked at me. "You've got your wires crossed, Al. It's not on the agenda."

"You're sure?"

"Sure, I'm sure!"

"Well, thanks a lot," I said. "Hope I can do something for you some day, Pete."

"You could do something for the Commissioner right now," he grinned.

"I know," I said. "Drop dead!"

I left Homicide, drove home and picked up the confidential file Snooks had sent me, then I drove back into town. I arrived at the offices of Hammond, Irvine and Snooks, snuck a quick look inside my own office and saw there was a small pile of memos asking me to ring Hammond, Irvine, Mrs. Byrne and Commissioner Lavers as soon as I got in. I took a raincheck on the lot, tucked the file firmly under my arm and rode the elevator two floors up.

I knocked on the door of Snooks' office and a moment later the blonde, Pauline, opened it. She was wearing an outfit that made business a pleasure—a black barathea suit with a blue silk shirt underneath. The shirt had a wide collar, and beneath the collar was the most interesting contour map in silk I'd seen since I left high school.

"Mr. Wheeler," she said. "This is a pleasant surprise."

"I'm glad to hear you say that," I said. "So few people do!"

"Mr. Snooks is out of the office for a moment," she said. "But he shouldn't be away very long. Would you care to come in and wait for him?"

"That would be enchanting," I said. "And if you pour me a drink—exotic!"

I followed her into Snooks' office and she closed the door, then went over to the bar. "Scotch, isn't it, Mr. Wheeler?"

"Why so formal?" I said. "Al is the name."

"Of course," she smiled. "Al Wheeler—the former unorthodox cop and hero of the Sunday supplements."

"And you're the girl who survived all those perils!" I grinned.

She wrinkled her nose. "All right, Al—you win!"

She handed me the drink.

"Thanks," I told her. "Aren't you drinking?"

"No," she said firmly. "Mr. Snooks has been trying to get me to have a drink in the office for the last twelve months. He says it's the first step." She looked up at the ceiling reflectively. "I'm a little uneasy about what he might term the second step—that's why I don't drink in the office."

"That's understandable," I said. "A guy like Snooks wouldn't sneak up on you. Before you knew where you were it would be too late—he would have snuck!"

Before Pauline had time to reply, the door opened and Snooks came in. "Ah," he smiled at me. "The virile young man is back."

"Have you been out buying yourself a new cap?" I asked him.

He shuffled over to his desk and sat down. "Pour me a drink, my dear," he said to Pauline. "A little brandy, I think."

He looked at me. "No cap," he said. "I'm too old for any more adventures." Pauline's silk shirt came into his line of vision as she bent forward to pick up a glass. "Well, almost," he corrected himself.

Pauline took the drink across to his desk, then took my glass and thoughtfully refilled it.

"That will be all for now, my dear," Snooks said, and Pauline smiled and went through the inner doorway presumably into her own office.

"Now," he said, sipping his drink and smacking his lips loudly. "To what do I owe the honour of your visit, Mr. Wheeler?"

"I am returning the file you so thoughtfully sent me," I said.

"Indeed? Did you find the contents interesting? I hope they passed a few pleasant minutes of your time for you, Wheeler?"

"You're one of the few assassins I've met that prefers a broad-sword to a knife."

He peered at me. "I don't quite follow you?"

"I can't make up my mind," I said slowly. "Whether you want Hammond convicted of murder because you don't like him—or because you think he is a murderer."

He made that rusty sound deep in his chest. "I see. Strong words, Wheeler. But then of course you were a police officer, no doubt used to strong language. But in the legal profession, we shudder at the use of any words that can be construed as having a definite meaning. Haven't you noticed the way lawyers always talk—it's a jargon all of its own."

"You still haven't answered my question," I pointed out.

He sighed and finished his drink. "I can see you are a man not to be denied, Wheeler," he said. "Would I were Pauline, I would tremble before you!"

"If you were Pauline, you would have no need to tremble!" I assured him.

The rusty noise came again. "Ah! That's rather good—I must remember that. Now, what were we talking about? Oh, the senior partner, of course."

"I was," I said. "You were dodging the question."

"Perhaps," he said. "Shall I put it to you this way, Wheeler? In a moment of sentimental weakness, celebrating my seventieth birthday, I decided to go into semi-retirement. I altered the structure of this organisation so that Hammond became the senior partner. Since it was virtually a gift that I gave him, I foolishly expected him still to consult me on matters of importance. He has done no such thing … he ignores me as far as he possibly can. He would ignore me altogether if I let him. So I'll agree with you I bear him a certain amount of animosity. But not enough to try and brand him a murderer—if he isn't. And I will be honest with you, Wheeler—I don't know that he is. I think he needs investigating a little. And since we now have our own investigator on the staff, then he's the man to do it."

I lit myself a cigarette. "If Wendy Martin was attempting to blackmail Byrne, then he had a motive. If he was framed with the blackmail note, then what happened to him when the murder took place, that he doesn't remember anything about it? Even if he'd been knocked out, he would have remembered that. So we could theorise that he's protecting somebody. Why? And who would have a motive for murdering Wendy Martin, or a motive for murdering her just to frame Byrne with the murder? Why not kill Byrne in the first place?"

I shook my head. "The whole thing is crazy and illogical once you discard Byrne as the prime suspect!"

Snooks nodded. "Then you think Byrne did kill her?"

"No," I said, "I don't. I wish I did—then I'd be thinking logically. The whole thing was too neat—the case against him—and now Delmar's been murdered, I'm even less inclined to think Byrne murdered the girl."

"Do you have any nominees?" he asked.

I shook my head. "They're all crazy people. His wife is crazy, his daughter is crazy, his butler is crazy, and his best friend Hammond is crazy. I don't know about Isobel Lamont, but I wouldn't be surprised!"

"Then perhaps, Wheeler, you had better start looking for a crazy motive?"

"There aren't many people commit murder with an insane motive. The trouble is, right now, I just don't see a motive at all."

He shuffled across to the bar and poured himself another drink.

"Well," he said. "This is most interesting, Wheeler. You must drop in again and tell me how your investigation is progressing."

"Thank you," I said. I got to my feet at the obvious cue to drift he'd just given me. "Don't go killing too many bears!"

I'd got as far as the door, had it halfway open when he cleared his throat with a noise like a powered wood-saw going through butter. "Er … Wheeler!"

I turned around and looked at him. "Mr. Snooks?"

"If I were investigating this thing—not that I'm anything like the expert you are, of course … I'd take a good look at United Steel. Their shareholders, the way the company is run … things like that."

"Thank you," I said.

"And I must confess," he said, "I did a little investigating of my own, just to prove a point."

"What was that?"

"Nothing very much—*Aloysius*!"

I still had my mouth hanging open when I got back to my office. The State's best-kept secret was Al Wheeler's full Christian name—so I'd thought.

CHAPTER 9

I picked up the sheaf of memos in one hand and the phone in the other. I rang Hammond first and a female glacier who I imagined was his secretary told me he was out and wouldn't be back until late in the afternoon. I rang Irvine who was also out, then Mrs. Byrne. Billings answered the phone, then connected me.

"I wanted to apologise, Al," she said softly, "for my behaviour last night. It was too stupid of me, but my nerves are over-wrought …"

"Don't let it worry you," I said. "How have you been?"

"Much better," she said. "I had a good night's sleep last night and nothing has happened … nothing to upset me. I've been thinking about things … I'd like to have another talk with you if I may?"

"Sure," I said. "When?"

"Tonight, perhaps?" she said. "Why don't you come for dinner? Say seven?"

"Fine," I said. "I'll be there."

I joggled the bar, then dialled Lavers' office. The familiar voice barked into my ear. "Lavers!"

"Mr. Commissioner," I heightened my voice to a falsetto. "We are conducting a public opinion survey. Do you prefer your eggs fried or poached?"

"Poached!" he growled.

"And how about your coffee? Do you take it with or without cream?"

"Without!" he said tersely.

"Just one more question, Mr. Commissioner?" I was having trouble maintaining the falsetto. "Do you remove your shoes or your trousers first when undressing?"

He thought for a moment. "Shoes!" he said finally.

"Thank you, Mr. Commissioner," I said. "According to the scale of marks awarded to your answers by our psychologists, you qualify as an idiot!"

There was a couple of moments' silence. "Wheeler!" he said disgustedly. "I might have known."

"I thought I'd make your day brighter," I said. "You were calling me— or was I just a wrong number?"

"I was calling you," he said. "Against my better judgment! I wanted to have a talk to you. Can you come over to my office?"

"Sure," I said. "When?"

"Any time this afternoon would suit me."

"Around four-thirty?"

"Fine. See you, Al." Then he hung up.

I put down the phone, wondering why he was being polite to me. I thought I'd done a good morning's work what with seeing Snooks and making four phone calls, and it was time I had some lunch.

By the time I'd finished lunch it was three-thirty, so I thought it wasn't worth going back to the office in case Hammond was back—I didn't really want to talk to Hammond just yet. And Irvine would be worrying about progress and there wasn't any, which would only worry him even more. So I walked a block down to a bar and had a couple of drinks until it was time to go and see the Commissioner.

The office didn't look any different. He had a new secretary, a redhead who was a little too buxom for the Californian climate, but who would have been a comfort in the Frozen North. She announced me and Lavers said for me to go right on in, so I did. He even offered me a chair and then sat down behind his desk, brooding behind a cigar.

"All right," he said finally. "I want your help."

I stared at him. "You're kidding."

"No," he said, "I mean it. If you were still working around here, I'd have called you in right now. But you're working for those lawyers now and they have a client. This could be in his interest."

"Tell me more," I said.

"The Byrne case," he said. "What do you know about it?"

"Not a thing that makes sense," I told him.

"You don't have to hold out on me, Al," he said wearily. "I don't think Byrne did it. There's a strong circumstantial case against him—almost too good a one—but since that Delmar got himself shot, I've had my doubts. But there aren't any facts to go on."

"I'll go along with that," I said.

He flipped the pages of the bulky folder on the desk in front of him. "I've got it all here," he said. "Hanlon's done a competent job by the copybook, but it doesn't get us anywhere. I could help you, Al, if you help me."

I told Lavers what I'd found out—or most of it, anyway. He nodded briefly when I got through.

"Have you found a motive, other than Byrne's, for the girl's murder?"

"No," I said. "I wish I had."

"That's the whole stumbling block," he grunted.

I sucked smoke into my lungs. "What about Delmar—any leads there?"

"A blind alley," he said. "Apparently he stayed back late at the office. The front door is never locked before eleven at night and anybody could have come in or out. The cleaners came on duty at ten. One of them found him in Byrne's office. Shot with a thirty-eight, from the slugs. Close range—four or five feet. Again, no apparent motive."

I lit myself a cigarette. "Did you dig up anything on the girl Martin?"

Lavers flipped open the pages of the folder. "It doesn't make pretty reading, Al," he said. "Wendy Martin and her brother ..."

"Skip that part," I cut in. "What's the dirt?"

"The Badger Game, Al!"

I whistled. "The Badger Game!"

"Yeah," he grunted. "She had two arrests and one conviction, did a year in Corona. We checked with the San Francisco boys."

"Poor Byrne," I muttered. "He was just another sucker who fell for a pretty babe until she starts in with the blackmail line."

"Could be, Al," he said. "But there's another thing."

"Yeah?"

"The owner of the nightclub in Frisco where Martin got picked up was ..."

"A doll by the name of Isabel Lamont," I finished for him.

Lavers' mouth dropped open. "How did you know?"

I grinned and tried to look modest. "Shucks, it wasn't nothin', Mr. Commissioner."

Lavers' face turned that underdone, off-beetroot colour.

I got out of the chair and headed for the door. "Thanks for your help. Be seeing you around!" I called back.

"But, but …" Lavers stammered. "You haven't told me …"

"But, sir, I told you everything," I crossed two fingers behind my back and added a silent "almost". "A smart cop like Hanlon should come up with the right answer."

I ran out of the office and across the street to where I'd parked the Jaguar. As I felt in my pockets for the keys, I remembered something. I figured I'd take a calculated risk on getting singed by Lavers' hot air. I walked slowly back to the office.

I glared at the blonde on the way through—which showed I meant business. I pushed open the door of Lavers' inner sanctum.

He rose to his feet. "You! What the hell do you want now? I wouldn't even have you on traffic detail in the force!"

I tried to smile demurely. "I just came back to apologise …"

Lavers sighed. "Look, Wheeler, I asked you here to give me some help, some suggestions. All you've done is make wisecracks and ask questions."

"I might have one suggestion … within the next twenty-four hours."

He looked hopeful. "Yes?"

"You won't like it," I said. "It's unorthodox."

"Were you ever anything else?" he growled. "What is it?"

"Maybe soon might be the right time to release Byrne on bail," I said. "Irvine is agitating for it, saying Delmar's murder must be connected with the Martin case and it therefore weakens the case against Byrne. You could go along with that a little and release him on bail."

"I could," Lavers said. "But why should I?"

"It's just a feeling I have," I said vaguely. "With Byrne out on bail things might start to happen, that's all."

"And a fine thing it'll be for me if he gets murdered while he's out on bail."

"At least you'll save the expense of his trial," I replied. "And know he's probably innocent. I think it might be an idea—not right now, but maybe soon."

"Is that the only constructive thought you have?"

"The only one," I agreed. "But I have another question." Lavers glowered, but I ignored the hint. "Have you found out anything about the guy Martin, the girl's brother?"

"No!" he snarled.

I turned to leave. "It was just a thought," I smiled politely.

Lavers' voice reverberated in my ears as I eased my way out the door. "Missing Persons can't find Martin—so you find him, Mister Unorthodox Wheeler!"

I went down to where I'd parked the car and got in. Just for the hell of it, I drove down to United Steel. I didn't stay very long—only long enough to learn that a Mr. Hammond, of legal fame, was also a vice-president of United Steel.

I left United Steel's office and made my way down to the street again. I had time to drive home and change leisurely for my dinner date with Mrs. Byrne. I had time to think too, and for the first time I could see a grain of sense in the whole affair. I was even looking forward to dinner—especially to seeing Billings, the butler.

CHAPTER 10

It was seven-thirty when I parked on the Byrne drive and got out of the Jaguar. Billings opened the door, every inch of him the perfect butler again.

"Good evening, sir," he said politely. "Mrs. Byrne is waiting for you in the bar."

"Fine," I gave him my hat. "You're still alive, I see?"

"I think you could say that is definite fact, sir," he said. "I am following the practice of sniffing before I drink."

"All the best wine-drinkers do that," I said. "Unless somebody else is paying for the bottle."

The bar was an annexe off the dining-room. A nice, intimate spot built for, at the most, about four. When I got there it made two, which is a figure that leads to even more intimacy in atmosphere.

Myra Byrne was wearing something she probably referred to as that old rag. That old rag was in heavy white sharkskin with a deep, scooped neckline, the whole gown relieved only by a dark blue orchid, pinned just below her left shoulder.

"You're late, Al," she smiled at me.

"Work," I said. "You know how it is. You look very beautiful tonight."

"My!" She raised her eyebrows a little. "That's not the sort of conversation I expected to hear from you, somehow."

"I've been losing my grip lately," I said. "Working too hard. From here on I intend to reform completely and utterly. The only pursuit I intend to indulge in is the straight line that leads from the cocktail-bar to the sofa."

"Well," she smiled, "I can't say I haven't been warned."

We had a couple of drinks, then went into the dining-room and sat down. Billings poured the wine, then served the meal. I talked to Myra about this and that and she talked to me about that and this. We finally got to the coffee and liqueur stage. We lit cigarettes and everything was still nice and cosy. Even Billings looked cosy as he came around with the silver coffee-pot to refill my cup.

"Tell me something, Billings," I said as he started to pour.

"Sir?"

"Are you back where you started from?"

His hand shook slightly and coffee spattered into the saucer. "I'm sorry, sir," he said evenly. "I'll get you a clean cup."

"Don't bother," I said. "You haven't answered my question yet."

"I'm afraid I couldn't quite understand it, sir. If you would be so good as to explain?"

I looked up at him. "It's a perfectly simple question. In fact, it's a quote from a very famous song—you must recognise it?"

"I'm afraid I don't, sir."

"Right out of, "California, Here I Come!"" I said. "Everybody knows that song."

"Of course, sir," he said. "It quite slipped my memory for the moment."

"It's been a long time," I said.

"A long time since what, Al?" Myra asked, a puzzled look on her face.

I leaned back in my chair. "Since Billings used to wear a top-hat and twirl a cane in his hand and sing, "California, Here I Come!""

She laughed. "I think you're just in a crazy mood tonight."

"Could be," I said. "See if you can dig up a couple of toppers and canes, Billings, and we'll see if we can knock out a double act. Who knows?"

"Yes, sir," he said. "Very good, sir." He went out of the room, taking the coffee-pot with him.

"Why are you teasing him like that?" Myra said. "It really isn't fair."

"Just the devil in me coming out," I said. "Within us all lurks the touch of sadism that has caused men to invent such things as telephones, television and peanut butter."

"Shall we sit in the sunroom?" she asked me. "Or would you rather go back to the bar?"

"The bar is closer, isn't it?" I said.

We went back to the bar. Myra poured us both a drink and I watched Billings come into the dining-room and clear the table. When he'd left again, I looked at her.

"Nothing else has happened since yesterday?" I asked.

"No," she said. "Do you think I was imagining it?"

"No, I don't think you were imagining it—but I have a feeling it won't happen again. I've also got some news for you."

"Good news, I hope?" she smiled.

I smiled back at her. "I certainly hope it is. I was talking to Commissioner Lavers this afternoon. Your husband will probably be released on bail sometime tomorrow."

"Oh!" The smile vanished from her face.

"You don't look as if that's good news," I said.

"Walter and I haven't been … very close, for quite some time," she said. "But of course I'm glad to hear the police are going to release him."

I lit myself a cigarette. "Do you mind if I ask you a couple of questions?"

"I thought you were intent on following a straight line to the nearest sofa?" she smiled.

"Just a couple of questions."

"All right," she sighed.

"You own a quarter share in the Due D'Or?"

"Yes. Why?"

I shrugged my shoulders. "It could be interesting. When did you put the money into the Due D'Or?"

She thought for a moment. "After the divorce with Hammond. As I remember it, my ex-husband had met this woman—Isabel Lamont—who had run a club on similar lines very successfully in San Francisco. The club premises were available at the sum for purchase and he put it up as a proposition to Walter. Walter was interested. The three of us put in an equal amount and gave Isabel Lamont a quarter share without her having to put up any hard cash. She was to run it. And I must say she has run it very successfully up to date."

I stubbed out my cigarette. "I'm surprised that Hammond remained so friendly with both you and your husband after you divorced him and married Walter."

"He isn't exactly friendly towards me," she said. "He is still Walter's friend, but he hardly speaks to me."

"Because of the divorce?"

"Because of the grounds," she replied. "We were washed up a long time before the divorce was sought. He raved about me charging him with gross cruelty and physical violence. He said it would ruin him professionally—it didn't, of course."

I nodded. "If you don't mind my asking … what are your feelings towards your husband now?"

"Indifference," she said. "I haven't been exactly lucky in either of my marriages. It's the curse of being a wealthy woman. You can never be sure if they're marrying you for your money or not."

"It must be tough," I said. "Just one more question. Why did you invite me over to dinner tonight?"

"I thought I should," she said. "To apologise for my stupid behaviour last night. My nerves were just overwrought, I guess."

"Like I said, don't worry about it. Are you going to divorce Walter when this murder problem is all wrapped up and put away?"

"That's really a leading question, Al."

"I know! Are you?"

"I haven't made up my mind," she said. "I may."

"You wouldn't have any trouble," I said. "Not with Wendy Martin to quote."

"I realise that," she said. "I suppose I should be able to get a laugh out of the thought of hiring Hammond for the job. My first husband obtaining a divorce from my second husband for me!"

I finished my drink and got to my feet. "Thanks for the dinner and the drinks," I said. "Both were very nice."

"You're going?"

"I have to," I said.

"That's a pity, Al," she said, and the scoop neckline scooped a little more. "You were just getting me interested in your straight line theory."

"Much as I hate to leave, I have to," I said. "Give me a ring if anything happens."

"I might even if it doesn't," she said. "Goodbye, Al."

"Goodbye, Myra," I said.

I went through the dining-room and into the hall and walked slowly along towards the front door. Billings came hurrying out of a side door with my hat in his hand, which he gave to me.

"I regret," he said with an expressionless face, "I was unable to find either a top-hat or a cane, sir."

"Too bad," I said. "We could have done a riot of a double act and called ourselves the Merry Martins, or something like that."

"I'm sure I would find this conversation even more entertaining if I knew what it was all about, sir?"

"Well," I said, "I'll tell you, Billings. I have a theory that either you killed your sister or you didn't. If you did, I'll dig up the proof sooner or later and you'll end up in the gas-chamber. If you didn't, I have an equally unpleasant theory."

"May I ask what the equally unpleasant theory is, sir?"

"Put it this way," I said. "If you didn't murder your sister, then I'd sleep with a gun under my pillow. And I'd grow eyes in the back of my head!"

Billings stared at me for a moment and there was a momentary flicker of something behind his eyes which could have been fear.

"Thank you for your advice, Mr. Wheeler," he said finally.

"There's just one other point," I said. "The police will probably release Mr. Byrne sometime tomorrow so that he should be home before evening."

"Is that why you're recommending I grow eyes in the back of my head?"

I shrugged my shoulders. "Could be. I'm not quite sure myself, it's just a feeling I have. I could be quite wrong, of course."

"What do you want of me?" he snarled.

"The truth," I said. "But you wouldn't give me that, would you?"

Then I opened the door and walked out into the night.

I drove home, put some Harry Belafonte on the hi-fi. I shuffled around the room in time to the music, more or less, and sang, "Stone cold dead in de apartment! I killed nobody but my lover!" Second verse: "Stone cold dead in de office! I killed nobody but my personal assistant!"

Then I got tired of playing Byrne and poured myself a drink. That was when I got to thinking again. By the time I was through, things were seeming a little clearer.

"Day-o, day-o," Belafonte sang powerfully. "Daylight come and we want to go home."

"Harry," I told him. "Before we can do that, there's a long night ahead of us."

CHAPTER 11

Miss Isobel Lamont gave me a smile that actually seemed to have some warmth in it, as I walked into her office.

"I'm so glad you called, Mr. Wheeler," she said. "I take it you have made up your mind about my little proposition?"

"You could say that," I agreed.

I sank into the nearest chair and lit myself a cigarette.

"I have good news for you, Miss Lamont. You don't have to worry about the police closing down your tables—they won't. You don't even have to pay me any money for the information. I had nothing to do with their decision."

She didn't look pleased. I wasn't sure if it was her hornrims or her eyes that glittered as she looked at me. Maybe it was both.

"How can you be so sure, Mr. Wheeler?" she asked. "Really, I would be a lot happier if you would take on the assignment. I would know then that our interests were being protected all the time."

"You don't have to worry," I assured her. "And that's straight from Wheeler's mouth, which is only half a size smaller than that of the horse."

She pursed her lips together tightly. "Very well, if you insist, Mr. Wheeler. And thank you for your information."

"It's a pleasure," I said. "I ask only one thing in return."

"Yes?" She brightened up a little.

"Some information from you," I said.

"Really!" Her fingers beat out that tattoo again. "I am quite sure I don't have any information that could be of interest to you, Mr. Wheeler."

"There," I said tenderly, "we disagree."

The fingers beat a faster tattoo.

"Did you meet Mr. Hammond here or in San Francisco?" I asked her.

"He came to my club a few times when he was in Frisco," she said. "We got to know each other there. I think I mentioned casually to him at one stage that I was leaving San Francisco. A couple of weeks later he wired me and said he had a proposition to open a club here—and the deal would include some stock for me. Naturally, I was interested enough to come here and talk to him about it. Is that what you wanted to know?"

I nodded encouragingly. "You're doing very well, Miss Lamont. That's some of what I wanted to know. The rest concerns the Merry Martins, really. You know how merry they could be. They certainly finished up merrily, didn't they? Wendy as a corpse and her brother as a butler. How merry can you get!"

"Really, Mr. Wheeler," she said. "I don't know what you're talking about!"

"Sometimes the naive approach becomes you, Isobel," I said.

"And sometimes it doesn't. This is one of the times it doesn't. Get out!"

"But I'm finding this conversation so interesting, Miss Lamont," I said coolly. "Now, how did you work things with the Martins in San Francisco? Did you pick out good prospects for them?"

"Prospects?" she said hoarsely.

"The Badger Game," I said gently. "That was their speciality, surely you remember?"

"Will you please leave my office!" she said.

"I will if you insist," I said. "But if I do, I'll ring the police right away and have them take you in for questioning. You just please yourself, Isobel. You talk to me here, or you talk to the boys in blue downtown."

Her shoulders slumped suddenly. "All right," she said. "What do you want to know?"

"If my theory is right, when you got here and opened this club Hammond would have told you about the Byrnes. About Myra who had all the money—and how she had been his wife, then divorced him."

"Yes," she nodded jerkily. "Is there anything wrong in that?"

"Not a thing," I said. "Except you have a brain like a rat-trap and a cash register instead of a heart. You'd hooked Hammond with your own appeal and then you wanted to cash in on the Byrnes."

The tattoo stopped for a while as her fingers nervously tucked a stray strand of hair back into place.

"That was why you brought the Martins down here," I went on. "They'd been useful to you in the past. Then you got enough knowledge of the Byrnes' background to know where to place the Martins. So you had them break their act. Wendy came into your chorus-line for the express intention of hooking Byrne. And her brother put on a monkey suit and got himself a job as butler at the Byrne house, for the express intention of hooking Myra Byrne."

I lit myself another cigarette and thought there wasn't much hope of her offering me a drink.

"Go on," she said in a dull voice.

"You knew it would take time," I said. "You were in no great hurry. Byrne set Wendy up in an apartment, Billings was doing fine with Mrs. Byrne. The stage was set the way you wanted it."

I sucked smoke deep into my lungs. "Now the thing blows up the wrong way. Wendy got sick of your cat and mouse tactics and decided to play in the big league. You found out that Wendy had sent Walter a black-mail note before you had given the word. That meant you were going to miss out on your cut, and your cash register mind didn't like that. So you thought you would fix things properly."

Isobel Lamont shook her head. "No," she said. "You're lying."

"So, Miss Lamont," I continued, "you hid in Wendy Martin's apartment one night and waited for her and Byrne to come home. When they arrived, you came out of hiding, shot Wendy and knocked out Byrne with the gun. You cleaned off the prints and carefully wrapped his fingers around the butt, then dropped the gun onto the floor. You rang the police anonymously and told them there had been a shooting."

"Lies!" she screamed. "All lies!"

I shrugged my shoulders again. "It's the truth, and you know it."

She put her head into her hands and began to weep bitterly. I lit one more cigarette and then the door behind her chair opened suddenly and Hammond stood there.

"Well," I grinned. "This is a surprise, Mr. Hammond. Good evening."

"Aren't you forgetting one thing in your wonderful theory, Wheeler?" he said coldly.

"You tell me," I said.

"Delmar's murder. Or do you think that was purely coincidental?"

He was so right!

I smiled weakly at him. "You could just have a point there."

"You fool!" he said. "Half-baked theories! I should think that Lavers was damned glad to see you leave his department!"

"You could have another point there, too," I admitted.

Isabel lifted her head slowly. "Darling!" she said to Hammond. "I'm so glad you came in. I thought I would have a complete breakdown the way Wheeler was hammering at me. All those fantastic lies! But he made them sound so logical at the time while he was saying them.”

She took off her glasses and began to polish them vigorously with a handkerchief. “I’m so glad you’re here, darling,” she said, looking up at him. “You know there isn’t one word of truth in what he said, don’t you?”

He looked down at her for a long moment, then shouted, “You scheming, conniving, filthy ...” He stopped himself with an effort. “Wheeler’s theory about you murdering the girl is ridiculous. I can alibi you for that—unfortunately. The rest isn’t. It makes sense. Horrible sense! The girl working here in the chorus—the butler working at Walter’s house!”

“Darling!” she moaned. “You can’t believe that! You know that all I’ve ever wanted since I’ve known you, was to protect your interests!”

“I don’t want to see or hear from you again,” he said tightly. “Don’t try and come near me because if you do, I’ll strangle you with my own hands!”

She staggered backwards across the room, and sank into a heap on the floor and began to whimper.

“Let’s get out of here, Wheeler,” Hammond said thickly. “Before I kill her!”

I took him back to my place. It seemed to be the easiest place we could go and get a drink, or get good and drunk if necessary without any interruptions.

Hammond hadn’t said a word since we left Isobel Lamont’s office, not even to ask where we were going. I sat him in an armchair, poured out two treble-strength Scotches and pushed one into his hand. He drained the glass in one long swallow and handed me back the glass. I refilled it for him and this time he drank it more slowly.

I drank some of my own drink, lit a cigarette and wondered if he would appreciate Sinatra on the hi-fi singing, “Thanks for the Memory”. I decided he probably wouldn’t.

Hammond cleared his throat suddenly with a rasping sound. “I’ve been a fool, Wheeler,” he said. “It isn’t easy for a man to admit that—particularly when it’s a woman who has made a fool out of him.”

“You aren’t unique,” I said consolingly. “It happens to a great number of people.”

“That doesn’t make it any easier,” he said. “I was a blind fool. I should have realised from the sort of woman she was, that she wouldn’t be content with just a quarter share in a nightclub—or even the income of a lawyer. She used me and my knowledge to get Walter and Myra into her clutches.”

“I wouldn’t worry too much,” I said. “It’s finished and you haven’t burned your fingers very badly, have you?”

“No,” he said slowly. “I suppose in a way I have been lucky.”

I finished my drink and refilled the glass. "I'm the guy who is really disappointed," I told him. "I thought I'd caught up with a murderer, but it turned out to be only a witch."

Hammond had finished his second treble and was definitely looking brighter. He got up out of the chair and helped himself to a third drink.

"No," he said. "When I think about it, I've a lot to be thankful for. I'm a lucky man, Wheeler. Lucky to be well out of the grasp of a scheming Jezebel such as Isobel Lamont."

"Viva!" I said.

He downed his third drink in a reflex action without noticing it. Correction—he did notice it enough to realise his glass was empty again, and refill it.

"Wheeler," He glared at me piercingly. "You are a definite asset to the organisation of Hammond, Irvine and Snooks. You are a man of keen foresight, undoubted ability and perceptive intuition. I salute you."

"Well, thank you," I said.

"If there is anything I, as the senior partner of our glorious organisation can do for you, just say the word."

"There is just one little thing," I said. "An expense account I ran up at the Due D'Or …"

"Unmasking that reptile disguised as a woman!" he said. "Send it up to my office first thing in the morning and pay no more attention to it!"

"Thank you, Mr. Hammond."

He polished off his fourth drink, refilled the glass and looked at me like a benign vulture.

"You're a genius, Wheeler," he said. "There is no doubt about it. The more I dwell on the point, the more I realise that's what you are—a genius! I shall nominate you for the next Nobel Prize. I salute you! The Man of the Year!"

He raised his glass exuberantly and carefully poured half its contents down his shirt-front. He frowned vaguely.

"Have you noticed something, Wheeler?" he asked confidentially. "These glasses—they're a couple of inches too short—they just don't reach your mouth!"

"I'll have them fixed right away," I assured him.

"Good fellow," he said. "Good fellow. I don't know many good fellows, Wheeler. Not many at all." A large tear dropped from his eye and splashed into his glass. "Hardly any, now that I come to think about it. You … who else? Irvine is not bad, but not what I'd call a good fellow and certainly not the Man of the Year. And Snooks!" He shuddered. "Like a hairy old goat sitting up there drinking himself to death and making eyes at a girl a third of his age. Disgusting, I call it. Sitting there like a great fat spider weaving his web of intrigue. He doesn't trust me—and that's a fact, Wheeler. Would you believe it—he doesn't trust me."

The tears were streaming down his face now. "He doesn't love me, Wheeler—and that's the truth of it. Nobody loves me. Snooks doesn't love me, Isobel didn't love me, Myra didn't love me. Nobody loves poor ol' Hammond. What did I do to deserve being one of the unloved ones, Wheeler? You can tell me, you're my friend. What did I do?"

"I'll call you a cab," I said. "Before you turn my living-room into an indoor pool."

I walked over to the phone and picked it up. He followed me, sobbing. "I don't care if I am making a pool," he said defiantly. "When it's deep enough I'm going to drown myself!"

I ordered the cab and replaced the phone.

"I don't suppose," I said casually, "that it was you who killed Wendy Martin and arranged for the note to be put into Byrne's drawer by Delmar, then had to kill him later to keep his mouth shut?"

He looked at me for a long time from under hooded lids. I thought he was thinking. It wasn't until he hit the floor I realised he was passing out.

The cab arrived and I bribed the driver to help me carry Hammond out. We bundled him into the back of the cab and I gave the driver Hammond's private address.

"See he gets there in one piece, Mac," I said, and bribed the driver some more.

"Sure," he grunted. "You don't have an empty bottle we could pour him into? He'd be easier to carry that way."

I watched the cab move out of sight, then went back into the house. I picked up Hammond's glass from the floor and cleaned up a little. Then I put some Julie London on the hi-fi and let her voice drown itself into my bloodstream, until the adrenalin was making like crazy.

One way and another, it had turned out to be quite a night.

CHAPTER 12

The hi-fi was halfway through Ellington's "Creole Love Call"—the original version which is all muted reeds—when I heard the Porsche bubble to a stop on the driveway. A couple of seconds later the door buzzer sounded.

I went and opened the door. Lucrece stormed past me into the living-room. I followed her in and found her pouring herself a Hammond-sized Scotch.

"I thought you were proving you could take that stuff or leave it alone?"

I said.

"I have reason!" she said stormily. "Of all the … I've a good mind to … I'll make her sorry! I'll …"

"Forgive me for being dense," I said. "But just what are you talking about?"

"That woman," she said. "That is, if she is a woman and not a bat in disguise!"

"Which bat in disguise is this?"

"Isobel Lamont!" she said. "The nerve of her."

I took a deep breath. "I am a patient man," I said. "So far we have worked out that you're talking about Isobel Lamont. What exactly did she do?"

"What did she do? She had the nerve to fire me tonight, that's what she did. Me, the best dancer in the chorus-line. With the best figure and legs of them all. Mr. Rogers even told me that! 'Kid!' he said. 'You're terrific!' he said. 'You've got the rest of 'em licked cold when it comes to curves and hoofing a routine.'"

"That's nice," I said. "Didn't he have anything to say when Isobel Lamont fired you? After all, if he thought that highly of you …"

"Ha!" she said bitterly. "You don't know that woman. She fired him, too. She's gone stark raving mad! She stormed into the dressing-room like a witch on a powered broomstick. 'You're fired!' she screamed at me. 'Get out!'

"I tell you, Al Wheeler, that dame is quite crazy—she's got woodpeckers inside her head and they're getting hungry for something to feed on. She ought to be put away somewhere out of sight."

"Maybe something happened to upset her?" I suggested.

"Something will happen to upset her!" she said venomously. "I can assure you of that, Al Wheeler."

I patted her shoulder. "If it makes you feel any better, I can tell you that you don't need to work at the club any longer. There's nothing there you could discover to help your father, so being fired saved you quitting the job."

"Oh?" she said. She turned and looked at me for the first time since she had stepped inside the house. "What makes you think that?" she said slowly.

"I was there earlier on tonight," I said. "Isobel Lamont is about two steps down from Simon Legree … but she didn't murder Wendy Martin and she doesn't know who did."

"Is this the celebrated Wheeler intuition?" she asked coldly. "Or have you facts to support your case?"

"I've got some facts," I said. "But not enough. When I've got enough I'll tell you the story—and anyway, there's more important news. Your father is coming home tomorrow."

Her mouth dropped open. "They're releasing him?"

"On bail," I said.

"That means they don't think he killed her."

"It means they have some doubts, that's all. They aren't withdrawing the charge of homicide against him."

"I've never heard of anyone accused of homicide getting bail before."

"It's unusual," I said easily. "But not unknown."

She snapped her fingers. "I bet I know who organised it!" She leaned forward and kissed the tip of my nose. "You're a genius, Al Wheeler!"

"Don't do that," I said irritably, rubbing my nose. "I'm too old to be cute!"

She tilted her head back, then looked out at me from under narrowed lids, her lips pursed thoughtfully. "I can see that you're right," she said. "You're old enough for the full treatment."

"Hey!" I said, but then it was too late. The next moment I was bent backwards over the table, held firmly in Lucrece's arms while she kissed me violently. And when I say violently, I'm not kidding!

But there is such a thing as male initiative. So I reversed the situation as soon as I got my breath back. I didn't make Lucrece's tactical error—I substituted the sofa for the table.

I was vaguely aware of Sinatra on the hi-fi, singing … "She Dances Overhead" … I had the thought that "McNamara's Band" would have been more appropriate … "The drums go bang and the cymbals clang …" But then maybe I was just being purist.

The next time I looked at my watch it was four-thirty in the morning, and Lucrece was sitting in a contented ball at one end of the sofa while I was pouring us both a drink.

"You should be going home," I said.

"Not worth it," Lucrece said complacently. "I'll get you some breakfast when the daylight appears."

"Won't they worry about you?"

"Myra? Billings?" She laughed. "What a keen sense of humour you've got, Al Wheeler."

"Okay," I said. "So it was a lousy thought."

I took the drinks back with me and sat down beside her on the sofa.

"Thanks," she said dreamily. "Being here with you makes up for that awful scene at the club tonight. I could have scratched her eyes out."

"Forget it, honey," I said. "It isn't important any more."

"You look tired," she said. "Why don't you lie down for a while?"

I stretched out on the sofa and put my head in her lap. She lit two cigarettes and put one in my mouth.

"Thanks," I grunted.

"Tell me about what happened tonight at the club," she said. "I can't stand you being so mysterious ... it makes me want to scream."

"Nothing terribly exciting," I said. I went on and told her the rest of it.

"The dirty, double-crossing ..." she said when I had finished telling her the story. "And that Billings—or should I call him Martin? Just wait till I get back to the house."

"Let us," I said coldly, "get one fact straight. On no account will you say anything to Billings or do anything that might let him know you know the story."

"Why not?"

I looked up at her face, looking down at me. And it was still immensely attractive, even upside-down. "Because that's the way I want it," I said. "Okay?"

"All right, genius," she sniffed. "I suppose so. But I'm strictly doing you a favour and I hope you appreciate it."

"I certainly do," I said. I finished the cigarette and the drink, settled my head more comfortably in her lap and closed my eyes.

"Would you like me to sing to you?" she asked in honey-sweet tones.

"If you can sing like Peggy Lee ... no, that would be asking too much," I said. I closed my eyes again and the universe was one well-sprung sofa and one so-comfortable lap.

When I opened my eyes, sunlight hit them. I screwed them tight shut again, then squinted cautiously. Finally, I sat up and yawned. I looked at my watch and it said nine-thirty.

"Hell, I'm late," I said. "And where's that breakfast that was coming at the first light of dawn?"

I looked around to where the lap should have been, but it had vanished along with the rest of Lucrece. There was a note on the table which said briefly: "You are the only man who ever went to sleep when I was close to him. Have gone home to look in the mirror and find out why!"

I staggered into the shower, turning on the needle-spray, but not being stupid enough to let the cold water run as well. After about ten minutes of steaming hot needles, I cautiously turned the control to cold, spent a stoic three seconds under the cold needles then leaped out screaming, "Uncle!"

I left the house just after ten, wearing the new grey suit that complemented the XK-SS. I got into the office at around twenty after ten. I sat down behind the desk and the phone rang.

I picked it up and said, "Wheeler," into it. One of these days I'm going to say, "Smith," for a change. But a habit is hard to change.

"This is Hammond," a cold voice said in my ear. "When will you appreciate that your working day starts at nine o'clock in the morning, Wheeler? Not ten-thirty!"

"Can I charge you overtime for last night?" I asked him.

"If that is meant to be a humorous remark, I do not appreciate it," he said heavily. "I have word from Commissioner Lavers that they will release Mr. Byrne on bail of ten thousand dollars this morning. I have fixed the time at eleven. Mr. Irvine is on his way down there now. I wanted you to go with him."

"I could catch up with him," I suggested. "He's driving Detroit machinery, isn't he?"

"I fail to understand the significance of that remark," he said. "I want you to meet them and escort Mr. Byrne to his home. I want you to stay out there with him. I have already spoken to Mrs. Byrne and she is quite agreeable to your staying there."

"Okay," I said. "But why do you want me out there?"

"It occurs to me that there could still be some danger for Mr. Byrne from the real murderer," he said. "That's why I want you close to him, Wheeler. Your main job for the time being is to make sure nothing happens to him."

"Sure," I said.

I heard his breathing at the other end of the line for a few moments. Finally he said, "I—ah—seem to remember quite well the incident at the Due D'Or last night. In fact, I can distinctly remember everything that happened—every word that was said. But after that, my mind is a blank …"

"You don't remember what you said about okaying my expense account?" I asked anxiously.

"I certainly don't remember anything about that. I woke up this morning in my apartment with all my clothes on. It has never happened before. I'd like an explanation if you can give me one, Wheeler?"

I thought what the hell? The expense account was obviously a lost cause.

"You came back with me to my house," I said courteously. "You got drunk on my liquor. Then you started crying and then you passed out cold on my carpet. I called a cab and the driver promised to see you got back to your own place in one piece. He obviously kept his word."

There was dead silence for five seconds, and then a crash that nearly broke my eardrum as he smashed the receiver back on the rest. I should worry about working for Hammond, Irvine and Snooks, I thought. I don't have to work for a living, I can always starve.

The phone rang again and I picked it up gingerly.

"Mr. Wheeler?" The voice was soft and feminine—soothing balm to an ear that had had too much of Hammond.

"It sure is, honey," I said warmly. "And did I ever tell you you're the most beautiful girl I ever met?"

"No," she said softly. "You didn't, Al. It just could be a slight exaggeration, though. If you'd said one of the two most beautiful girls you'd ever met, I would have believed you."

"Who is this speaking?"

"You would have to go and spoil it," she said. "This is Pauline Whitby here and I'm hurt!"

"Hello, Miss Pauline hurt Whitby," I said. "I was just kidding. I knew it was you all the time. The glorious blonde with the skin that's a shade too tight."

"Back to business, I think," she said demurely. "Mr. Snooks wants to see you urgently."

"That makes it tough," I said. "I've just had urgent instructions from Mr. Hammond to proceed urgently to the Homicide Bureau, where Mr. Irvine is in the process of bailing out Mr. Byrne."

"Well, you make up your own mind, Al," she said. "But if you want to still be working here this afternoon, my advice is to come right up and see Mr. Snooks now."

"You don't scare me!" I said. "And tell Mr. Snooks I'll be right up."

Five minutes later I was inside his office. He was sitting behind his desk as usual, an idiotic smile on his face. Proudly he turned his head so I got the profile. Perched on top of his head was a cap.

"How do you like it, Aloysius?" he asked proudly. "Thinkin' I'll likely go out an' shoot me a b'ar today!"

"You look exactly the way Davy Crockett would look," I said admiringly. "If he was still alive."

"What about your hunting?" he asked. "Any progress?"

"Some," I said.

I told him the story of the previous night—as far as the Due D'Or was concerned, anyway. I considered Hammond's crying was his own business as Lucrece was my own business. He listened attentively until I'd finished.

"Well," he said finally, "that is most interesting. I think it calls for a drink."

"Much as I love drinking," I told him, "I'll have to regretfully decline. I am supposed to be protecting Walter Byrne with my own life right now. Hammond's direct orders … delivered in person."

"Do you really think Byrne is in any danger for the next half hour?" he asked.

"No," I said.

"Then we'll consider the subject closed." He pressed a button and a few moments later Pauline came into the office.

"I've got my fellow soak with me again," Snooks chuckled. "So don't be light-handed in the pouring."

"Casanova Wheeler," she said darkly. "The man who knows so many beautiful women, he doesn't even remember which one he is talking with on the phone."

She poured the drinks, gave Snooks his and brought mine over to me. She bent forward to hand me the glass and the wrinkles in her silk blouse all vanished.

"You take one deep breath and you'll really be in trouble!" I said interestedly.

"Take one deep breath, Pauline," Snooks said hopefully. "And that's an order."

"I think you are both nothing but a couple of dirty old men!" she said coldly, heading back towards her own office.

"He might be old," I said. "But me!"

"Correction," she said. "I think Mr. Snooks is a dirty old man. I think you, Mr. Aloysius Wheeler, are a dirty middle-aged man!"

The door slammed behind her.

Snooks chuckled. "Pauline likes you, Aloysius. She only gets flustered by men she likes."

"That's ridiculous," I said. "She was even flustered with you a moment back."

"You heard what I said," he snorted.

I drank some of the Scotch. "I don't think I agree with your theory about the two murders, Mr. Snooks."

"My theory?"

"That our senior partner committed them."

"Did I say that?"

"No," I admitted. "You just implied it in a rather unsubtle way."

"I think you must have misconstrued my thoughts," he said placidly. "You seem to be travelling fast with your eliminations, Aloysius. Let's see now—you've eliminated Isobel Lamont and that butler fellow, Billings. Now you've eliminated Hammond. I presume you have already eliminated Myra and Lucrece Byrne? Who have you got left in the running?"

"I haven't eliminated anybody, with the possible exception of Isobel Lamont," I said patiently. "Hammond has alibied her, and the way he feels about Isobel Lamont he isn't likely to be lying."

"Now we're both being cautious," he told me. "Maybe I'm a cynical old man, Wheeler, but I feel that there are very few, if any, stronger motives for murder than money. And money is the tie-up between our senior partner, Walter Byrne and Myra Byrne. With Myra, who has the real money, right in the centre.

"I personally would doubt very much if Walter Byrne is in any danger at all, but I wouldn't be quite so sure about his wife. That was what I wanted to see you about. It was my suggestion that you be sent out to stay at the Byrne home for a time. I suggested it to Hammond, saying that it would be protection for Walter Byrne, knowing he'd agree to it—inside of ten minutes he would be convinced it was his own idea, in any case. But I wanted to see you before you left and tell you to keep one and a half eyes on Myra. Half an eye for Walter will be plenty."

"Yes, sir," I said.

"When you come back, we'll have a welcome home for you," he chuckled. "I'll shoot a b'ar and Pauline will bake a cake. Give you something to look forward to, eh?"

"I shall tremble with joy every time I think of it," I told him.

"Good! Have a nice time at the Byrne home. Most everybody does, they tell me—except the Byrnes, of course. And ask Billings or Martin or whatever his name is, if he'd consider a new partner in his double act. Instead of the topper and cane, I would wear a cap and a long-barrelled rifle. Do you think he would be interested?"

"No, sir," I said flatly.

"Oh? Why not?"

"Your legs aren't good enough for tights!" I told him.

CHAPTER 13

I checked with Homicide and found Irvine and Walter Byrne had left there half an hour before. I pushed the Jag along a little and arrived at the Byrne house ten minutes after they did. Irvine looked quite relieved to see me when I walked into the living-room.

"Been wondering where you'd got to," he said. "Mr. Hammond has been quite worried about you."

"Traffic," I said vaguely.

"I'll give him a ring and let him know you're here," he said, then went out of the room.

Walter Byrne smiled at me wearily. There were fine lines at the corners of his eyes, and the eyes themselves were haunted by something I couldn't see.

"I appreciate you being here, Mr. Wheeler," he said. "Though I must say I think Hammond is exaggerating the possible dangers somewhat."

"You could be right, Mr. Byrne," I said. "But it's better to play these things on the safe side."

"I suppose so," he said. "You'll need some clothes if you're going to stay here, won't you?"

"I brought a suitcase with me," I said. "I stopped off at my house for a couple of minutes on the way over. Billings took it for me."

"Good," he nodded, his attention wandering away from me. "I understand he's fixed a room for you."

Irvine came back and glared at me. "Mr. Hammond hopes you will not be late again in any vital duty such as this, Wheeler," he said stiffly.

I looked appealingly at the ceiling. "In the fine print on my contract," I said, "which is not by document but by gentlemen's agreement, it says something to the effect that given any assignment, I have the right to handle it in my own way."

Irvine coloured a little. "That is true, of course," he said. "But you could be a little more tactful in the way you handle the senior partner."

"I'd be wasting my time," I said. "I don't even look like Isobel Lamont!"

The lawyer turned his back on me deliberately and spoke to Byrne. "Now that Wheeler's here, Walter, I'd better be getting back to the office. You just take it easy for a couple of days and relax. We're going to make sure you never go back behind bars!"

"Thanks," Byrne said and shook hands with Irvine. The lawyer barely nodded to me on his way out.

After he'd gone, Byrne lit himself a cigarette.

"I suppose I should let you know what I'm going to do—or where I will be all the time?" he asked dubiously.

"That isn't necessary, Mr. Byrne," I told him. "I'd only like to know when you're leaving the house for any reason."

"Good." He looked relieved. "I'll certainly do that. I'll just wander out into the sunroom. I think my wife is out there."

"You go right ahead," I said. "After all, this is your house."

He walked out of the room into the hall. I lit a cigarette and wondered if life was going to be exciting as a house-guest of the Byrnes. I began to doubt it. I smoked the cigarette down to a butt, ground it out in an ashtray, looked out of the window at the lawn and the garden beyond, lit another cigarette and saw all of fifteen minutes had gone by since Byrne had left the room. It began to look like a long day.

I went out into the hall and saw Billings coming towards me from the kitchen.

"Which is my room, Billings?"

"Turn to your left at the head of the stairs, sir," he said. "And then the last but one door to your right. I've put your clothes away, sir."

"Thanks very much," I said.

"A pleasure, sir," he said woodenly, then waited until I turned away towards the stairs before he went on his way down the hall.

I climbed the stairs, walked down to the last but one door on my right, and opened it. It was quite a nice room, complete with bed, wardrobe, chest of drawers and an extra door on the inside wall, which apparently connected my room with the last one to the right.

I walked over and tried the handle of the door—it was locked on the other side. I went back to the bed, tested it with my hand and at least the springs didn't make any chiming noises. I lay down on it, lit another cigarette and thought if anybody thought life was dull in Little Rock, they ought to change places with me.

I was still staring up at the ceiling when I heard the sound of a key turning in a lock. I sat up to see the connecting door swing open.

I watched, fascinated; seeing the trim leg that appeared first, followed by an exceedingly trim figure not quite robed in a thin silk robe.

"Hello," Lucrece said. "Comfy?"

"I should have known!" I said.

"I arranged it with Billings," she said complacently. "You had better be nice to me, Al Wheeler … the key is my side of the door!"

The world was suddenly a righter place.

"I didn't know you were home," I said.

"It's an occasion," she told me. "The return of the wandering father."

"I thought you liked him?"

"I do," she said indifferently. "Only it's all highly embarrassing at the moment. Myra's still making up her mind whether to speak to him or not, and she's scared sick I'll tell on her and Billings. And Billings looks as if he isn't quite sure whether it's Sunday or Coney Island. I'm glad you came, Al. I can use a little light relief around here."

"Honey," I sighed deeply. "Me, too!"

She came over and sat down on the bed beside me. The robe, close up, looked even more fragile than it had at a distance. If distance makes the heart grow fonder, the close-up makes the heart beat faster.

"I never got any breakfast this morning," I said in an injured voice.

"I was never so insulted in all my life!" she said. "You—going to sleep on me like that! Just passing out cold. And snoring!"

"I never snore," I said defensively. "I may breathe loudly but snore, never!"

"What are you doing here, anyway?"

"Hammond's idea," I said. "Guard your father with my very life."

"Whatever from?"

I shrugged my shoulders. "I wouldn't know. Hammond seems to think that the murderer, whoever that may be, is only waiting for the chance to murder your father. I am here for protection, laughter will not be appreciated."

"I don't understand how he works that out," Lucrece said. "If the murderer had wanted to kill Father, he would have killed him in the first place and not Wendy Martin, wouldn't he?"

"Put it that way and it sounds logical," I said: "But who am I to argue with the senior partner?"

"Anyway," she snuggled closer to me, "I'm glad you are here, Al. It makes the house much more exciting. So far it's been like a morgue."

"Don't say that," I told her.

"Well, it is! Myra walking around like she's hearing the voice of doom announcing a special commercial aimed entirely at her. And Father looks as if he's seeing ghosts in every corner of the room. Billings looks as if he's in a trance … Did you ever wonder if he's a zombie? He might have been dead for months and we've never known it."

"You're giving me goose-pimples where they have no right to be," I said. "Let's talk about something more cheerful."

"What you really mean is, don't let's talk," she said. "And I am for that motion, Mr. Wheeler. Would you mind locking your door?"

I never did get downstairs for lunch that day, but I was down in plenty of time for dinner. I walked into the living-room about six-thirty. Myra and Walter were already there, and so was Hammond. Billings was serving martinis from a tray and I thought I'd arrived at the right time. I lifted a glass from the tray and smiled at the Byrnes. They smiled back, then their faces relapsed into blankness.

"Good evening, Mr. Hammond," I said.

"Evening, Wheeler," he said coldly. "I hope you've taken all the necessary precautions to protect Mr. Byrne's life?"

"Yes, sir," I said. "Six bloodhounds are patrolling the grounds. I've run a high-voltage cable around the outside wall. The sixty-eight patrolmen and one boy are riding in a continuous circle on their motor-bikes outside the property. The helicopter equipped with radar, of course, should arrive overhead at any moment."

Hammond looked as if he was going to have a stroke. "Look! I've had just about enough …"

"Take it easy," Walter Byrne said, a genuine smile on his face for the first time since I'd known him. "Mr. Wheeler just put the thing in its right perspective. It's quite ridiculous, the whole idea, and you know it."

"If you think that," Hammond said stiffly, "I can send Wheeler home."

"No!" Myra Byrne said suddenly. "I don't think it's absurd at all. The trouble is we're all just sitting around here waiting for something frightful to happen and we're getting on each other's nerves. We should try relaxing a little. Let's have another drink for a start."

"I think that's a wonderful idea!" Lucrece said from the door.

Everyone watched her as she walked into the room. She was wearing a gown gunmetal in colour, off-the-shoulder and fitting her in a skin-tight sheath right down below her knees, where it kicked out a hem so that she could walk. I could almost hear Hammond panting beside me.

Lucrece lifted a martini from Billings' tray. "This is a celebration, isn't it? The return of the prodigal father!"

"Lucrece," Hammond said heavily. "My dear, I think …"

"I doubt it!" she said brightly. "Well, here's to crime!" She drained her glass and put it back onto Billings' tray, then helped herself to a full glass.

It looked as if the party was going to brighten up quite suddenly. Billings discreetly disappeared with his tray, but not before I had lifted another full glass from it.

"No conversation?" Lucrece said. "No idle chatter? This isn't my idea of a party. I know." She nodded wisely. "We need some conversational gambits. Mr. Hammond … who have you been robbing lately?"

Hammond opened his mouth in a gallant attempt at a smile but didn't make it; so he closed it again like a steel vice.

"No good?" Lucrece said, her eyebrows raised delicately. "I'll have to start again …"

"Dinner is served, Madame," Billings announced from the door that led to the dining-room. You could almost hear the sigh of relief that went up.

Lucrece was quiet while she was eating and I imagined that everyone blessed her appetite. Billings served the meal, course by course, and cleared away the debris. We reached the coffee stage and Billings was serving Lucrece when she came to life again.

"Will you be leaving us now that my father is back, Billings?" she asked him in a voice brimming over with childish innocence.

"No, Miss," he said.

"Oh?" She looked at him archly. "You are brave, aren't you!"

"I'm afraid I don't understand, Miss," he said, and moved down the table to serve Hammond's coffee. His hands were slightly unsteady, I noticed.

"You're just being bashful, Billings!" Lucrece said. "You know very well what I mean—doesn't he, Myra?"

Myra Byrne looked murder at her. "I don't think it's very nice to tease Billings," she said coldly. "Be rude to us if you wish, but not to Billings. It isn't really fair."

"You haven't changed much, have you, Lucrece?" Walter said bitterly.

"Of course I've changed, Daddy dear," she said. "I'm all grown up now. Quite old enough to understand about you and Wendy Martin. And my dear stepmother and the butler."

"What!" Byrne gasped.

"Don't pay any attention to her, Walter," Myra said quickly. "She's lying. Can't you see that? She wants to cause trouble, she enjoys it. So you're only pandering to her if you give her any attention."

Lucrece smiled. "I don't see what you're annoyed about, Stepmother dear," she said sweetly. "I think it was jolly nice of Billings to look after you while Daddy was away—keep you from being lonely—cuddling you and kissing you and everything."

"I can't stand any more of this!" Myra said. She got to her feet and walked quickly out of the room.

"If you'll excuse me," Hammond muttered. "Just remembered, have to ring the office."

"I'd keep an eye on that ex-husband if I were you, Daddy," Lucrece said. "Now that I've eliminated the competition from the butler, the ex-husband might think he's in the running again."

Byrne got slowly to his feet. "I've had just about enough for one night," he said. "Go to your room, Lucrece, and stay there, or I won't be responsible for my actions."

"You sound so mid-Victorian," she said. "I really think ..."

He raised his hand and Lucrece stood there for a moment, looking at him disbelievingly, then suddenly burst into tears and ran from the room.

Byrne let his hand drop to his side. "I'm sorry, Wheeler," he said. "Terribly sorry."

"Why don't we have a drink?" I suggested.

He smiled wanly. "That's the most brilliant piece of conversation I've heard tonight."

We went into the bar and Byrne pushed a bottle of Scotch towards me. "Help yourself," he said.

"Thanks," I said. I poured out a generous measure, then passed the bottle back to him. He helped himself and added ice to the glass.

"Lucrece is my fault," he said. "Her mother died when she was quite young and I just didn't have the time to look after her properly. I'm reaping the years of neglect."

"She'll get over it," I said.

"I suppose so," Byrne said slowly. "But at the moment she's emotionally disturbed and hurt—and her stepmother's attitude doesn't help."

"Talking of Myra, Mr. Byrne," I changed the subject. "Not that I'm a pessimist, but supposing we can't get you out of this mess and a smart D.A. gets you convicted for Wendy Martin's murder ..."

"Supposing, Wheeler?" he asked.

"Your wife would then be an extremely wealthy woman, Mr. Byrne, wouldn't she have her own personal fortune plus your large stock holdings?"

"I don't quite follow you, Wheeler," he said. "Granted Mrs. Byrne gets all my money when I die—and that would make her very well off, to say the least. But at the moment, Mrs. Byrne hasn't a dime to her name. Except, of course," he added quickly, "for the generous allowance I give her."

"But what about her quarter share in the Due D'Or?" I blurted out.

"Oh, that," Byrne smiled. "She bought that from the settlement money after the divorce from Hammond. The income from that wouldn't keep Myra in champagne for the year. You see, Mr. Wheeler, Myra is somewhat of a luxury product ..."

"Gift wrapped in the twenty-four carat gold class—and then some," I finished for him.

"That's one way to put it," Byrne agreed.

"Then why does she go to such pains to pretend she's so wealthy?" I asked. "And she makes sure everyone believes it."

Byrne shrugged. "Some sort of complex, I suppose, but believe me ..."

Byrne was still speaking when the two shots sounded from somewhere upstairs.

CHAPTER 14

I went up the stairs three at a time, with Walter Byrne close behind me. We stopped on the landing for a moment, then I heard the hysterical sobs coming from a room down to my right. I ran towards it, seeing that the door was open. I ran into the room and stopped suddenly.

It was Myra Byrne's bedroom, quite obviously. A room full of feminine accoutrements—the only thing out of place was Billings' corpse on the floor. Myra was stretched out across the bed, face down, sobbing hysterically.

I knelt down beside Billings and turned him over onto his back gently. Both bullets had gone into his chest at close range. He was quite dead. Quite dead with a look of blank surprise on his face. I wondered about that look.

I got to my feet again and Byrne looked at me haggardly. "Is he dead?"

"Sure," I nodded. "Quite dead." I looked around the floor and didn't see any gun.

Heavy footsteps hurried down the passage outside and then Hammond appeared, breathing hard. "Shots," he said. "I thought I heard shots!"

Then he saw Billings on the floor and his face blanched. "What happened?" he quavered.

"We don't know yet," I said. Then the outside door buzzer sounded.

Hammond looked at me blankly. "Who the hell can that be?"

"I'll go and find out," I said. "You'd better try and quieten your wife, Mr. Byrne."

"Yes," he said dully. "Yes, of course."

I went downstairs, along the hall to the front door and opened it. Isobel Lamont stood there. She looked as surprised to see me as I was her.

"Is Mrs. Byrne home?"" she asked.

"I guess so," I said.

"Thank you," she said coldly. Then she stepped past me into the hall. "Would you tell her I'm here, please?"

"Mrs. Byrne is indisposed at the moment," I said. "There's just been an accident …"

"Oh," she bit her lip. "Mrs. Byrne rang me half an hour ago and asked me to come out here immediately. She said it was most urgent—a matter of life or death! I came right away."

"She must have had a premonition," I said. "Somebody just shot Billings twice."

"Is he hurt?"

"He's not hurt," I told her. "He's dead!"

I managed to catch her as she swooned gracefully into my arms. I carried her back up the stairs with me and along to the bedroom. Hammond and Byrne stared at me, fish-eyed, as I put my burden alongside Myra on the bed.

"She was calling on Mrs. Byrne," I said evenly. "Mrs. Byrne rang her half an hour ago and told her to come here immediately. That it was a matter of life or death."

Slowly Myra pulled herself up to a sitting position and looked at me. "But I didn't," she said in a small voice. "I never rang her. What on earth would I ring her for?"

"What happened here, Mrs. Byrne?" I asked her. "How did Billings get himself killed?"

She shook her head. "I don't know. When I left the dining room, I came up here to my room. A couple of minutes later there was a knock on the door. I opened it and Billings was there. He asked could he speak to me, so I told him to come into the room. I didn't close the door—I thought, after Lucrece's remarks at the table, that it would be wrongly construed if anyone came along and found me with the butler behind a closed door.

"Billings talked to me about the things Lucrece had said. He was most upset and wanted to quit his job and leave right away. I told him to ignore them, that no one could believe such an impossible fantasy as that. I told him that Mr. Byrne wouldn't take it seriously and then," her voice broke. "From behind me, I heard the sound of a gun being fired. For a moment, I thought whoever it was firing the gun intended to kill me and there was nothing I could do about it. Then Billings just slumped to the floor and when I managed to look around, the passage was empty behind me. I guess

I just gave out then … I know I started to scream and cry—I fell onto the bed …”

Walter Byrne took a deep breath. “I think you had better call the police, Hammond,” he said quietly. “And Myra, will you stay here and look after Miss Lamont for a few moments?”

She nodded. “Of course.”

“Mr. Wheeler,” he said softly. “Would you come with me, please? It won’t take very long.”

“Sure,” I said.

Byrne walked out of the room and I followed him. He went down to the end of the passage and knocked on Lucrece’s door.

“Come in,” she called listlessly.

He turned the handle, pushed the door open, then walked into the room with me following. Lucrece was sitting on her bed and as she looked up at us, I saw the tears staining her cheeks.

Byrne looked at her for a long time before he said anything, then finally he said, “Where did you put the gun?”

“Gun?” she said blankly. “What gun?”

“The one you shot Billings with,” he said in a tired voice. “I can’t take any more, Lucrece. I’ve stood enough. That is two, or is it three people you’ve killed? It can’t go on any more.”

“What are you talking about?” she whispered.

He lit himself a cigarette, took a deep drag, then looked at me. “You might as well know the truth, Wheeler. The night Wendy Martin was murdered, I was in her apartment—as you know. There was a knock on the door. I opened it and Lucrece came in. She had obviously found out about Wendy and myself. That night Lucrece had been drinking, so she came to the apartment and stormed at both of us. She had a right to be angry, I suppose. But I got rid of her as quickly as I could. Five minutes later there was another knock on the door. I guessed it would be Lucrece back again and I begged Wendy not to answer it, but she insisted.”

“Go on, Mr. Byrne,” I said.

“The next thing I heard was a revolver shot and then Wendy collapsed on the floor—dead. I knew then that Lucrece, in one of her violent fits of rage induced by her wild drinking, had killed Wendy Martin.”

“This is a most enlightening story, Mr. Byrne.” I glared at Lucrece. “Please continue.”

“When the police arrived and found me with Wendy’s body, and the gun with my fingerprints on it—I’d automatically picked it up from where Lucrece had dropped it—the whole case was open and shut. Either I accused my daughter of murder or faced the charge myself.”

“Did you actually see Lucrece?” I asked him.

"No, but ..."

"It makes sense, Mr. Byrne," I said.

"Father!" Lucrece's voice was frightened. "You're lying!"

He shook his head slowly. "I could pray that I were," he said bitterly.

There was a look of blank horror on Lucrece's face as she stared at me. "You can't mean this, Al!" she said. "You can't believe I killed her!"

I ignored her, concentrating on Walter Byrne.

"But, Mr. Byrne, I think you have been too generous in your description of Lucrece's motive. You've told me that Mrs. Byrne inherits your fortune, and on her death I would presume that the money automatically reverts to Lucrece."

Byrne nodded slowly.

"There have been some attempts made on your wife's life, fake attempts. No one who was really trying could miss three times in a row. They were made by Lucrece. She hoped that Myra would believe it was Billings so that when she ultimately did murder Myra, Billings would be blamed. I think that's what happened tonight—she was overwrought, overtense—when she fired the gun she missed her target. She missed Myra and killed Billings by mistake!"

Byrne lowered his head. "The trouble is," he said brokenly, "it is all my fault."

"Where's the gun, Lucrece?" I asked casually.

"I haven't got it," she said. "I didn't think you'd turn against me, Al Wheeler! I guess when I think about it, I can expect my own father to turn against me—but I thought you came out of a different box!"

"The gun?" I repeated. "What did you do with it?"

There was a knock on the door.

"Wheeler!" It was Hammond's voice. "Wheeler! Are you in there?"

"Sure," I called back. "What is it?"

"I've found the gun!" he said. "On the floor in Myra's room—it must have been tossed on the floor and skidded under the bed."

"I guess we should go take a look," I said to Byrne.

"I suppose so," he said.

He turned round to face the door, his fingers reaching out to the handle, and I chopped him scientifically across the back of the neck with the side of my hand. He dropped to the floor without making any noise at all.

Lucrece stared at me, open-mouthed.

"You did go to Wendy Martin's apartment on the night of the murder, didn't you?" I asked her quietly.

"Yes, but I swear I never came back a second time to kill ..."

"Okay," I whispered at her. "Make like a clam and keep that way."

I eased Byrne to one side of the door, then opened it, stepping outside and closing the door again with a smooth, quick movement so that Hammond had no chance of seeing what went on inside.

He looked at me uncertainly. "Is Walter in there?"

"He's talking to his daughter," I told him. "She's the murderer, Hammond. She's the reason he wouldn't say what happened in Wendy Martin's apartment the night of the murder. His own daughter killed her."

"It's unbelievable," Hammond said.

"Sure," I agreed. "Like soap opera!"

I pushed past him and back into the bedroom. Isobel Lamont was sitting on the bed, a small mirror in one hand and a lipstick in the other. She must have recovered from her faint, I thought. Myra was standing over by the dressing-table, a dazed look still in her eyes.

I moved into the room, and a moment later Hammond came in and stood beside me. "It's shocking," he said heavily. "An appalling story."

"What is?" Isobel Lamont asked sharply.

"Wheeler just told me," Hammond said. "Byrne revealed that it was Lucrece who shot Wendy Martin—as it obviously was Lucrece who shot Billings tonight."

Then he stared at me for a moment, his eyes widening. "And she must have killed Delmar as well!"

"She is nothing if not a busy girl," I said.

I lit a cigarette carefully, feeling Hammond still staring at me.

"I suppose you're hardened to this sort of thing," he said. "But the thought of a young and beautiful girl like Lucrece being a cold-blooded murderess is something I can't just casually accept."

"Neither can I," I said. "I don't accept it at all, in fact."

"What are you talking about?" he demanded sharply.

"Since this thing started," I said, "there have been more lies and more conflicting statements than you'd find in Khruschev's autobiography!"

I looked at Isobel Lamont. "You," I said, "are the main maggot in the woodpile!"

"How dare you!" She quivered with indignation. "How dare you speak to me like that!"

"I haven't really started yet," I said. "I'm just thinking of some of the things you told me the other night at the club. You are a very dangerous woman, Isobel—about ninety per cent of what you told me was probably the truth. And when somebody comes close to telling you the whole truth, you're inclined to take it as the whole truth."

She just glared murder at me, while Hammond shuffled his feet impatiently. Myra still had no apparent interest in what was going on. I lit another cigarette from the stub of the first.

"Let's take Delmar's murder first," I said. "For the benefit of those of you present who didn't know Isobel Lamont, she was an expert at organising a pastime known as the Badger Game. She had as her two accomplices, Wendy Martin and her brother, alias the late Cedric Billings."

Myra began to sit up and take an active interest. "You mean, Al," she said in a low voice, "that our butler Billings was Wendy Martin's brother?"

"Correct," I said. "Now Isobel Lamont had very cleverly hooked our legal friend, Mr. Hammond. Her motives were simple enough. Hammond could provide her with pocket money and the odd fur coat, and he could also unknowingly supply leads for Isobel's next victims in the Badger Game. After an unfortunate episode with the police in San Francisco, Hammond suggested that Isobel come here and helped her to organise backers for a nightclub. These backers, Mr. and Mrs. Byrne, were made to measure as Badger Game victims."

"Really, Wheeler!" Hammond nearly choked. "I hardly think it necessary—"

"Do shut up!" I said wearily. "You're paying me to deduct, now let me do it!"

I got on with my story. "So Billings was set up as a butler in the Byrne household and ordered to make a play for Mrs. Byrne. And Walter Byrne, unhappily married, was an easy catch for Wendy Martin."

"You're sure of this, Al?" Myra Byrne swallowed a couple of times.

"Never surer," I replied. "When the news of Wendy Martin's murder hit the streets and with it the news of the blackmail note, Isobel realised that Wendy had double-crossed her. It was a blow to her cash register mind, of course, but nothing serious as there were other girls willing to take Wendy's place."

I took a deep drag on my cigarette. That much I knew for certain, now I had to play it by ear for a while.

"Then even Isobel's trashcan brain was surprised when she received a visit from a certain Mr. Delmar, who introduced himself as Walter Byrne's personal assistant. Delmar, though not sure who had murdered Wendy, had found out enough to threaten exposing Isobel to the police as the organiser of the Badger Game if she didn't part with some hard cash."

Isobel Lamont's face was a chalky-grey colour and her right eyelid twitched spasmodically.

"Isobel would sooner murder than part with her money—and that's precisely what she did."

"You mean Isobel murdered Delmar?" Mr. Hammond sounded incredulous.

I didn't really have to answer the question. The sound of Isobel hitting the floor in a dead faint was sufficient. But just for the record, I gave it to

Hammond straight.

"Check," I nodded. "I'm just trying to think the way Isobel would have thought. It means corkscrewing your brain and dipping it in a trashcan, but I'm being well paid. Isobel had one trump card still up her sleeve. Billings was getting along just fine with Mrs. Byrne, and the time was ripe to put on the screws."

"Ugh!" Myra squirmed. "That horrible Lamont woman!"

I let that one slide. "But the joke was on Isobel, because Mrs. Byrne is not the wealthy woman she claims to be. In fact, Isobel could have twisted the screws to the end of the thread, but she wouldn't have got a dime out of Mrs. Byrne. Would she, Myra?"

"I—I—" Myra stammered.

"Really, Wheeler!" Hammond cut in. "Haven't you taken this thing far enough? We all know that Lucrece murdered ..."

"Lucrece nothing!" I snarled. "Myra Byrne murdered Wendy Martin for the sole purpose of framing her husband. She thought it was the subtle way to do it! Once Walter was dead, all Myra's make believe dreams of being a wealthy woman would become a reality."

"It's a lie!" Myra screamed.

"And," I went on, "you also murdered Billings less than half an hour ago!"

Myra made a desperate effort to control herself. She got slowly to her feet. "It's all quite absurd," she said. "You don't have a shred of proof!"

"Science is a wonderful thing, Myra," I replied. "A laboratory test within the next hour or two can prove whether you have fired a gun recently. Minute grains of powder always stick to the palm."

Well, sometimes they do, more often they don't, but I didn't imagine that was the sort of knowledge Myra Byrne would have.

But Hammond was a stickler for facts. "It all seems absurd to me, Wheeler. Granted that Myra might have killed Walter. But why did she kill Billings?"

"Wendy Martin wasn't the only one who was double-crossing Isobel," I said. "Billings had told Myra the whole story behind Isobel Lamont, and together they cooked up the plot to get rid of Walter."

"You mean, Billings could tell Myra where Wendy Martin's apartment was and what their moves were to be that evening?"

"You legal eagles catch on fast, Mr. Hammond," I said. "But Myra hadn't told Billings she intended being so subtle and murdering his sister Wendy. Billings wouldn't have approved of that. But after it was done, Billings was in too deep to get out, so he had to play things Myra's way."

Myra was almost foaming at the mouth. "You won't get away with this, Wheeler!"

I ignored the comment. "Billings and Myra made a clever pair. They knew there was always the danger of Lucrece finding out too much and if she did she would have to be killed. So they laid their plans very carefully, each telling me the story that someone was trying to murder them. And that also helped to confuse the issue.

"When a major snag arose, I scared the hell out of Billings by saying that I knew he was Martin. Billings got cold feet—he was ready to crack. Myra was able to bolster up his courage for a while, but the strain of the last couple of days proved too much. I'd say that Billings, having telephoned Isobel Lamont, came to Myra's room after dinner this evening and told her that he'd had enough. Myra was desperate, they quarrelled and Myra shot him. But Myra was made of tough stuff and she tried to bluff it out. She almost succeeded when Byrne decided that his daughter had done enough damage and accused her point blank of murdering Billings."

I stopped speaking suddenly as the door burst open. Lucrece was desperately trying to stop her father coming into the room.

"What the hell do you mean by slugging me, Wheeler?" Byrne shouted.

"I tried to stop him coming, Al," Lucrece said. "I guessed you didn't want him here."

"He could have loused things up before, but he can stay now," I grinned. "It's all over bar the pellet dropping!"

"You don't mean that surely, Mr. Wheeler?" a cool voice said from behind me.

I spun round, but Myra Byrne had the situation well in hand. She also had a gun in the same place, the barrel resting cosily between two of my ribs.

"You were all so interested in the new arrivals that I thought I'd stop my gun gathering dust on the floor," she said.

I winced loudly—and me an ex-cop!

"Look here, Myra," Hammond said suddenly. "You won't get away with it!"

Myra smiled coolly. "I think I will—if Mr. Wheeler has any respect for his midsection!"

She edged the barrel a little more firmly between the two ribs. I fluffed my cue in a series of gurgles.

"Move over to the corner of the room," Myra told the other three. Isobel still seemed a heap on the floor.

"And you, Mr. Wheeler," Myra cooed, "will ..."

I jerked my body sideways as Isobel's arms came hurtling over Myra's head, deflecting the gun in the opposite direction to my body action. A bullet dug a hole in the wall above Lucrece's head.

I lashed out with my foot, aiming for the gun between the two struggling women and I connected with Isobel's face.

A second shot sounded loud in the room.

I saw Isobel step backwards suddenly and Myra Byrne, a look of horror in her eyes, crumbling to the floor, her hands clutched tight to her midriff.

I stooped quickly to pick the gun off the floor.

"It went off," Isobel said flatly. "Fortunately, the barrel was pressing into her stomach at the time. She couldn't get away if I—"

There was a sharp clunk and Isobel grunted and slumped to the floor. I spun round and saw Lucrece with a smile of triumph on her face and a spike-heeled shoe held by the toe, in her hand.

"Honey," I grinned at her, "the timing's way off, but the killer instinct's great!"

Byrne scuttled out of his corner like a frightened borer beetle.

"Get Homicide!" I yelled at Hammond. "Get hold of Hanlon. Tell him he'd better let Commissioner Lavers know—he might care to come along."

"All right," he said dully. "What about Isobel?"

I grinned at him. "Isobel will be all right," I said. "I'll take good care of her. I'd hate to see her miss the gas-chamber!"

Hammond went out of the room at a lumbering trot.

Inside ten minutes the house was swarming with cops. I figured this wasn't the time or the place for mere ex-cops. I told Hanlon the story, then I collected Lucrece and we headed back to my house in the Jag.

"Honey," I said, "you were wonderful!"

"Sure," Lucrece replied. "And you're my hero, too."

I figured if this mutual admiration society held out until we reached the house, we'd really have something to celebrate.

I closed the front door firmly and did a double-check to see if the bolt was holding. Lucrece settled herself down on the divan while I mixed drinks for two.

I gave Lucrece her drink and fixed some Ellington on the hi-fi. Lucrece had come a long way since the night I figured "Danse Macabre" as her theme. As I sank back on the divan beside her, "Creole Love Call" piped smoothly through the hi-fi.

"Well," Lucrece said hesitantly, "I guess this evening sort of winds up everything."

"I guess it calls for a toast," I grinned, moving my arm firmly around Lucrece's waist.

"To the smartest and most unorthodox ex-cop I know!" She raised her glass and drank slowly.

"Why, thank you, Miss Byrne," I said modestly. "Now maybe we can relax for a little while."

"Relax?"

"Sure." I put my fingers around her chin and turned it gently so she faced me. "Don't tell me you don't know how to relax?" I kissed her gently on the lips.

"I don't think I do," she murmured. "Teach me, Al."

"There is absolutely no charge," I murmured. "And although I say it myself," I kissed her again, "you have come to the master."

Her lips pouted slightly. "Don't talk so much, maestro," she whispered.

THE END

Alan Geoffrey Yates Bibliography
(1923-1985)

**As Carter Brown/
Peter Carter Brown**

Series:

Al Wheeler (no U.S. edition unless
otherwise stated through to
Chorine Makes a Killing)

The Wench is Wicked (1955)
Blonde Verdict (1956; revised for
  the U.S. as The Brazen, 1960)
Delilah Was Deadly (1956)
No Harp for My Angel (1956)
Booty for a Babe (1956)
Eve, It's Extortion (1957; revised
  as Walk Softly Witch!, 1959,
  and further revised for the U.S.
  as The Victim, 1959)
No Law Against Angels (1957;
  revised for the U.S. as The Body,
  1958; 1st U.S. Wheeler)
Doll for the Big House (1957;
  revised for the U.S. as The
  Bombshell, 1960)
Chorine Makes a Killing (1957)
The Unorthodox Corpse (1957;
  revised for the U.S., 1961)
Death on a Downbeat (1958;
  revised for the U.S. as The
  Corpse, 1958)
The Blonde (1958; reprinted in
  the U.S., 1958)
The Lover (1958)
The Mistress (1959)
The Passionate (1959)
The Wanton (1959)
The Dame (1959)
The Desired (1959)

The Temptress (1960)
Lament for a Lousy Lover (1960)
  [includes Mavis Seidlitz]
The Stripper (1961)
The Tigress (1961; reprinted in
  the UK as Wildcat, 1962)
The Exotic (1961)
Angel! (1962)
The Hellcat (1962)
The Lady Is Transparent (1962)
The Dumdum Murder (1962)
Girl in a Shroud (1963)
The Sinners (1963; reprinted in
  U.S. as The Girl Who Was
  Possessed, 1963)
The Lady Is Not Available (1963;
  reprinted in U.S. as The Lady Is
  Available, 1963)
The Dance of Death (1964)
The Vixen (1964; reprinted in the
  U.S. as The Velvet Vixen, 1964)
A Corpse for Christmas (1965)
The Hammer of Thor (1965)
Target for Their Dark Desire
  (1966)
The Plush-Lined Coffin (1967)
Until Temptation Do Us Part
  (1967)
The Deep Cold Green (1968)
The Up-Tight Blonde (1969)
Burden of Guilt (1970)
The Creative Murders (1971)
W.H.O.R.E. (1971)
The Clown (1972)
The Aseptic Murders (1972)
The Born Loser (1973)
Night Wheeler (1974)
Wheeler Fortune (1974)
Wheeler, Dealer! (1975)

The Dream Merchant (1976)
Busted Wheeler (1979)
The Spanking Girls (1979)
Model for Murder (1980)
The Wicked Widow (1981)
Stab in the Dark (1984; Australia only)

Larry Baker

Charlie Sent Me (1965; revised from Swan Song for a Siren, 1955)
No Blonde Is an Island (1965)
So What Killed the Vampire? (1966)
Had I But Groaned (1968; reprinted in the UK as The Witches, 1969)
True Son of the Beast (1970)
The Iron Maiden (1975)

Barney Blain (no U.S. editions)

Madam, You're Mayhem (1957)
Ice Cold in Ermine (1958)

Danny Boyd

Tempt a Tigress (1958; no U.S.)
So Deadly, Sinner! (1959; reprinted in the U.S. as Walk Softly, Witch, 1959, 1st U.S. Boyd; different version of the Wheeler title)
Suddenly by Violence (1959)
Terror Comes Creeping (1959)
The Wayward Wahine (1960; published in Australia as The Wayward, 1962)
The Dream Is Deadly (1960)
Graves, I Dig (1960; revised from

Cutie Wins a Corpse (1957)
The Myopic Mermaid (1961, revised from A Siren Sounds Off, 1958)
The Ever-Loving Blues (1961; revised from Death of a Doll, 1956)
The Seductress (1961; published in the U.S. as The Sad-Eyed Seductress, 1961)
The Savage Salome (1961; revised from Murder is My Mistress, 1954)
The Ice-Cold Nude (1962)
Lover Don't Come Back (1962)
Nymph to the Slaughter (1963)
Passionate Pagan (1963)
Silken Nightmare (1963)
Catch Me a Phoenix! (1965)
The Sometime Wife (1965)
The Black Lace Hangover (1966)
House of Sorcery (1967)
The Mini-Murders (1968)
Murder Is the Message (1969)
Only the Very Rich (1969)
The Coffin Bird (1970)
The Sex Clinic (1971)
Angry Amazons (1972) [includes Randy Roberts]
Manhattan Cowboy (1973)
So Move the Body (1973)
The Early Boyd (1975)
The Savage Sisters (1976)
The Pipes Are Calling (1976)
The Rip Off (1979)
The Strawberry-Blonde Jungle (1979)
Death to a Downbeat (1980)
Kiss Michelle Goodbye (1981)
The Real Boyd (1984; Australia only)

Paul Donavan

Donavan (1974)
Donovan's Day (1975)
Chinese Donavan (1976)
Donavan's Delight (1979)

Max Dumas (no U.S. editions)

Goddess Gone Bad (1958)
Luck Was No Lady (1958)
Deadly Miss (1958)

Mike Farrel

The Million Dollar Babe (1961;
    revised from Cutie Cashed His
    Chips, 1955)
The Scarlet Flush (1963; revised
    from Ten Grand Tallulah and
    Temptation, 1957)

Rick Holman

Zelda (1961; 1st U.S. Holman)
Murder in the Harem Club,
    1962; reprinted in the U.S. as
    Murder in the Key Club, 1962)
The Murderer Among Us (1962)
Blonde on the Rocks (1963)
The Jade-Eyed Jinx (1963;
    reprinted in the U.S. as The
    Jade-Eyed Jungle, 1964)
The Ballad of Loving Jenny
    (1963; reprinted in the U.S. as
    The White Bikini, 1963)
The Wind-Up Doll (1963)
The Never-Was Girl (1964)
Murder Is a Package Deal (1964)
Who Killed Doctor Sex? (1964)
Nude—with a View (1965)
The Girl from Outer Space (1965)

Blonde on a Broomstick (1966)
Play Now… Kill Later (1966)
No Tears from the Widow (1966)
The Deadly Kitten (1967)
Long Time No Leola (1967)
Die Anytime, After Tuesday!
    (1969)
The Flagellator (1969)
The Streaked-Blond Slave (1969)
A Good Year for Dwarfs? (1970)
The Hang-up Kid (1970)
Where Did Charity Go? (1970)
The Coven (1971)
The Invisible Flamini (1971)
The Pornbroker (1972)
The Master (1973)
Phreak-Out! (1973)
Negative in Blue (1974)
The Star-Crossed Lover (1974)
Ride the Roller Coaster (1975)
Remember Maybelle? (1976)
See It Again, Sam (1979)
The Phantom Lady (1980)
The Swingers (1980)

Andy Kane

The Hong Kong Caper (1962;
    revised from Blonde, Bad and
    Beautiful, 1957)
The Guilt-edged Cage (1963;
    revised from That's Piracy, My
    Pet, 1957; published in
    Australia as Bird in a Guilt-
    Edged Cage)

Ivor MacCallum
(no U.S. editions)

Sweetheart You Slay Me (1952)
Blackmail Beauty (1953)

Randy Roberts

Murder in the Family Way (1971)
The Seven Sirens (1972)
Murder on High (1973)
Sex Trap (1975)

Mavis Seidlitz

Honey, Here's Your Hearse
  (1955; no U.S.)
The Killer is Kissable (1955; no
  U.S.)
A Bullet For My Baby (1955; no
  U.S.)
Good Morning, Mavis! (1957; no
  U.S.)
Murder Wears a Mantilla (1957;
  revised for U.S. as same title,
  1962)
The Loving and the Dead (1959;
  1st U.S. Seidlitz)
None But the Lethal Heart (1959;
  reprinted as The Fabulous,
  1961)
Tomorrow Is Murder (1960)
Lament for a Lousy Lover (1960)
  [includes Al Wheeler]
The Bump and Grind Murders
  (1964)
Seidlitz and the Super Spy (1967;
  published in the UK as The
  Super-Spy, 1968)
Murder Is So Nostalgic (1972)
And the Undead Sing (1974)

Unrelated Novels/Novelettes (all
non-U.S. unless otherwise noted)

Death Date for Dolores (1951)
Designed to Deceive (1951)

Duchess Double X (1951)
Forever Forbidden (1951)
The Lady Is Murder (1951;
  reprinted as Lady is a Killer
  with Murder by Miss Take,
  1958)
Three Men, One Love (1951)
Uncertain Heart (1951)
Your Alibi Is Showing (1951)
Alias a Lady (1952)
Blackmail for a Brunette (1952)
Blondes Prefer Bullets (1952)
Hands Off the Lady (1952)
Kiss Life Goodbye (1952)
Larceny Was Lovely (1952)
Meet Miss Mayhem (1952)
Murder Sweet Murder (1952)
She Wore No Shroud (1952)
Sssh! She's a Killer (1952)
Chill on Chili/Butterfly Nett
  (1953)
Cyanide Sweetheart (1953)
Dead Dolls Don't Cry (1953)
Dimples Died De-Luxe (1953)
Judgement of a Jane (1953)
Kidnapper Wears Curves (1953)
The Lady Wore Nylon (1953)
The Lady's Alive (1953)
Lethal in Love (1953; reprinted as
  The Minx is Murder, 1956)
Madame You're Morgue-Bound
  (1953)
Meet a Body (1953)
The Mermaid Murmurs Murder
  (1953)
Model for Murder (1953;
  different from 1980 Al Wheeler
  title)
Moonshine Momma (1953)
Murder is a Broad (1953)

Penthouse Pass-Out (1953;
  reprinted as Hot Seat for a
  Honey, 1956)
Rope for a Redhead (1953;
  revised as Model of No Virtue,
  1956)
Slightly Dead (1953)
Stripper You're Stuck (1953)
Widow is Willing (1953)
The Black Widow Weeps (1954)
Felon Angel (1954)
Floozies Out of Focus (1954)
The Frame is Beautiful (1954)
Fraulein is Feline (1954; reprinted
  with Moonshine Momma &
  Slaughter in Satin, 1955)
Good-Knife Sweetheart (1954)
Honky Tonk Homicide (1954;
  reprinted with Chill on Chili &
  Butterfly Nett, 1955)
Homicide Harem (1954; reprinted
  with Good-Knife Sweetheart &
  Poison Ivy, 1955; with Felon
  Angel, 1965)
The Lady is Chased (1954;
  reprinted as Trouble is a Dame,
  1957)
A Morgue Amour (1954)
Murder—Paris Fashion (1954)
Murder! She Says (1954)
Nemesis Wore Nylons (1954)
Pagan Perilous (1954)
Perfumed Poison (1954)
Poison Ivy (1954)
Shady Lady (1954)
Sinsation Sadie (1954)
Slaughter in Satin (1954)
Strip Without Tease (1954;
  reprinted as Stripper, You've
  Sinned, 1959)
Trouble is a Dame (1954)
Wreath for Rebecca (1954)

Venus Unarmed (1954)
Yogi Shrouds Yolande (1954;
  reprinted with Poison Ivy, 1965)
Curtains for a Chorine (1955)
Curves for a Coroner (1955)
Cutie Cashed His Chips (1955;
  revised for U.S. as The Million
  Dollar Babe, 1961, as Farrel
  series)
Homicide Hoyden (1955)
Kiss and Kill (1955; reprinted
  with Cyanide Sweetie, 1958)
Kiss Me Deadly (1955; reprinted
  as Lipstick Larceny, 1958)
Lead Astray (1955)
Lipstick Larceny (1955)
Maid for Murder (1955)
Miss Called Murder (1955)
Shamus, Your Slip Is Showing
  (1955; reprinted with A Morgue
  Amour, 1957)
Shroud for My Sugar (1955)
Sob-Sister Cries Murder (1955)
The Two Timing Blonde (1955)
Baby, You're Guilt-Edged (1956;
  reprinted with Pagan Perilous,
  1959)
Bid the Babe Bye-Bye (1956)
Blonde, Beautiful, and – Blam!
  (1956)
The Bribe Was Beautiful (1956)
Caress Before Killing (1956)
Darling You're Doomed (1956)
Donna Died Laughing (1956)
The Eve of His Dying (1956)
Hi-Jack for Jill (1956)
The Hoodlum Was a Honey
  (1956)
The Lady Has No Convictions
  (1956; reprinted with Slightly
  Dead, 1959)
Meet Murder, My Angel (1956)

Murder By Miss-Demeanour (1956)
My Darling Is Deadpan (1956)
No Halo For Hedy (1956)
Strictly for Felony (1956)
Sweetheart, This is Homicide (1956)
Bella Donna Was Poison (1957)
Cutie Wins a Corpse (1957; revised for U.S. as Graves, I Dig!, 1960, as Boyd series)
Last Note for a Lovely (1957)
Lethal in Love (1957; different than 1953 title)
Sinner, You Slay Me (1957)
Ten Grand Tallulah and Temptation (1957; revised as The Scarlet Flush, 1963, Farrel series)
That's Piracy, My Pet (1957; revised as Bird in a Guilt-Edged Cage, 1963, as Kane series)
Wreath for a Redhead (1957)
The Charmer Chased (1958)
Cutie Takes the Count (1958)
Deadly Miss (1958)
Hi-Fi Fadeout (1958)
High Fashion in Homicide (1958)
No Body She Knows (1958; with Slaughter in Satin, 1960)
No Future Fair Lady (1958)
Sinfully Yours (1958)
A Siren Signs Off (1958; with Moonshine Momma; revised for U.S. as The Myopic Mermaid, 1961, as Boyd series)
So Lovely She Lies (1958)
Widow Bewitched (1958)
The Blonde Avalanche (1984)

As Tod Conway (western stories)

As Caroline Farr

The Intruder (1962)
House of Tombs (1966)
Mansion of Evil (1966)
Villa of Shadows (1966)
Web of Horror (1966; reprinted in the U.S. as A Castle in Spain, 1978)
Granite Folly (1967)
The Secret of the Chateau (1967)
Witch's Hammer (1967)
So Near and Yet... (1968)
House of Destiny (1969)
The Castle on the Lake (1970)
The Secret of Castle Ferrara (1970)
Terror on Duncan Island (1971)
The Towers of Fear (1972)
A Castle in Canada (1972)
House of Dark Illusions (1973)
House of Secrets (1973)
Dark Mansion (1974)
Mansion Malevolent (1974)
The House on the Cliffs (1974)
Dark Citadel (1975)
Mansion of Peril (1975)
Castle of Terror (1975)
The Scream in the Storm (1975)
Chateau of Wolves (1976)
Mansion of Menace (1976)
Brecon Castle (1976)
The House of Landsdown (1977)
House of Treachery (1977)
Ravensnest (1977)
The House at Lansdowne (1977)
Sinister House (1978)
House of Valhalla (1978)
Heiress Of Fear (1978)
Room Of Secrets (1979)
Island of Evil (1979)
A Castle on the Rhine (1979)

The Castle on the Loch (1979)
The Secret at Ravenswood (1980)

As Raymond Glenning (stories)

Ghosts Don't Kill (1951)
Seven for Murder (1951)

As Sinclair Mackellar

Prompt for Murder (1981)

As Dennis Sinclair

Temple Dogs Guard My Fate
  (1968)
Third Force (1976)
The Friends of Lucifer (1977)
Blood Brothers (1977)

As Paul Valdez
(stories & novelettes)

Hypnotic Death (1949)
The Fatal Focus (1950)
Outcasts of Planet J (1950)
Jetbees from Planet J (1951)
Escape to Paradise (1951)
Fugitives from the Flame World
  (1951)
Kidnapped in Chaos (1951)
Killer by Night (1951)
Suicide Satellite (1951)
The Time Thief (1951)
Flight Into Horror (1951)
Murder Gives Notice (1951)
The Corpse Sat Up (1951)
The Maniac Murders (1951)
Satan's Sabbath (1951)
You Can't Keep Murder Out
  (1951)
Kill Him Gently (1951)

Feline Frame-Up (1951)
Celluloid Suicide? (1951)
The Murder I Don't Remember
  (1952)
Kidnapped in Space (1952)
There's No Future in Murder
  (1952)
The Crook Who Wasn't There
  (1952)
Maniac Murders (1952)
The Mad Meteor (1952)
Operation Satellite (1952)

As A. G. Yates

The Cold Dark Hours (1958)

As Alan Yates

Novel:

Coriolanus, the Chariot (1978)

Stories & Novelettes:

Client for Murder (Leisure
  Detective #7, 195?)
The Corpse on the Carpet
  (Leisure Detective #8, 195?)
Farewell, My Lady of Shalott!
  (Action Detective Magazine #6,
  1952)
Hush-a-Buy Homicide (Leisure
  Detective #9, 195?)
Margie (Action Detective
  Magazine #5, 1952)
Merger with Death (Leisure
  Detective #12, 195?)
Murder in the Family (Leisure
  Detective #11, 195?)
Murder Needs Education (Action
  Detective Magazine #2, 1952)

Murder! She Says
  (Detective Monthly #2, 195?)
My Love Lies Murdered (Action
  Detective Magazine #7, 1952)
Nemesis for a Nude! (Leisure
  Detective #10, 195?)

Genie from Jupiter (Thrills
  Incorporated #14, 1951)
Goddess of Space (Thrills
  Incorporated #20, 1952)
No Pixies on Pluto (Thrills
  Incorporated #22, 1952)

Planet of the Lost (Thrills
  Incorporated #17, 1951)
A Space Ship Is Missing
  (Thrills Incorporated #16, 1951)
Spacemen Spoofed (Thrills
  Incorporated #23, 1952)

Autobiography

Ready when you are, C.B.!: The
  autobiography of Alan Yates
  alias Carter Brown (1983)

Follow the previous capers of Al Wheeler from the irrepressible...

Carter Brown

The Wench is Wicked / Blonde Verdict / Delilah Was Deadly

978-1-944520-33-5 $19.95

Al Wheeler #1-3.

"All fans of crime fiction should take this opportunity to rediscover Brown and Al Wheeler, and experience what kind of stories kept readers happily turning pages when paperback originals first ruled the market." —Alan Cranis, *Bookgasm.*

No Harp for My Angel / Booty for a Babe / Eve, It's Extortion

978-1-944520-44-1 $19.95

Al Wheeler #4-6.

"These three novels are testaments to Brown's authorial leanness... With succulent descriptions of succulent women, two-fisted action, twists and turns, and Wheeler's irrepressible attitude, there's nothing *not* to like in Brown's series about this rakish police officer." —Kristofer Upjohn, *Noir Journal.*

"A mix of sex, violence, mystery, and police procedural all wrapped in a pure pulp bundle." —*Just a Guy That Likes to Read*

STARK HOUSE PRESS
1315 H Street, Eureka, CA 95501
griffinskye3@sbcglobal.net
www.StarkHousePress.com

Available from your local bookstore, or order direct or via our website.